Praise for *New York Times* bestselling author

LINDA HOWARD

"You can't read just one Linda Howard!"
—*New York Times* bestselling author Catherine Coulter

"Linda Howard writes with power, stunning sensuality
and a storytelling ability unmatched in the romance genre.
Every book is a treasure for the reader to savor again and again."
—*New York Times* bestselling author Iris Johansen

"This master storyteller takes our breath away."
—*RT Book Reviews*

Praise for *New York Times* bestselling author

MARIE FORCE

"This book starts out strong and keeps getting better. Marie Force is
one of those authors that will be on my must-read list in the future."
—*The Romance Studio* on *Fatal Affair*

"The author makes the reader part of the action, effortlessly weaving
the world of politics and murder in which the characters come alive
on the pages. The plot was addictive and scandalous with so many
family secrets....Drama, passion, suspense. *Fatal Affair* has it all!"
—*Book Junkie*

"Marie Force's second novel in the Fatal series is an
outstanding romantic suspense in its own right; that it follows
the fantastic first installment only sweetens the read."
—*RT Book Reviews*, 4½ stars, on *Fatal Justice*

LINDA HOWARD

— AND —

MARIE FORCE

DANGEROUS
GAMES

HARLEQUIN® HQN™

Recycling programs
for this product may
not exist in your area.

ISBN-13: 978-0-373-77824-9

DANGEROUS GAMES

Copyright © 2013 by Harlequin Books S.A.

The publisher acknowledges the copyright holders of the individual works as follows:

COME LIE WITH ME
Copyright © 1984 by Linda Howington

FATAL JUSTICE
Copyright © 2011 by Marie Sullivan Force

Printed in U.S.A.

COME LIE WITH ME

LINDA HOWARD

CHAPTER 1

The ocean had a hypnotic effect. Dione gave in to it without a struggle, peacefully watching the turquoise waves roll onto the blindingly white sand. She wasn't an idle person, yet she was content to sit on the deck of her rented beach house, her long, honey-tanned legs stretched out and propped on the railing, doing nothing more than watching the waves and listening to the muted roar of water coming in and going out. The white gulls swooped in and out of her vision, their high-pitched cries adding to the symphony of wind and water. To her right, the huge golden orb of the sun was sinking into the water, turning the sea to flame. It would have made a stunning photograph, yet she was disinclined to leave her seat and get her camera. It had been a glorious day, and she had done nothing more strenuous than celebrate it by walking the beach and swimming in the green-and-blue-streaked Gulf of Mexico. Lord, what a life. It was so sweet, it was almost sinful. This was the perfect vacation.

For two weeks she had wandered the sugar-white sands of Panama City, Florida, blissfully alone and lazy. There wasn't a clock in the beach house, nor had she even wound her watch since she'd arrived, because time didn't matter. No matter what time she woke, she knew that if she was hungry and didn't feel like cooking, there was always a place within walking distance where she could get something to eat. During the summer, the Miracle Strip didn't sleep. It was a twenty-four-hour party that constantly renewed itself from the end of school through the Labor Day weekend. Students and singles looking for a good time found it; families looking for a carefree vacation found it; and tired professional women wanting only a chance to unwind and relax beside the dazzling Gulf found that, too. She felt completely reborn after the past two delicious weeks.

A sailboat, as brightly colored as a butterfly, caught her attention, and she watched it as it lazily tacked toward shore. She was so busy watching the boat that she was unaware of the man approaching the deck until he started up the steps and the vibration of the wooden floor alerted her. Without haste she turned her head, the movement graceful and unalarmed, but her entire body was suddenly coiled and ready for action, despite the fact that she hadn't moved from her relaxed posture.

A tall, gray-haired man stood looking at her, and her first thought was that he didn't belong in this setting. P.C., as the vacation city was known, was a relaxed, informal area. This man was dressed in an impeccable three-piece gray suit, and his feet were shod in supple Italian leather. Dione reflected briefly that his shoes would be full of the loose sand that filtered into everything.

"Miss Kelley?" he inquired politely.

Her slim black brows arched in puzzlement, but she withdrew her feet from the railing and stood, holding out her hand to him. "Yes, I'm Dione Kelley. And you are...?"

"Richard Dylan," he said, taking her hand and shaking it firmly. "I realize that I'm intruding on your vacation, Miss Kelley, but it's very important that I speak with you."

"Please, sit down," Dione invited, indicating a deck chair

beside the one she had just vacated. She resumed her former position, stretching out her legs and propping her bare feet on the railing. "Is there something I can do for you?"

"There certainly is," he replied feelingly. "I wrote to you about six weeks ago concerning a patient I'd like you to take on—Blake Remington."

Dione frowned slightly. "I remember. But I answered your letter, Mr. Dylan, before I left on vacation. Haven't you received it?"

"Yes, I have," he admitted. "I came to ask you to reconsider your refusal. There are extenuating circumstances, and his condition is deteriorating rapidly. I'm convinced that you can—"

"I'm not a miracle worker," she interrupted softly. "And I do have other cases lined up. Why should I put Mr. Remington ahead of others who need my services just as badly as he does?"

"Are they dying?" he asked bluntly.

"Is Mr. Remington? From the information you gave me in your letter, the last operation was a success. There are other therapists as well qualified as I am, if there's some reason why Mr. Remington has to have therapy this very moment."

Richard Dylan looked out at the turquoise Gulf, the waves tipped with gold by the sinking sun. "Blake Remington won't live another year," he said, and a bleak expression crossed his strong, austere features. "Not the way he is now. You see, Miss Kelley, he doesn't believe he'll ever walk again, and he's given up. He's deliberately letting himself die. He doesn't eat; he seldom sleeps; he refuses to leave the house."

Dione sighed. Depression was sometimes the most difficult aspect of her patients' conditions, taking away their energy and determination. She'd seen it so many times before, and she knew that she'd see it again. "Still, Mr. Dylan, another therapist—"

"I don't think so. I've already employed two therapists, and neither of them has lasted a week. Blake refuses to cooperate at all, saying that it's just a waste of time, something to keep him occupied. The doctors tell him that the surgery was a success, but he still can't move his legs, so he just doesn't believe them. Dr. Norwood suggested you. He said that you've had remarkable success with uncooperative patients, and that your methods are extraordinary."

She smiled wryly. "Of course he said that. Tobias Norwood trained me."

Richard Dylan smiled briefly in return. "I see. Still, I'm convinced that you're Blake's last chance. If you still feel that your other obligations are more pressing, then come with me to Phoenix and meet Blake. I think that when you see him, you'll understand why I'm so worried."

Dione hesitated, examining the proposal. Professionally, she was torn between refusing and agreeing. She had other cases, other people who were depending on her; why should this Blake Remington come before them? But on the other hand, he sounded like a challenge to her abilities, and she was one of those high-powered individuals who thrived on challenges, on testing herself to the limit. She was very certain of herself when it came to her chosen profession, and she enjoyed the satisfaction of completing a job and leaving her patient better able to move than before. In the years that she had been working as a private therapist, traveling all over the country to her patients' homes, she had amassed an amazing record of successes.

"He's an extraordinary man," said Mr. Dylan softly. "He's engineered several aeronautical systems that are widely used now. He designs his own planes, has flown as a test pilot on some top-secret planes for the government, climbs mountains, races yachts, goes deep-sea diving. He's a man who was at home on land, on the sea, or in the air, and now he's chained to a wheelchair and it's killing him."

"Which one of his interests was he pursuing when he had his accident?" Dione asked.

"Mountain climbing. The rope above him snagged on a rock, and his movements sawed the rope in two. He fell forty-five feet to a ledge, bounced off it, then rolled or fell another two hundred feet. That's almost the distance of a football field, but the snow must have cushioned him enough to save his life. He's said more than once that if he'd fallen off that mountain during the summer, he wouldn't have to spend his life as a cripple now."

"Tell me about his injuries," Dione said thoughtfully.

He rose to his feet. "I can do better than that. I have his file, complete with X-rays, in my car. Dr. Norwood suggested that I bring it."

"He's a sly fox, that one," she murmured as Mr. Dylan disappeared around the deck. Tobias Norwood knew exactly how to intrigue her, how to set a particular case before her. Already she was interested, just as he had meant her to be. She'd make up her mind after seeing the X-rays and reading the case history. If she didn't think she could help Blake Remington, she wouldn't put him through the stress of therapy.

In just a moment Mr. Dylan returned with a thick, manila envelope in his grasp. He released it into Dione's outthrust hand and waited expectantly. Instead of opening it, she tapped her fingernails against the envelope.

"Let me study this tonight, Mr. Dylan," she said firmly. "I can't just glance over it and make a decision. I'll let you know in the morning."

A flicker of impatience crossed his face; then he quickly mastered it and nodded. "Thank you for considering it, Miss Kelley."

When he was gone, Dione stared out at the Gulf for a long time, watching the eternal waves washing in with a froth of turquoise and sea-green, churning white as they rushed

onto the sand. It was a good thing that her vacation was ending, that she'd already enjoyed almost two full weeks of utter
contentment on the Florida panhandle, doing nothing more
strenuous than walking in the tide. She'd already lazily begun
considering her next job, but now it looked as if her plans had
been changed.

After opening the envelope she held up the X-rays one by
one to the sun, and she winced when she saw the damage that
had been done to a strong, vital human body. It was a miracle
that he hadn't been killed outright. But the X-rays taken after
each successive operation revealed bones that had healed better
than they should have, better than anyone could have hoped.
Joints had been rebuilt; pins and plates had reconstructed his
body and held it together. She went over the last set of X-rays
with excruciating detail. The surgeon had been a genius, or
the results were a miracle, or perhaps a combination of both.
She could see no physical reason why Blake couldn't walk
again, provided the nerves hadn't been totally destroyed.

Beginning to read the surgeon's report, she concentrated
fiercely on every detail until she understood exactly what
damage had been done and what repairs had been made. This
man *would* walk again; she'd make him! The end of the report
mentioned that further improvement was prevented by the patient's lack of cooperation and depth of depression. She could
almost feel the surgeon's sense of frustration as he'd written
that; after all his painstaking work, after the unhoped-for success of his techniques, the patient had refused to help!

Gathering everything together, she started to replace the
contents in the envelope and noticed that something else was
inside, a stiff piece of paper that she'd neglected to remove.
She pulled it out and turned it over. It wasn't just a piece of
paper; it was a photograph.

Stunned, she stared into laughing blue eyes, eyes that sparkled and danced with the sheer joy of living. Richard Dylan

was a sly one, too, knowing full well that few women would be able to resist the appeal of the dynamic man in the photograph. It was Blake Remington, she knew, as he had been before the accident. His brown hair was tousled, his darkly tanned face split by a rakish grin which revealed a captivating dimple in his left cheek. He was naked except for a brief pair of denim shorts, his body strong and well muscled, his legs the long, powerful limbs of an athlete. He was holding a good-sized marlin in the picture, and in the background she could make out the deep blue of the ocean; so he went deep-sea fishing, too. Wasn't there anything the man couldn't do? Yes, now there was, she reminded herself. Now he couldn't walk.

She wanted to refuse to take the case just to demonstrate to Richard Dylan that she couldn't be manipulated, but as she stared at the face in the photograph she knew that she would do just as he wanted, and she was disturbed by the knowledge. It had been such a long time since she'd been interested in any man at all that she was startled by her own reaction to a simple photograph.

Tracing the outline of his face with her fingertip, she wondered wistfully what her life would have been like if she'd been able to be a normal woman, to love a man and be loved in return, something that her brief and disastrous marriage had revealed to be impossible. She'd learned her lesson the hard way, but she'd never forgotten it. Men weren't for her. A loving husband and children weren't for her. The void left in her life by the total absence of love would have to be filled by her sense of satisfaction with her profession, with the joy she received from helping someone else. She might look at Blake Remington's photograph with admiration, but the daydreams that any other woman would indulge in when gazing at that masculine beauty were not for her. Daydreams were a waste of time, because she knew that she was incapable of attracting a man like him. Her ex-husband, Scott Hayes, had taught her with pain and humiliation the folly of enticing a man when she was unable to satisfy him.

Never again. She'd sworn it then, after leaving Scott, and she swore it again now. Never again would she give a man the chance to hurt her.

A sudden gust of salty wind fanned her cheeks, and she lifted her head, a little surprised to see that the sun was completely gone now and that she had been squinting at the photograph, not really seeing it as she dealt with her murky memories. She got to her feet and went inside, snapping on a tall floor lamp and illuminating the cool, summery interior of the beach house. Dropping into a plumply cushioned chair, Dione leaned her head back and began planning her therapy program, though of course she wouldn't be able to make any concrete plans until she actually met Mr. Remington and was better able to judge his condition. She smiled a little with anticipation. She loved a challenge more than she did anything else, and she had the feeling that Mr. Remington would fight her every inch of the way. She'd have to be on her toes, stay in control of the situation and use his helplessness as a lever against him, making him so angry that he'd go through hell to get better, just to get rid of her. Unfortunately, he really would have to go through hell; therapy wasn't a picnic.

She'd had difficult patients before, people who were so depressed and angry over their disabilities that they'd shut out the entire world, and she guessed that Blake Remington had reacted in the same way. He'd been so active, so vitally alive and in perfect shape, a real daredevil of a man; she guessed that it was killing his soul to be limited to a wheelchair. He wouldn't care if he lived or died; he wouldn't care about anything.

She slept deeply that night, no dreams disturbing her, and rose well before dawn for her usual run along the beach. She wasn't a serious runner, counting off the miles and constantly reaching for a higher number; she ran for the sheer pleasure of it, continuing until she tired, then strolling along and letting the silky froth of the tide wash over her bare feet. The sun was piercing the morning with its first blinding rays when she returned to the beach house, showered and began packing. She'd made her decision, so she saw no need to waste time. She'd be ready when Mr. Dylan returned.

He wasn't even surprised when he saw her suitcases. "I knew you'd take the job," he said evenly.

Dione arched a slim black brow at him. "Are you always so sure of yourself, Mr. Dylan?"

"Please, call me Richard," he said. "I'm not always so certain, but Dr. Norwood has told me a great deal about you. He thought that you'd take the job because it was a challenge, and when I saw you, I knew that he was right."

"I'll have to talk with him about giving away my secrets," she joked.

"Not all of them," he said, and something in his voice made her wonder just how much he knew. "You have a lot of secrets left."

Deciding that Richard was far too astute, she turned briskly to her cases and helped him take them out to his car. Her own car was a rental, and after locking the beach house and returning the car to the rental office, she was ready to go.

Later, when they were in a private jet flying west to Phoenix, she began questioning Richard about her patient. What did he like? What did he hate? What were his hobbies? She wanted to know about his education, his politics, his favorite colors, the type of women he had dated, or about his wife if he were married. She'd found that wives were usually jealous of the close relationship that developed between therapist and patient, and she wanted to know as much as she could about a situation before she walked into it.

Richard knew an amazing amount about Mr. Remington's

personal life, and finally Dione asked him what his relationship was to the man.

The firm mouth twisted. "I'm his vice president, for one thing, so I know about his business operations. I'm also his brother-in-law. The only woman in his life who you'll have to deal with is my wife, Serena, who is also his younger sister."

Dione asked, "Why do you say that? Do you live in the same house with Mr. Remington?"

"No, but that doesn't mean anything. Since his accident, Serena has hovered over him, and I'm sure she won't be pleased when you arrive and take all of his attention. She's always adored Blake to the point of obsession. She nearly went insane when we thought he would die."

"I won't allow any interference in my therapy program," she warned him quietly. "I'll be overseeing his hours, his visitors, the food he eats, even the phone calls he receives. I hope your wife understands that."

"I'll try to convince her, but Serena is just like Blake. She's both stubborn and determined, and she has a key to the house."

"I'll have the locks changed," Dione planned aloud, perfectly serious in her intentions. Loving sister or not, Serena Dylan wasn't going to take over or intrude on Dione's therapy.

"Good," Richard approved, a frown settling on his austere brow. "I'd like to have a wife again."

It was beginning to appear that Richard had some other motive for wanting his brother-in-law walking again. Evidently, in the two years since Blake's accident, his sister had abandoned her husband in order to care for him, and the neglect was eroding her marriage. It was a situation that Dione didn't want to become involved in, but she had given her word that she would take the case, and she didn't betray the trust that people put in her.

Because of the time difference, it was only midafternoon when Richard drove them to the exclusive Phoenix suburb where Blake Remington lived. This time his car was a white Lincoln, plush and cool. As he drove up the circular drive to the hacienda-style house, she saw that it looked plush and cool, too. To call it a house was like calling a hurricane a wind; this place was a mansion. It was white and mysterious, keeping its secrets hidden behind its walls, presenting only a grateful facade to curious eyes. The landscaping was marvelous, a blend of the natural desert plants and lush greenery that was the product of careful and selective irrigation. The drive ran around to the back, where Richard told her the garage area was, but he stopped before the arched entry in front.

When she walked into the enormous foyer Dione thought she'd walked into the garden of paradise. There was a serenity to the place, a dignified simplicity wrought by the cool brown tiles on the floor, the plain white walls, the high ceiling. The hacienda was built in a U, around an open courtyard that was cool and fragrant, with a pink marble fountain in the center of it spouting clear water into the air. She could see all of that because the inner wall of the foyer, from ceiling to floor, was glass.

She was still speechless with admiration when the brisk clicking of heels on the tiles caught her attention, and she turned her head to watch the tall young woman approaching. This had to be Serena; the resemblance to the photo of Blake Remington was too strong for her to be anyone else. She had the same soft brown hair, the same dark blue eyes, the same clear-cut features. But she wasn't laughing, as the man in the photo had been; her eyes were stormy, outraged.

"Richard!" she said in a low, wrathful tone. "Where have you been for the past two days? How dare you disappear without a word, then turn up with this...this gypsy in tow!"

Dione almost chuckled; most women wouldn't have attacked so bluntly, but she could see that this direct young woman had her share of the determination that Richard had attributed to Blake Remington. She opened her mouth to tell the truth of the matter, but Richard stepped in smoothly.

"Dione," he said, watching his wife with a cold eye, "I'd like to introduce my wife, Serena. Serena, this is Dione Kelley. I've hired Miss Kelley as Blake's new therapist, and I've been to Florida to pick her up and fly her back here. I didn't tell anyone where I was going because I had no intention of arguing over the matter. I've hired her, and that's that. I think that answers all of your questions." He finished with cutting sarcasm.

Serena Dylan wasn't a woman to be cowed, though a flush did color her cheeks. She turned to Dione and said frankly, "I apologize, though I refuse to take all of the blame. If my husband had seen fit to inform me of his intentions, I wouldn't have made such a terrible accusation."

"I understand." Dione smiled. "Under the same circumstances, I doubt that my conduct would have been as polite."

Serena smiled in return, then stepped forward and gave her husband a belated peck on the cheek. "Very well, you're forgiven." She sighed. "Though I'm afraid you've wasted your time. You know that Blake won't put up with it. He can't stand having anyone hover over him, and he's been pushed at and pounded on enough."

"Evidently not, or he'd be walking by now," Dione replied confidently.

Serena looked doubtful, then shrugged. "I still think you've wasted your time. Blake refused to have anything to do with the last therapist Richard hired, and he won't change his mind for you."

"I'd like to talk to him myself, if I may," Dione insisted, though in a pleasant tone.

Serena hadn't exactly stationed herself like a guard before the throne room, but it was evident that she was very protective of her brother. It wasn't all that unusual. When someone had been in a severe accident, it was only natural that the members of the family were overprotective for a while. Perhaps, when Serena found that Dione would be taking over the vast majority of Blake's time and attention, she would give her own husband the attention he deserved.

"At this time of day, Blake is usually in his room," Richard said, taking Dione's arm. "This way."

"Richard!" Again color rose in Serena's cheeks, but this time they were spots of anger. "He's lying down for a nap! At least leave him in peace until he comes downstairs. You know how badly he sleeps—let him rest while he can!"

"He naps every day?" Dione asked, thinking that if he slept during the day, no wonder he couldn't sleep at night.

"He tries to nap, but he usually looks worse afterward than he did before."

"Then it won't matter if we disturb him, will it?" Dione asked, deciding that now was the time to establish her authority. She caught a faint twitch of Richard's lips, signaling a smile, then he was directing her to the broad, sweeping stairs with his hand still warm and firm on her elbow. Behind them, Dione could feel the heat of the glare that Serena threw at them; then she heard the brisk tapping of heels as Serena followed.

From the design of the house, Dione suspected that all of the upstairs rooms opened onto the graceful gallery that ran along the entire U of the house, looking down on the inner courtyard. When Richard tapped lightly on a door that had been widened to allow a wheelchair to pass easily through it, then opened it at the low call that permitted entrance, she saw at once that, at least in this room, her supposition was correct. The enormous room was flooded with sunlight that streamed through the open curtains, though the sliding glass doors that opened onto the gallery remained closed.

The man at the window was silhouetted against the bright

sunlight, a mysterious and melancholy figure slumped in the prison of a wheelchair. Then he reached out and pulled a chord, closing the curtains, and the room became dim. Dione blinked for a moment before her eyes adjusted to the sudden darkness; then the man became clear to her, and she felt her throat tighten with shock.

She'd thought that she was prepared; Richard had told her that Blake had lost weight and was rapidly deteriorating, but until she saw him, she hadn't realized exactly how serious the situation was. The contrast between the man in the wheelchair and the laughing man in the photo she'd seen was so great that she wouldn't have believed them to be the same man if it hadn't been for the dark blue eyes. His eyes no longer sparkled; they were dull and lifeless, but nothing could change their remarkable color.

He was thin, painfully so; he had to have lost almost fifty pounds from what he'd weighed when the photo had been taken, and he'd been all lean muscle then. His brown hair was dull from poor nutrition, and shaggy, as if it had been a long time since he'd had it trimmed. His skin was pale, his face all high cheekbones and gaunt cheeks.

Dione held herself upright, but inside she was shattering, crumbling into a thousand brittle pieces. She inevitably became involved with all her patients, but never before had she felt as if she were dying; never before had she wanted to rage at the injustice of it, at the horrible obscenity that had taken his perfect body and reduced it to helplessness. His suffering and despair were engraved on his drawn face, his bone structure revealed in stark clarity. Dark circles lay under the midnight blue of his eyes; his temples had become touched with gray. His once powerful body sat limp in the chair, his legs awkwardly motionless, and she knew that Richard had been right: Blake Remington didn't want to live.

He looked at her without a flicker of interest, then moved

his gaze to Richard. It was as if she didn't exist. "Where've you been?" he asked flatly.

"I had business to attend to," Richard replied, his voice so cold that the room turned arctic. Dione could tell that he was insulted that anyone should question his actions; Richard might work for Blake, but he was in no way inferior. He was still angry with Serena, and the entire scene had earned his disapproval.

"He's so determined." Serena sighed, moving to her brother's side. "He's hired another therapist for you, Miss...uh, Diane Kelley."

"Dione," Dione corrected without rancor.

Blake turned his disinterested gaze on her and surveyed her without a word. Dione stood quietly, studying him, noting his reaction, or rather, his lack of one. Richard had said that Blake had always preferred blondes, but even taking Dione's black hair into consideration, she had expected at least a basic recognition that she was female. She expected men to look at her; she'd grown used to it, though once an interested glance would have sent her into panic. She was a striking woman, and at last she had been able to accept that, considering it one of nature's ironies that she should have been given the looks to attract men when it was impossible for her to enjoy a man's touch.

She knew what he saw. She'd dressed carefully for effect, realizing that her appearance would either be intimidating or appealing; she didn't care which, as long as it gave her an edge in convincing him to cooperate. She'd parted her thick, vibrant black hair in the middle and drawn it back in a severe knot at the nape of her neck, where she'd secured it with a gold comb. Gold hoop earrings dangled from her ears. Serena had called her a gypsy, and her warm, honey-tanned skin made it seem possible. Her eyes were cat's eyes, slanted, golden, as mysterious as time and fringed with heavy black lashes. With her high cheekbones and strong, sculptured jawline, she looked Eastern and exotic, a prime candidate for a lusty sheik's harem, had she been born a century before.

She'd dressed in a white jumpsuit, chic and casual, and now she pushed her hands into the pockets, a posture that outlined her firm breasts. The line of her body was long and clean and sweeping, from her trim waist to her rounded bottom, then on down her long, graceful legs. Blake might not have noticed, but his sister had, and Serena had been stirred to instant jealousy. She didn't want Dione around either her husband or her brother.

After a long silence Blake moved his head slowly in a negative emotion. "No. Just take her away, Richard. I don't want to be bothered."

Dione glanced at Richard, then stepped forward, taking control and focusing Blake's attention on her. "I'm sorry you feel that way, Mr. Remington," she said mildly. "Because I'm staying anyway. You see, I have a contract, and I always honor my word."

"I'll release you from it," he muttered, turning his head away and looking out the window again.

"That's very nice of you, but *I* won't release *you* from it. I understand that you've given Richard your power of attorney, so the contract is legal, and it's also ironclad. It states, simply, that I'm employed as your therapist and will reside in this house until you're able to walk again. No time limit was set." She leaned down and put her hands on the arms of his wheelchair, bringing her face close to his and forcing him to give her his attention. "I'm going to be your shadow, Mr. Remington. The only way you'll be able to get rid of me is to walk to the door yourself and open it for me. No one else can do it for you."

"You're overstepping yourself, Miss Kelley!" Serena said sharply, her blue eyes narrowing with rage. She reached out and thrust Dione's hands away from the wheelchair. "My brother has said that he doesn't want you here!"

"This doesn't concern you," Dione replied, still in a mild tone.

"It certainly does! If you think I'll let you just move in here…why, you probably think you've found a meal ticket for life!"

"Not at all. I'll have Mr. Remington walking by Christmas. If you doubt my credentials, please feel free to investigate my record. But in the meantime, stop interfering." Dione straightened to her full height and stared steadily at Serena, the strength of her willpower blazing from her golden eyes.

"Don't talk to my sister like that," Blake said sharply.

At last! A response, even if it was an angry one! With secret delight Dione promptly attacked the crack in his indifference. "I'll talk to anyone like that who tries to come between me and my patient," she informed him. She put her hands on her hips and surveyed him with a contemptuous curl to her mouth. "Look at you! You're in such pitiful shape that you'd have to go into training to qualify for the ninety-eight-pound weakling category! You should be ashamed of yourself, letting your muscles turn into mush. No wonder you can't walk!"

The dark pupils of his eyes flared, a black pool in a sea of blue. "Damn you," he choked. "It's hard to do calisthenics when you're hooked up to more tubes than you have places for, and nothing except your face works when you want it to!"

"That was then," she said relentlessly. "What about now? It takes muscles to walk, and you don't have any! You'd lose a fight with a noodle, the shape you're in now."

"And I suppose you think you can wave your magic wand and put me into working order again?" he snarled.

She smiled. "A magic wand? It won't be as easy as that. You're going to work harder for me than you've ever worked before. You're going to sweat and hurt, and turn the air blue cussing me out, but you're going to work. I'll have you walking again if I have to half kill you to do it."

"No, you won't, lady," he said with cold deliberation. "I don't care what sort of contract you have—I don't want you in my house. I'll pay whatever it takes to get rid of you."

"I'm not giving you that option, Mr. Remington. I won't accept a payoff."

"You don't have to give me the option! I'm *taking* it!"

Looking into his enraged face, flushed with anger, Dione abruptly realized that the photograph of the laughing, relaxed man had been misleading, an exception rather than the rule. This was a man of indomitable will, used to forcing things to go his way by the sheer power of his will and personality. He had overcome every obstacle in his life by his own determination, until the fall down the cliff had changed all that and presented him with the one obstacle that he couldn't handle on his own. He'd never had to have help before, and he hadn't been able to accept that now he did. Because he couldn't make himself walk, he was convinced that it wasn't possible.

But she was determined, too. Unlike him, she'd learned early that she could be struck down, forced to do things she didn't want to do. She'd pulled herself out of the murky depths of despair by her own silent, stubborn belief that life *had* to be better. Dione had forged her strength in the fires of pain; the woman she had become, the independence and skill and reputation she'd built, were too precious to her to allow her to back down now. This was the challenge of her career, and it would take every ounce of her willpower to handle it.

So, insolently, she asked him, "Do you *like* having everyone feel sorry for you?"

Serena gasped; even Richard made an involuntary sound before bringing himself back under control. Dione didn't waste a glance on them. She kept her eyes locked with Blake's, watching the shock in them, watching the angry color wash out of his face and leave it utterly white.

"You bitch," he said in a hollow, shaking voice.

She shrugged. "Look, we're getting nowhere like this. Let's make a deal. You're so weak, I'll bet you can't beat me at arm wrestling. If I win, I stay and you agree to therapy. If you win, I walk out that door and never come back. What do you say?"

CHAPTER 2

His head jerked up, his eyes narrowing as they swept over her slender form and graceful, feminine arms. Dione could almost read his thoughts. As thin as he was, he still outweighed her by at least forty, possibly even fifty, pounds. He knew that even if a man and a woman were the same weight, the man would be stronger than the woman, under normal circumstances. Dione refused to let a smile touch her lips, but she knew that these weren't normal circumstances. Blake had been inactive for two years, while she was in extremely good shape. She was a therapist; she had to be strong in order to do her job. She was slim, yes, but every inch of her was sleek, strong muscle. She ran, she swam, she did stretching exercises regularly, but most important, she lifted weights. She had to have considerable arm strength to be able to handle patients who couldn't handle themselves. She looked at Blake's thin, pale hands, and she knew that she would win.

"Don't do it!" Serena said sharply, twisting her fingers into knots.

Blake turned and looked at his sister in disbelief. "You think she can beat me, don't you?" he murmured, but the words were more a statement than a question.

Serena was tense, staring at Dione with an odd, pleading look in her eyes. Dione understood: Serena didn't want her brother humiliated. And neither did she. But she did want him to agree to therapy, and she was willing to do whatever was necessary to make him see what he was doing to himself. She tried to say that with her eyes, because she couldn't say the words aloud.

"Answer me!" Blake roared suddenly. Every line of him was tense.

Serena bit her lower lip. "Yes," she finally said. "I think she can beat you."

Silence fell, and Blake sat as though made of stone. Watching him carefully, Dione saw the moment he made the decision. "There's only one way to find out, isn't there?" he challenged, turning the wheelchair with a quick pressure of his finger on a button. Dione followed him as he led the way to his desk and positioned the wheelchair beside it.

"You shouldn't have a motorized wheelchair," she observed absently. "A manual chair would have kept your upper body strength at a reasonable level. This is a fancy chair, but it isn't doing you any good at all."

He shot her a brooding glance, but didn't respond to her comment. "Sit down," he said, indicating his desk.

Dione took her time obeying him. She felt no joy, no elation, in knowing that she would win; it was something she had to do, a point that she had to make to Blake.

Richard and Serena flanked them as they positioned themselves, Blake maneuvering himself until he was satisfied with his location, Dione doing the same. She propped her right arm on the desk and gripped her biceps with her left hand. "Ready when you are," she said.

Blake had the advantage of a longer arm, and she realized

that it would take all of the strength in her hand and wrist to overcome the leverage he would have. He positioned his arm against hers and wrapped his fingers firmly around her much smaller hand. For a moment he studied the slim grace of her fingers, the delicate pink of her manicured nails, and a slight smile moved his lips. He probably thought it would be a cake walk. But she felt the coldness of his hands, indicating poor circulation, and knew the inevitable outcome of their little battle.

"Richard, you start it," Blake instructed, lifting his eyes and locking them with hers. She could feel his intensity, his aggressive drive to win, and she began to brace herself, concentrating all her energy and strength into her right arm and hand.

"Go," said Richard, and though there was no great flurry of movement between the two antagonists, their bodies were suddenly tense, their arms locked together.

Dione kept her face calm, revealing nothing of the fierce effort it took to keep her wrist straight. After the first moments, when he was unable to shove her arm down, Blake's face reflected first astonishment, then anger, then a sort of desperation. She could feel his first burst of strength ebbing and slowly, inexorably, she began forcing his arm down. Sweat broke out on his forehead and slipped down one side of his face as he struggled to reverse the motion, but he had already used his meager strength and had nothing in reserve. Knowing that she had him, and regretting her victory even though she knew it was necessary, Dione quickly settled the matter by forcing his arm down flat on the desk.

He sat in his wheelchair, a shattered expression in his eyes for a flashing moment before he closed himself off and made his face a blank wall.

The silence was broken only by his rapid breathing. Richard's face was grim; Serena looked torn between the desire to comfort her brother and a strong inclination to throw Dione out herself.

Dione moved briskly, rising to her feet. "That settles that," she said casually. "In another two months I won't be able to do that. I'll put my things in the room next to this one—"

"No," said Blake curtly, not looking at her. "Serena, give Miss Kelley the guest suite."

"That won't do at all," Dione replied. "I want to be close enough to you that I'll be able to hear you if you call. The room next door will do nicely. Richard, how soon can you have those changes made that I stipulated?"

"What changes?" Blake asked, jerking his head up.

"I need some special equipment," she explained, noting that the diversion had worked, as she'd intended it to. He'd already lost that empty look. She'd evidently made the right decision in being so casual about beating him at arm wrestling, treating the incident as nothing unusual. Now was not the time to rub it in, or to let him know that there were a lot of men walking the earth who couldn't match her in arm wrestling. He'd find out soon enough when they got into the weight-lifting program.

"What sort of special equipment?" he demanded.

She controlled a smile. His attention had certainly been caught by the possibility of any changes in his beloved home. She outlined her needs to him. "A whirlpool is a necessity. I'll also need a treadmill, weight bench, sauna, things like that. Any objections?"

"There might be. Just where do you plan to put all this?"

"Richard said he could outfit a gym for me on the ground floor, next to the pool, which will be very convenient, because you'll be doing a lot of work in the pool. Water is a great place for calisthenics," she said enthusiastically. "Your muscles still get the workout, but the water supports your weight."

"You're not putting in a gym," he said grimly.

"Read my contract." She smiled. "The gym is going in. Don't make such a fuss—the house won't be disfigured, and the equipment is necessary. An Olympic trainee won't be getting the workout you're facing," she said with quiet truth. "It's going to be hard work, and it's going to be painful, but you'll do it if I have to drive you like a slave. You can put money on it—you'll be walking by Christmas."

A terrible longing crossed his face before he brought his thin hand up to rub his forehead, and Dione sensed his indecision. But it wasn't in him to give in to anyone else easily, and he scowled. "You won the right to stay here," he said grudgingly. "But I don't like it, and I don't like you, Miss Kelley. Richard, I want to see that contract she keeps harping about."

"I don't have it with me," Richard lied smoothly, taking Serena's arm and edging her toward the door. "I'll bring it with me the next time I'm over."

Serena had time for only an incoherent protest before Richard had her out the door. Trusting Richard to keep his wife away, at least for the time being, Dione smiled at Blake and waited.

He eyed her warily. "Don't you have something else to do besides staring at me?"

"I certainly do. I was just waiting to see if you have any questions. If you don't, I need to be unpacking."

"No questions," he muttered.

That wouldn't last long, she thought, leaving him without another word. When he found out the extent of her therapy, he'd have plenty to say about it.

It was evidently up to her to find her way around the house, but because the design was so simple, she had no difficulty exploring. Her suitcases were sitting in the foyer, and she took them upstairs herself, finally examining the room she'd chosen for her own. It was a room for a man, done in masculine browns and creams, but it was comfortable and suited her; she wasn't picky. She unpacked, a chore that didn't take long because she didn't burden herself with a lot of clothing. What she had was good and adaptable, so she could use one outfit for several different things just by changing a few accessories. The way she traveled around, from one case to another, a lot of clothing would have been a hindrance.

Then she went in search of the cook and housekeeper; a house that size had to have some sort of staff, and she needed everyone's cooperation. It might have been easier if Richard had remained to introduce her, but she was glad that he'd taken Serena out of the way.

She found the kitchen without difficulty, though the cook who occupied it was something of a surprise. She was tall and lean, obviously part Indian, despite the pale green of her eyes. Though her age was impossible to determine, Dione guessed her to be at least in her fifties, possibly sixties. Her raven-black hair didn't hint at it, but there was something in the knowledge in her eyes, the dignity of her features, that suggested age. She was as imperial as a queen, though the look she turned on the intruder into her kitchen wasn't haughty, merely questioning.

Quickly Dione introduced herself and explained why she was there. The woman washed her hands and dried them with unhurried motions, then held her hand out. Dione took it. "My name is Alberta Quincy," the cook said in a deep, rich voice that could have been a man's. "I'm glad that Mr. Remington has agreed to therapy."

"He didn't exactly agree," Dione replied honestly, smiling. "But I'm here anyway, and I'm staying. I'll need everyone's cooperation to handle him, though."

"You just tell me what you want," Alberta said with pure confidence. "Miguel, who takes care of the grounds and drives Mr. Remington's car, will do as I tell him. My stepdaughter, Angela, cleans the house, and she'll also do as I say."

Most people would, Dione thought privately. Alberta

Quincy was the most regal person she'd ever met. There wasn't much expression in her face and her voice was even and deliberate, but there was a force to the woman that most people wouldn't be able to resist. She would be an indispensable ally.

Dione outlined the diet she wanted Blake to follow, and explained why she wanted changes made. The last thing she wanted to do was offend Alberta. But Alberta merely nodded. "Yes, I understand."

"If he gets angry, put all the blame on me," Dione said. "At this point, I *want* him to be angry. I can use anger, but I can't work with indifference."

Again Alberta nodded her regal head. "I understand," she said again. She wasn't a talkative woman, to understate the matter, but she did understand, and to Dione's relief she didn't express any doubts.

There was one other problem, and Dione broached it cautiously. "About Mr. Remington's sister…"

Alberta blinked once, slowly, and nodded. "Yes," she said simply.

"Does she have a key to the house?" Gold eyes met green ones, and the communication between the two women was so strong that Dione had the sudden feeling that words were unnecessary.

"I'll have the locks changed," Alberta said. "But there'll be trouble."

"It'll be worth the benefits. I can't have his routine interrupted once I get him started on it, at least until he can see some improvement for himself and will want to continue with it. I think Mr. Dylan can handle his wife."

"If he even wants to any longer," Alberta said calmly.

"I think he does. He doesn't seem like a man to give up very easily."

"No, but he's also very proud."

"I don't want to cause trouble between them, but Mr. Remington is my concern, and if that causes friction, then they have to handle it as best they can."

"Mrs. Dylan worships her brother. He raised her. Their mother died when Mrs. Dylan was thirteen."

That explained a lot, and Dione spared a moment of sympathy for both Serena and Richard; then she pushed thoughts of them away. She couldn't consider them; Blake would take all her concentration and energy.

Suddenly she was very tired. It had been a full day, and though it was only late afternoon, she needed to rest. The battle would begin in earnest in the morning, and she'd need a good night's sleep in order to face it. Starting tomorrow, her hands would be full.

Alberta saw the sudden fatigue that tightened Dione's features and within minutes had a sandwich and a glass of milk sitting on the table. "Eat," she said, and Dione knew better than to argue. She sat down and ate.

Dione's alarm clock went off at five-thirty the next morning. She rose and took a shower, her movements brisk and certain from the moment she got out of bed. She always woke instantly, her mind clear, her coordination in perfect sync. It was one reason why she was such a good therapist; if a patient needed her during the night, she didn't stumble around rubbing her eyes. She was instantly capable of doing whatever was required of her.

Something told her that Blake wouldn't be such a cheerful riser, and she could feel her heartbeat speeding up as she brushed her long hair and braided it in one thick braid. Anticipation of the coming battle ran through her veins like liquid joy, making her eyes sparkle and giving a rosy flush to her skin.

The morning was still cool, but she knew from experience that exertion would make her warm, so she dressed in brief blue shorts, a sleeveless cotton shirt with cheerful polka dots

in red, blue and yellow, and an old pair of tennis shoes. She
touched her toes twenty times, stretching her back and legs,
then did twenty sit-ups. She was capable of many more than
that, but this was only a quick routine to warm up.

She was smiling when she entered Blake's room after a
quick tap on the door. "Good morning," she said cheerfully
as she crossed the floor to the balcony and opened the curtains, flooding the room with light.

He was lying on his back, his legs positioned a little awkwardly, as if he'd tried to move them during the night. He
opened his eyes, and Dione saw the flare of panic in them.
He twitched and tried to sit up, groping at his legs; then he
remembered and fell back, his face bleak.

How often did that happen? How often did he wake, not
remembering the accident, and panic because he couldn't move
his legs? He wouldn't do that for very much longer, she determined grimly, going over to sit on the bed beside him.

"Good morning," she said again.

He didn't return the greeting. "What time is it?" he snapped.

"About six o'clock, maybe a little earlier."

"What're you doing here?"

"Beginning your therapy," she replied serenely. He was
wearing pajamas, she saw, and wondered if he were able to
completely dress himself or if someone had to help him.

"No one's up at this hour," he grumbled, closing his eyes
again.

"I am, and now you are. Come on, we've got a lot to do
today." She rolled the wheelchair to the side of the bed and
threw the covers back, revealing his pitifully thin legs clad in
the pale blue pajamas. His feet were covered with white socks.

He opened his eyes and the anger was there again. "What're
you doing?" he snarled, reaching out an arm to whip the covers back over himself again.

He didn't want her to see him, but she couldn't permit any

modesty to interfere. Before long she'd be as familiar with his body as she was with her own, and he had to realize that. If he were ashamed of his physical condition, then he'd simply have to work to improve it.

She snatched the covers away again, and with a deft movement scooped his legs around until they were hanging off the side of the bed. "Get up," she said relentlessly. "Go to the bathroom before we get started. Do you need any help?"

Pure fire sparked from his blue, blue eyes. "No," he growled, so angry that he could barely speak. "I can go to the bathroom by myself, Mama!"

"I'm not your mother," she returned. "I'm your therapist, though the two do have a lot in common."

She held the chair while he levered himself into it; then he shot across the room and was in the adjoining bathroom before she could react. She laughed silently to herself. When she heard the lock click she called out, "Don't think you can lock yourself in there all morning! I'll take the door off the hinges if I have to."

A muffled curse answered her, and she laughed again. This was going to be interesting!

By the time he finally came out she had begun to think she really would have to take the door down. He'd combed his hair and washed his face, but he didn't look any more pleased with being awake than he had before.

"Do you have any underwear on?" she asked, not making any comment on the length of time he'd spent in the bathroom. He'd timed that very nicely, stalling as long as he could, but coming out just before she did something about it.

Shock froze his features. "What?" he asked.

"Do you have any underwear on?" she repeated.

"What business is it of yours?"

"Because I want your pajamas off. If you don't have any

underwear on, you may want to put on a pair, but it really doesn't matter to me. I've seen naked men before."

"I'm sure you have," he muttered snidely. "I have underwear on, but I'm not taking my pajamas off for you."

"Then don't. I'll take them off for you. I think you learned yesterday that I'm strong enough to do it. But those pajamas are coming off, the easy way or the hard way. Which is it?"

"Why do you want them off?" he stalled. "It can't be so you can admire my build," he said bitterly.

"You're right about that," she said. "You look like a bird. That's why I'm here. If you didn't look like a bird, you wouldn't need me."

He flushed.

"The pajamas," she prodded.

Furiously he unbuttoned the shirt and threw it across the room. She could sense that he would have liked to do the same to the bottoms, but they were a bit more difficult to remove. Without a word Dione helped him back onto the bed, then pulled the garment down his thin legs and draped it over the arm of the wheelchair. "On your stomach," she said, and deftly rolled him over.

"Hey!" he protested, his face smothered in the pillow. He swept the pillow aside. He was shaking with fury.

She popped the elastic waistband of his shorts. "Calm down," she advised. "This will be painless this morning."

Her impertinent little gesture made his temper flare so hotly that his entire torso flushed. Smiling at his response, she began to firmly knead his shoulders and back.

He grunted. "Take it easy! I'm not a side of beef!"

She laughed. "How delicate you are!" she mocked. "There's a reason for this."

"Like what? Punishment?"

"In a word, circulation. Your circulation is terrible. That's why your hands are cold, and why you have to wear socks to keep your feet warm, even in bed. I'll bet they're icy cold right now, aren't they?"

Silence was her answer.

"Muscles can't work without a good blood supply," she commented.

"I see," he said sarcastically. "Your magical massage is going to zip me right onto my feet."

"No way. My magical massage is mere groundwork, and you should learn to like it, because you're going to be getting a lot of it."

"God, you're just loaded down with charm, aren't you?"

She laughed again. "I'm loaded down with knowledge, and I also come equipped with a thick hide, so you're wasting your time." She moved down to his legs; there was no flesh there to massage. She felt as if she were merely moving his skin over his bones, but she kept at it, knowing that the hours and hours of massage that she would give him would eventually pay off. She pulled his socks off and rubbed his limp feet briskly, feeling some of the chill leave his skin.

The minutes passed as she worked in silence. He grunted occasionally in protest when her vigorous fingers were a little too rough. A fine sheen of perspiration began to glow on her face and body.

She shifted him onto his back and gave her attention to his arms and chest and his hollow belly. His ribs stood out white under his skin. He lay with his eyes fixed on the ceiling, his mouth grim.

Dione moved down to his legs again.

"How much longer are you going to keep this up?" he finally asked.

She looked up and checked the time. It had been a little over an hour. "I suppose that's enough for right now," she said. "Now we do the exercises."

She took first one leg, then the other, bending them, forcing his knees up to his chest, repeating the motion over and over. He bore it in silence for about fifteen minutes, then suddenly rolled to a sitting position and shoved her away.

"Stop it!" he shouted, his face drawn. "My God, woman, do you have to keep on and on? It's a waste of time! Just leave me alone!"

She regarded him in amazement. "What do you mean, 'a waste of time'? I've just started. Did you really expect to see a difference in an hour?"

"I don't like being handled like so much putty!"

She shrugged, hiding a smile. "It's almost seven-thirty anyway. Your breakfast will be ready. I don't know about you, but I'm hungry."

"I'm not hungry," he said, and then a startled look crossed his face and she knew that he'd just realized that he *was* hungry, probably for the first time in months. She helped him to dress, though her aid managed to send him off into a black temper again. He was as sullen as a child when they entered the elevator that had been installed especially for him.

But the sullenness fled when he saw what was on his plate. Watching him, Dione had to bite her lip to keep from laughing aloud. First horror, then outrage contorted his features. "What's that mess?" he roared.

"Oh, don't worry," she said casually. "That's not all you're getting, but that's what you'll start off with. Those are vitamins," she added in a helpful tone.

They could have been snakes from the way he was staring at them. She had to admit that the collection was a little impressive. Alberta had counted them out exactly as Dione had instructed, and she knew that there were nineteen pills.

"I'm not taking them!"

"You're taking them. You need them. You'll need them even more after a few days of therapy. Besides, you don't get anything to eat until after you've taken them."

He wasn't a good loser. He snatched them up and swallowed them several at a time, washing them down with gulps of water. "There," he snarled. "I've taken the damned things."

"Thank you," she said gravely.

Alberta had evidently been listening, because she promptly entered with their breakfast trays. He looked at his grapefruit half, whole wheat toast, eggs, bacon and milk as if it were slop. "I want a blueberry waffle," he said.

"Sorry," Dione said. "That's not on your diet. Too sweet. Eat your grapefruit."

"I hate grapefruit."

"You need the vitamin C."

"I just took a year's supply of vitamin C!"

"Look," she said sweetly, "this is your breakfast. Eat it or do without. You're not getting a blueberry waffle."

He threw it at her.

She'd been expecting something like that, and ducked gracefully. The plate crashed against the wall. She collapsed against the table, the laughter that she'd been holding in all morning finally bursting out of her in great whoops. His hair was practically standing on end, he was so angry. He was beautiful! His cobalt-blue eyes were as vivid as sapphires; his face was alive with color.

As dignified as a queen, Alberta marched out of the kitchen with an identical tray and set it before him. "She said you'd probably throw the first one," she said without inflection.

Knowing that he'd acted exactly as Dione had predicted made him even angrier, but now he was stymied. He didn't know what to do, afraid that whatever he did, she would have anticipated it. Finally he did nothing. He ate silently, pushing the food into his mouth with determined movements, then balked again at the milk.

"I can't stand milk. Surely coffee can't hurt!"

"It won't hurt, but it won't help, either. Let's make a deal," she offered. "Drink the milk, which you need for the calcium, and then you can have coffee."

He took a deep breath and drained the milk glass.

Alberta brought in coffee. The remainder of the meal passed in relative peace. Angela Quincy, Alberta's stepdaughter, came in to clear the mess that Blake had made with his first breakfast, and he looked a little embarrassed.

Angela, in her way, was as much of an enigma as Alberta was. She showed her age, unlike Alberta; she was about fifty, as soft and cuddly as Alberta was lean and angular. She was very pretty, could even have been called beautiful, despite the wrinkling of her skin. She was the most serene person Dione had ever seen. Her hair was brown, liberally streaked with gray, and her eyes were a soft, tranquil brown. She had once been engaged, Dione would learn later, but the man had died, and Angela still wore the engagement ring he'd given her so many years before.

She wasn't disturbed at all by having to clean egg off the wall, though Blake became increasingly restless as she worked. Dione leisurely finished her meal, then laid her napkin aside.

"Time for more exercises," she announced.

"No!" he roared. "I've had enough for today! A little of you goes a long way, lady!"

"Please, call me Dione," she murmured.

"I don't want to call you anything! My God, would you just leave me alone!"

"Of course I will, when my job is finished. I can't let you ruin my record of successful cases, can I?"

"Do you know what you can do with your successful record?" he snarled, sending the chair jerking backward. He jabbed the forward button. "I don't want to see your face again!" he shouted as the chair rolled out of the room.

She sighed and lifted her shoulders helplessly when her eyes met Angela's philosophic gaze. Angela smiled, but didn't say anything. Alberta wasn't talkative, and Angela was even less so. Dione imagined that when the two of them were together, the silence was deafening.

When she thought that Blake had had enough time to get over his tantrum, she went upstairs to begin again. It would probably be a waste of time to try his door, so she entered her room and went straight through to the gallery. She tapped on the sliding glass doors in his room, then opened them and stepped in.

He regarded her broodingly from his chair. Dione went to him and placed her hand on his shoulder. "I know it's difficult," she said softly. "I can't promise you that any of this will be easy. Try to trust me. I really am good at my job, and at the very worst you'll still be in much better health than you are now."

"If I can't walk, why should I care about my health?" he asked tightly. "Do you think I want to live like this? I would rather have died outright on that cliff than have gone through these past two years."

"Have you always given up so easily?"

"Easily!" His head jerked. "You don't know anything about it! You don't know what it was like—"

"I can tell you what it wasn't like," she interrupted. "I can tell you that you've never looked down at where your legs used to be and seen only flat sheet. You've never had to type by punching the keys with a pencil held in your teeth because you're paralyzed from the neck down. I've seen a lot of people who are a lot worse off than you. You're going to walk again, because I'm going to make you."

"I don't want to hear about how bad other people have it! They're not *me!* My life is my own, and I know what I want out of it, and what I can't…what I *won't* accept."

"Work? Effort? Pain?" she prodded. "Mr. Remington, Richard has told me a great deal about you. You lived life to the fullest. If there were even the slimmest chance that you could do all of that again, would you go for it?"

He sighed, his face unutterably weary. "I don't know. If I really thought there was a chance… But I don't. I can't walk, Miss Kelley. I can't move my legs at all."

"I know. You can't expect to move them right now. I'll have to retrain your nerve impulses before you'll be able to move them. It'll take several months, and I can't promise that you won't limp, but you *will* walk again…if you cooperate with me. So, Mr. Remington, shall we get started again on those exercises?"

CHAPTER 3

He submitted to the exercises with ill grace, but that didn't bother her as long as he cooperated at all. His muscles didn't know that he lay there scowling the entire time; the movement, the stimulation, were what counted. Dione worked tirelessly, alternating between exercising his legs and massaging his entire body. It was almost ten-thirty when she heard the noise that she'd been unconsciously listening for all morning: the tapping of Serena's heels. She lifted her head, and then Blake heard it, too. "No!" he said hoarsely. "Don't let her see me like this!"

"All right," she said calmly, flipping the sheet up to cover him. Then she walked to the door and stepped into the hallway, blocking Serena's way as she started to enter Blake's room.

Serena gave her a startled look. "Is Blake awake? I was just going to peek in. He usually doesn't get up until about noon."

No wonder he'd been so upset when I got him up at six! Dione thought, amused. To Serena she said blandly, "I'm giving him his exercises now."

"So early?" Serena's brows arched in amazement. "Well, I'm certain you've done enough for the day. Since he's awake early he'll be ready for his breakfast. He eats so badly. I don't want him to miss any meals. I'll go in and see what he'd like—"

As Serena moved around Dione to enter Blake's bedroom, Dione deftly sidestepped until she once more blocked the door. "I'm sorry," she said as gently as possible when Serena stared at her in disbelief. "He's already had his breakfast. I've put him on a schedule, and it's important that he stay on it. After another hour of exercise we'll come downstairs for lunch, if you'd like to wait until then."

Serena was still staring at her as if she couldn't believe what she was hearing. "Are you saying…" she whispered, then stopped and began again, her voice stronger this time. "Are you saying that I can't see my brother?"

"At this time, no. We need to complete these exercises."

"Does Blake know I'm here?" Serena demanded, her cheeks suddenly flushing.

"Yes, he does. He doesn't want you to see him right now. Please, try to understand how he feels."

Serena's marvelous eyes widened. "Oh! Oh, I see!" Perhaps she did, but Dione rather doubted it. Hurt shimmered in Serena's eyes for a moment; then she shrugged lightly. "I'll…see him in an hour, then." She turned away, and Dione watched her for a moment, reading wounded emotions in every line of her straight back. It wasn't unusual for the one closest to the patient to become jealous of the intimacy that was necessary between patient and therapist, but Dione never failed to feel uncomfortable when it happened. She knew that the intimacy was only fleeting, that as soon as her patient was recovered and no longer needed her services, she would go on to some other case and the patient would forget all about her. In Blake's case, there was nothing to be jealous of anyway. The only emotion he felt for her was hostility.

When she reentered the bedroom he twisted his head around to stare at her. "Is she gone?" he questioned anxiously.

"She's going to wait downstairs to eat lunch with you," Dione answered, and saw the relief that crossed his face.

"Good. She…nearly went to pieces when this happened to me. She'd be hysterical if she saw what I really look like." Pain darkened his eyes. "She's special to me. I practically raised her. I'm all the family she has."

"No, you're not," Dione pointed out. "She has Richard."

"He's so wrapped up in his work, he seldom remembers that she's alive," he snorted. "Richard's a great vice president, but he's not a great husband."

That wasn't the impression Dione had gotten from Richard; he'd seemed to her to be a man very much in love with his wife. On the surface Richard and Serena were opposites; he was reserved, sophisticated, while she was as forceful as her brother, but perhaps they were each what the other needed. Perhaps her fire made him more spontaneous; perhaps his reserve tempered her rashness. But Dione didn't say anything to Blake. She began the repetitious exercises again, forcing his legs through the same motions.

It was tiring, boring work; tiring for her, boring for him. It made him irritable all over again, but this time when he snapped at her to stop, she obeyed him. She didn't want to browbeat him, to force her wishes on him in everything. He'd put in the most active morning he'd had since the accident, and she wasn't going to push him any further. "Whew!" She sighed, wiping her forehead with the back of her hand and feeling the moisture there. "I need a shower before lunch! Breaking off a little early is a good idea."

He looked at her, and his eyes widened in surprise. She knew that he didn't really see her all morning; he'd been preoccupied with his own condition, his own despair. She'd told him that he'd have to work hard, but now for the first time he realized that she'd be working hard, too. It wasn't going to be a picnic for her. She knew that she looked a mess, all sweaty and flushed.

"A bath wouldn't hurt you," he agreed dryly, and she laughed.

"Don't be such a gentleman about it," she teased. "You just wait. I won't be the only one working up a sweat before long, and I won't show you any mercy!"

"I haven't noticed you showing any, anyway," he grumbled.

"Now, I've been very good to you. I've kept you entertained all morning; I made certain you had a good breakfast—"

"Don't push your luck," he advised, giving her a black look, which she rewarded with a smile. It was important that he learn to joke and laugh with her, to ease the stress of the coming months. She had to become the best friend he had in the world, knowing as she did so that it was a friendship that was doomed from the outset, because it was based on dependence and need. When he no longer needed her, when his life had regained its normal pace, she would leave and be promptly forgotten. She knew that, and she had to keep a part of herself aloof, though the remainder of her emotions and mental effort would be concentrated entirely on him.

While she was helping him to dress, a process that didn't anger him as it had that morning, he said thoughtfully, "You'll be spending most of your time dressing and undressing me, it seems. If this is the routine you're going to be following it'll save a lot of time if I just wear a pair of gym shorts. I can put on a robe before we eat, and Alberta can bring trays up here."

Dione successfully hid her delight, merely saying, "That's your second good idea of the day." Secretly she was elated. From a practical standpoint he was right: it would save a lot of time and effort; however, it would also exclude Serena from most of their meals. That would be a big help.

It wasn't that she disliked Serena; if she had met her under different circumstances, Dione felt that she would have liked

Serena very much. But Blake was her concern now, and she
didn't want anyone or anything interfering with her work.
While she was working on a case she concentrated on her
patient to the extent that everyone else faded into the background, became gray cardboard figures rather than three-
dimensional human beings. It was one of the things that made
her so successful in her field. Already, after only one morning, Blake so filled her thoughts, and she was so much in tune
with him, that she felt she knew him inside and out. She could
practically read his mind, know what he was going to say before he said it. She ached for him, sympathized with him, but
most of all she was happy for him, because she could look at
his helplessness now and know that in a few months he would
be strong and fit again. Already he was looking better, she
thought proudly. It was probably due more to his anger than
her efforts, but his color was much improved. He could stay
angry with her for the entire time if it would keep him active and involved.

She was feeling satisfied with the morning's work as she
walked beside him into the dining room, but that feeling was
shattered when Serena plunged toward Blake, her lovely face
bathed in tears. "Blake," she said brokenly.

Instantly he was alert, concerned, as he reached for her
hand. "What is it?" he asked, a note of tenderness creeping
into his voice, a particular tone that was absent when he talked
to everyone else. Only Serena inspired that voice of love.

"The patio!" she wailed. "Mother's bench…it's ruined!
They've turned the pool into a madhouse! It looks awful!"

"What?" he asked, his brows snapping together. "What're
you talking about?"

Serena pointed a shaking finger at Dione. "*Her* gym!
They've torn up the entire patio!"

"I don't think it's that bad," Dione said reasonably. "It may
be disorganized now, but nothing should be torn up. Richard's

overseeing the installation of the equipment, and I'm sure he wouldn't let anything be damaged."

"Come see for yourself!"

Dione checked her watch. "I think we should have lunch first. The patio isn't going anywhere, but the food will be cold."

"Stalling?" Blake inquired coldly. "I told you, Miss Kelley, that I don't want this house changed."

"I can neither deny nor confirm what changes have been made, because I haven't been outside. I've been with you all morning. However, I trust Richard's good sense, even if you don't," she said pointedly, and Serena flushed furiously.

"It isn't that I don't trust my husband," she began heatedly, but Blake cut her off with a lifted hand.

"Not now," he said shortly. "I want to see the patio."

Serena fell into immediate silence, though she looked sulky. Evidently Blake was still very much the big brother, despite his obvious ill health. His voice carried the unmistakable ring of command. Blake Remington was accustomed to giving orders and having them carried out immediately; his morning with Dione must have gone completely against the grain.

It was the first time Dione had been on the patio, and she found it beautifully landscaped, cool and fragrant, despite the brutal Arizona sun. Yucca plants and different varieties of cactus grew in perfect harmony with plants normally found in a much more congenial climate. Careful watering explained the unusual variety of plants, that and the well-planned use of shade. White flagstones had been laid out to form a path, while a central fountain spewed its musical water upward in a perfect spray. At the back of the patio, where a tall gate opened onto the pool area, was a beautifully carved bench in a delicate pearl-gray color. Dione had no idea what type of wood it was, though it was gorgeous.

The patio *was* disorganized; evidently the workers Richard

had hired had used the patio to store the pool furniture that was in the way, and also the materials that they didn't need at the moment. However, she saw that they had been careful not to disturb any of the plants; everything was placed carefully on the flagstones. But Serena ran to the lovely bench and pointed out a long gouge on its side. "See!" she cried.

Blake's eyes flashed. "Yes, I see. Well, Miss Kelley, it looks as if your workers have damaged a bench that I consider priceless. My father gave it to my mother when they moved into this house. She sat here every evening, and it's here that I see her in my mind. I want this whole thing called off before something else is ruined, and I want you out of my house."

Dione was distressed that the bench had been damaged, and she opened her mouth to apologize; then she saw the flash of triumph in Serena's eyes and she paused. To give herself time to think, she walked to the bench and bent down to examine the scarred wood. Thoughtfully she ran a finger over the gouge; a quick glance at Serena caught a hint of apprehension in those amazingly expressive eyes. What was Serena worried about? Looking back at the bench, the answer became readily apparent: the bench was undoubtedly damaged, but the gouge was old enough to have weathered. It certainly hadn't been done that morning.

She could have accused Serena of deliberately trying to cause trouble, but she didn't. Serena was fighting for the brother she loved, and though her battle was useless, Dione couldn't condemn her for it. She would just have to separate Serena from Blake so her work could continue without a constant stream of interruptions. Richard would have to bring that laser brain of his into use and keep his wife occupied.

"I can understand why you're both upset," she said mildly, "but this gouge wasn't done tonight. See?" she asked, pointing at the wood. "It isn't a fresh scar. I'd guess that this has been here for several weeks."

Blake moved his wheelchair closer and leaned down to in-spect the bench for himself. He straightened slowly. "You're right." He sighed. "In fact, I'm afraid I'm the culprit."

Serena gasped. "What do you mean?"

"A few weeks ago I was out here and I bumped the wheel-chair into the bench. You'll notice that the gouge is the same height as the hub of my wheel." He rubbed his eyes with a thin hand that trembled with strain. "God, I'm sorry, Serena."

"Don't blame yourself!" she cried, rushing to his side and clutching his hand. "It doesn't matter. Please don't be upset. Come inside and let's have lunch. I know you must be tired. It can't do any good for you to tire yourself out like this. You need to rest."

Dione watched as Serena walked beside the wheelchair, all concern and love. Shaking her head a little in amused exas-peration, she followed them.

Serena remained close by Blake's side for the rest of the day, fussing over him like a hen with one chick. Blake *was* tired after his first day of therapy, and he let her coddle him. Though Dione had planned to have another session of exer-cise and massage, she let it go rather than fight a battle to do it. Tomorrow...well, tomorrow would be another story.

Richard arrived for dinner, a practice that Alberta had told Dione was the usual whenever Serena came over, which was every day. He watched silently as Serena hovered anxiously over Blake, and though Richard had the original poker face, Dione sensed that he wasn't happy with the situation. After dinner, while Serena got Blake settled in his study, Dione took the opportunity to speak privately to Richard.

They went out to the patio and sat on one of the benches that were scattered around. Dione looked up at the countless stars that were visible in the clear desert night. "I'm having a problem with Serena," she said without preamble.

He sighed. "I know. I've had a problem with her since Blake

had his accident. I understand how she feels, but it's still driving me crazy."

"He said something today about raising her."

"Practically. Serena was thirteen when their mother died, and it was quite a shock to her. It was weeks before she could bear for Blake to be out of her sight. It must've seemed to her as if everyone she loved was dying. First her father, then her mother. She was especially close to her mother. I know that she's terrified something will happen to Blake, but at the same time I can't help resenting it."

"'Forsaking all others,'" Dione quoted, a little sadly.

"Exactly. I want my wife back."

"Blake said that you don't pay any attention to her, that you're wrapped up in your work."

He rubbed the back of his neck with restless fingers. "I have a lot of work to do, with Blake like he is. My God, what I wouldn't give to go home to just a little of the tender loving care that she smothers Blake with every day!"

"I spoke to Alberta about having the locks on the doors changed, but the more I think about it, the more I think it isn't such a good idea," she confessed. "Blake would be furious if anyone locked his sister out of his house. The problem is, I can't keep him on a schedule if she keeps interrupting."

"I'll see what I can do," he said doubtfully. "But any suggestion that will keep her away from Blake will go over like an outbreak of plague." He looked at her, and his teeth suddenly flashed white as he grinned. "You must have the steadiest nerves I've ever seen. Was it interesting today?"

"It had its moments," she replied, laughing a little. "He threw his breakfast at me."

Richard laughed aloud. "I wish I could've seen that! Blake's always had a hot temper, but for the past year he's been so depressed that you couldn't make him angry if you tried all day. It would've been like old times if I had been here to see him."

"I hope I can get him to the point where he doesn't need to be angry," she said. "I'm certain that he'll progress more rapidly if we aren't interrupted. I'm relying on you to think of something that'll keep Serena occupied."

"If I could, I'd have used it before now," he said in disgust. "Short of kidnapping her, I can't think of anything that will work."

"Then why don't you?"

"What?"

"Kidnap her. Take her on a second honeymoon. Whatever it takes."

"The second honeymoon sounds good," he admitted. "But there's no way I can get free until Blake returns to work and takes over again. Any more ideas?"

"I'm afraid you'll have to think of something on your own. I don't know her that well. But I need privacy to work with Blake."

"Then you'll have it," he promised after a moment's thought. "I don't know what I'll do, but I'll keep her away as much as I can. Unless Blake's completely dead, it shouldn't take him long to realize that he'd rather have you fussing over him than his sister, anyway."

At the obvious admiration in his voice, Dione shifted uncomfortably. She was aware of her looks, but at the same time she didn't want anyone to comment on them. Blake was her patient; it was out of the question for her to become involved with him in any sort of sexual relationship. Not only was it against her professional ethics, it was impossible for her. She no longer woke up in the middle of the night trying desperately to scream, her throat constricted by sheer terror, and she wasn't going to do anything to reawaken those nightmares. She'd put the horror behind her, where it had to stay.

Sensing her unease, Richard said, "Dione?" His voice was low, puzzled. "Is something wrong?" He put his hand on her arm, and she jumped as if she'd been stung, unable to bear the touch. He got to his feet, alarmed by her action. "Dione?" he asked again.

"I…I'm sorry," she murmured, wrapping her arms tightly around herself in an effort to control the trembling that had seized her. "I can't explain…. I'm sorry—"

"But what's wrong?" he demanded, reaching out his hand to her again, and she drew back sharply, jumping to her feet.

She knew that she couldn't explain, but neither could she stand there any longer. "Good night," she said rapidly, and walked away from him. She entered the house and almost bumped into Serena, who was stepping out onto the patio.

"There you are," she said. "Blake's gone to bed. He was so tired."

"Yes, I thought he would be," Dione said, gathering her composure enough to answer Serena evenly. Suddenly she felt very tired, too, and she was unable to stifle a yawn. "I'm sorry," she said. "It's been a long day."

Serena gave her an odd, considering look. "Then Richard and I will be leaving. I don't want to keep you up. I'll see Blake tomorrow."

"I'll be increasing his exercises tomorrow," Dione informed her, taking the opportunity to let Serena know that her presence would hinder rather than help. "It would be better if you waited until late afternoon, say after four."

"But that's too much!" Serena gasped. "He isn't strong enough!"

"At this point, I'm doing most of the work," Dione reassured her dryly. "But I'll be careful not to let him do too much."

If Serena heard the sarcasm that Dione couldn't quite suppress, she didn't let on. Instead she nodded. "I see," she said coldly. "Very well. I'll see Blake tomorrow afternoon."

Well, will wonders never cease, Dione thought wryly to herself as she made her way upstairs. All she'd had to do was mention that Blake would be busy, and though Serena hadn't been happy with the situation, she'd agreed to it.

After she'd gotten ready for bed, she tapped lightly on Blake's door; when she didn't hear an answer she opened the door just enough to peek inside. He was sound asleep, lying on his back, his head rolled against his shoulder. With only the light from the hallway on him, he looked younger, the lines of suffering not visible now.

Quietly she closed the door and returned to her room. She was tired, so tired that her limbs ached, but after she was in bed she found that sleep eluded her. She knew why, and lay awake staring at the ceiling, knowing that she might not sleep at all that night. Such a silly, trivial thing...just because Richard had touched her.

Yet it wasn't trivial, and she knew it. She might have pushed the nightmare away, she might have restructured her life completely, but her past was hers, a part of her, and it hadn't been trivial. Rape wasn't trivial. Since that night she hadn't been able to bear for anyone to touch her. She'd worked out a compromise with herself, satisfying her human need for warmth and touching by working with her patients, touching them, but she could bear the contact only as long as she was the one in control.

On the surface she had recovered completely; she had built a wall between who she was now and who she had been then, never dwelling on what had happened, literally forcing herself to gather together the shattered pieces of her life and, with fierce concentration and willpower, actually mending the pieces into a stronger fabric. She could laugh and enjoy life. More important, she had learned how to respect herself, which had been the hardest task of all.

But she couldn't tolerate a man's touch.

That night had effectively prevented her from marrying and having a family. Since that part of life was denied her, she ignored it, and never cried for what might have been. Instead she became a vagabond of sorts, traveling around the country and helping other people. While she was on a case she had an intense relationship full of love and caring, but without any sexual overtones. She loved her patients, and, inevitably, they loved her...while it lasted. They became her family, until the day when it was over and she left them with a smile on her face, ready to continue on to her next case and her next "family."

She had wondered, when she began her training, if she would ever be able to work with a man at all. The problem worried her until she decided that, if she couldn't, she would be handicapping her career terribly and made up her mind to do what was necessary. The first time she worked with a man she'd had to grit her teeth and use all her considerable determination to make herself touch him, but after a few minutes she had realized that a man who needed therapy obviously wasn't in any shape to be attacking her. Men were human beings who needed help, just like everyone else.

She preferred working with children, though. They loved so freely, so wholeheartedly. A child's touch was the one touch she could tolerate; she had learned to enjoy the feel of little arms going about her neck in a joyous hug. If there was one regret that sometimes refused to go away, it was the regret that she would never have children of her own. She controlled it by channeling extra devotion into her efforts for the children she worked with, but deep inside her was the need to have someone of her own, someone who belonged to her and who she belonged to, a part of herself.

Suddenly a muffled sound caught her attention, and she lifted her head from the pillow, waiting to see if it was repeated. Blake? Had he called out?

There was nothing but silence now, but she couldn't rest until she had made certain that he was all right. Getting out of bed, she slipped on her robe and walked silently to the room next door. Opening the door enough to look inside, she saw him lying in the same position he'd been in before. She was about to leave when he tried to roll onto his side, and when his legs didn't cooperate, he made the same sound she'd heard before, a half sigh, half grunt.

Did no one ever think to help him change his position? she wondered, gliding silently into the room on her bare feet. If he'd been lying on his back for two years, no wonder he had the temperament of a water buffalo.

She didn't know if he were awake or not; she didn't think so. Probably he was just trying to change positions as people do naturally during sleep. The light in the hallway wasn't on now, since everyone was in bed, and in the dim starlight coming through the glass doors she couldn't see well enough to decide. Perhaps, if he were still asleep, she could gently adjust his position without his ever waking up. It was something she did for most of her patients, a gesture of concern that they usually never realized.

First she touched his shoulder lightly, just placing her hand on him and letting his subconscious become accustomed to the touch. After a moment she applied a little pressure and he obeyed it, trying to roll to his right side, facing her. Gently, slowly, she helped him, moving his legs so they didn't hold him back. With a soft sigh he burrowed his face into the pillow, his breathing becoming deeper as he relaxed.

Smiling, she pulled the sheet up over his shoulder and returned to her room.

Blake wasn't like her other patients. Still lying awake over an hour later, she tried to decide why she was so determined to make him walk again. It wasn't just her normal devotion to a patient; in some way she didn't yet understand, it was important to her personally that he once again become the man he had been. He had been such a strong man, a man so vi-

brantly alive that he was the center of attention wherever he
went. She *knew* that. She had to restore him to that.

He was so near to death. Richard had been correct in saying that he wouldn't live another year the way he was. Blake
had been willing himself to die. She had gotten his attention
that morning with her shock tactics, but she had to keep it
until he could actually see himself progressing, until he realized that he could recover. She would never be able to forgive
herself if she failed him.

She finally slept for about two hours, rising before dawn
with a restless anticipation driving her. She would have loved
to run on the beach, but Phoenix didn't have a beach, and she
didn't know the grounds well enough to go trotting around
them in the dark. For all she knew Blake had attack dogs pa-
trolling at night. But despite her lack of sleep she was brim-
ming with energy. She tried to burn off some of it by doing a
brisk routine of exercises, but the shower she took afterward
so refreshed her that she felt she was ready to tackle the world.
Well, at least Blake Remington!

It was even earlier than it had been the morning before
when she gave in to her enthusiasm and bounded into his
room, snapping on the light as she did, because it was still dark.

"Good morning," she chirped.

He was still on his side; he opened one blue eye, surveyed
her with an expression of horror, then uttered an explicit word
that would have gotten his mouth washed out with soap if
he'd been younger. Dione grinned at him.

"Are you ready to start?" she asked innocently.

"Hell, no!" he barked. "Lady, it's the middle of the night!"

"Not quite. It's almost dawn."

"*Almost?* How close to almost?"

"In just a few minutes," she soothed, then ruined it by
laughing as she threw the covers off him. "Don't you want
to see the sunrise?"

"No!"

"Don't be such a spoilsport," she coaxed, swinging his legs off the bed. "Watch the sunrise with me."

"I don't want to watch the sunrise, with you or anyone else," he snarled. "I want to sleep!"

"You've been asleep for hours, and you don't want to pass this sunrise up. It's going to be a special one."

"What makes this sunrise so special? Does it mark the beginning of the day you're going to torture me to death?"

"Only if you *don't* watch it with me," she promised him cheerfully, catching his hand and urging him upright. She helped him into the wheelchair and covered him with a blanket, knowing that the air would feel cool to him. "Where's the best place to watch it from?" she asked.

"By the pool," he grunted, rubbing his face with both hands and mumbling the words through his fingers. "You're crazy, lady—a certified lunatic if I've ever seen one."

She smoothed his tousled hair with her fingers, smiling down at him tenderly. "Oh, I don't know about that," she murmured. "Didn't you sleep well last night?"

"Of course I did!" he snapped. "You had me so tired I couldn't hold my head up!" As soon as the words left his mouth a sheepish expression crossed his face. "All right, so it was the best night I've had in two years," he admitted, grudgingly, it was true, but at least he said it.

"See what a little therapy can do for you?" she teased, then changed the subject before he could flare up at her again. "You'll have to lead the way to the pool. I don't want to go through the courtyard, since the workers have put so much of their equipment there. It could be tricky in the dark."

He wasn't enthusiastic, but he put the chair in motion and led her through the silent house to the rear entrance. As they circled around the back to the pool, a bird chirped a single, liquid note in greeting of the new day, and his head lifted at the sound.

Had it been two years since he'd heard a bird sing?

Sitting beside the pool, with the quiet ripple of the water making its own music, they silently watched the first graying of dawn; then at last the first piercing ray of the sun shot over the rim of the mountains. There were no clouds to paint the sky in numberless hues of pink and gold, only the clear, clear blue sky and the white-gold sun, but the utter serenity of the new day made the scene as precious as the most glamorous sunrise she'd ever seen. As fast as that, the day began to warm, and he pushed the blanket down from his shoulders.

"I'm hungry," he announced, a prosaic concern after the long silence they had shared.

She looked at him and chuckled, then rose from her cross-legged position on the concrete. "I can see how much you appreciate the finer things in life," she said lightly.

"If you insist on getting me up at midnight, naturally I'm hungry by the time dawn rolls around! Am I getting the same slop today that I had yesterday morning?"

"You are," she said serenely. "A nutritious, high-protein breakfast, just what you need to put weight on you."

"Which you then try your damnedest to beat off of me," he retorted.

She laughed at him, enjoying their running argument. "You just wait," she promised. "By this time next week you're going to think that yesterday was nothing!"

CHAPTER 4

Dione lay awake, watching the patterns of light that the new moon was casting on the white ceiling. Richard had worked miracles and informed her at dinner that night that the gym was now ready for use, but her problem was with Blake. Unaccountably he'd become withdrawn and depressed again. He ate what Alberta put before him, and he lay silent and uncomplaining while Dione exercised his legs, and that was all wrong. Therapy wasn't something for a patient to passively accept, as Blake was doing. He could lie there and let her move his legs, but when they started working in the gym and in the pool, he'd have to actively participate.

He wouldn't talk to her about what was bothering him. She knew exactly when it had happened, but she couldn't begin to guess what had triggered it. They had been sniping at each other while she gave him a massage before beginning the exercises, and all of a sudden his eyes had gotten that blank, empty look, and he'd been unresponsive to any of her gibes since then. She didn't think it was anything she'd said; her teasing that day had been lighthearted, because of his greatly improved spirits.

Turning her head to read the luminous dial of the clock, she saw that it was after midnight. As she had done every night, she got up to check on Blake. She hadn't heard the sounds that he usually made when he tried to turn over, but she'd been preoccupied with her thoughts.

As soon as she entered his room she saw that his legs had that awkward, slightly twisted look that meant he'd already tried to shift his position. Gently she put her left hand on his shoulder and her right on his legs, ready to move him.

"Dione?"

His quiet, uncertain voice startled her, and she leaped back. She'd been so intent on his legs that she hadn't noticed his open eyes, though the moonlight that played across the bed was bright enough for her to see him.

"I thought you were asleep," she murmured.

"What were you doing?"

"Helping you to roll over onto your side. I do this every night. This is the first time you've been disturbed by it."

"No, I was already awake." Curiosity entered his tone as he shifted his shoulders restlessly. "Do you mean you come in here in the middle of every night and roll me around?"

"You seem to sleep better on your side," she said by way of explanation.

He gave a short, bitter laugh. "I sleep better on my stomach, or at least I did before. I haven't slept on my stomach in two years now."

The quiet intimacy of the night, the moonlit room, made it seem as if they were the only two people on earth, and she was aware of a deep despair in him. Perhaps he felt a special closeness with her, too; perhaps now, with the darkness as a partial shield, he would talk to her and tell her what was bothering him. Without hesitation she sat down on the edge of the bed and pulled her nightgown snugly around her legs.

"Blake, what's wrong? Something's bothering you," she said softly.

"Bingo," he muttered. "Did you take psychology, too, when you were in training to be Superwoman?"

She ignored the cut and put her hand on his arm. "Please tell me. Whatever it is, it's interfering with your therapy. The gym is ready for you, but you aren't ready for it."

"I could've told you that. Look, this whole thing is a waste of time," he said, and she could almost feel the weariness in him, like a great stone weighing him down. "You may feed me vitamins and rev up my circulation, but can you promise that I'll ever be exactly like I was before? Don't you understand? I don't want just 'improvement,' or any other compromise. If I can't be back, one hundred percent, the way I was before, then I'm not interested."

She was silent. No, she couldn't honestly promise him that there wouldn't always be some impairment, a limp, difficulties that would be with him for the rest of his life. In her experience, the human body could do wonders in repairing itself, but the injuries it suffered always left traces of pain and healing in the tissue.

"Would it matter so much to you if you walked with a limp?" she finally asked. "I'm not the way I would like to be, either. Everyone has a weakness, but not everyone just gives up and lets himself rot because of it, either. What if your position were reversed with say, Serena? Would you want her to just lie there and slowly deteriorate into a vegetable? Wouldn't you want her to fight, to try as hard as she could to overcome the problem?"

He flung his forearm up to cover his eyes. "You fight dirty, lady. Yes, I'd want Serena to fight. But I'm not Serena, and my life isn't hers. I'd never really realized, before the accident, how important the quality of my life was. The things I did were wild and dangerous, but, my God, I was alive! I've never been a nine-to-five man. I'd rather be dead, even though I know that millions of people are perfectly happy and content with that kind of routine. That's fine for them, but it's not *me*."

"Would a limp prevent you from doing all those things again?" she probed. "You can still jump out of airplanes, or climb mountains. You can still fly your own jets. Is the rhythm of your walk so important to you that you're willing to die because of it?"

"Why do you keep saying that?" he asked sharply, jerking his arm down and glaring at her. "I don't remember heading my wheelchair down the stairs, if that's what you're thinking."

"No, but you're killing yourself just as surely in a different way. You're letting your body die of neglect. Richard was desperate when he tracked me down in Florida. He told me that you wouldn't live another year the way you were going, and after seeing you, I agree with him."

He lay in silence, staring up at the ceiling that he had already looked at for more hours than she could imagine. She wanted to gather him into her arms and soothe him as she did the children she worked with; he was a man, but in a way he was as lost and frightened as any child. Confused suddenly by the unfamiliar need to touch him, she folded her hands tightly in her lap.

"What's your weakness?" he asked. "You said that everyone has one. Tell me what torments you, lady."

The question was so unexpected that she couldn't stop the welling of pain, and a shudder shook her entire body. His weakness was obvious, there for everyone to see in his limp, wasted legs. Hers was also a wound that had almost been fatal, for all that it couldn't be seen. There had been a dark time when death had seemed like the easiest way out, a soft cushion for a battered mind and body that had taken too much abuse. But there had been, deep inside her, a bright and determined spark of life that had kept her from even the attempt, as if she knew that to take the first step would be one step too many. She had fought, and lived, and healed her wounds as best she could.

"What's wrong?" he jeered softly. "You can pry into everyone else's secrets, so why can't you share a few of your own? What are your weaknesses? Do you shoplift for kicks? Sleep with strangers? Cheat on your taxes?"

Dione shuddered again, her hands clenched so tightly that her knuckles were white. She couldn't tell him, not all of it, yet in a way he had a right to know some of her pain. She had already witnessed a lot of his, knew what he thought, knew his longing and despair. None of her other patients had demanded so much from her, but Blake wasn't like the others. He was asking for more than he knew, just as she was asking him for superhuman effort. If she put him off now, she knew in her bones that he wouldn't respond to her anymore. His recovery depended on her, on the trust she could foster between them.

She was shaking visibly, her entire body caught up in the tremors that shook her from head to foot. She knew that the bed was vibrating, knew that he could feel it. His brows snapped together and he said uncertainly, "Dione? Listen, I—"

"I'm illegitimate," she ground out, her teeth chattering. She was panting with the effort it took her to speak at all, and she felt a film of perspiration break out on her body. She sucked in her breath on a sob that shuddered through her; then with a grinding force of will she held her body still. "I don't know who my father was. My mother didn't even know his name. She was drunk, he was there, and presto! She had a baby. Me. She didn't want me. Oh, she fed me, I suppose, since I'm alive to tell about it. But she never hugged me, never kissed me, never told me that she loved me. In fact, she went out of her way to tell me that she hated me, hated having to take care of me, hated even seeing me. Except for the welfare check she got for me, she would probably have dumped me in a trash can and left me."

"You don't know that!" he snapped, heaving himself up on one elbow. She could tell that he was taken aback by the harsh bitterness in her voice, but now that she had started, she couldn't stop. If it killed her, the poison had to spew out now.

"She told me," she insisted flatly. "You know how kids are. I tried every way I knew how to make her love me. I couldn't have been more than three years old, but I can remember climbing up on chairs, then onto the cabinets so I could reach the whiskey bottle for her. Nothing worked, of course. I learned not to cry, because she slapped me if I cried. If she wasn't there, or if she was passed out drunk, I learned to eat whatever I could. Dry bread, a piece of cheese, it didn't matter. Sometimes there wasn't anything to eat, because she'd spent all the check on whiskey. If I waited long enough she'd go off with some man and come back with a little money, enough to get by until the next check, or the next man."

"Dee, stop it!" he ordered harshly, putting his hand on her arm and shaking her. Wildly she jerked away from him.

"You wanted to know!" she breathed, her lungs aching with the effort they were making to draw air into her constricted chest. "So you can hear it!… Whenever I made the mistake of bothering her, which didn't take much, she slapped me. Once she threw a whiskey bottle at me. I was lucky that time, because all I got was a little cut on my temple, though she was so angry at the wasted whiskey that she beat me with her shoe. Do you know what she told me, over and over? 'You're just a bastard, and nobody loves a bastard!' Over and over, until finally I had to believe it. I know the exact day when I learned to believe it. My seventh birthday. I'd started to go to school, you see, and I knew then that birthdays were supposed to be something special. Birthdays were when your parents gave you presents to show you how much they loved you. I woke up and went running into her room, sure that today was the day that she would finally love me. She slapped me for waking her up and shoved me into the closet. She kept me locked in the closet all day long. That's what she thought of my birthday, you see. She hated the sight of me."

She was bent over, her body tight with pain, but her eyes were dry and burning. "I was living in the streets by the time I was ten," she whispered, her strength beginning to leave her. "It was safer than home. I don't know what happened to her. I went back one day, and the place was empty."

Her rasping breath was the only sound in the room. He lay as if he had been turned to stone, his eyes burning on her. Dione could have collapsed, she was suddenly so tired. With an effort she drew herself upright. "Any more questions?" she asked dully.

"Just one," he said, and her body clenched painfully, but she didn't protest. She waited, wondering in exhaustion what he would ask of her next.

"Were you eventually adopted?"

"No," she breathed, closing her eyes, swaying a little. "I eventually wound up in an orphanage, and it was as good a place as any. I had food, and a place to sleep, and I was able to go to school regularly. I was too old for adoption, and no one wanted me as a foster child. My looks were too odd, I suppose." Moving like an old woman, she got to her feet and slowly left the room, knowing that the air was still heavy with questions that he wanted to ask, but she'd remembered enough for one night. No matter what she had accomplished, no matter how many years had passed since she was a lonely, bewildered child, the lack of her mother's love was still an emptiness that hadn't been filled. A mother's love was the basis of every child's life, and the absence of it had left her crippled inside just as surely as the accident had crippled Blake's legs.

Not surprisingly, she fell facedown on her bed and slept

heavily, without dreaming, to awaken promptly when the alarm went off. She had learned, over the years, how to function even when she felt as if a part of her had been murdered, and she did so now. At first she had to force herself to go through the regular routine, but in only a moment the hard self-discipline had taken over, and she shoved the crisis of the night away. She would *not* let it drag her down! She had a job to do, and she'd do it.

Perhaps something of her determination was written on her face when she entered Blake's bedroom, because he promptly raised his hands and said mildly, "I surrender."

She stopped in her tracks and regarded him quizzically. He was smiling a little, his pale, thin face weary, but no longer locked in a mask of detachment. "But I haven't even attacked yet," she protested. "You're taking all the fun out of it."

"I know when I'm outgunned." He grimaced and admitted, "I don't see how I can give up without at least trying again. You didn't give up, and I've never been a man to back down from a challenge."

The hard knot of apprehension that had been tied in her stomach since he'd lapsed into depression slowly eased, then relaxed completely. Her spirits soared, and she gave him a blinding smile. With his cooperation, she felt that she could do anything.

At first he was capable of very little with the weights. Even the smaller ones were too much for him, though he kept gritting his teeth and trying to continue even when she wanted him to stop. *Stubborn* was too mild a word to describe him. He was hell-bent and determined to push himself to the limits of his endurance, which unfortunately wasn't far. It always took a long session in the whirlpool afterward to ease the pain from his tortured muscles, but he kept at it, even knowing that he was going to have to pay with pain.

To her relief he asked no more questions and in no way referred to what she'd told him of her childhood. Because of the extra demand he was making on his body, he was always sound asleep when she checked on him at night, so there were no repeats.

Over Serena's protests Dione also began giving him therapy in the pool. Serena was terrified that he'd drown, since his legs were useless and he obviously couldn't kick, but Blake himself overruled her objections. He'd said that he liked challenges, and he wasn't backing off from this one. With his engineering expertise, he designed and directed the construction of a system of braces and pulleys that enabled Dione to lower him into the pool and hoist him out when the session was ended, something that he would soon be able to do for himself.

One morning, after she'd been there a little over two weeks, Dione watched him as he devoured the breakfast that Alberta had prepared. Already it seemed that he was gaining weight. His face had fleshed out and wasn't as gray as it had been. He'd burned a little during the first few days he'd been in the sun, but he hadn't peeled, and now the light tan he'd acquired made his blue eyes seem even bluer.

"What're you staring at?" he demanded as Alberta removed the plate before him and replaced it with a bowl of fresh strawberries in cream.

"You're gaining weight," Dione told him with immense satisfaction.

"Shouldn't wonder," Alberta snorted as she left the room. "He's eating like a horse."

Blake scowled at her, but dipped his spoon into the bowl and lifted a plump strawberry. His white teeth sank into the red fruit; then his tongue captured the juice that stained his lips. "That's what you wanted, isn't it?" he demanded grumpily. "To fatten me up?"

She smiled and didn't reply, watching as he demolished the

fruit. Just as he was finishing Angela glided in with a telephone, which she placed on the table before him. After plugging it in, she gave him a shy smile and left.

Blake sat there, staring at the phone. Dione hid a grin. "I think that means you have a call," she prompted.

He looked relieved. "Good. I was afraid you wanted me to eat it."

She chuckled and got to her feet. As he lifted the receiver and put it to his ear, she touched his shoulder lightly and murmured, "I'll be in the gym. Come down when you're finished."

He met her eyes and nodded, already embroiled in conversation. She heard enough to know that he was talking to Richard, and just the thought of Richard was enough to pucker her brow in a line of worry.

Serena had been very good after that first day; she'd come to see Blake only in the late afternoon, when Dione had completed her schedule for the day. She'd also learned not to wait until too late to arrive, or Blake would already be asleep. Most nights, Richard also arrived for dinner.

Richard was a witty, entertaining man, with a dry sense of humor and a repertoire of jokes that often had her chuckling in her seat, but which couldn't be repeated when Blake or Serena asked what was so funny.

Dione couldn't say that Richard had been less than a gentleman. In no way had he said or done anything that could be termed suggestive. It was just that she could read the deepening admiration in his eyes, sense the growing gentleness in the way he treated her. She wasn't the only one who felt that perhaps Richard was becoming too fond of her; Serena was subtle, but she watched her husband sharply when he was talking with Dione. In a way, Dione was relieved; it meant that Serena was at least paying attention to her husband. But she didn't want complications of that sort, especially when there was nothing to it.

She didn't feel that she could say anything to Richard about it, either. How could she scold him when he'd been nothing but polite? He loved his wife, she was sure. He liked and admired his brother-in-law. But still, he responded to Dione in a way that she knew she hadn't mistaken.

She'd been the object of unwanted attention before, but this was the first time that attention hadn't been obvious. She had no idea how to handle it. She knew that Richard would never try to force himself on her, but Serena was jealous. Part of Dione, the deeply feminine part of her, was even flattered by his regard. If Serena had been giving her husband the attention he deserved, none of this would be happening.

But they weren't important, she told herself. She couldn't let them be important to her. Only Blake mattered. He was coming out of the prison of his disability, more and more revealing himself as the man he'd been before the accident. In another month she hoped to have him standing. Not walking, but standing. Letting his legs get used to supporting the weight of his body again. What she was doing now was dealing with the basics, restoring him to health and building his strength up enough that he would be able to stand when she demanded it of him.

She ran hot water in a plastic container and set the flask of oil that she used down in it to warm it for the massage that she always gave him before he went in the pool, in an effort to protect him from any chill. Not that a chill was likely in the hundred-plus-degree heat of a summer day in Phoenix, she thought wryly, but he was so thin, still so weakened, that she didn't take any chances with him. Besides, he seemed to enjoy the feel of the warm oil being massaged into him, and he had little enough joy in his life.

She was restless, and she prowled aimlessly about the converted game room, pausing to stretch her body. She needed a good workout to release some of her energy, she decided, and positioned herself on the weight bench.

She liked lifting weights. Her aim was strength, not bulk, and the program that she followed was designed with that in mind. For Blake, she was altering the program enough to build up the bulk of his muscles without pumping him up like a Mr. Universe. Carefully regulating her breathing, concentrating on what she was doing, she began her sets. Up, down. Up, down.

She finished her leg sets and adjusted the system of pulleys and weights to what she wanted for her arms. Puffing, she began again. The demand she was making on her muscles reached a plateau that was almost pleasure. Again. Again.

"You damned cheat!" The roar startled her, and she jerked upright, alarm skittering across her features. Confused, she stared at Blake. He sat in his wheelchair, just inside the door, his face dark red and contorted with fury.

"What?" she spluttered.

He pointed at the weights. "You're a weight lifter!" he bellowed, so furious that he was shaking. "You little cheat. You knew the day you beat me at arm wrestling that you'd win! Hell, how many men *could* beat you?"

She blushed. "Not everyone," she said with modesty, which seemed to make him even angrier.

"I can't believe it!" He was yelling, getting louder and louder. "Knowing how it would make me feel that a woman could beat me at arm wrestling, you made a bet on it anyway, and you *rigged* it!"

"I never said that I wasn't good at it," she pointed out, trying to keep the laughter out of her voice. He looked wonderful! If sheer rage could have put him back on his feet, he'd have been walking right then. A giggle escaped her control, and at the sound of it he began pounding his fist on the arm of the wheelchair; unfortunately he was pounding on the controls, and the chair began jumping back and forth like a bronc trying to rid itself of an unwanted rider.

Dione couldn't help it; she gave up even trying to keep a straight face and laughed until tears ran down her face. She howled. She beat the weight bench with her fist in mute mockery of the way he'd pounded the wheelchair controls; she clutched her arms across her stomach, gasping for breath, and every new eruption of rage from him sent her off into renewed paroxysms.

"Stop laughing!" he thundered, his voice booming off the walls. "Sit down! We'll see who wins this time!"

She was so weak that she had to haul herself to the massage table where he'd propped his elbow and was waiting for her with a face like doom. Still giggling, she collapsed against the table.

"This isn't fair!" she protested, putting her hand in his grip. "I'm not ready. Wait until I stop laughing."

"Was it fair when you let me think I was wrestling a frail, *normal* woman?" he seethed.

"I'm perfectly normal!" she hooted. "You got beat fair and square, and you know it!"

"I don't know any such thing! You cheated, and I want a rematch."

"All right, all right. Just give me a minute." Quickly she squelched the remaining laughter that wanted to bubble out and flexed her hand in his. She began tightening her muscles. "Okay. I'm ready."

"On the count of three," he said. "One...twothree!"

It was fortunate that she was ready for the quick count he gave. She threw her entire body into the effort, realizing that the extra weight he'd gained and the few days of workouts that he'd had with the weights had increased his strength. Not by much, perhaps, but with the added impetus of his anger and the laughter that had weakened her, perhaps it would be enough to win the match for him.

"You cheated!" she accused in turn, gritting her teeth as she bore down with all her strength against the force of his arm.

"You deserved it!"

They panted and huffed and grunted for several minutes, and sweat began to run down their faces. They were close together, almost face-to-face, as their locked arms strained harder and harder. Dione groaned aloud. His initial burst of strength had been greater than hers, but not enough to make a quick end to it. Now it was a matter of stamina, and she thought that she could outlast him. She could have let him win, to soothe his ego, but it wasn't in her to trick him that way. If he won, it would be despite everything she could do.

Something of her determination must have shown in her face, because he growled, "Damn it, this is the part where you're supposed to let me win!"

She puffed, sucking in much-needed oxygen. "If you want to beat me, you're going to have to work for it," she panted. "I don't *let* anybody win!"

"But I'm a patient!"

"You're an opportunist!"

He ground his teeth and pushed harder. Dione ducked her head, a movement that placed her head in the hollow of his shoulder, and counteracted his move with everything she had. Slowly, slowly, she felt his arm begin to move back. The rush of strength that winning always gave her zoomed through her veins, and with a cry she slammed his arm down flat on the table.

Their panting breaths filled the room, and her heartbeat thundered in her ears like the hoofbeats of a galloping horse. She was still slumped against him, her head on his shoulder, and she could feel the pounding of his heart throughout his entire body. Slowly she pushed herself off him, letting her weight fall against the table. Like a rag doll, he slumped forward onto the table, too, his color fading almost to normal as he sucked in deep breaths of air.

After a moment he propped his chin on his folded arm and regarded her out of dark blue eyes that still held storm clouds.

Dione drew a deep breath, staring at him. "You're beautiful when you're angry," she told him.

He blinked in astonishment. Stunned, he stared at her for a long, long minute that hung suspended in time; then an odd little gurgle sounded in his throat. He gulped. The next sound was a full-throated roar of laughter. He threw his head back and clutched helplessly at his stomach. Dione began to giggle again.

He was rolling, howling with mirth, rocking back and forth. The abused controls of the wheelchair caught the impact of his fist again, and this time the jerky movements combined with his back and forth motion to pitch him out on his face. It was lucky that he wasn't hurt, because Dione couldn't have stopped laughing if her life had depended on it. She fell off her stool to lie beside him, drawing her legs up to her stomach. "Stop it! Stop it!" she shrieked as tears rolled down her face.

"Stop it! Stop it!" he mimicked, catching her and digging his fingers into her ribs.

In all her life, Dione had never been tickled. She'd never known what it was to play. She was so startled by the unbearably ticklish sensation of his fingers on her ribs that she couldn't even be alarmed at his touch. She was screaming her head off, rolling helplessly in an effort to get away from those tormenting fingers, when another voice intruded on them.

"Blake!" Serena didn't stop to interpret the scene before her. She saw her brother on the floor, she heard Dione screaming and she immediately assumed that a terrible accident had happened. She added her despairing cry to the din and dived for him, her desperate hands catching him and rolling him to her.

Though Serena wasn't supposed to be there during the day, Dione was grateful to her for the interruption. Shakily she rolled away from Blake and sat up, only then realizing that Serena was almost hysterical.

"Serena! There's nothing wrong," Blake was saying strongly, deliberately, having sensed his sister's state of mind before Dione had. "We were just playing around. I'm not hurt. I'm not hurt," he repeated.

Serena calmed down, her white face regaining some of its color. Blake pushed himself to a sitting position and reached for the blanket that usually covered his legs. As he covered himself, he demanded harshly, "What're you doing here? You know you're not supposed to come during the day."

She looked as if he'd slapped her, drawing back sharply and staring at him with a stunned look in her eyes. Dione bit her lip. She knew why he'd spoken so sharply. He'd become used to her seeing him, and in her presence he could sit around wearing nothing but a pair of briefs or gym shorts, but he was still sensitive about his body with everyone else, Serena most of all.

Serena recovered, lifting her chin proudly. "I thought this was supposed to be therapy, not play period." She lashed out as sharply as he had, and rose to her feet. "Excuse me for interrupting. I had a reason for seeing you, but it can wait."

Her outraged temper was evident in every line of her straight back as she marched out the door, ignoring Blake's rueful call.

"Damn!" he said softly. "Now I'll have to apologize. It's just so awkward explaining...."

Dione chuckled. "She's definitely your sister, isn't she?"

He eyed her warningly. "Don't be acting so cocky, young lady. I've found the weakness in your fortress, now. You're as ticklish as a baby!"

She prudently scooted out of his reach. "If you tickle me

again I'll sneak up on you when you're asleep and pour ice water on you."

"You would, too, you wretch," he snorted, and glared at her. "I want a rematch in two weeks."

"You're a glutton for punishment, aren't you?" she asked gleefully, getting to her feet and contemplating the problem of getting him from the floor to the table.

"Don't even try it," he ordered, seeing the speculative look on her face as she looked at him. She smiled sheepishly, because she'd been about to try lifting him herself. "Call Miguel to help you."

Miguel was Blake's chauffeur, handyman and, Dione suspected, bodyguard. He was short and lean, as hard as rock, and his dark face was marred by a scar that puckered his left cheek. No one had said how Blake had acquired his services, and Dione wasn't sure she wanted to know. She didn't even know where Miguel was from; it could have been any Latin nation. She did know that he spoke Portuguese as well as Spanish and English, so she suspected that he was from South America, but again, no one volunteered the information and she didn't ask. It was enough that he was dedicated to Blake.

Miguel wasn't one for asking questions, either. If he was surprised to find his employer on the floor, none of that surprise was reflected on his face. Together he and Dione lifted Blake and put him on the table.

"Miguel, I need another contraption rigged for me in here like the one by the pool," Blake instructed. "We can bolt a bar across the ceiling, this way," he said, indicating the length of the room. "With the pulley arm swinging in any direction we want, and running the length of the bar, I can get myself up and down as I please."

Miguel studied the ceiling, getting in his mind exactly what Blake wanted. "No problem," he finally allowed. "Will tomorrow be soon enough?"

"If you can't do it any faster than that, I suppose it will."

"You're a brutal slave driver," Dione told him as she was massaging his back with the warm oil.

"I've been taking lessons from you," he murmured sleepily, burrowing his head deeper into the cradle of his arm. The comment earned him a pinch on his side, and he laughed. "One thing about it," he continued. "I haven't been bored since you bulldozed into my life."

CHAPTER 5

He was already awake the next morning when she went into his room; he was bending from the waist and rubbing his thighs and calves. She regarded him with satisfaction, glad that he was taking an active part in his recovery.

"I had a long talk with Serena last night," he grunted, not looking up from what he was doing.

"Good. I expect the apology was good for your soul," she said, slipping behind him and kneading his back and shoulders.

"She was upset. It seems Richard has been leaving again as soon as he takes her home at night, and she thinks he's seeing another woman."

Dione's fingers stilled. Was it possible? She hadn't thought him the type to sneak around. It seemed so tawdry, and Richard wasn't a tawdry man.

Blake swiveled his head around to look at her. "Serena thinks he's seeing you," he said bluntly.

She resumed the motion of her fingers. "What did you tell her?" she asked, trying to stay calm. She concentrated on the feel of his flesh under her hands, noting that he didn't feel as bony as he had at first.

"I told her that I'd find out and stop it if he was," he replied. "Don't look so innocent, because we both know that Richard's attracted to you. Hell, he'd have to be dead not to be. You're the type of woman who has men swarming around her like bees around a honey pot."

Richard had said much the same thing about Blake, she thought, and smiled sadly at how far they both were from the truth.

"I'm not seeing Richard," she said quietly. "Aside from the fact that he's married, when would I have time? I'm with you all day long, and I'm too tired at night to put forth the energy that sneaking around would take."

"Serena said that she saw you on the patio one night."

"She did. We were talking about you, not making love. I know that Richard's unhappy with Serena—"

"How do you know that?"

"I'm not blind. She's devoted the last two years to you and virtually ignored her husband, and naturally he resents it. Why do you think he was so determined to find a therapist for you? He wants you walking again so he can have his wife back." Perhaps she shouldn't have told him that, but it was time Blake realized that he'd been dominating their lives with his physical condition.

He sighed. "All right, I believe you. But just in case you start thinking how attractive Richard is, let me tell you now that the one thing I won't tolerate is for Serena to be hurt."

"She's a big girl, Blake. You can't run interference for her for the rest of her life."

"I can do it as long as she needs me, and as long as I'm able. When I think of how she was after our mother died... I swear, Dee, I think I'd kill to keep her from ever looking like that again."

At least she'd had a mother who loved her. The words were on Dione's lips, but she bit them back. It wasn't Serena's fault

that Dione's mother hadn't been loving. Her burden of bitterness was her own, not something to be loaded onto someone else's shoulders.

She pushed it away. "Do you think he really is seeing someone else? In a way, I can't see it. He's so besotted with Serena
that no one else registers."

"*You* register with him," Blake insisted.

"He's never said anything to me," Dione replied honestly,
though she was still stretching the truth a little. "How do you
know? Male intuition?"

"If you want to call it that," he murmured, leaning back
against her as he tired. Her soft breasts supported his weight.
"I'm still a man, even if I couldn't chase a turtle and catch
it. I can look at you and see the same thing he sees. You're
so damned beautiful, so soft and strong at the same time. If I
could chase you, lady, you'd have the race of your life."

The soft words alarmed her in a way that was different
from the panic she normally felt when faced with a prowl-
ing, hunting male. Her hands were still on his shoulders, and
his weight was resting on her; his body was as familiar to her
as her own, the texture of his skin, even the smell of him. It
was as if he were a part of her, because she was building him,
remaking him, shaping him into the gorgeous man he'd been
before the accident. He was her creation.

She suddenly wanted to rest her cheek on his shaggy head,
feel the silky texture of his hair. Instead she denied the impulse, because it was so foreign to her. Yet his head beckoned,
and she moved her hand from his shoulder to touch the dark
strands.

"You're beginning to look like a sheepdog," she told him,
her voice a little breathless and tinged with the laughter that
they shared so often now.

"Then cut it for me," he said lazily, letting his head find a
comfortable position on her shoulder.

"You'd trust me to cut your hair?" she asked, startled.

"Of course. If I can trust you with my body, why not my hair?" he reasoned.

"Then let's do it now," she said, slapping his shoulder. "I'd like to see if you have ears. Come on, get off me."

A shudder rippled down him, and he turned his eyes to her, eyes as blue as the deepest sea, and as primal. She knew what he was thinking, but she turned her gaze away and refused to let the moment linger.

A nameless intimacy had enfolded them. She was jittery, yet she couldn't say that she was really frightened. It was...*odd,* and her forehead was furrowed with a pensive frown as she plied the scissors on his thick hair. He was a patient, and she'd learned not to be afraid of her patients. He'd gotten closer to her than she'd ever allowed anyone else to get, even the children who had tugged the most strongly at her heartstrings. He was the challenge of her career; he'd become so much to her, but he was still a man, and she couldn't understand why she didn't get that icy, sick feeling she normally got when a man got close to her. Blake could touch her, and she couldn't tolerate the touch of any other man.

Perhaps, she decided, it was because she knew that she was safe with him. As he'd pointed out, he wasn't in any condition to do any chasing. Sexually, he was as harmless as the children she'd hugged and comforted.

"You look like Michelangelo, agonizing over the final touches to a statue," he said provokingly. "Have you cut a big gap in my hair?"

"Of course not!" she protested, running her fingers through the unruly pelt. "I'm a very good barber, for your information. Would you like a mirror?"

He sighed blissfully. "No, I trust you. You can shave me now."

"Like heck I will!" With mock wrath she practically slapped

the loose hair off his shoulders. "It's time for your session on the rack, so stop trying to stall!"

In the days that followed nothing else was said about the situation between Serena and Richard, and though the couple continued to have dinner with Blake and Dione, the coolness between them was obvious. Richard treated Dione with a warmth that never progressed beyond friendliness, though Dione was certain that Serena wasn't convinced that the situation between them was innocent. Blake watched everything with an eagle eye and kept Dione close by his side.

She understood his reasons for doing so, and as it suited her to be with him, she let him be as demanding of her company as he wanted. She liked being with him. As he grew stronger his rather devilish personality was coming out, and it took all her concentration to stay one step ahead of him. She had to play poker with him; she had to play chess with him; she had to watch football games with him. There were a million and one things that took his interest, and he demanded that she share them all. It was as if he'd been in a coma for two years and had come out of it determined to catch up on everything he'd missed.

He pushed himself harder than she ever would have. Because she could lift more weight than he could, he worked for hours with the weights. Because she could swim longer and faster than he could, he pushed himself to do lap after lap, though he still couldn't use his legs. And every week they had a rematch at arm wrestling. It was their fifth match before he finally defeated her, and he was so jubilant that she let him have blueberry waffles for breakfast.

Still, she was nervous when she decided that it was time for him to begin using his legs. This was the crux of the entire program. If he couldn't see some progress now in his legs, she knew that he'd lose hope and sink into depression again.

She didn't tell him what she had planned. After he'd done

his sets on the weight bench she got him back into the wheelchair and guided the chair over to the parallel bars that he would use to support himself while she reeducated his legs in what they were expected to do. He looked at the bars, then at her, his brows lifted in question.

"It's time for you to stop being so lazy," she said as casually as possible, though her heart was pounding so loudly it was a miracle he couldn't hear it. "On your feet."

He swallowed, his eyes moving from her to the bars, then back to her.

"This is it, huh? D-day."

"That's right. It's no big deal. Just stand. No trying to walk. Let your legs get accustomed to holding your weight."

He set his jaw and reached out for the bars. Bracing his hands on them, he pulled himself out of the wheelchair.

The weight lifting came in handy as he pulled himself up, using only the strength in his shoulders and arms. Watching him, Dione noted the way his muscles bunched and played. He had real muscles now, not just skin over bone. He was still thin, too thin, but no longer did he have the physique of a famine victim. Even his legs had responded to the forced exercises she gave him every day by forming a layer of muscle.

He was pale, and sweat dripped down his face as Dione positioned his feet firmly under him. "Now," she said softly, "let your weight off your hands. Let your legs hold you. You may fall—don't worry about it. Everyone falls when he reaches this phase of therapy."

"I won't fall," he said grimly, throwing his head back and clenching his teeth. He was balancing himself with his hands, but his weight was on his feet. He groaned aloud. "You didn't say it would hurt!" he protested through his teeth.

Dione's head jerked up, her golden eyes firing with excitement. "Does it hurt?"

"Like hell! Hot needles—"

She let out a whoop of joy and reached for him, drawing back as she remembered his precarious balance. Unbidden, her eyes moistened. She hadn't cried since she was a child, but now she was so proud she was helpless against the tears that formed. Still, she blinked them back, though they shimmered like liquid gold between her black lashes as she offered him a tremulous smile. "You know what that means, don't you?"

"No, what?"

"That the nerves are working! It's all working! The massages, the exercises, the whirlpool...*your legs!* Don't you understand?" she shrieked, practically jumping up and down.

His head jerked around to her. All the color washed out of his face, leaving his eyes glowing like blue coals. "Say it!" he whispered. "Spell it out!"

"You're going to walk!" she screamed at him. Then she couldn't control the tears any longer and they trickled down her face, blurring her vision. She brushed them away with the back of her hand and gave a watery chuckle. "You're going to walk," she said again.

His face twisted, contorted by an agony of joy; he let go of the bars and reached for her, falling forward as his body pitched off-balance. Dione caught him, wrapping her arms tightly around him, but he was too heavy for her now, and she staggered and went down under his weight. He had both arms around her, and he buried his face in her neck. Her heart gave an enormous leap, her blood turned by icy terror into a sluggish river that barely moved. "No," she whispered, her mind suddenly blanking, and her hands moved to his shoulders to push him off.

There was an odd quivering to his shoulders. And there was a sound...it wasn't the same sound of her nightmares.

Then, like someone throwing a light switch and changing a room from dark to light, she knew that this was Blake, not

Scott. Scott had hurt her; Blake never would. And the strange sound was the sound of his weeping.

He was crying. He couldn't stop the tears of joy any more than she'd been able to a moment before; the heaving sobs that tore out of him released two long years of torment and despair. "My God," he said brokenly. "My God."

It was like a dam bursting inside her. A lifetime of holding her hurts inside, of having no one to turn to for comfort, no one to hold her while *she* cried, was suddenly too much. A great searing pain in her chest rose into her throat and burst out in a choked, anguished cry.

Her body shuddered with the force of her sobs, and her enormous golden eyes flooded with tears. For the first time in her life she was being held close in someone's arms while she cried, and it was too much. She couldn't bear the bittersweet pain and joy of it, yet at the same time she felt as if something had changed inside her. The simple act of weeping together had torn down the wall that kept her isolated from the rest of the world. She had existed on only a surface level, never letting anything get too close to her, never letting herself feel too deeply, never letting anyone know the woman behind the mask, because the woman had been hurt so badly and feared that it could happen again. She'd developed quite a defense mechanism, but Blake had somehow managed to short-circuit it.

He was different from every other man she knew. He was capable of loving; he was at once a laughing daredevil and a hard-hitting businessman. But most of all, he needed her. Other patients had needed her, but only as a therapist. Blake needed *her,* the woman she was, because only her personal strengths had enabled her to help him with her trained skills and knowledge. She couldn't remember anyone ever needing *her* before.

She cuddled him close to her, stunned by the slowly increas-

ing warmth inside her that was gradually melting the frozen
pain that had dominated her for so long. She wanted to weep
some more, because she was both frightened and excited by
her new freedom to touch and be touched. Her hand stroked
his hair, her fingers lacing themselves in the silky waves, as
his tears finally stopped and he lay sweetly, limply against her.

He lifted his head to look at her. He wasn't ashamed of the
tears that wet his face and glittered in his blue eyes. Very gently he rubbed his wet cheek against hers, a subtle caress that
mingled their happiness as well as their tears.

Then he kissed her.

It was a slow, wondering kiss, a gentle touch that sought but
didn't pursue, a delicate tasting of her lips that lacked any aggressive, masculine need. She quivered in his arms, her hands
automatically moving to his shoulders to shove him away if
he progressed beyond the still-guarded borders of intimacy
that she could accept. But he didn't try to deepen the kiss. He
raised his mouth and instead touched his nose to hers, rolling his head back and forth in a light, brushing movement.

After a long moment he drew back slightly and let his gaze
roam over her face with a certain curiosity. Dione couldn't
look away from his eyes, watching the irises expand until they
had almost swallowed the blue. What was he thinking? What
caused that sudden flash of desperation that startled her, the
shadow that crossed his face? His eyes lingered on the soft,
trembling fullness of her lips, then slowly lifted to meet her
gaze and lock in place. They stared at each other, so close that
she could see her reflection in his eyes and knew that he could
see himself in hers.

"Your eyes are like melted gold," he whispered. "Cat eyes.
Do they shine in the dark? A man could get lost in them," he
said, his voice suddenly rough.

Dione swallowed; her heart seemed to be rising to stick
in her throat. Her hands were still on his shoulders; beneath

the warmth of his flesh she could feel the flexing of his muscles as he levered himself up on his elbows, the weight of his body still pressed into hers from the waist down. She shivered, faintly alarmed by their posture, but too bemused by the emotional intimacy quivering between them to push him away.

"You're the loveliest thing I've ever seen," he murmured. "As exotic as Salome, as graceful as a cat, as simple as the wind...and so damned mysterious. What goes on behind those cat eyes? What are you thinking?"

She couldn't answer; instead she shook her head blindly as fresh tears made her eyes glitter. He sucked in his breath, then kissed her again, this time parting her lips and slowly penetrating her mouth with his tongue, giving her the time to decide if she would accept the caress. She was trembling in his arms, afraid to let herself be tempted by the gentle touch, yet she *was* tempted, terribly so. Her tongue moved hesitantly and touched his, withdrew, returned for another shy taste, and finally lingered. He tasted marvelous.

He deepened the kiss, exploring the ridges of her teeth, the softness of her mouth. Dione lay quietly beneath him, unaware of the growing force of his passion until suddenly his mouth turned hard and demanding, asking for more than she could give, reminding her abruptly and with chilling clarity how it had been with Scott— The black pit of her nightmares loomed before her, and she squirmed under him, but he didn't feel the sudden tension in her body. His hands grasped her with the roughness of desire, and the last thread holding her control snapped.

She tore her mouth from his with a raw cry. "No!" she shrieked, sudden fear giving her strength. She shoved him away with all the considerable power of her arms and legs, and he rolled across the floor, bumping into the wheelchair and sending it flying across the room.

He pulled himself into a sitting position and seared her

with a scathing, furious look. "Don't bother screaming," he snapped bitterly. "It's a cinch that nothing's going to happen."

"You can bet on it!" she snapped in return, scrambling to her feet and straightening her blouse and shorts, which had somehow become twisted. "I'm a therapist, not a…a convenience!"

"Your professional integrity is safe," he muttered. "From me, at any rate. You might want to try someone like Richard if you're really serious with your kisses, though I warn you right now, all of his parts are in working order and he might not be so easy to throw off!"

It was evident that his ego had been bruised, because she'd tossed him off so easily; he hadn't even noticed the wild expression that had touched her face. She gave silent thanks, then calmly retrieved the wheelchair and placed it beside him. "Stop feeling sorry for yourself," she said curtly. "We have work to do."

"Sure, lady," he snarled. "Anything you say. You're the therapist."

He pushed himself so hard for the rest of the day that Dione had to lose her temper with him that afternoon to make him stop. He was in the foulest mood she'd ever seen him in, surly and bleak. Even Serena was unable to coax him into a better mood that night over dinner, and he excused himself shortly afterward, uttering that he was tired and going to bed.

Serena's brows lifted, but she didn't protest. Richard got to his feet and said, "Let's go into the study for a minute, Blake. There are some things that I need to talk over with you. It won't take long."

Blake nodded briefly, and the two men left the room. Silence fell between Dione and Serena, who had never had much to say to each other.

Serena was apparently engrossed with the strappy white sandal she was dangling from her toes. Without looking up from it, she asked casually, "What's wrong with Blake tonight? He's like a hornet."

Dione shrugged. She wasn't about to tell Serena about the kisses that day, or the reason for Blake's ill humor. Instead she passed along the encouraging news that Blake, for some reason, hadn't. "He stood today. I don't know why he's so grouchy— he should be on top of the world."

Serena's eyes lit up, and her pretty face glowed. "He stood?" she cried, dropping the sandal to the floor and sitting upright. "He actually stood?"

"He had his weight on his legs, yes, and he could feel it," Dione clarified.

"But that's wonderful! Why didn't he tell me?"

Again Dione shrugged.

Serena made a rueful face. "I know—you think I make too much of a fuss over him. I do; I admit it. I…I'm sorry for my attitude when you first came. I didn't think you'd be able to help him, and I didn't want him to get his hopes up, only to be disappointed again. But even if he doesn't walk again, I can see that therapy has been good for him. He's gained weight and he's looking so healthy again."

Surprised by the apology, Dione didn't know what to say beyond the conventional disclaimer, "That's all right."

"No, it isn't all right. Richard's barely speaking to me, and I can't say that I blame him. I've treated him like the invisible man for the two years since Blake had the accident. God knows how he's been as patient as he has. But now I can't get close to him again, and it's all my fault. Still, I'm irrational where Blake's concerned. He's my security, my home base."

"Perhaps Richard wants that distinction," Dione murmured, not really wanting to get into a discussion of Serena's marital problems. She hadn't forgotten that Serena thought Richard might be seeing another woman, namely herself, and she didn't think that involving herself with them would be smart. She liked Richard enormously, and Serena had be-haved remarkably well since their bad beginning, but still, she felt uneasy discussing Richard as if she knew him a lot better than she actually did.

"Oh, I know he does! The trouble is, Blake's such a hard act for any man to follow. He was the perfect older brother." She sighed. "Strong, affectionate, understanding. When Mother died he became my rock. Sometimes I think that if anything happened to Blake, I'd die on the spot."

"Not a very considerate thing to do," Dione commented, and Serena looked at her sharply before giving a laugh.

"No, it wouldn't be, would it?"

"I've been jealous of you," Serena continued after a mo-ment, when Dione showed no signs of picking up the conver-sational threads. "I'd been with Blake almost constantly since the accident. Then you practically forbade me to come over except at a time *you* decided would be all right. I was livid! And almost from the beginning, Blake has been engrossed with his therapy, which has taken his attention away from me even when I am with him. He was so close to you, so obvi-ously taken with you. You could get him to do all the things the other therapists couldn't even get him to think about."

Dione shifted uncomfortably, afraid that Serena was going to start talking about Richard. It looked as if there was noth-ing she could do to prevent it, so she decided she might as well hold up her end of the conversation. Lifting her head, she turned somber golden eyes on the other woman.

"I knew you felt that way. I regretted it, but there was noth-ing I could do about it. Blake had to come first—you were interfering, and I couldn't let you do that."

Serena arched her dark brows in a manner so like Blake's that Dione stared at her, taken by their similarities. "You were entirely right," Serena said firmly. "You were doing what you were supposed to do. It took about two weeks before I began to see the difference in Blake, and then I had to admit that I was resenting you on *my* behalf, not his. If I really loved Blake, then I had to stop acting like a spoiled brat. I'm sorry, Dione. I'd really like to be friends with you."

Dione was startled again; she wondered briefly if Serena's apology had any ulterior motive, but decided to take the younger woman at face value. When all was said and done, she herself was there only temporarily, so anything Serena said wouldn't affect Dione beyond the moment. Lifelong friendships didn't come Dione's way, because she'd learned not to let anyone get too close to her. Even Blake—however close they might be right now, no matter how well she knew him or how much he knew about her—when this was all over, she would be gone and very probably never see him again. She didn't make a habit of keeping in touch with her ex-patients, though she did sometimes receive cards from some of them at Christmas.

"If you'd like," she told Serena calmly. "An apology really wasn't necessary."

"It was for *me*," Serena insisted, and perhaps it had been. She was Blake's sister, and very like him. Blake didn't back down from anything unpleasant, either.

Dione was tired after the emotional impact of the day, and she didn't look in on Blake before she went to bed. The mood he'd been in, he was probably lying awake waiting for her to stick her head in so he could bite it off. Whatever was bothering him, she'd worry about it in the morning. She fell into a deep sleep, untroubled by dreams.

When she was jerked awake by her name being called, she had the feeling that the sound had been repeated several times before it penetrated her sleep. She scrambled out of bed as it came again. "Dione!"

It was Blake, and from the hoarse strain in his voice, he was in pain. She ran to his room and approached the bed. He was writhing, trying to sit up. What was wrong with him? "Tell me," she said insistently, her hands on his bare shoulders, easing him back.

"Cramps," he groaned.

Of course! She should have realized! He'd pushed himself far too hard that day, and now he was paying the price. She ran her hands down his legs and found the knotted muscles. Without a word she got on the bed with him and began to knead the cramps away, her strong fingers working efficiently. First one leg relaxed, then the other, and he sighed in relief. She kept massaging his calves, knowing that a cramp could return. His flesh was warm under her fingers now, the skin roughened by the hair on his legs. She pushed the legs of his pajamas up over his knees and continued with her massage. Perhaps he would go back to sleep under the soothing touch....

Abruptly he sat up and thrust her hands away from his legs. "That's enough," he said curtly. "I don't know what kind of a thrill you get out of handling cripples, but you can play with someone else's legs. You might try Richard. I'm sure he could do you more good than I can."

Dione sat there astonished, her mouth open. How could he *dare* to say something like that? She'd pulled her nightgown up to give her legs more freedom of movement when she'd climbed on his bed, and now she thrust the cloth down to cover her long legs. "You need slapping," she said, her voice shaking with anger. "Damn it, what's wrong with you? You know I'm not seeing Richard, and I'm sick of you throwing him up to me! *You* called *me,* remember? I didn't sneak in here to take advantage of you."

"You'd have a hard time doing that," he sneered.

"You're pretty sure of yourself since you've gotten stronger, aren't you?" she said sarcastically. It made her doubly angry that he'd act like that after what they'd shared earlier. He'd kissed her. Of course, he couldn't possibly know that he was the only man to have touched her since she was eighteen, which had been twelve years before, but still…the injustice of it made her get to her knees on the bed, leaning forward as she jabbed a finger at him.

"You listen to me, Mr. Grouch Remington! I've been driving myself into the ground trying to help you, and you've fought me every step of the way! I don't know what's eating you and I don't care, but I won't let it interfere with your therapy. If I think your legs need massaging, then I'll do it, if I have to tie you down first! Am I getting through that hard head of yours?"

"Who do you think you are? God?" he roared, his face darkening so much that she could see it even in the dim light that came through his windows. "What do you know about what *I* want, what *I* need? All you think about is that damned program you've mapped out. There are other things that I need, and if I can't—"

He stopped, turning his head away. Dione waited for him to continue, and when he didn't she prompted, "If you can't… what?"

"Nothing," he muttered sullenly.

"Blake!" she said in utter exasperation, reaching out and grasping his shoulders and shaking him. "What?"

He shrugged away from her grip and lay back down, his expression bleak as he turned his face back to the windows. "I thought that learning to walk again would be the answer," he whispered. "But it's not. My God, woman, you've been around me for weeks now, running around in almost nothing sometimes, and those see-through nightgowns of yours the rest of the time. Haven't you noticed yet that I can't…"

When his voice trailed off again Dione thought she'd explode. "Can't what?" she tried again, forcibly keeping her tone level.

"I'm impotent," he said, his voice so low that she had to lean closer to hear him.

She sat back on her heels, stunned.

Once he'd said the words aloud, the rest poured out of him in a torrent, as if he couldn't control it. "I didn't think about it before, because what was there to arouse me? It didn't matter, if I couldn't walk, but now I find that there's an opposite side of the coin. If I can't live life as a man instead of a sexless gelding, then it doesn't matter if I walk or not."

Dione's mind went blank. She was a physical therapist, not a sex therapist. It was ironic that he should even mention the subject to *her,* of all people. She was in the same boat he was in; perhaps she'd sensed that from the beginning, and that was why she hadn't been frightened of him.

But she couldn't let this prey on his mind or he'd give up. Desperately she tried to think of something to tell him.

"I don't see why you'd even think you should be aroused by me," she blurted. "I'm a therapist. It's totally unethical for there to be any sort of relationship except a professional one between us. I certainly haven't been trying to seduce you, or even interest you! You shouldn't think of me like that! I...I'm more of a mother figure than I am anything else, so I'd think it was odd if you responded physically to me."

"You *don't* remind me of my mother," he said heavily.

Again she searched for something to say. "Did you really expect all of your capabilities to return immediately, just because you put your weight on your legs today?" she finally asked. "I would've been surprised if you had been...er, responding like that. You've had a lot on your mind, and you've been in terrible physical shape."

"I'm not in terrible physical shape now," he pointed out tiredly.

No, he wasn't. Dione considered him as he lay there, wearing only the bottoms of his pajamas. He'd started leaving off the tops several weeks ago. He was still lean, but now it was the leanness of a hard layer of muscle. Even his legs had fleshed out some as he gained weight, and thanks to the rigorous program he'd been following, he even had muscles in his legs, despite his inability to command movement from them yet. He was a natural athlete anyway, and his body had responded promptly to the training. His arms and shoulders and chest were showing the benefits of weight lifting, and the hours in the pool had given his skin a glowing bronze color. He looked incredibly healthy, all things considered.

What could she say? She couldn't reassure him that his mind and body would recover and let him respond normally, because recovery hadn't happened yet for her. She couldn't even say that she wanted to "recover." Perhaps she missed out on a great deal of human warmth by living the way she did, but she also avoided the pain of human cruelty. Until the accident, Blake had led a charmed life. He had loved, and been loved, by more women than he could probably remember. To him, life wasn't complete without sex. To her, life was much safer without it. How could she even begin to convince him of something she didn't believe in herself?

At last she said cautiously, "You're better, yes, but you're not in top physical condition yet. The body is a series of complementary systems—when any part of it is hurt, all the systems cooperate in helping to speed healing. With the therapy program you've been following, you've focused your mind and body on retraining your muscles. It's part of the recovery process, and until you've progressed enough that such intense concentration isn't needed, I think you're being unrealistic to expect any sexual responses. Let things happen in their own time." After considering him for another minute, she tilted her head sideways. "I estimate that you're at about sixty-five percent of your normal strength. You're expecting too much."

"I'm expecting what any normal man expects in his life,"

Blake said harshly. "You were bubbling over with self-confidence when you promised me that I'd walk again, but you're not sure about this, are you?"

"I'm not a sex therapist," she snapped. "But I do have common sense, and I'm trying to use it. There's no physical reason why you shouldn't be able to have sex, so I'd advise you to stop worrying about it and concentrate on walking. Nature will take care of everything else."

"Stop worrying!" he muttered under his breath. "Lady, it's not the weather we're talking about! If I can't function as a man, what's the use in living? I'm not talking about just sex. There'd be no marriage for me, no children, and while I've never wanted to marry anyone yet, I've always thought that I'd like to have a family someday. Can't you understand that? Haven't you ever wanted a husband, children?"

Dione winced, physically shrinking away from him. He had an uncanny knack of hitting her where she was most vulnerable. Before she could stop herself, she blurted out thickly, "I've always wanted children. And I *was* married. It just didn't work out."

His chest rose and fell as he drew in a deep breath, and she could feel his gaze searching her face in the darkness. Surely he couldn't see anything more than an outline, since she was sitting out of the dim light coming through the windows, so why did she feel as if he could tell exactly how her lower lip was trembling, or see the sudden pallor of her cheeks?

"Damn," he said softly. "I've done it again, haven't I? Every time I say something, I stick my foot in my mouth."

She shrugged, trying not to let him know how thin her armor was. "It's all right," she murmured. "It was a long time ago. I was just a kid, too young to know what I was doing."

"How old were you?"

"Eighteen. Scott—my ex-husband—was twenty-three, but neither of us was ready for marriage."

"How long did it last?"

A harsh laugh tore from her throat. "Three months. Not a record-setting length of time, was it?"

"And since then? Haven't you been in love with anyone else?"

"No, and I haven't wanted to be. I'm content the way I am." The conversation had gone on long enough; she didn't want to reveal any more than she already had. How did he keep chipping away at the wall she'd built around her past? Most people never even realized it was there. She uncoiled her legs and crawled off the bed, tugging her nightgown down when it tried to crawl up to her hips.

Blake said a harsh expletive. "You're running, Dee. Do you realize how long you've been here without receiving a single phone call or a letter, without even going shopping? You've sealed yourself in this house with me and shut the world out. Don't you have any friends, any boyfriends on a string? What is it out there that you're afraid of?"

"There's nothing out there that frightens me," she said quietly, and it was true. All of her terrors were locked within herself, frozen in time.

"I think everything out there frightens you," he said, stretching out his arm and snapping on the bedside lamp. The soft glow drove away the shadows and illuminated her as she stood there in her white gown with her long, black hair streaming down her back. She looked medieval, locked away in a fortress of her own making. His blue eyes seared over her as he said softly, "You're afraid of life, so you don't let anything touch you. You need therapy as much as I do. My muscles won't work, but you're the one who doesn't feel."

CHAPTER 6

She didn't sleep that night; she lay awake, feeling the seconds and minutes ticking away, becoming hours. He was right; she *was* afraid of life, because life had taught her that she would be punished if she asked for too much. She had learned not to ask for anything at all, thereby risking nothing. She had denied herself friends, family, even the basic comfort of her own home, all because she was afraid to risk being hurt again.

It wasn't in her character to deny the truth, so she looked it in the face. Her mother wasn't a typical example of motherhood; her husband hadn't been a typical husband. Both of them had hurt her, but she shouldn't shut everyone else out because of them. Serena had made an overture of friendship, but Dione had backed away from it, doubting the other woman's motives. Those doubts were just an excuse for her own instinctive reaction to withdraw whenever anyone got too close to her. She had to take risks, or her life would be just a mockery, no matter how many patients she helped. She needed help just as much as Blake did.

But facing the truth and dealing with it were two very different things. Just the thought of lowering her defenses and letting anyone get close to her gave her a sick feeling. Even the little things were more than she had ever had, and more than she could handle. She'd never giggled with a girlfriend far into the night, never gone to a party, never learned *how* to be with people in the normal manner. She'd had her back to the wall for her entire life, and self-protection was more than a habit: it was a part of her, branded into her cells.

Perhaps she was beyond changing; perhaps the bitter horror of her childhood had altered her psyche so drastically that she'd never be able to rise above the murky pit of her memories. For a moment she had a vision of her future, long and bleak and solitary, and a dry sob wrenched at her insides. But she didn't cry, though her eyes burned until her lids felt scorched. Why waste tears on years that stretched away emptily for as far as she could see? She was used to being alone, and at least she had her work. She could touch people through her work, giving them hope, helping them; perhaps it wasn't enough, but surely it was better than the sure destruction that awaited her if she allowed someone to hurt her again.

Suddenly a memory of Scott flashed into her mind and she almost cried out, her hands rising in the dark to push him away. The sickness in her changed to pure nausea, and she had to swallow convulsively to control it. For a moment she wavered on the edge of a black abyss, memories rising like bats from a rancid cave to dart at her; then she clenched her teeth on the wild cry that was welling up in her and reached out a trembling hand to turn on the lamp. The light drove away the horrors, and she lay staring at the shadows.

To combat the memories she deliberately pushed them aside and called up Blake's face as a sort of talisman against the evils of the past. She saw his blue eyes, burning with despair, and her breath caught. Why was she lying there worrying about herself when Blake was teetering on the edge of his own abyss?

Blake was the important one, not her! If he lost interest now, it would wreck his recovery.

She'd trained herself for years to push her personal interests and problems aside and concentrate entirely on her patient. Her patients had reaped the benefits, and the process had become a part of her inner defenses when things threatened to become too much for her. She used it now, ruthlessly locking out all thoughts except those of Blake, staring at the ceiling so intently that her gaze should have burned a hole in it.

On the surface the problem seemed to be simple: Blake needed to know that he could still respond to a woman, still make love. She didn't know why he couldn't now, unless it was because of the common-sense reasons she'd given him just a few hours before. If that were the case, as his health improved and he gained strength, his sexual interest would reawaken naturally, if he had someone to interest him.

That was a problem Dione chewed on her lower lip. Blake obviously wasn't going to start dating now; his pride wouldn't allow him to be helped in and out of cars and restaurants, even if Dione would allow him to disrupt his schedule so drastically, which was out of the question. No, he *had* to stay in therapy, and they were just now getting into the toughest part of it, which would require more time and effort, and pain, from him.

There simply was a shortage of available women in his life right now, a necessary shortage, but there nevertheless. Besides Serena, Alberta and Angela, there was only herself, and she automatically discounted herself. How could she attract anyone? If any man made a move toward her, she reacted like a scalded cat, which wasn't a good start.

A frown laced her brows together. That was true with all men…except Blake. Blake touched her, and she wasn't frightened. She had wrestled with him, romped on the floor with him…kissed him.

The idea that bloomed was, for her, so radical that when it first entered her consciousness she dismissed it, only to have it return again and again, boomeranging in her mind. Blake needed help, and she was the only woman available to help him. If she could attract him…

A shudder rose from her toes and flowed upward to shake her entire body, but it wasn't from revulsion or fear, except perhaps fear at her own daring. Could she do it? How could she do it? How could she possibly manage such a thing? It wouldn't do Blake any good if he made a pass at her and she ran screaming from the room. She didn't think she would do that with him, but just the thought of trying to attract a man was so foreign to her that she couldn't be sure. Could she tempt him enough to prove to him that he was a man?

She couldn't let the situation progress into anything concrete; she knew that not only was it something she wasn't ready for, but an affair with a patient was totally against her professional integrity. Besides, she wasn't Blake's type, so there was little chance of anything serious happening. She tried to decide if he would find her so lacking in expertise that she wouldn't appeal to him at all, or if his isolation for the past two years would blind him to her inexperience. He was fast leaving behind his morose preoccupation with his invalidism, and she knew that she wouldn't be able to fool him for long. Every day he became more himself—the man in the photo that Richard had shown her, with a biting intellect and a driving nature that swept everyone along with him like the force of a tidal wave.

Could she do it?

She trembled at the thought, but she was so shaken by what he'd said that night that she didn't push the idea away as she would have before. For the first time in her life Dione decided to try to attract a man. It had been so long since she'd cut herself off from sexual contact with anyone that she had no idea if she could do it without looking obvious and silly. She was thirty years old, and she felt as inexperienced and awkward as any young girl just entering her teens. Her brief marriage to Scott didn't count at all; far from trying to attract Scott, after her wedding night she'd gone out of her way to avoid him. Blake was a mature, sophisticated man, used to having any woman he wanted before the accident had robbed him of the use of his legs. Her only advantage was that she was the only available woman in his life right then.

She just didn't know how to arouse a man.

That unusual problem, one she'd never thought she'd face, was the reason she was standing hesitantly before the mirror the next morning, long past the time when she usually woke Blake. She hadn't even dressed; she was staring at herself in the mirror, chewing on her lower lip and frowning. She knew that men usually liked the way she looked, but were looks enough? She wasn't even blond, as Blake preferred his women to be. Her thick black hair swirled over her shoulders and down her back; she'd been about to braid it out of her way when she'd paused, staring at herself, and she still held the brush in her hand, forgotten, as she intensely surveyed the ripe figure of the woman in the mirror. Her breasts were full and firm, tipped with cherry nipples, but perhaps she was too bosomy for his tastes. Perhaps she was too athletic, too strong; perhaps he liked dainty, ultrafeminine women.

She groaned aloud, twisting around to study herself from the back. So many ifs! Maybe he was a leg man; she had nice legs, long and graceful, smoothly tanned. Or maybe… Her bottom, covered only by wispy, pink silk, was curvy and definitely feminine.

Her clothes were another problem. Her everyday wardrobe consisted mostly of things that were comfortable to work in: jeans, shorts, T-shirts. They were neat and practical, but not enticing. She did have good clothes, but nothing that could be worn while working and be practical, too. Her dresses weren't sexy, either, and her nightgowns were straight out of a convent, despite Blake's comment about her "running around in see-through nighties." She needed new clothes, things that were sexy but not transparently so, and definitely a real see-through nightie.

She was so preoccupied that she hadn't heard the sounds of Blake in his bedroom; when his rumbling, early-morning voice broke into her thoughts with an ill-tempered, "Lazybones, you overslept this morning!" she whirled to face the door as it swung open and Blake rolled his wheelchair through the doorway.

They both froze. Dione couldn't even raise her arms to cover her bare breasts; she was stunned by the shock of his entrance, so lost in her thoughts that she was unable to jerk herself back to reality and take any action. Neither did Blake appear capable of moving, though good manners demanded that he leave the room. He didn't; he sat there with his blue eyes becoming even bluer, a dark, stormy expression heating his gaze as it raked down her almost naked body, then rose to linger over her breasts.

"Good Lord," he whispered.

Dione's mouth was dry, her tongue incapable of moving. Blake's intent look was as warm as a physical touch, and her nipples shrank into tiny points, thrusting out at him. He sucked in an audible breath, then slowly let his eyes dip lower, down the curve of her rib cage, the satiny smoothness of her stomach; his gaze probed the taut little indentation of her navel and finally settled on the juncture of her thighs.

An unfamiliar curling sensation low in her stomach frightened her, and she was finally able to move. She whirled away from him with a low cry, belatedly raising her arms to cover herself. Standing rigidly with her back to him, she said in a voice filled with mortification, "Oh, no! Please, get out!"

There was no obedient whir of an electric motor as he sent the wheelchair into motion, and she knew that he was still sitting there.

"I've never seen anyone blush all over before," he said, his voice deep and filled with an almost tangible male amusement. "Even the backs of your knees are pink."

"Get out," she cried in a strangled voice.

"Why are you so embarrassed?" he murmured. "You're beautiful. A body like that just begs for a man to stare at it."

"Would you please just leave?" she begged. "I can't stand here like this all day!"

"Don't hurry on my account," he replied with maddening satisfaction. "I like the back view as well as I did the front. It's a work of art, the way those long legs of yours sweep up into that perfect bottom. Is your skin as satiny as it looks?"

Embarrassment finally turned to anger and she stomped her foot, although it was largely a wasted effort, as the thick carpet muffled any sound her bare foot might have made. "Blake Remington, I'll get back at you for this!" she threatened, her voice trembling with anger.

He laughed, the deep tone vibrating in the quiet morning air. "Don't be such a sexist," he taunted. "You've seen me in only a pair of undershorts, so why be shy about my seeing you wearing only panties? You don't have anything to be ashamed of, but you have to know that already."

He evidently wasn't going to leave; he was probably enjoying himself, the wretch! She sidled around until she could reach her nightgown, where she had thrown it across the bed. She was careful to keep her back to him, and she was so fiercely preoccupied with reaching that nightgown that she didn't hear the soft whir of the wheelchair as it came up behind her. Just as she touched the nightgown a much larger hand appeared from behind and anchored the garment to the bed.

"You're beautiful when you're angry," he jibed, returning

the teasing compliment she'd given him the day he'd become enraged when he had discovered that she lifted weights.

"Then I must be the world's most beautiful woman right now," she fumed, then added, "because I'm getting madder by the minute."

"Don't waste your energy," he crooned, and she jumped as his hard hand suddenly swatted her on the bottom, then lingered to mold the round, firm cheek with his long fingers. He finished with an intimate pat, then removed his hand from the nightgown.

"I'll be waiting for you at breakfast," he said smoothly, and she heard him chuckling as he left the room.

She wadded up the nightgown and threw it at the closed door. Her face felt as if it were on fire, and she pressed her cold hands to her cheeks. Furiously she considered ways of paying him back, but she had to stop short of physical harm, and that left out all the most delicious schemes she could imagine. It would probably be impossible to embarrass him in return; since he was in so much better condition now, she doubted if it would bother him if she saw him stark naked. In fact, from the way he'd acted that morning, he'd probably enjoy it and proudly let her look all she wanted!

She was seething, until the thought came to her that her scheme to attract him couldn't have gotten off to a better start. He hadn't been thinking about sex, really; he'd been indulging a streak of pure devilry, but the end result was that he'd become aware of her as a woman. There was the added advantage of the entire scene being totally spontaneous without any of the stiffness that would probably result from any effort she deliberately made.

That thought enabled her to get through the day, which was a difficult one. He watched her like a hawk, waiting for her to betray by either action or word that she was still embarrassed by the morning's incident. She was as cool and impersonal as she knew how to be, deliberately working him as hard as her conscience would allow. He spent more time than the day before at the bars, balancing himself with his hands while his legs bore his weight. He kept up a continuous stream of cursing at the pain he endured, but he didn't want to stop, even when she decided to go on to other exercises. She moved his feet in the first walking motions they'd made in two years; sweat poured off of him at the pain in his muscles, unaccustomed to such activity.

That night the cramps in his legs kept him awake for hours, and Dione massaged him until she was so weary she could hardly move. There were no intimate discussions in the dark that night; he was in pain, barely getting relaxed after one cramp was relieved before another one would knot in his legs. Finally she took him down and put him in the whirlpool, which relieved the cramps for the night.

She really did oversleep the next morning, but she had been careful to lock her door before she went to bed, so she wasn't afraid of an interruption. When she did wake, she lay there with a smile on her face as she relished how he would react to the interruption in his route that she planned.

Over breakfast she said casually, "May I borrow one of your cars? I need to do some shopping today."

Startled, he looked up; his eyes narrowed thoughtfully. "Are you doing this because of what I said the other night?"

"No, of course not," she lied with admirable ease. "I do need some things, though. I'm not much on shopping, but like every woman I have necessities."

"Do you know anything about Phoenix?" he asked, reaching for the glass of milk that he now drank without protest at every meal.

"Nothing," she admitted cheerfully.

"Do you even know how to get downtown?"

"No, but I can follow signs and directions."

"No need to do that. Let me give Serena a call. She loves shopping, and she's been at loose ends lately."

At first the thought of shopping in Serena's company dampened Dione's enthusiasm for her project, but she realized that she would probably need another woman's opinion, so she agreed to his suggestion. Serena did, too; he'd barely mentioned it to her over the phone before he hung up the receiver, a wry smile tugging at his chiseled mouth. "She's on her way." Then the smile gave way to a sharply searching look. "You didn't seem very enthusiastic," he remarked. "Did you have some other plans?"

What did he mean by that? "No, it's just that I had something else on my mind. I'm glad you thought of asking Serena. I could use her opinion on some things."

The searching look disappeared, to be replaced by one of lively curiosity. "What things?"

"Nothing that concerns you," she replied promptly, knowing that her answer would drive him crazy. He wanted to know the whys and wherefores of everything. He'd probably dismantled every toy he'd received as a child, and now he was trying to do the same thing to her. He probably did it to everyone. It was one of the characteristics that had made him such an innovative engineer.

As she quickly dressed for her shopping trip, she realized that lately Blake had shown signs of becoming more interested in his work again. He talked to Richard on the phone more than he had before, and designing the pulley system at the pool and in the gym had piqued his interest even more. Every night after dinner he made some mysterious doodles on a pad in his study, random drawings that resembled nothing Dione recognized, but Richard had seen the pad one evening and made a comment on it. The two men had then embarked on a highly technical conversation that had lasted until Dione put an end to it by signaling that it was time for Blake to go to bed. Richard had caught the signal and understood it immediately, giving her a quick wink.

The Phoenix heat prompted her to wear the bare minimum of clothing: a white sundress; the necessary underwear, which wasn't much; and strappy sandals. The weeks had slipped away, taking the summer with it, but the changing season wasn't yet reflected by any dip in the temperature. When she went downstairs to meet Serena, Blake gave her a quick comprehensive look that seemed to take inventory of every garment she had on. Dione shivered at the fleeting expression in his eyes. He knew what she looked like now, and every time he saw her he was imagining her without any clothes. She should probably be glad, as that was what she wanted, but it still made her uneasy.

Serena drove, as Dione knew absolutely nothing about Scottsdale or Phoenix. The pale blue Cadillac slipped as silently as oiled silk past the array of expensive millionaires' homes that decorated Mount Camelback. Overhead, a sparkle of silver in the pure blue of the sky, one of the innumerable jets from the air bases in the Phoenix area, painted a white streak directly above their path.

"Blake said you had shopping to do," Serena said absently. "What sort of shopping? Not that it matters. If it exists, I know a shop that carries it."

Dione gave her a wry glance. "Everything," she admitted. "Dresses, underwear, sleepwear, bathing suits."

Serena arched her slim, dark brows in an astonished movement. "All right," she said slowly. "You asked for it."

By the time they'd had lunch several hours later, Dione firmly believed that Serena knew the location of every shop in Arizona. They had been in so many that she couldn't keep straight just where she had bought what, but that didn't really matter. What mattered was the steadily growing mound of bags and packages, which they made regular trips to the car to stow in the trunk.

Dione systematically tried on dresses that made the most of her dark coloring and tall, leggy build. She bought skirts that were slit up the side to showcase her long, slender legs; she bought real silk hosiery and delicate shoes. The nightgowns she chose were filmy, flimsy pieces of fabric that were held on her body more by optimism than any other means. She bought sexy lace panties and bras, wickedly seductive teddies, shorts and T-shirts that clung to her body, and a couple of bikinis that stopped just short of illegal.

Serena watched all of this in amazed silence, offering her opinion whenever Dione asked it, which was often. Dione couldn't quite decide if a garment was sexy without being blatant, so she yielded to Serena's taste. It was Serena who chose the bikinis, one a delicate shell-pink and the other a vibrant blue, both of which glowed like jewels on Dione's honey-tanned body.

"You know," Serena mused as she watched Dione choose a skin-toned teddy that, from a distance, made her look as if she had nothing on at all, "this looks like war."

Dione was feeling a little frantic and out of touch by that time, and she merely gave Serena a blank look.

"I could almost pity Blake for being the target of such firepower," the other woman continued, laughing a little. "Almost, but not quite. From the effort you're making, Dione, I think you're out for unconditional surrender. Are you in love with Blake?"

That got Dione's attention with the force of a punch in the jaw. In love? Of course not! It was impossible. Blake was her patient; falling in love with him would be against every professional ethic that she had. Not only that, how could she be in love with him? Couldn't Serena see that it was totally out of the question? she wondered distractedly. It was just that

Blake's was such a demanding case. She'd rebuilt him almost literally, molded him from a basket case into a strong, healthy man; she couldn't let him give up now, couldn't let all of that sweat and effort go to waste.

But suddenly, seeing through Serena's eyes the staggering amount of clothing she'd bought in one day, she realized what a hopeless effort it was. How could she ever have imagined that she'd be able to physically attract Blake Remington? Not only did she not know how to do it, but she'd probably go into screaming hysterics if she succeeded!

She sagged into a chair, crumpling the flesh-colored teddy in her lap. "It's no use," she muttered. "It'll never work."

Serena eyed the teddy. "If he's human, it will."

"All of these props are useless, if the actors can't perform," Dione said in self-disgust. "I don't know how to seduce any-one, least of all a man who's been around as much as Blake has!"

Serena's eyes widened. "Are you serious? The way you look, you don't *have* to seduce anyone. All you have to do is stand still and let him get to you."

"Thanks for the pep talk, but it's not that easy," Dione hedged, unable to tell Blake's sister the entire story. "Some men like my looks, but I know that Blake's always preferred blondes. I'm not his type at all."

"How you can look in a mirror and still worry about not being blonde is more than I can understand," Serena said im-patiently. "You're…sultry. That's the only word I can think of to describe the way you look. If he hasn't made a pass at you yet, it's because you haven't given him a go-ahead sig-nal. Those clothes will do it for you. Then just let things de-velop naturally."

If only they would! Dione thought as she paid for the teddy and a bottle of heady perfume that the saleswoman had sworn drove her husband mad with lust.

She didn't want Blake mad with lust, just aroused. What a dilemma for her to be in! Life was just full of little ironies, but she couldn't find this one very amusing.

Blake wasn't in evidence when they arrived back at the house, and Dione could only be thankful for that. She didn't want him to have any idea of the extent of her shopping trip. Angela silently helped Dione and Serena carry all the packages up to Dione's room, and when asked about Blake's whereabouts, the woman smiled shyly and murmured, "In the gym," before quickly walking out.

Serena gave a little laugh after Angela had left the room. "She's something, isn't she? I think Blake picked his entire staff on the basis of how much they talk, or rather, don't talk." Before Dione could make any comment, Serena changed the subject. "Do you mind if I stay for dinner? I know you probably want to start your campaign, but Richard told me this morning that he'd be late coming home tonight, and I'm at loose ends."

Far from being anxious to begin her "campaign," Dione was dreading it, and gladly asked Serena to stay. As she usually had dinner with them, Blake might think something was off if all of a sudden she stopped the practice.

While Serena went to the den to entertain herself, Dione made her way down to the pool and entered the gym. She stopped abruptly. Blake was on the bars, balancing himself with his hands, while Alberta was on her knees, moving his feet in walking motions. From the looks of him, he'd been hard at it since she'd left with Serena that morning, and poor Alberta was frazzled, too. Blake wore only a brief pair of blue gym shorts, and he'd tied his shirt around his forehead to keep the sweat from getting into his eyes. He was literally dripping as he strained, trying to force his muscles to do his bidding. Dione knew that he had to be in a great deal of pain; it was revealed in the rigid set of his jaw, his white lips. The fact that he'd enlisted Alberta's help instead of waiting for her to return said something about his determination, but she was afraid that he'd tried to do too much. He'd paid for his excesses the night before with agonizing cramps, and she had the feeling that tonight would be a repeat.

"Time for the whirlpool," she said easily, trying not to sound anxious. Alberta looked up with an expression of acute relief, and achingly got to her feet. Blake, on the other hand, shook his head.

"Not yet," he muttered. "Another half hour."

Dione signaled to Alberta, who quietly left the room. Taking a towel from the stack she always kept handy, she went up to him and wiped his face, then his shoulders and chest. "Don't push it so hard," she advised. "Not yet. You can do yourself more harm than good at this stage. Come on, into the whirlpool. Give your muscles a rest."

He sagged against the bars, panting, and Dione quickly brought the wheelchair over to him. He levered himself into it; he seldom needed her help moving himself around now, since he was so much stronger. She switched the whirlpool on and turned around to find that he'd been staring at her bottom as she bent over. Wondering how much she'd exposed in the unaccustomed dress, she flushed pink.

He gave her a wicked little smile, then grasped the pulley and swung himself over the pool, letting himself down expertly into the water. He sighed in relief as the pulsing water eased his tired, strained muscles.

"I didn't expect you to be gone all day," he said, closing his eyes wearily.

"I only shop once a year." She lied without compunction. "When I shop, it's an endurance event."

"Who won, you or Serena?" he asked, smiling as he lay there, his eyes still closed.

"I think Serena did," she groaned, stretching her tight muscles. "Shopping uses an entirely different set of muscles than weight lifting does."

He opened one eye a slit and surveyed her. "Why not join me?" he invited. "As the old saying goes, 'Come on in, the water's fine.'"

It was tempting. She looked at the swirling water, then shook her head regretfully as she thought of the many things that she needed to do. She didn't have time to relax in a whirl-pool.

"Not tonight. By the way," she added, changing the subject, "how did you talk Alberta into helping you with your exercises?"

"A mixture of charm and coercion," he replied, grinning a little. His gaze slipped over the bodice of her dress; then he closed his eyes again and gave himself up to the bliss of the whirlpool.

Dione moved around the room, putting everything in place and preparing for the massage she'd give him when he left the whirlpool, but her actions were purely automatic. Their conversation had been casual, even trivial, but she sensed an entirely different mood under the cover of their words. He was looking at her, he was seeing her, as a woman, not a therapist. She was both frightened and exhilarated at her success, because she'd expected it to take much longer before she got his attention. The intent way he stared at her was sending messages that she wasn't trained to interpret. As a therapist, she knew instinctively what her patient needed; as a woman, she was completely in the dark. She wasn't even completely certain that he wasn't staring at her with derision.

"All right, that's enough," he said huskily, breaking her train of thought. "I hope Alberta's not going to hold a grudge against me, because I'm hungry. Do you think she'll feed me?"

"Serena and I will let you have our scraps," Dione offered generously, earning a wryly appreciative glance from him.

A few minutes later he lay on his stomach on the table with a towel draped over his hips, sighing in contentment as her strong fingers worked their magic on his flesh. He propped his chin on his folded arms, the look on his face both absent and absorbed, a man concentrating on his inner plans. "How long before I'll be able to walk?" he asked.

Dione continued manipulating his legs as she considered the answer. "Do you mean until you take your first steps, or walk without aid?"

"The first steps."

"I'll take a stab and say six weeks, though that's only a rough guess," she warned him. "Don't hold me to it. You could do it in four or five, or it could be two months. It really depends on how well I've planned your therapy program. If you push too hard and injure yourself, then it'll take longer."

"When will the pain ease?"

"When your muscles are accustomed to your weight and the mechanics of movement. Are your legs still numb?"

"Hell, no," he growled feelingly. "I can tell when you're touching me now. But after those cramps last night, I'm not certain I want to feel."

"The price to pay," she taunted gently, and slapped him on the bottom. "Time to turn over."

"I like that dress," he said when he was lying on his back and could stare at her. Dione didn't glance up, consciously keeping the flexing of her fingers in an unbroken rhythm. When she failed to comment he pushed a little harder. "You've got great legs. I see you every day, dressed in next to nothing, but I hadn't realized how good your legs are until I saw you in a dress."

She quirked one eyebrow. That statement alone verified her suspicion that he hadn't been aware of her as a woman, not really. She half-turned her back to him as she rubbed her hands down the calf of his right leg, hoping that the vigorous massage would lessen any cramps he might have. When the warm touch of his hand rested on her bare thigh, under her skirt, she gave a stifled half scream and jerked up straight.

"Blake!" she yelped, pushing frantically at his hand in an effort to dislodge it from under her dress. "Stop it! What are you doing?"

"You're playing with *my* legs," he retorted calmly. "Turnabout's fair play."

His fingers were between her legs while his thumb was on the outside of her thigh, and she flinched from the feel of his hand as her other leg instinctively pressed against him to halt the upward movement. Her face flushed brightly.

"I like that," he said huskily, his eyes bright. "Your legs are so strong, so sleek. Do you know what you feel like? Cool satin."

She twisted, trying to loosen his grip, and to her dismay his fingers slid even higher. She sucked in a lungful of air and held it, going still, her eyes wide and alarmed as she tried to still the flare of panic in her stomach. Her heart lurched drunkenly in her chest.

"Let me go, please," she whispered, hoping that the trembling of her voice wouldn't be as noticeable if she didn't try to talk loudly.

"All right," he agreed, a little smile moving his lips. Just as she began to sag in relief, he added, "If you'll kiss me."

Now her heart was slamming so wildly that she pressed her hand to her chest in an effort to calm it. "I... Just one kiss?"

"I can't say," he drawled, staring at her lips. "Maybe, maybe not. It depends on how well we like it. For God's sake, Dee, I've kissed you before. You won't be violating any sacred vow not to become involved with a patient. A kiss isn't what I'd term an involvement."

Despite her efforts to hold her legs together and trap his wandering hand, he somehow moved a little higher.

"It's only a kiss," he cajoled, holding his left hand out to her. "Don't be shy."

She wasn't shy, she was terrified, but she could still hold on to the thought that Blake wasn't Scott. That alone gave her the courage to lean down and touch her lips to his as lightly, as delicately, as a breath of air. She drew back and stared down at him. His hand remained on her leg.

"You promised," she reminded him.

"That wasn't a kiss," he replied. The expression in his eyes was intent, watchful. "A real kiss is what I want, not a child's kiss. I've been a long time without a woman. I need to feel your tongue on mine."

Weakly she leaned against the table. *I can't handle this,* she thought wildly, then stiffened as the thought formed in her brain. Of course she could; she could handle anything. She'd already been through the worst that could happen to her. This was just a kiss, that was all...

Though her soft, generous mouth trembled against his, she gave him the intimate kiss he'd requested, and she was startled to feel him begin to shake. He removed his hand from her leg and placed both arms around her, but he held her without any real force, only a warm sort of nearness that failed to alarm her. The hair on his bare chest was tickling her above the fabric of her sundress; the faintly musky smell of him filled her lungs. She became aware of the warmth of his skin, the roughness of his chin against her smooth skin, the light play of his tongue against hers. Her eyes had been open, but now they slowly closed, and she became lost in a world of sensation, the light only a redness against her lids, her senses of touch and smell intensified by the narrowing of her concentration.

That was what she wanted, she reminded herself dimly. She hadn't thought she would enjoy herself in the process, but the excitement that was beginning to course through her veins brought with it a warmth that could only be pleasure.

"God, you smell good," he breathed, breaking the kiss to nuzzle his face in the soft hollow of her throat. "What perfume is that?"

Giddily she remembered all the perfumes she'd tried. "It's a mixture of everything," she admitted in a bemused tone.

He chuckled and turned his head to claim her mouth again. This time the kiss was deeper, harder, but she didn't protest. Instead she kissed him back as strongly as he kissed her, and he finally fell back onto the table, gasping.

"You're taking advantage of a starving man," he groaned, and she gave a spurt of laughter.

"I hope Alberta doesn't feed you anything," she told him, and turned away to hide the color that she knew still tinted her cheeks. She fussed over several insignificant details, but when she turned back he wasn't paying attention to her. She disciplined her face into smoothness and helped him to dress, but there was a sense of determination about him that bothered her. It nagged at her all during dinner, where Serena entertained Blake with a wholly fictitious tale of their shopping trip.

What was he up to? She'd agonized over her scheme, gone to ridiculous lengths to put it into action, but somehow she still had the feeling that he was the one who was scheming, not her.

CHAPTER 7

"Dione, may I talk to you? In private, please." Richard's face was tight with strain, and Dione looked at him sharply, wondering at the bitterness that was so evident in his expression. She looked past him to the study door, and he read her mind.

"She's playing chess with Blake," he said heavily, thrusting his hands into his pockets and moving to the doors that opened onto the courtyard.

Dione hesitated only a moment, then followed him. She didn't want anything to be said about her being in his company, but on the other hand, she knew that Richard wasn't going to make a pass at her, and she resented feeling guilty for being friendly to him. Serena had continued her efforts at friendship, and Dione found that she really liked the younger woman; Serena was a lot like Blake, with his directness, his willingness to accept challenges. Sometimes Dione had the uneasy thought that Serena could check on her more easily under the guise of friendship, but more and more it seemed that the thought came from her own wariness, not any premeditated action on Serena's part.

"Aren't things going well?" she asked Richard quietly.

He gave a bitter laugh, rubbing the back of his neck. "You know they're not. I don't know why," he said wearily. "I've tried, but it's always in the back of my mind that she'll never love me the way she loves Blake, that I'll never be as important to her as he is, and it makes me almost sick to touch her."

Dione chose her words carefully, picking them like wildflowers. "Some resentment is only natural. I see this constantly, Richard. An accident like this really shakes up everyone connected to the patient. If it's a child who's injured, it can cause resentment between the parents, as well as the other children. In circumstances like these, one person gets the lion's share of the attention, and others don't like it."

"You make me sound so small and petty," he said, one corner of his stern mouth curving upward.

"Not that. Just human." Her voice was full of warmth and compassion, and he stared at her, his eyes moving over her tender face. "It'll get better," she reassured him.

"Soon enough to save my marriage?" he asked heavily. "Sometimes I almost hate her, and it's damned peculiar, because what I'm hating her for is not loving me the way I love her."

"Why make her take all the blame?" Dione probed. "Why not put some of that resentment on Blake? Why not hate him for taking her attention?"

He actually laughed aloud. "Because I'm not in love with him." He chuckled. "I don't care what he does with his attention…unless he hurts you with it."

Shock rippled through her, widening her enormous eyes. In the dimness of twilight they gleamed darkly gold, as deep and bottomless as a cat's. "How can he hurt me?" she asked, her voice husky.

"By making you fall in love with him." He was too astute, capable of summing up a situation in a glance. "I've been watching you change these last couple of weeks. You were beautiful before, God knows, but now you're breathtaking. You…glow. Those new clothes of yours, the look on your face, even the way you walk…all of that has changed. He needs you now so intensely that everyone else is wiped out of his mind, but what about later? When he can walk again, will he still watch you as if his eyes are glued on you?"

"Patients have fallen in love with me before," she pointed out.

"I don't doubt that, but have you ever fallen in love with a patient before?" he asked relentlessly.

"I'm not in love with him." She had to protest the idea, had to thrust it away from her. She couldn't be in love with Blake.

"I recognize the symptoms," Richard said.

As sticky as the conversation was when they were discussing Serena, Dione infinitely preferred it to the current line, and she moved jerkily away. "I don't have any sand castle built," she assured him, clenching her hands into fists in an effort to keep herself from trembling. "When Blake's walking, I'll move on to another job. I know that. I've known it from the beginning. I *always* get personally involved with my patients," she said, laughing a little. That was all it was, just her normal intense concentration on her patient.

Richard shook his head in amusement. "You see so clearly with everyone else," he said, "to be so blind about yourself."

The old, blind panic, familiar in form but suddenly unfamiliar in substance, clawed at her stomach. *Blind.* That word, the one Richard had used. No, she thought painfully. It wasn't so much that she was blind as that she deliberately didn't see. She had built a wall between herself and anything that threatened her; she knew it was there, but as long as she didn't have to look at it, she could ignore it. Blake had forced her on two occasions to face the past that she'd put behind her, never realizing what the ordeal had cost her in terms of pain. Now Richard, though he was using his coolly analytical brain instead of the gut instincts Blake operated on, was trying to do the same.

"I'm not blind," she denied in a whisper. "I know who I am, and what I am. I know my limits. I learned them the hard way."

"You're wrong," he said, his gray eyes thoughtful. "You've only learned the limits that other people have placed on you."

That was so true that she almost winced away from the thrust of it. Instinctively she pushed the thought away, drew herself up, marshaling her inner forces. "I think you wanted to talk to me about Serena," she reminded him quietly, letting him know that she wasn't going to talk about herself any longer.

"I did, but on second thought, I won't bother you with it. You have more than enough on your mind now. In the end, Serena and I will have to settle our differences on our own, so it's useless to ask anyone else's advice."

Walking together, they reentered the house and went into the study. Serena was sitting with her back to them, though her posture of concentration told them exactly what expression was on her face. She hated to lose, and she poured all her energies into beating Blake. Although she was a good chess player, Blake was better. She was usually wild with jubilation whenever she managed to beat him.

Blake, however, looked up as Richard and Dione came in together, and a hard, determined expression pulled his face into a mask. His blue eyes narrowed.

Later that night, when she poked her head into his bedroom to tell him good-night, he said evenly, "Dee, Serena's marriage is hanging by a thread. I'm warning you—don't do anything to break that thread. She loves Richard. It'll kill her if she loses him."

"I'm not a home wrecker or a slut," she retorted, stung. Anger brought red spots to her cheeks as she stared at him.

He had left the lamp on, evidently waiting until she told him good-night, as she usually did, so she could see exactly how forbidding he looked. Bewildered pain mingled with her anger to make her tremble inside. How could he even think… "I'm not like my mother," she blurted, her voice stifled, and she whirled, slamming the door behind her and fleeing to her own room despite the sound of her name being called demandingly.

She was both hurt and furious, but years of self-discipline enabled her to sleep dreamlessly anyway. When she woke hours later, just before her alarm went off, she felt better. Then she frowned. It seemed as if her subconscious could hear the echo of her name being called. She sat up, tilting her head as she listened.

"Dee! Damn it to hell!"

After weeks of hearing that particular note in his voice when he called her, she knew that he was in pain. Without her robe, she ran to his room.

She turned on the light. He was sitting up, rubbing his left calf, his face twisted in a grimace of pain. "My foot, too," he gritted. Dione seized his foot and forcefully returned his toes to their proper positions, digging her thumbs into the ball of his foot and massaging. He fell back against his pillow, his chest rising and falling swiftly as he gulped in air.

"It's all right," she murmured, moving her soothing hands up his ankle to his calf.

She devoted her attention to his leg, unaware of the fixed way he watched her. After several minutes she straightened out his leg and patted his ankle, then pulled the sheet over him. "There," she said, smiling as she looked up, but the smile faded as she met his gaze. Those dark blue eyes were as fierce and compelling as the sea, and she faltered in the face of his regard, her soft lips parting. Slowly his eyes dipped downward, and she was abruptly aware of her breasts, thrusting against the almost transparent fabric of her nightgown. A throbbing ache in her nipples made her fear that they had hardened, but she didn't dare glance down to confirm it. Her new nightgowns didn't hide a lot; they merely veiled.

Suddenly she couldn't withstand the force of his gaze and she averted her eyes, her thick lashes dropping to shield her thoughts. His body was in her line of vision, and abruptly her eyes widened. She almost gasped, but controlled her reaction at the last second.

Jerkily she got to her feet, forgetting about how much the nightgown revealed. She'd accomplished her aim, but she didn't feel smug about it; she felt stunned, her mouth dry, her pulses hammering through her veins. She swallowed, and her voice was too husky to be casual when she said, "I thought you said you were impotent."

It was a moment before her words registered. He looked as stunned as she felt, then he glanced down at himself. His jaw hardened and he swore aloud.

A hot blush suddenly burned her face. It was ridiculous to stand there, but she couldn't move. She *was* fascinated, she admitted, completely bewildered by her reaction, or rather, her lack of it. As fascinated as a bird before a cobra, and that was a Freudian simile if ever she'd heard one.

"I must be psychic," he whispered rawly. "I was just thinking that that little bit of nothing you have on would rouse the dead."

She couldn't even smile. Abruptly, though, she was able to move, and she left the room as swiftly as she could without actually running.

That disturbing dryness was still in her mouth as she dressed, pulling out her old clothes rather than the clinging new garments she'd been wearing. There was no need to dress seductively now; that particular milestone was behind him, and she knew better than to play with fire.

The only problem was, she discovered as the days passed,

that Blake didn't seem to notice that she'd reverted to her old clothes, her modest nightgowns. He didn't say anything, but she could always feel the blue fire of his gaze on her when they were together. In the course of therapy she was constantly touching him, and she gradually became accustomed to the way he'd wrap his fingers around her leg while she massaged him, or the frequency with which their bodies rubbed together when they were swimming.

Much sooner than she'd expected, he stood alone, not using his hands. He swayed for a moment, but his legs held and he regained his balance. He worked harder than any patient she'd had before, determined to end his dependency on the wheelchair. He paid for his determination every night with the torturous cramps that he suffered, but he didn't let up the killing pace he'd set for himself. Dione no longer organized his therapy; he pushed himself. All she could do was try to prevent him from doing so much that he harmed himself, and soothe his muscles at the end of every workout with massages and sessions in the whirlpool.

Sometimes she got a lump in her throat as she watched him straining himself to the limit, his teeth clenched, his neck corded with effort. It would soon be over, and she'd move on to another patient. He was already an entirely different man from the one she'd first seen almost five months before. He was as hard as a rock, tanned the color of teak, his body rippling with lean muscles. He'd regained all of his weight, and possibly more, but it was all muscle, and he was as fit as any professional athlete. She couldn't analyze the emotions that quivered through her when she watched him. Pride, of course, even some possessiveness. But there was also something else, something that made her feel warm and languid; yet at the same time she was more alive now than she'd ever been. She watched him, and she let him touch her, and she felt closer to him than she'd ever thought possible. She *knew* this man, knew his fierce pride, the daredevil in him that thumbed his nose at danger and laughingly accepted any challenge. She knew his swift, cutting intelligence, the blast of his temper, his tenderness. She knew the way he tasted, the strength of his mouth, the texture of his hair and skin beneath her hesitant fingers.

He was becoming so much a part of her that, when she allowed herself to think about it, it frightened her. She couldn't let that happen. Already he needed her less and less, and one day in the near future he would return to his work and she would be gone. For the first time the thought of moving on was painful. She loved the huge, cool hacienda, the smooth tiles underfoot, the serene expanses of white wall. The long summer days she'd spent in the pool with him, the laughter they'd shared, the hours of work, even the sweat and tears, had forged a bond that linked him to her in a way she didn't think she could bear.

It wasn't easy admitting that she loved him, but as the gilded fall days slipped past, she stopped trying to hide it from herself. She'd faced too much in the past to practice self-deception for long. The knowledge that at last she loved a man was bittersweet, because she didn't expect anything to come of it. Loving him was one thing; allowing him to love her was quite another. Her golden eyes were haunted as she watched him, but she threw herself into their remaining time together with a single-minded determination to gather all the memories she could, to let no shadows darken the time she had left. Like pieces of gold, she treasured his deep chuckles, the blistering curses he used whenever his legs wouldn't do as he wanted, the way the virile groove in his cheek deepened into a dimple when he would look up at her, elated, at every triumph.

He was so vitally alive, so masculine, that he deserved a woman in every sense of the word. She might love him, but she knew that she wouldn't be able to satisfy him in the way that was most important to him. Blake was a very physical man; that was a part of his character that became more and more evident with each passing day as he regained command of his body. She wouldn't burden him with the tangle of somber memories that lay just under the calm exterior she presented to the world; she wouldn't make him feel guilty that she'd come to love him. If it killed her, if it tore her to pieces inside, she'd keep their relationship on an even keel, guide him through the last weeks of his therapy, celebrate with him when he finally took those first, all-important steps, then quietly leave. She'd had years of practice in doing just that, devoting herself body and soul to her patient...no, the relentlessly honest side of her corrected. Never before had she devoted herself *body* and soul to anyone else, only to Blake. And he'd never know. She would smilingly say goodbye, walk away, and he'd pick up his life again. Perhaps sometimes he'd think of the woman who'd been his therapist, but then again, perhaps he wouldn't.

Her eyes were cameras, hungrily catching images of him and etching them permanently into her brain, her dreams, the very fiber of her being. There was the morning she went into his room and found him lying on his back, staring at his feet with fierce concentration. "Watch," he grunted, and she watched. Sweat beaded on his face, his fists clenched...and his toes moved. He threw his head back, giving her a blinding smile of triumph, and her built-in shutter clicked, preserving another memory; there was the scowl he gave her one night when she bested him in a long-fought game of chess, and he acted as outraged as he had when he'd discovered that she lifted weights. Laughing or frowning, he was the most beautiful thing that had ever happened to her, and she watched him constantly.

It simply wasn't fair that one man should be so rich with all the treasures of manhood, tempting her with his strength and laughter, when she knew that he was forbidden to her.

The depths of her fey golden eyes held a world of silent suffering, and though she was very controlled whenever she thought anyone was looking at her, in repose her features reflected the sadness she felt. She was so engrossed with the discovery of her love, and regret for what could never be, that she failed to notice the sharp blue eyes that watched her in return, read the pain she felt and determined to find the cause.

As the early days of November brought the sizzling Phoenix heat down into the comfortable mid-seventies, the milestone that she had dreaded, yet worked for so determinedly, was finally reached. He'd been on the bars all morning, literally dragging his feet along, and he was so wet with sweat that his dark blue shorts were soaked and clinging to him. Dione was exhausted by the effort of crouching beside him, moving his feet in the proper motions, and she sank to the floor.

"Let's rest a minute," she said, her voice muffled by fatigue.

His nostrils flared, and he made a sound that was almost a snarl. With his hands clenched around the bars, his teeth bared with determination, he flexed his muscles and bore down with the strain. His right foot moved erratically forward. A feral cry tore itself from deep in his chest and he sagged on the bars, his head falling forward. Trembling, Dione scrambled to her feet and reached out for him, but before she could touch him, he pulled his shoulders back and began the agonizing process with his left foot. His head arched back and he gulped in air; every muscle in his body stood out from the strain he was subjecting himself to, but at last the left foot moved, dragging more than the right foot had, but it moved. Dione stood rooted beside him, her face wet with silent, unnoticed tears as she watched him.

"Damn it," he whispered to himself, shuddering with the effort it cost him as he tried to take another step. "Do it again!"

She couldn't take it any longer; with a choked cry she hurled herself at him, wrapping her arms around his taut waist and burying her face in the sweaty hollow of his shoulder. He wavered, then regained his balance, and his sinewed arms locked around her, holding her so tightly that she moaned from the exquisite pain of it.

"You witch," he muttered thickly, burrowing his fingers under her tumbled mane of hair and twisting his hand in the black mass of it. He exerted just enough pressure to lift her face out of his shoulder and turn it up to him so he could see her wet cheeks, her drowning, glittering eyes and trembling lips. "You stubborn, beautiful witch, you all but jerked me out of that wheelchair by the hair on my head. Shh, don't cry," he said, his tone changing to one of rustling tenderness. He bent his head and slowly kissed the salty tears from her lashes. "Don't cry, don't cry," he crooned, his lips following the tracks of her silvery tears down her cheek, sliding to her lips, where his tongue licked them away. "Laugh with me, lady. Celebrate with me. Let's break out the champagne—you don't know what this means to me…lady… No more tears," he whispered, sighing the words against her face, her lips, and as the last one became sound he settled his mouth firmly over hers.

Blindly she clung to him, hearing the tone of his voice, though the words didn't make any sense. His arms were living shackles, holding her to him, his long, bare legs pressing against hers, her breasts crushed into the dark curls that decorated his chest, and she wasn't afraid. Not of Blake. The taste of him was wild and heady, his tongue strong and insistent as it moved into her mouth and tasted her deeply, possessively. Instinctively she kissed him in return, making her own discoveries, her own explorations. He bit gently at her tongue, then sucked it back into his mouth when she began a startled withdrawal. Dione's knees buckled and she sagged against him, which was enough to upset his precarious balance. He lurched sideways, and they stumbled to the floor in a tangle of arms and legs, but not once did he release her. Again and again his mouth met hers, demanding things that she didn't know how to give, and giving her a wild, alien pleasure that set her to trembling like a tree in a hurricane.

Her nails dug into his shoulders and she strained against him, mindlessly seeking to intensify the contact with him. Not once did she think of Scott. Blake filled her world. The sweaty male scent of him was in her nostrils, the slippery texture of his hot skin under her hands; the unbearably erotic taste of his mouth lay sweetly on her tongue. At some unknown point his kisses had slipped past celebration and become intensely male, demanding, giving, thrilling. Perhaps they'd never been celebration kisses at all, she thought fuzzily.

Suddenly he removed his mouth from hers and buried his face in the curve of her neck. When he spoke his voice was shaky, but husky with an undertone of laughter. "Have you noticed how much time we spend rolling around on the floor?"

It wasn't that funny, but in her sensitized state it struck her as hilarious, and she began to chuckle helplessly. He propped himself up on his elbow and watched her, his blue eyes lit by a strange light. His hard, warm hand went to her stomach and slid under the thin fabric of her T-shirt top, resting lightly but soothingly on her bare flesh. The intimate but unthreatening touch calmed her almost immediately, and she quieted, lying there and watching his face with huge, fathomless eyes, in which her tears still glittered.

"This definitely calls for champagne," he murmured, leaning over to crush his lips lightly over hers, then withdrawing before the contact could start anew the searing fire of discovery.

Dione was under control again, and the therapist in her began to take over. "Definitely champagne, but first let's get off the floor." She rolled gracefully to her feet and extended her hand to him. He used his hands to place his feet in a secure position, then placed his forearm against hers, his hand cupping her elbow. She stiffened her arm, and he used the leverage to pull himself up, swaying for a moment before he found his balance.

"What now?" he asked.

Someone else might have thought he was asking about the immediate future, but Dione was so attuned to him that she knew he was asking about his progress. "Repetition," she replied. "The more you do it, the easier it'll be. On the other hand, don't push yourself too hard, or you could hurt yourself. People get clumsy when they're tired, and you could fall, break an arm or a leg, and the lost time would really hurt."

"Give me a time," he insisted, and she shook her head at his persistence. He didn't know how to wait; he pushed things along, impatient even with himself.

"I'll be able to give you a ballpark figure in a week," she said, not letting him push *her*. "But I'll definitely be able to keep my promise that you'll be walking by Christmas."

"Six weeks," he figured.

"With a cane," she threw in hastily, and then he glared at her.

"Without a cane," he insisted. She shrugged. If he set his mind to walking without a cane, he probably would.

"I've been thinking of going back to work," he said, startling her. She looked up and was tangled in the web of his blue gaze; it captured her as surely as a spider caught a helpless fly. "I could do it now, but I don't want to interfere with my therapy. What do you say about the first of the year? Will I be far enough along that working won't interfere with my progress?"

Her throat clogged. By the first of the year she'd be gone. She swallowed and said in a low but even voice, "You'll be out of therapy by then and can resume your normal schedule. If you want to continue your exercise program, that's up to you. You have all of the equipment here. You won't have to work as hard as you have, because I was building you up from a very low point. All you have to do now, if you want to continue, is maintain the level you're at now, which won't require such intensive training. If you'd like, I'll draw up a program for you to follow to stay in your present shape."

Blue lightning suddenly flashed from his eyes. "What do you mean, for me to follow?" he demanded harshly, his hand darting out to grip her wrist. Despite her strength, her bones were slender, aristocratic, and his long fingers more than circled her flesh.

Dione could feel her insides crumbling; hadn't he realized that when his therapy was completed, she'd be leaving? Perhaps not. Patients were so involved with themselves, with their progress, that the reality of other responsibilities didn't occur to them. She'd been living for weeks with the pain of knowing that soon she'd have to leave him; now he had to realize it, too.

"I won't be here," she said calmly, straightening her shoulders. "I'm a therapist. It's what I do for a living. I'll be on another case by then. You won't need me anymore. You'll be walking, working, everything you did before...though I think you should wait a while before climbing another mountain."

"You're *my* therapist," he snapped, tightening his grip on her wrist.

She gave a sad laugh. "It's normal to be possessive. For months we've been isolated in our own little world, and you've depended on me more than you have on any other person in your life, except your mother. Your perspective is distorted now, but when you begin working again, everything will right itself. Believe me, by the time I've been gone a month, you won't even think about me."

A dark red flush ran up under his tan. "Do you mean you'd

just turn your back on me and walk away?" he asked in a dis-believing tone.

She flinched, and tears welled in her eyes. She'd gone for years without crying, having learned not to when she was a child, but Blake had shattered that particular control. She'd wept in his arms...and laughed in them. "It...it's not that easy for me, either," she quivered. "I get involved, too. I always... fall a little in love with my patients. But it passes.... You'll pick up your life and I'll move on to another patient—"

"I'll be damned if you're going to move in with some other man and fall in love with him!" Blake interrupted hotly, his nostrils flaring.

Despite herself, Dione laughed. "Not all of my patients are men. I have a large percentage of children."

"That's not the point." His flesh was suddenly taut over his cheekbones. "*I* still need you."

"Oh, Blake," she said in a half sob, half chuckle. "I've been through this more times than I can remember. I'm a habit, a crutch, nothing more, and I'm a crutch that you don't even need now. If I left today, you'd do just fine."

"That's a matter of opinion," he snapped. He shifted his grasp on her wrist and brought her hand up, cradling it to his beard-roughened cheek for a moment before touching his mouth to her knuckles. "You shoved your way into my life, lady, took over my house, my routine, me.... Do you think people forget volcanoes?"

"Maybe you won't forget me, but you'll discover, one day soon, that you don't need me anymore. Now," she said briskly, deliberately inserting cheer into her voice, "what about that champagne?"

They had champagne. Blake rounded up everyone, and between them they drank the entire bottle. Angela received the news of Blake's progress by gently crying; Alberta forgot herself so far as to give Dione a smile of self-satisfied complicity and drank three glasses of champagne; Miguel's dark face suddenly lit, the first smile Dione had ever seen from him, and he toasted Blake with a silently raised glass, the two men's eyes meeting and communicating as memories flashed between them.

There was another bottle of champagne at dinner that night. Serena hurled herself into Blake's arms when he broke the good news to her, wrenching sobs of relief shaking her body. It took some time to quiet her; she was almost wild with the joy of it. Richard, whose face had become more and more strained as the weeks passed, suddenly looked as if the weight of the world had been lifted from his shoulders. "Thank God," he said with heartfelt sincerity. "Now I can have that nervous breakdown I've been putting off for two years."

Everyone laughed, but Blake said, "If anyone deserves a long vacation, it's you. As soon as I get back into harness, you're relieved of duty for at least a month."

Richard moved his shoulders tiredly. "I won't refuse it," he said.

Serena looked at her husband with determined cheerfulness. "How about Hawaii?" she asked. "We could spend the whole month lying on the beach in paradise."

Richard's mouth thinned. "Maybe later. I think I just need to be by myself for a while."

Serena drew back as though he'd slapped her, and her cheeks paled. Blake looked at his sister, reading the dejection in her, and anger brightened the dark blue of his eyes. Dione put her hand on his sleeve to restrain him. Whatever problems Richard and Serena were having, they had to work them out by themselves. Blake couldn't keep smoothing the path for Serena; that was a large part of the trouble. He was so important to her that Richard felt slighted.

In only a moment Serena gathered herself and lifted her head, smiling as though Richard's comment had completely missed her. Dione couldn't help but admire her grit. She was a proud, stubborn woman; she didn't need big brother to fight her battles for her. All she had to do was realize that for herself, and make Blake realize it, too.

Dinner was an astonishing melange of items that weren't normally served together, and Dione suspected that Alberta was still celebrating. When the cornish hen was followed by fish, she knew that the three glasses of champagne had been too much. She made the mistake of glancing at Blake, and the barely controlled laughter on his face was too much for her. Suddenly everyone at the table was laughing, effectively banishing the silence that had fallen after Richard's rejection of Serena.

To keep from hurting Alberta's feelings, they made a valiant effort at eating everything placed before them, though she'd evidently gotten carried away and prepared much more than she normally did. If she hadn't been such a good cook, even when she was tipsy, it would have been impossible.

They could hear occasional bursts of song from the kitchen, and just the thought of Alberta, of all people, singing, was enough to bring on fresh bouts of hilarity. Dione laughed until her stomach muscles were sore. The champagne was having its effect on them, too, and she suspected that anything would have made them laugh at that point.

It was much later than usual when Serena and Richard left, and if nothing else, the champagne had destroyed the distance between them. Richard had to support his wobbly wife for the short distance to the car, and Serena was frankly hanging on him, laughing like a maniac. Dione was still sober enough to be glad that Richard handled his alcohol well, since he was driving, but she was also tipsy enough to fall into gales of laughter at the thought that it was a good thing Blake was still in a wheelchair; he'd never have made it up the stairs if he'd been walking.

He insisted that she help him undress, and she put him to bed as if he were a child. As she leaned over him to adjust the sheet, he caught her hand and pulled it. After the champagne, her balance wasn't the best it had ever been, and she tumbled across him. He stopped her giggles by kissing her slowly, sleepily, then settling her in his arms. "Sleep with me," he demanded, then closed his eyes and fell immediately to sleep himself.

Dione smiled a little sadly. The lights were still blazing, and she was dressed in the royal blue dress she'd put on to celebrate the occasion. She hadn't had *that* much to drink. After a few moments she gently extricated herself from his sleep-relaxed grip and slid from the bed. She turned out the lights, then made her way to her own room and removed the dress, dropping it carelessly on the floor. She, too, slept deeply, and woke the next morning with a headache that tempted her to just stay in bed.

With admirable, if painful, self-discipline, she got out of bed and showered, then went about her normal activities. The champagne hadn't affected Blake as much as it had her, and he was as clear-eyed as usual, ready to begin his exercises. After helping him to warm up, she left him to it and went to take a couple of aspirin.

Serena came in just as she was about to go downstairs—a radiant Serena, whose mouth seemed curved in a permanent smile. "Hi," she said cheerfully. "Where's Blake?"

When Dione told her, she said, "Good, I came to see you, not him. I just wanted to ask you how the chase is going."

It took a moment before Dione realized what she meant; her "scheme" to attract Blake had been so short-lived that, in retrospect, it seemed silly that she'd gotten so upset over something so trivial. Other worries had taken over her time and attention. "Everything's fine," she said, forcing herself to smile. "I think everything's fine with you, too. You look better than I'd expected you to look this morning."

Serena gave her a wink. "I hadn't had that much to drink," she admitted without a hint of shame. "It just seemed like too good an opportunity to pass up. You inspired me. If you could go after the man you wanted, why couldn't I? He's my husband, for heaven's sake! So I seduced him last night."

Despite her headache Dione chuckled. Serena grinned. "The war isn't won yet, but I've recaptured some lost territory. I've decided that I'm going to get pregnant."

"Is that wise?" So many things could go wrong. If the marriage failed, then Serena would be left to raise the child alone. Or Richard might stay because of the child, but that seemed like a hellish situation for all concerned.

"I know Richard," said Serena with confidence. "I've offended him, and it'll take him a while to forgive me, but I really think that he loves me. Having his baby will show him how much I love him, too."

"What he really needs is to know that you love him more than you love Blake," Dione said. She felt a little uneasy at giving advice; what did she know about handling a love life? Her own brief experience with marriage had been disastrous.

"I *do!* I love Richard in an entirely different way from the way I love Blake."

"If you were faced with a situation where you could save one of them, but not both of them, which one would you save?"

Serena paled, staring at her.

"Think it over," Dione said gently. "That's what Richard wants. Your wedding vows were to forsake all others."

"You're telling me that I have to let Blake go, to cut him out of my life."

"Not entirely—just change the amount of time that you devote to him."

"I shouldn't have dinner over here every night, should I?"

"I'm sure Richard wonders which house you consider your home."

Serena was a fighter; she absorbed Dione's words, and for a moment she looked frightened. Then her shoulders straightened and her chin went up. "You're right," she said forcefully. "You're a dear!" She startled Dione by giving her a fierce hug. "Poor Richard won't know what's hit him. I'm going to positively smother him with tender loving care! You can be the baby's godmother," she added with a wicked twinkle.

"I'll remember that," said Dione, but after Serena had left she wondered if Serena would remember. By that time, Dione would be long gone.

CHAPTER 8

The next day, without mentioning it to anyone, Dione began making arrangements to take another case. She'd give herself time to recover from the pain of losing Blake, time to adjust to waking up without knowing that he was in the next room. She'd begin at the end of January, she thought. Blake would be returning to work after the first of January, and she'd probably leave sometime around then.

Now that success was in his grasp, Blake pushed himself harder. Dione gave up even trying to rein in his energy. She watched him force himself along the bars, sweating, cursing steadily as an antidote against the pain and weariness, and when he was too tired to continue she'd massage his exhausted body, put him in the whirlpool, then give him another massage. She watched his diet more closely than ever, knowing how badly he needed extra nutrition now. When cramps knotted his legs in the night, she rubbed them out for him. There was no stopping him.

It was time for him to leave the wheelchair behind. She brought in a walker, a four-legged half cage that provided him with the balance and stability he needed, and the pleasure of getting around under his own power was so great that he gladly endured the slow pace, the strain.

He didn't mention Serena's sudden absence from the dinner table, though Alberta immediately adjusted both her menus and the amount she cooked. The full dinners almost ceased; instead she began preparing small, light dinners, and Dione often found the table set with candles and a decanter of wine. The intimate atmosphere was another spike that crucified her heart, but as Blake welcomed the pain of therapy, she welcomed the hurt of his company. This was all she had, and the days were trickling away so swiftly that she felt as if she were grasping at shadows.

On Thanksgiving Day, following Blake's directions, she drove them to Serena's house for dinner. Except for being transferred from the hospital to home, it was the first time he'd been out since his accident, and he sat turned to stone, his entire body tense as his senses struggled to take everything in. In two years Scottsdale had changed, cars had changed, clothing had changed. She wondered if the desert sky seemed bluer to him, the sun brighter.

"When will I be able to drive?" he asked abruptly.

"When your reflexes are fast enough. Soon," she promised absently. She seldom drove, and she had to concentrate on what she was doing. She jumped when his hand rested on her knee, then slid up under the skirt she was wearing to pat her thigh.

"Next week we'll start practicing," he said. "We'll go out in the desert, away from all the traffic."

"Yes, fine," she said, her voice taut with tension caused by the warm hand on her leg. He touched her constantly, bestowing kisses and pats, but somehow his hand seemed much more intimate when she had on a skirt.

A smile twitched at his lips. "I like that dress," he said.

She gave him a harried glance. He liked every dress she wore, evidently. He was definitely a leg man. He slid closer and bent his head to inhale the perfume she'd used in honor of the occasion, his warm breath caressing her collarbone just before he pressed his lips into the soft hollow. Simultaneously his hand slid higher, and the car wobbled dangerously before Dione straightened it.

"Stop it!" she fumed, pushing uselessly at his hand. "You're making me nervous! I don't drive that well anyway!"

"Then put both hands on the wheel," he advised, laughing. "I'm in the same car, remember? I'm not going to do anything that'll cause you to crash."

"You wretch!" she shouted as his fingers began stroking back and forth over her thigh. "Damn it, Blake, would you stop it! I'm not a doll for you to play with!"

"I'm not playing," he murmured. His fingers circled higher.

Desperately Dione released the wheel and grabbed his wrist with both hands. The car veered sideways, and with a curse he finally moved his hand, grabbing the steering wheel and bringing the car back under control. "Maybe I'd better start driving *now*," he panted.

"You're going to be walking to Serena's!" she yelled, her face scarlet.

He threw his head back and laughed. "You don't know how good that sounds, lady! It would take me a while, but I could do it! God, I feel like a human being again!"

Abruptly she realized that his spirits were sky-high, the natural result of his victory and the experience of being away from the house. He was delirious with pleasure, drunk on his newfound freedom from the prison of his own body. Still, she was driving, and she was afraid that he was going to make her run into something.

"I mean it, stop fooling around!" she said sharply.

He gave her a lazy smile, a heart-stopping smile. "Lady, if I decided to fool around, you'd be the first to know."

"Why don't you go back to work tomorrow?" she demanded in sudden exasperation.

"We're closed for the holidays. I wouldn't have anything to do."

"I'm going to give you something to do," she muttered.

"Like what?"

"Picking your teeth up off the pavement," she said.

He threw his hands up in mock alarm. "All right, all right! I'll be good. Next thing I know, you'll be sending me to bed without my supper. I wouldn't really mind, though, because you always come to tuck me in, and I get to watch you running around in those thin nightgowns of yours that you think are so modest.... Serena's house is the solar redwood and rock one."

He threw in the last sentence just as she opened her mouth to blast him again, and she maneuvered the Audi up the steep drive to where the house nestled against the mountain. By the time she'd gotten out of the car and gone around to help Blake wrestle with the walker, Serena and Richard had come out to greet them.

The steps were a problem for Blake, but he mastered them. Serena watched, an anxious look on her face, but she didn't run to help him. Instead she stayed firmly by Richard's side, her arm looped through his. Dione remained a step behind Blake, not out of servitude but to catch him in case he started to tumble. He looked over his shoulder at her and grinned. "Not bad, huh?"

"A regular goat," she replied, and only he caught her hidden meaning.

He gave her another of his breathtaking smiles. "Don't you mean mountain goat?"

She shrugged. "A goat is a goat is a goat."

His eyes promised retribution, but she felt safe from him

for the time being. If he started anything on the drive back home, *she'd* get out and walk!

The traditional dinner had all of them groaning before it was over. Blake and Richard then retired to talk business, and Dione helped Serena clear the table. Serena had a cook, but she told Dione that everything had been prepared the day before and she'd given the cook the rest of the week off. "I don't mind being alone in the house with Richard," she said, laughing a little.

"Is Operation Manhunt going well?" asked Dione.

"At times." Serena laughed. "Sometimes I…ah…undermine his resistance. Then he'll freeze up on me again. But I think I'm winning the battle. He noticed that I've stopped going to Blake's every day."

"Did he ask you about it?"

"Richard? Not a chance! But he calls me almost every afternoon about some little something, as if he's checking on me."

They traded a few comments on the mule-headedness of men in general and finished cleaning the kitchen. When they finally emerged they discovered that the men were still deep in conversation about the company, with Richard going over some sort of electronic blueprint with Blake. Dione looked at Serena, and they both shrugged. Kicking off their shoes, they sat down, and Serena used the remote control to turn on the television set, which revealed two football teams tearing into each other.

Within ten minutes the men had left their technical conversation and were sitting beside the women. Dione liked football, so she didn't mind watching the game, and evidently Serena shared the same fondness for it. At first Dione didn't pay attention to the hand that touched her shoulder, lying absently over it so that the fingers touched her collarbone. Gradually the touch firmed, shifted and exerted pressure. Without quite knowing how it had happened, she suddenly realized that she was leaning back in the circle of Blake's arm, resting against his chest while his arm kept her firmly anchored there.

The startled movement of her body brought a knowing smile to his lips, but he merely held her more closely than before. "Shh. Just watch the game," he murmured.

She was so rattled that nothing sank into her consciousness, but eventually the warmth of his body began to relax her. He would behave himself here, so she was free to enjoy the sensation, let herself drown in the heady scent of his skin. All too soon she would have only the memories of him to take out and savor.

The time passed swiftly. Incredibly they became hungry again, so everyone raided the refrigerator and constructed enormous sandwiches of turkey, lettuce, tomato and anything else they could find. Blake's sweet tooth demanded feeding, and he devoured what was left of the strawberry pie. The atmosphere was easy, comfortable, and he commented on it when they were driving home late that night.

"Serena and Richard seem to have patched up their differences," he said, watching her sharply in the dim light from the dash.

"I think they're well on their way," she said, carefully keeping her tone bland. She wasn't about to divulge anything Serena had told her.

When they got home Dione looked him squarely in the eye and smiled. "I really don't think there's any need for me to tuck you in any longer," she said sweetly. "You're perfectly mobile now. I'll see you in the morning. Good night."

As she let herself into her room she heard him doing a perfect imitation of a chicken clucking, and she had to bite her lip to stifle her laughter. The monster!

But when he called her several hours later, jerking her out of a sound sleep, she didn't hesitate. She hurried to his room and flipped on the light switch. He was lying on his stomach, hopelessly tangled in the sheet as he tried to reach his left leg.

"Easy," she crooned, finding the cramp and briskly rubbing the muscle of his calf between her hands. He went limp with relief as the pain eased away.

"How much longer will this go on?" he muttered into his pillow.

"Until your muscles are used to the demands you're making on them," she said. "It's not as bad as it was. You seldom have a cramp in your right leg now."

"I know. My left leg drags more than the right. I'll always limp, won't I?"

"Who knows? It won't matter, though. You'll look smashing with a cane."

He laughed and rolled over on his back, tangling the sheet even more. Despite what she'd said earlier, Dione bent over him and automatically began straightening the sheet. "You managed to make a disaster area of your bed," she complained.

"I was restless tonight," he said, his voice suddenly strained.

Dione glanced up, and her hands froze at their task. He was staring at her, his gaze locked on her breasts. A look of such raw hunger was in his eyes that she would have flinched away if she'd had any strength in her limbs. But she continued to sit on the side of his bed, mesmerized by the way his gaze moved lovingly, longingly, over her female curves.

"Lady, what you do to me is almost criminal," he groaned in a shaky voice.

An odd tightening in her breasts made her close her eyes. "I've got to go," she said weakly, but for the life of her she couldn't make herself move.

"No, don't go," he pleaded. "Let me touch you...my God, I've got to touch you!"

Dione caught her breath on a sob as she felt his fingertips trace lightly over her breast, and she squeezed her eyes shut even more tightly than before. For a moment the awful unfamiliarity of a man's touch on her breast brought back a nightmare of pain and humiliation, and she made a choked sound of protest.

"Dee, honey, open your eyes. Look at me—look at how I'm shaking. Touching you makes me dizzy," he whispered fiercely. "I get drunk on the very smell of you."

Dione's eyes fluttered open, and she found that he'd moved closer, until his face was filling her vision. It was Blake's face, not Scott's, and his blue eyes were as dark and stormy as the sea, full of incredible hunger. His trembling fingers were still moving only lightly over her breasts, though the heat of his hand burned her even through her nightgown.

"That…that's enough," she said, her voice thin, wavering out of control. "This isn't right."

"I need you," he cajoled. "It's been so long… Can't you tell how much I need you? Please. Let me touch you, really touch you. Let me unbutton this granny gown and see you."

Even as the words were tumbling harshly from his lips, his agile fingers were slipping the tiny buttons of her nightgown free of the buttonholes. The buttons ran down to her waist, and he undid every one of them while she sat helplessly transfixed by the primitive call of his need. Slowly, with rapt attention, he opened the gown and pushed it off her smoothly tanned shoulders, dropping the cloth around her arms and baring her to the waist.

"I've dreamed of this," he whispered harshly. "I saw you that morning…. You were so perfect, so damned *female,* that you took my breath away." Gently he cupped a breast in his palm, curving his fingers over its ripe curve as if he were measuring the heft of it.

Dione began to tremble, wild little tingles of sensation shooting through her body. She didn't know what to do, how to handle him. She had no experience with men other than her husband, and that had been a horror from start to finish, nothing that compared to the sweet pain of Blake's touch. Sweet, yes…and not really pain. Incredible. Unknown. A primitive exultation raced along her veins, heating her blood, making her feel stupidly, happily weak. She wanted to sink down beside him on the bed, but she couldn't do that. Despite the joy her body was feeling, her mind was still locked away from even the possibility of it.

Now both of his hands were on her, holding her breasts together. His head bent, and she sucked in a convulsive breath, staring down at his dark hair with terrified fascination. His tongue darted out and washed a cherry nipple, then he blew his warm breath across it, watching with delight as it tightened and thrust out at him. "That's beautiful," he breathed, and tasted the other one.

At last she could move, and her fingers threaded through his hair. She thought dimly that she'd pull his head away, but instead her palms pressed against his warm skull and held him to her, held his mouth to the tender flesh he was suckling as fiercely as any starving infant.

He released her nipple from his mouth and lay back, his hands sliding to her ribs and drawing her with him, pulling her down until she lay half-across him. He began kissing her with short, hard kisses that stung her lips. "I need you," he panted. "Please. I want you so much. Let me make love to you."

Dione moaned, a high, keening sound that reflected both the tumult he'd stirred in her and her fear of going any further. "I can't," she cried, tears suddenly stinging her eyes. "You don't know what you're asking of me."

"Yes, I do," he whispered, moving his mouth down to the line of her jaw, nipping at her with his teeth. "I'm asking you to let me love you. I want you so much that I'm aching all over. I can't sleep for dreaming about you. Let me be a man

with you. Let me bury myself in you and forget about the past
two years. Make me whole again," he pleaded.

She'd spent too long nurturing this man, agonized over
him too much, felt his pain, celebrated his triumphs, loved
him. How could she refuse him now? She'd be leaving soon,
and she'd never know the heady taste of him again. But she
was shaking, almost convulsed with the fear of what he'd do
to her. For him, she'd bear it, this one last time. The scars
that Scott had left on her mind had ruined her forever, kept
her from feeling the total pleasure of a man, and when Blake
rolled, deftly placing himself above her, the nauseating panic
that beat its wings in her stomach threatened to overtake her.

He saw the fixed expression in her enormous golden eyes
and began to speak softly to her, making her realize his iden-
tity. With silent desperation she stared at him, her nails digging into his shoulders.

"It's all right," he murmured soothingly. "You know I won't
hurt you; I'd never hurt you. Let's get you out of this," he said
as he began thrusting the bunched cloth at her waist down over
her hips, then stroking it away from her thighs. He leaned on
his elbow and looked at her, drinking in and savoring all the
details that he'd only dreamed about before. He steadied his
shaking hand by flattening his palm on her stomach and sliding it over her satiny skin. One finger dipped into the tight
little hollow of her navel, and she gasped again, but though
her nails were digging so deeply into his shoulders that she'd
broken the skin, the blind fear had left her face. Her eyes were
locked on him, letting him know that for him, she would do
this. Though she was afraid, she trusted him, and she would
give him this one last gift, the pleasure of her body.

His hand slid lower, insinuating itself between her thighs
and exploring, as he'd tried to do so many times before. She
clenched her teeth in shock and tried to control her body's

instinctive movement, but her thighs tightened as she tried to dislodge the alien touch.

"Honey, don't!" he cried. "I won't hurt you, I swear."

Dione swallowed and slowly regained control of herself, forcing her legs to relax. He was shaking all over, his body dewed with sweat, the color in his face as florid as if he burned with fever; she felt the heat of his skin beneath her hands and wondered vaguely if he weren't really fevered after all. His blue eyes were glittering wildly, and his lips were red, swollen. She removed one trembling hand from his shoulder and touched his face, placing her fingertips on his lips. "It's all right," she whispered thinly. "I'm ready."

"Oh, God, no, you're not," he groaned, kissing her fingers. "I wanted to wait, but I don't think I can."

"It's all right," she repeated, and with a muffled cry he moved to lie fully over her.

All of the love she felt for him welled up and made her body pliable for his touch; with her eyes wide-open and locked on his face, she knew that this was Blake, and that she would do anything for him. Though her heart was slamming against her ribs with almost shattering force, though her entire body shook, she clutched his shoulders and drew him tightly to her.

He tried to be gentle, but the years of celibacy had destroyed a great deal of his normal self-control. When he parted her legs and felt the silkiness of her thighs cradle his hips, he moaned deep in his chest and took her with a single strong movement.

Hot tears burned her lids, then slid down her cheeks. This wasn't the agony she'd expected, but her body had been untouched for twelve years, and the pain and shock of his entry were all too real. To her astonishment, her flesh didn't flinch from him; she still lay soft and willing beneath him. She began to weep in earnest, not from the pain, which was already fading, but because suddenly she realized that Blake had given her as much as he was taking. He'd given her back her womanhood. The years had wrought their healing miracle, after all; it had taken Blake to make her realize it, Blake to make her love enough to overcome the past.

He lifted his head from her throat and saw the tears, and he paled. "No," he croaked. "Dee, what have I done? I'll stop—"

Inexplicably the tears mingled with laughter, and she caught him tightly, preventing the removal of his body. "Don't stop!" she said joyously, the words clogging in her throat. "I didn't know... I had no idea! No, don't ever stop—"

He caught the babbling words in his mouth, kissing her wildly and deeply, relief making him drunk. "I'm going to have to stop," he panted, beginning to move rhythmically on her. "It's been over two years, darling. I don't think I can wait—"

"Then don't wait," she said softly, her eyes shining. "This is for you."

He kissed her again, even harder than before. "The next one's for you," he promised hoarsely, just before he slid over the edge of control. Dione hugged him to her, accepting his body and his desperate, almost violent movements, cradling him, soothing him, and in a moment the storm had passed and he sagged against her.

She could feel the heavy pounding of his heart as he lay on her in the silent aftermath, feel the heat of his breath on her shoulder, the trickle of sweat that ran from his side and slipped down her ribs. She smoothed his tousled dark hair, adjusted his head more comfortably on her shoulder. He murmured something and his hand came up to cover her breast. She waited, lying there pressed into the bed by his weight, as his body relaxed and he drifted slowly, easily into sleep.

She stared up at the light that still blazed brightly; turning out the light hadn't occurred to either of them.

Exhaustion made her body heavy, but she couldn't sleep. The night had been a major turning point in her life, but she didn't know what direction to take. Or was it such a major turning point? Blake had taught her that she no longer needed to fear the touch of a man, but what difference did it make? If the man weren't Blake, then she didn't want him. It was the love that she felt for him that had enabled her to tear down her prison of fear, and without that love she simply wasn't interested.

Nor, she realized suddenly, could it ever happen again. She couldn't afford to let it happen. She was a therapist, and Blake was her patient. She'd violated her own professional code, totally forgotten the rules and standards that she'd set for herself. This was the worst mistake she'd ever made and she felt sick with remorse.

Whatever happened, she had to remember that soon she'd be leaving, that she was only a temporary part of Blake's life. She'd have to be stupid to jeopardize her career for something that she knew was only a moment out of time. *I should have seen it coming,* she thought tiredly. Of course Blake had been attracted to her; she was the only woman available to him. But she'd been so engrossed in her own misery and attraction that she hadn't realized that his actions hadn't been meant merely to tease.

Gently she shifted him to one side, and he was sleeping so deeply that he didn't flicker an eyelash. With slow, careful movements she sat up and reached for her discarded nightgown, pulling it over her head before she got to her feet. As she stood she winced at the unfamiliar soreness of her body, but forced herself to walk silently to the door and leave, turning out the light as she passed the switch.

In her own room she stared at her bed, but realized that it would be a waste of time to return to it. She'd never be able to sleep. Too many sensations, too many memories, were warring in her mind and body. Her bedside clock told her that it was a little after three; she might as well stay up the rest of the night.

She felt oddly empty, her regret canceling out the bittersweet pleasure she'd found in his embrace and leaving her
with nothing. For a short while, in his arms, she'd felt wildly
alive, as if all her fetters had fallen away. Reality was something less than that. Reality was knowing that the night meant
nothing to him beyond the immediate satisfaction of his sex-
starved body. She'd seen it coming from a mile away and still
hadn't had the sense to duck; no, she'd taken the punch full
on the jaw.

But mistakes were something to learn from, better text-
books than anything that ever got put into print. She'd picked
herself up before and gone on, and she'd do it again. The trick
was to remember that there was an end to everything, and
the end of her time with Blake was coming at her with the
speed of a jet.

She cringed inwardly at the thought, and in agitation
walked out to the gallery. The desert air was cold, and she
shivered when it touched her heated skin, but she welcomed
the shock of it. The night had been an emotional roller coaster,
a ride that had left her stunned, bewildered. She'd gone from
fear to acceptance, then to joy, followed by regret and a rerun
of acceptance, and now she was afraid again, afraid that she
wouldn't be able to pick up the pieces, afraid that life after
Blake would be so hollow that it would be useless. Afraid,
even, of the possibility that the fear he'd destroyed had been
her strongest defense.

CHAPTER 9

The sudden lancing of light across the dark gallery made her heart leap into her throat, and she turned her head to the left to wearily eye the sliding doors to Blake's room, where the light was coming from. What had awakened him? When the glass doors remained closed, she turned back to stare out again into the blackness of the garden. She hoped he wouldn't come looking for her; she didn't think she could face him right then. Perhaps in the morning, when she was dressed in her familiar "therapist uniform" of shorts and a T-shirt and they were involved in the routine of exercise. Perhaps then she'd have herself under control and could act as if nothing unusual had happened. But now she felt raw and bleeding, every nerve exposed. Wearily she leaned her head against the railing, not even feeling how cold she'd become.

A whirr came to her ears and she lifted her head, frowning. It was coming from her room…then it stopped just behind her, and she knew. Blake had used the wheelchair, because he could get around faster in it than he could using the walker. Her entire body tensed as she listened to him getting out of the chair, struggling for balance, but she didn't dare look around.

She kept her forehead pressed against the cold metal of the railing, hoping without belief that he'd realize she didn't want to be disturbed and leave her alone.

First she felt his hands, gripping her shoulders, then the hard, warm press of his body against her back and the stirring of his breath in her hair. "Dee, you're freezing," he murmured. "Come inside. We'll talk there, and I'll get you warm."

She swallowed. "There's nothing to talk about."

"There's everything to talk about," he said, a hardness that she'd never heard before in his voice making her shudder in reaction. He felt the ripple of her muscles under his fingers and pulled her closer to him. "Your skin is icy, and you're coming in with me now. You're in shock, honey, and you need to be taken care of. I thought I understood, but you threw me for a loop tonight. I don't know what it is you're hiding, what you're afraid of, but I'm damned well going to find out before this night is over."

"The night *is* over," she told him thinly. "It's morning now."

"Don't argue with me. In case you haven't noticed, I don't have a stitch of clothing on and I'm freezing, but I'm staying right here with you. If you don't come inside I'll probably catch pneumonia and undo all the progress you've worked for. Come on," he said, his tone changing into one of cajolery. "You don't have to be afraid. We'll just talk."

She shook her head, her long hair flying wildly and striking him in the face. "You don't understand. I'm not afraid of you. I never have been."

"Well, that's something," he muttered, dropping his arm to her waist and urging her to turn. She gave up and dully let him guide her inside, with him using her for balance. His pace was slow but remarkably steady, and he didn't really put any of his weight on her. He stopped to close the sliding doors, then guided her to the bed.

"Here, get under the covers," he ordered as he bent down to switch on the lamp. "How long have you been out there? Even the room is cold."

She shrugged; it didn't really matter how long it had been, did it? She did as he said and crawled into the bed, pulling the thick comforter up to her neck. Blake studied her pale, set expression for a moment, and his lips pressed grimly together. He lifted the cover and slid into the bed next to her, and she stared at him in shock.

"I'm cold, too," he said, and it was only half a lie. He slid his arm under her neck and curved his other hand around her waist, pulling her into the cocoon of his body heat. At first she was rigid; then the warmth began to penetrate her chilled skin and she started to shiver. His hand exerted just the slightest pressure and she moved with it, unconsciously pressing more closely to him in search of extra heat. When he had her settled, her head cradled on his shoulder and her legs tangled with his, he stroked the heavy black hair away from her face and she felt the pressure of his mouth on her forehead.

"Are you comfortable?" he murmured.

Comfortable wasn't the word for it; she was so tired that her limbs lay heavily, without strength. But she nodded, as he seemed to want an answer. What did it matter? She was just so tired....

After a moment he said with misleading mildness, "I thought you said you'd been married."

Surprise made her lift her head and stare at him. "I was." What did he mean?

Gently he threaded his fingers through her hair and forced her head back to his shoulder. "Then why was it so...painful for you?" he asked, his voice a rumble under her ear. "I damned near fainted, thinking that you'd been a virgin."

For a moment her mind was blank, struggling to understand what he was saying; then realization came abruptly and a hot

flush warmed her cold cheeks. "I wasn't a virgin," she assured
him huskily. "It's just that I haven't… It's been a long time."

"How long?"

With rising alarm she heard the determination in his voice,
barely masked by the quietness of his tone. He meant to know
everything, to uncover all her secrets. Twice before he'd torn
away the protection of her forgetfulness, forcing her to remember the pains and failures that she'd tried so hard never
to think of again. Did he like causing her pain?

"How long?" he repeated inexorably. "Talk to me, honey,
because you're not leaving this bed until I know."

Dione closed her eyes in despair, swallowing in an effort to
relieve the dryness of her mouth. She might as well tell him
and get it over with. "Twelve years," she finally admitted, the
words muffled against his skin because as she said them, she
turned her face into his throat.

"I see." Did he? Did he really see? Could any man really understand what went through a woman's mind when her body
was violated? A wild bitterness sprang out of the well of pain
that she usually kept covered. He didn't care if he explored
the clock's workings until it could no longer tick, as long as he
discovered what had made it tick in the beginning. Her hands
stiffened against him and she pushed, but now he was much
stronger than she was, and held her welded tightly to him, his
body hard and unyielding against hers. After a moment she
gave up the futile effort and lay beside him in rigid rejection.

He curved his long fingers over her smooth shoulder and
tucked her even closer to him, as if to shield her. "Twelve
years is a long time," he began easily. "You had to be just a
kid. How old are you now?"

"Thirty." She heard the ragged edge of panic in her voice,
felt the way her heart began to skitter, the increased rhythm
of air rushing in and out of her lungs. She'd already told him

too much; he could put the pieces of the puzzle together now and read the whole ugly story.

"Then you had to be just eighteen.... You told me that you got married when you were eighteen. Haven't you been in love since then? I know men have been attracted to you. You've got a face and body that turn my insides into melted butter. Why haven't you let someone love you?"

"That's my business," she cried sharply, trying again to roll away from him. He held her without hurting her, gently subduing her with his arms and legs. Goaded, maddened by the bonds that held her, she shrieked, "Men don't *love* women! They hurt them, humiliate them, then say, 'Whatsamatter? You frigid?' *Let me go!*"

"I can't," he said, his voice catching oddly. She was in no state to pay any attention to how her words had affected him; she began to fight in earnest, kicking at his legs, trying to scratch his face, her body arching wildly in an effort to throw herself off the bed. He snatched her hands away from his cheeks before she could do any damage, then wrestled her around until she was beneath him, his weight holding her captive.

"Dione, stop it!" he yelled. "Damn it, talk to me! *Were you raped?*"

"Yes!" she screamed, a sob tearing out of her throat. "Yes, yes, yes! Damn you! I didn't want to remember! Can't you understand that? It kills me to remember!" Another tearing, aching sob wrenched its way out of her chest, but she wasn't crying. Her eyes were dry, burning, yet still her chest heaved convulsively and the awful sounds, like someone choking on a pain too large to be swallowed, continued.

Blake's head fell back and he ground his teeth in a primal snarl, his neck corded with the rage that surged through him. His muscles trembled with the need to vent his fury physically, but a despairing whimper from the woman in his arms made him realize the need to control himself, to calm her. He held her and stroked her, sliding his palms down her body and feeling the marvelous tone of her sleek muscles even through the fabric of her gown. His lips nuzzled into her hair, moved on to discover the softness of her eyelids, the satin stretch of skin over her exotic cheekbones, the intoxicating bloom of her soft, generous mouth. He whispered to her, crooned endearments, reassured her with broken phrases that told her how lovely she was, how much he wanted her. He promised her with his words and his body that he wouldn't hurt her, reminding her over and over of the hour not long past when she'd trusted him enough to let him make love to her. The memory of that joining burned over his skin, but his need for her could wait. *Her* needs came first, the needs of a woman who had known too much pain.

Gradually she calmed; gradually she reached out to him, by slow degrees curling her arms around his muscular back. She was tired, so worn out from the emotional strain of the night that she was limp against him, but he had to know, so he said again, "Tell me about it."

"Blake, no," she moaned, turning her head weakly away from him. "I can't...."

"You can. You have to. Was that why you got divorced? Couldn't your husband handle what had happened to you?" His questions fell on her like rocks, bruising her, and she flinched in his arms. He caught her chin and turned it back to him so he could read the nuances of her expression. "What kind of bastard was he, to turn his back on you when you needed him most? Did he think it was your fault?"

A high, strained peal of laughter escaped her, and she shut it off abruptly by clapping her hand over her mouth, afraid of the rising hysteria in her. "He... Oh, this is funny! He didn't have any trouble handling what happened to me! *He* did it. My husband was the one who raped me!"

Blake went rigid, stunned both by her words and the way she began to laugh, gasping shrieks of laughter that again she shut off, visibly clenching herself in an effort to regain control. She attained it, but she used all of the inner strength she possessed, and as she lay in his arms she could feel the emotion draining away from her, leaving her heavy, spent...

"Tell me," he insisted, his voice so hoarse that she didn't recognize it.

Her heartbeat had changed from a frantic sledgehammer pounding to a ponderous rhythm; dimly she wondered at it, but what did it really matter? What did anything really matter? She'd had all she could bear tonight....

"Dione," he prodded.

"I don't know why I married him," she said dully. "I don't think I ever loved him. But he was handsome and he had money, something I'd never had. He dazzled me with it. He bought me things, took me places, told me how much he loved me. I think that was it—he told me that he loved me. No one had ever told me that before, you see. But I was still stand-offish with him, and Scott couldn't stand that. I don't think anyone had ever said no to him before. So he married me."

Blake waited a moment for her to resume, and when she didn't he jostled her lightly. "Go on."

Her eyelids lifted slowly. She stared at him with half-veiled eyes, the glimmering, mysterious golden pools darkened to amber by the shadow of her lashes. "On our wedding night, he hurt me," she said simply. "He was so rough...I started fighting him. I was strong even then, and I knocked him off of me. He went wild.... He forced me to have sex with him, and he wasn't gentle. It was my first time, and I thought I was dying.

"I knew then that the marriage was an awful mistake, that I wanted out, but he wouldn't let me go. Every night I'd fight him again, and he'd force me again. He was going to teach me how to be a woman if he had to break every bone in my body, he said. I couldn't stop fighting him," she muttered to herself. "I never could just lie there and let him get it over with. I *had* to fight back, or I felt like something in me would die. So I fought, and the more I fought, the rougher he got. He started...hitting me."

Blake cursed violently and she jumped, throwing her arm up to cover her face. She was so deep inside her bitter memories that she was reacting as she had then, defending herself. His curse changed into a groan and he cuddled her, coaxing her to lower her arm. "I'm sorry, darling, I didn't mean to startle you," he panted. "When he started hitting you, why didn't you turn him in to the police?"

"I didn't know that he couldn't do that," she said tiredly. "I was so dumb. I read a lot of things about it afterward, but at the time I thought he had a legal right to do what he wanted with me, short of murder. He got worse and worse. He almost stopped wanting sex. He'd just start right in hitting me. Sometimes he'd go ahead and rape me, as roughly as he could, but most of the time he didn't."

"You stayed with him for three months? Isn't that how long you told me your marriage lasted?"

"Not even that long. That I stayed with him, I mean. I can't remember.... He pushed me down the steps one night, and I landed in the hospital with a broken arm and a concussion. I was there for several days, and a nurse figured out that I hadn't simply tripped while going down the steps. She talked to me, and a counselor talked to me. I didn't go back to Scott. When I was released from the hospital, the nurse let me stay with her."

She was calmer now, the memories easier to bear. In her normal voice she said, "Scott's family was horrified by what had happened. They were good people, and when I filed for divorce they forced Scott to go along with it. They gave me a lot of support, paid for my training as a therapist, kept Scott away from me, even got him into psychiatric counseling. It must have worked. He's remarried now, and they seem very happy. He has two daughters."

"Have you kept in touch with him?" Blake asked incredulously.

"Oh, no!" she denied, shaking her head. "But while his mother was alive she kept track of me, sort of looked after me like a guardian angel. She never got over what had happened to me, as if it were her fault because Scott was her son. She told me when he remarried, and when her grandchildren were born. She died a couple of years ago."

"So he lived happily ever after, and you've been dragging a ball and chain around with you for all these years," he said angrily. "Afraid to let anyone touch you, keeping people pushed away at a safe distance...only half-alive!"

"I haven't been unhappy," she said wearily, her lashes sweeping down. She was so tired.... He knew all of it now, and she felt so empty, as if all the terror that had filled her for so long had seeped away, leaving her hollow and lost. The warmth of Blake's body was so comforting in the chilly room; the steady rumble of his heartbeat in his strong chest was so reassuring. She could feel the iron in the bands of flesh that wrapped around her, feel the security of his strength. She'd given him that strength; it was only right that she rely on it now. She turned her face against him, inhaling and tasting on her tongue the heady scent of his body. He smelled of man, of sweat, of a clean grassy scent that eluded her when she tried to search it out. He had the musky smell of sex, a reminder of the incredible night. With a slow, gentle sigh, she slept, all of her senses filled with him.

When she woke she was alone in the bed and the brightness of the room told her that the morning was almost over. She wasn't fortunate enough to forget, even for a moment, the events of the night. Her eyes went to the gallery, but the wheelchair was gone, and she wondered how Blake could have left her bed and taken the wheelchair without waking her; she was normally the lightest of sleepers, coming awake at any unusual noise. But she'd been so tired...she was still tired, her body heavy and clumsy-feeling, her reactions slow.

She eased out of bed, wincing at the unfamiliar soreness of her body. How could she have been so stupid that she'd let Blake make love to her? She was trying to get through these last days with him with the least amount of emotional damage, and she'd made it impossibly complicated. She should never have tried to arouse him; she didn't know anything about handling men, or handling herself, if it came to that. He'd said, "I need you," and she'd melted. A real pushover, she told herself contemptuously. He must have seen her coming a mile away. Then, to top it all off, she'd told him about Scott.

She writhed inwardly with embarrassment. She'd managed for years to control herself, to keep herself from wallowing in the slimy pool of the past. So she hadn't been comfortable with men; what of it? A lot of women managed very well without men. When she thought of the way she'd clung to him, weeping and moaning, she wanted to die of shame. Her solitary nature hated the thought of displaying so much of herself to anyone, even the man who had taken up her days and nights for months.

Willpower had a lot to say for itself; it steadied her nerves, gave her the courage to shrug her shoulders and step into the shower as if there was nothing unusual about that morning. She dressed as she normally did, then went straight to the gym, where she knew she'd find Blake. There was no point in putting off their meeting, because time wouldn't make it any easier. It was best to face him and get it over with.

When she opened the door he glanced at her but didn't say anything; he was lying on his stomach, lifting weights with his legs, and he was counting. He was totally engrossed in the demands he was making of his body. With a slow but steady rhythm he lifted each leg in turn.

"How long have you been doing that?" Dione asked sternly, forgetting her discomfort as her professional concern surfaced.

"Half...an...hour," he grated.

"That's enough. Stop right now," she ordered. "You're over-doing it. No wonder your legs give you fits! What are you trying to do, punish your legs for the years they didn't work?"

He relaxed with a groan. "I'm trying to get away from the walker," he said irritably. "I want to walk alone, without lean-ing on anything."

"If you tear a muscle you're going to be leaning on some-thing for a lot longer than necessary," she snapped back. "I've watched you push yourself past the bounds of common sense, but no more. I'm a therapist, not a spectator. If you're not going to follow my instructions, then there's no use in my staying here any longer."

His head jerked around, and his eyes darkened to a stormy color. "Are you telling me that you're leaving?"

"That's up to you," she returned stonily. "If you'll do as you're told and follow your training program, I'll stay. If you're going to ignore everything I say and do what you want, there's no point in my wasting my time here."

He flushed darkly, and she realized that he still wasn't used to giving in to anyone. For a moment she expected him to tell her to pack her bags, and she pulled herself up, braced for the words that would end her time with him. Then he clenched his jaw and snapped, "All right, lady, you're the boss. What's the matter with you today? You're as touchy as a rattler."

Absurd relief washed over her, at both her reprieve from exile and the familiar, comforting ill temper apparent in his words. She could handle that; but she knew beyond a doubt that she wouldn't have been able to handle the situation if he'd made any reference to the intimacy of the night, if he'd tried to kiss her and act like a lover.

She was so determined to regain the therapist-patient relationship that during the day she resisted his teasing and efforts to joke with her, turning a cold face to his laughing eyes. By the time they had finished they were snarling at each other like two stray dogs. Dione, having eaten nothing all day, was so hungry that she was almost sick, and that only added to the hostility she felt.

Her body was rebelling against her misuse of it when it was finally time for dinner. On wobbly legs she made her way down the stairs, her head whirling in a nauseating manner that made her cling to the banisters. She was so preoccupied with the task of getting down the stairs in one piece that she didn't hear Blake behind her, didn't feel his searing blue gaze on her back.

She made it to the dining room and fell into her chair with relief at not having sprawled on the floor. After a moment Blake made his way past her and went into the kitchen; she was too sick to wonder at that, even though it was the first time she'd seen him enter the kitchen in the months she'd been living there.

Alberta came out promptly with a steaming bowl of soup, which she placed before Dione. "Eat that right now," she ordered in her gruff, no-nonsense voice.

Slowly Dione began to eat, not trusting her queasy stomach. As she ate, though, she began to feel better as her stomach settled; by the time she'd finished the soup the trembling in her body was subsiding and she wasn't as dizzy. She looked up to find Blake seated across from her, silently watching her eat. A wave of color heated her face, and she dropped her spoon, embarrassed that she'd begun eating without him.

"Lady," he said evenly, "you give the word *stubborn* a whole new meaning."

She lowered her eyes and didn't respond, not certain if he were talking about how hungry she'd been or something else; she feared it was the "something else," and she just couldn't carry on a calm, ordinary conversation about what had happened between them.

She made an effort to call a truce between them, though without lowering her guard an inch. She couldn't laugh with him; her nerves were stretched too tightly, her emotions were too ravaged. But she did smile and talk, and generally avoided meeting his eyes. In that manner she made it safely through the evening until it was time to go to bed and she could excuse herself.

She was already in bed, staring at the ceiling, when she heard him call. It was like an instant replay of the night before and she froze, a film of perspiration breaking out on her body. She couldn't go in there, not after what had happened the last time. He couldn't have cramps in his legs, because she'd heard him come up not five minutes before. He wasn't even in bed yet.

She lay there telling herself fiercely that she wouldn't go; then he called her name again and years of training rose up to do battle with her. He was her patient, and he was calling her. She could just check and make certain that he was all right, and leave again if there was nothing wrong.

Reluctantly she climbed out of bed, this time reaching for her robe and belting it tightly around her. No more going into his room wearing only her nightgown; the thought of his hands on her breasts interfered with the rhythm of her breathing, and an odd ache began in the flesh that he had touched.

When she opened the door to his bedroom she was surprised to see that he was already in bed. "What did you want?" she asked coolly, not leaving her position by the door.

He sighed and sat up, stuffing his pillows behind his back. "We have to talk," he said.

She froze. "If you like to talk so much, maybe you should join a debating team," she retorted.

"I made love to you last night," he said bluntly, going straight to the heart of the issue and watching as she flinched against the door. "You had a rough deal with your ex-husband, and I can understand that you're wary, but last night wasn't a total disaster for you. You kissed me, you responded to me. So why are you acting today as if I'd raped you?"

Dione sighed, shaking her long hair back. He'd never understand something that she didn't really understand herself; she only knew that, in her experience, caring led to pain and rejection. It wasn't so much a physical distance she wanted from him as an emotional one, before he took everything she had and left her only a shell, empty and useless. But there was something he *would* understand, and at last she met his eyes.

"What happened last night won't happen again," she said, her voice low and clear. "I'm a therapist, and you're my patient. That's the only relationship that I can allow between us."

"You're closing the barn door after the horse is already out," he said with maddening amusement.

"Not really. You had doubts about your ability to have sex after the accident, and that was interfering with your training. Last night removed those doubts. That was the beginning and end of anything sexual between us."

His face darkened. "Damn it," he growled, all amusement gone. "Are you telling me that last night was just a therapeutic roll in the hay?"

Her lips tightened at his crudity. "Bingo," she said, and stepped out of his room, closing the door firmly behind her.

She returned to bed, knowing it was useless to think of sleep, but making the effort anyway. She had to leave. She simply couldn't stay until the first of the year, not with things as strained as they were now. Blake was almost fully recovered;

time and practice would accomplish the rest of it. He didn't need her any longer, and there were other people who did.

Her bedroom door opened and he stood there, without the walker, moving slowly and carefully as he closed the door and crossed the room to her.

"If you want to run, I can't catch you," he said flatly.

She knew that, but still she lay where she was, watching him. He was nude, his tall, perfect body shamelessly exposed to her gaze. She looked at him and couldn't help feeling a thrill of pride at the ripple of muscles, the fluid grace of his body. He was beautiful, and she'd created him.

He lifted the sheet and got into bed beside her, immediately enveloping her in the warmth of his body. She wanted to sink into his flesh, but instead she made one more effort to protect herself. "This can't work," she said, her voice cracking with pain.

"It already has. You just haven't admitted it yet." He put his hand on her hip and pulled her to him, nestling her against him down the entire length of his body. She sighed, her soft breath tickling the hairs on his chest; her body relaxed in traitorous contentment.

He tilted her chin up and kissed her, his lips gentle, his tongue dipping into her mouth briefly to taste her, then withdrawing. "Let's get one issue settled right now," he murmured. "I've been lying to you, but I thought it best to keep from frightening you. I wanted you since…hell, it seems like from the first time I saw you. Definitely since I threw my breakfast at you, and you laughed the most beautiful laugh I'd ever heard."

Dione frowned. "Wanted me? But you couldn't—"

"That's what I've been lying about," he admitted, kissing her again.

She jerked back, her cheeks going scarlet. "What?" she

gasped, mortified when she thought of the effort she'd made to arouse him, and the money she'd spent on seductive clothes.

Wryly he surveyed her furious face, but braved the wildcat's claws and pulled her back into his arms. "Several things you did made me think that you might have been mistreated," he explained.

"So you decided to show me what I'd been missing," she exploded, pushing at his chest. "Of all the sneaky, egotistical snakes in the world, you're at the top of the heap!"

He chuckled and gently subdued her, using the strength that she'd given him. "Not quite. I wanted you, but I didn't want to frighten you. So I pretended that I couldn't make love to you. All I wanted was for you to get to know me, learn to trust me, so I'd have a chance at least. Then you started dressing in those thin shirts and shorts, and I thought I'd go out of my mind. You damn near killed me!" he said roughly. "You touched me constantly, driving me so wild I'd almost exploded out of my skin, and I'd have to hide my reaction from you. Didn't you wonder why I'd been working like a maniac?"

She sucked in a shaky breath. "Is that why?"

"Of course it is," he said, touching her lip with his finger. "I tried to get you used to my touch, too, and that only made my problem worse. Every time I kissed you, every time I touched your legs, I was driving myself crazy."

Closing her eyes, she remembered all the times when he'd stared at her with that peculiar, hot light in his eyes. A woman with any real experience would have known immediately that Blake wasn't impotent, but she'd been the perfect, all-time sucker for that line. "You must have laughed yourself sick at me," she said miserably.

"I haven't been in any shape to laugh, even if it had been a laughing matter. Which it wasn't," he said. "The thought that someone had hurt you made me so furious I wanted to tear the guy apart. Whoever he was, *he* was the reason you were frightened of me, and I hated that. I'd have done anything to make you trust me, let me love you."

She bit her lip, wishing that she could believe him, but how could she? He made it sound as if he'd been so concerned for her, and all he'd really been concerned with was his own sexual appetite. She knew how touchy he'd been about letting even Serena see him while he was less than perfect; he wouldn't want to make love to a woman who might pity him for the effort it took him to walk, or, even worse, might want him because of a morbid curiosity. Dione was the one safe female of his acquaintance, the one who knew everything about him already and was neither shocked, curious, nor pitying. "What you're saying is that you wanted sex, and I was handy," she said bitterly.

"My God, Dee!" He sounded shocked. "I'm not getting through to you, am I? Is it so hard for you to believe that I want *you,* not just sex? We've been through a lot together. You've held me when I hurt so much I couldn't stand it any longer, and I held you last night when you were afraid, but trusted me with yourself anyway. You're not just a sexual outlet for me; you're the woman I want. I want all of you—your temper, your contrariness, your strength, even your downright bitchiness, because you're also an incredibly loving woman."

"All right, I absolve you," she said wearily. "I don't want to talk about it now. I'm tired and I can't think straight."

He looked down at her, and impatience flickered across his face. "There's no reasoning with you, is there?" he asked slowly. "I shouldn't have wasted my time talking to you. I should have just shown you, like I'm going to do now."

CHAPTER 10

Dione drew back sharply, her golden eyes flashing. "Do all men use force when a woman isn't willing?" she said between clenched teeth. "I warn you, Blake, I'll fight. Maybe I can't stop you, but I can hurt you."

He laughed softly. "I know you can." He lifted one of her fists and carried it to his lips, where he kissed each knuckle in turn. "Darling, I'm not going to force you. I'm going to kiss you and tell you how lovely you are, and do everything I can think of to give you pleasure. The first time was for me, remember, but the second time is for you. Don't you think I can show you?"

"You're trying to seduce me," she snapped.

"Mmm. Is it working?"

"No!"

"Damn. Then I'll have to try something else, won't I?" He laughed again, and pressed his warm lips to her wrist. "You're so sweet, even when you're mad at me."

"I am not!" she protested, practically insulted by his compliment. "There's not a 'sweet' bone in my body!"

"You're sweet-smelling," he countered. "And sweet-tasting.

And the feel of you is sweet torment. Your name should be Champagne instead of Dione, because you make me so drunk I barely know what I'm doing."

"Liar."

"What did I do for excitement before I met you?" he asked wryly. "Fighting with you makes mountain climbing pale in comparison."

The amusement in his voice was more than she could bear; she was so confused and upset, but he seemed to think it was funny. She turned her head away to hide the tears that welled up. "I'm glad you're getting such a kick out of this," she muttered.

"We'll talk about that later," he said, and kissed her. She lay rigidly in his arms, refusing to let her mouth soften and mold itself to his, and after a moment he drew back.

"Don't you want me at all?" he whispered, nuzzling her hair. "Did I hurt you last night? Is that what's wrong?"

"I don't know what's wrong!" she shouted. "I don't understand what I want, or what *you* want. I'm out of my depth, and I don't like it!" The frustration she felt with herself and with him came bubbling out of her, but it was nothing less than the truth. Her mind was so muddled that nothing pleased her; she felt violent, but without a safe outlet for that violence. She'd been violated, hurt, and though years had passed, only now was the anger breaking out of the deep freeze where she'd locked her emotions. She wanted to hurt him, hit him, because he was a man and the symbol of what had happened to her, but she knew that he was innocent, at least of that. But he had dominated her last night, manipulated her with his lies and his truths, and now he was trying to dominate her again.

Furiously she shoved at him, rolling him over on his back. Before he could react she was astride him, her face pagan with the raw force of her emotions. "If there's any seducing to be done, I'll do it!" she raged at him. "Damn you, don't you dare move!"

His blue eyes widened, and a rich understanding crossed his face. "I won't," he promised, a little hoarsely.

With a sensual growl she assaulted him, using her mouth, her hands, her entire body. A man's sexuality had always been denied to her, but now this man offered himself in spread-eagled sacrifice, and she explored him with voracious hunger. Much of his body she already knew; the sleek strength of his muscles under her fingers; the roughness of the hair on his chest and legs; the male scent that made her nostrils flare. But now she learned the taste of him as she nibbled at his ears, his chin, his mouth; she pressed her lips against the softness of his temple and felt his pulse hammering madly. She kissed his eyes, the strong column of his throat, the slope of his shoulder, the sensitive inside of his elbow.

His palms twitched as her tongue traced across them, and he groaned aloud when she sucked on his fingers. "Hush!" she said fiercely, crouching over him. She didn't want any break in her concentration. As she learned him, her body was coming alive, warming and glowing like something long frozen and slowly beginning to thaw. She moved upward, licked the length of his collarbone, then snaked her tongue downward through the curls of hair until she found the little nipples that hid there. They were tight, as hard as tiny diamonds, and when she bit them he shuddered wildly.

His flat stomach, ridged with muscles that were now writhing under her touch, beckoned her marauding mouth. She traced the arrow of downy hair, played a wet game of sneak attack with his navel, then slithered downward. Her silky hair draped across him as she kissed his legs from thigh to foot, biting the backs of his knees, dancing her tongue across his instep, then working her way back up.

He was shaking in every muscle, his body so taut that only

his heels and shoulders were touching the bed. He was gripping the bedposts, his arms corded as he writhed in tormented ecstasy. "Please…please!" he begged hoarsely. "Touch me! Damn it, I can't take any more!"

"Yes, you can!" she insisted, panting for breath. She touched him, her hand learning him, stroking him, and something close to a howl broke from his throat.

Suddenly she knew. For such vital strength, for such tender power, there was only one resting place, and that was the mysterious depth of her femininity. Male and female, they had been created to join together, the two halves to make a whole. She felt breathless, stunned, as if suddenly the world had shifted and nothing was the same as it had been.

His body was a bow, taut and aching. "Take…me!" he rasped, both in plea and demand, and Dione smiled a radiant, mysterious smile that almost blinded him with the joy of it.

"Yes," she said, and with aching tenderness moved over him. She accepted him easily. He cried out, but lay still, letting her move as she wished. She looked at him, and golden eyes met blue, communicating wordlessly. She was awed by the rightness of their union, by the heated flares of pleasure that shot through her body. All the barriers were gone now; the fears and nightmares that had prevented her from letting herself enjoy the magic of giving herself to the man she loved had disappeared. She was sensual by nature, but events had taught her to deny that part of herself. No longer. Sweet heaven, no longer. He freed her, not only allowing her to be herself, but glorying in the woman she was. It was evident in the lost, rapt look he wore, the mindless undulating of his body.

She reveled in him. She adored him, she used him, she sank deeply into the whirlpool of the senses and welcomed the drowning. She was burning alive in the heat of her own body as the pleasure intensified and became unbearable, but still she couldn't stop. The moans and gasping cries that kept forcing themselves from his throat as he fought for control were matched by her own sounds of pleasure, until that pleasure became wildfire and she was consumed by it. She heard a wordless cry lingering in the night air and didn't recognize it was hers, or realize that it was joined by a deeper cry as Blake finally released himself from his sweet torture. She sank down, a long, long way, and sprawled weakly on him. His arms swept up and held her safely, securely in place.

He was kissing her, his mouth all over her face before finally settling on her lips and drinking deeply. She met his tongue with her own, and they lay together for a long time exchanging tired, leisurely kisses.

"You took me apart," he murmured.

"I put you together again," she said sleepily.

"I'm not talking about Humpty Dumpty, lady bird, I'm talking about what you did to me."

"Didn't you like it?"

"I loved it." A deep chuckle rumbled through his chest. "As if you had to ask." Then he sobered and pushed her hair away from her face so he could read her eyes. "Was it good for you?"

She smiled and ducked her head against him. "As if you had to ask."

"No bad moments?"

"None," she said, and yawned.

"Wretch, are you going to sleep on me?" he demanded in mock indignation, but his hands were tender as he stroked her. "You're tired, aren't you? Then sleep, darling. I'll hold you. Just don't move. I want to stay inside you all night."

She would have blushed, but she was too tired, too satisfied, and he made a wonderful bed. She was boneless, draped over him, protected by him. She eased into sleep with the steady throb of his heartbeat in her ear.

He woke her at dawn with his slow, tender movements. The room was chilled, but they were warm, heated by the excitement that began to curl inside. There was no urgency, no need to hurry. He talked to her and teased her, told her jokes that made her laugh, and her laughter somehow increased her inner heat. He knew her body as well as she knew his, knew how to touch her and make her writhe with pleasure, knew how to gradually move her up the plane to satisfaction. Her trust was a tangible thing between them, evident in her clear, shining eyes as she allowed him to handle her as he pleased. Even when he rolled her onto her back and pinned her with his weight, no shadow of ancient fear darkened her joy. He had earned her trust the night before when he had offered his own body for her enjoyment. How could she deny him the pleasure of hers?

There was pleasure for her, too, a deep and shining pleasure that took her breath away. It was so intense that she almost cried out her love for him, but she clenched her teeth on the words. The time with him was golden but transient, and there was no need to burden him with an emotion that couldn't be returned.

"I'd like to stay in bed with you all day," he whispered against her satiny skin. "But Alberta will be up here soon if we don't put in an appearance. She was worried about you yesterday, almost as much as I was."

She buried her hands in his thick, dark hair. "Why were you worried? You knew why I was upset."

"Because I never meant to upset you. I didn't want to remind you of anything that had hurt you, but I did. You were so pale and cold." He kissed the enticing slope of her breast and smiled at the ripple of response that was evident under her skin.

They showered together; then he sprawled on the bed and directed her dressing. He wanted her to wear the slinky, seductive shorts she'd worn before, and his eyes glittered as he watched her pull them on. He had to return to his room to dress, as he'd come to her stark naked, and stark naked he walked down the hall, moving slowly but with increasing confidence and grace. Tears of pride stung her eyes as she watched him.

"It's a beautiful day," Alberta said with an odd smugness as she served breakfast, and it was so unusual for Alberta to make small talk that Dione glanced at her sharply, but could read nothing in the woman's stoic face.

"Beautiful," Blake echoed gravely, and gave Dione a slow smile that started her blood racing.

Their workouts were leisurely and remarkably short; Blake seemed more interested in watching her than in lifting weights or walking on the treadmill. He was relaxed, satisfaction lying on him like a golden glow. Instead of trying to slow him down, Dione scolded him for doing so little. "I'm going to have to cut down on the amount you're eating if you aren't going to work any more than this."

"Whatever you say," he murmured, his eyes on her legs. "You're the boss."

She laughed and gave up. If he weren't going to work out, he might as well be walking. It was warmer out than it had been recently, so they walked around the grounds; the only support he used was his arm around her waist. She noticed that he was limping less; even his left leg moved without dragging as badly as it had.

"I've been thinking," he announced as they returned to the house. "There's no use in waiting until the first of the year before I go back to work. I'm going back Monday. I'll get myself accustomed to the place and what's going on, before Richard takes off."

Dione stopped and stared at him, her cheeks paling. He saw her expression and misunderstood it; he laughed as he hugged her to him. "I'm not going to hurt myself," he assured her.

"I'll just work in the mornings. Half a day, I promise. Then I'll come home and put myself in your hands again, and you can work me until I drop if that's what you want."

She bit her lip. "If you're capable of returning to work, then there's no need for me to stay at all," she said quietly.

He frowned, his hands tightening on her. "There's all the need in the world. Don't even think about leaving me, honey, because I won't let you. You're part of me. We've already been through this once, and it's settled. You're staying here."

"Nothing's settled," she denied. "I have to work, to support myself—"

"By all means, work if you want," he interrupted. "But you don't *have* to. I can support you."

She jerked back, indignant color staining her face. "I'm not a call girl," she snapped. "Or a lap dog."

He put his hands on his hips. "I'll agree with that, but I'm not talking about either of those," he said, his own temper rising. "I'm talking about marriage, lady, the 'till death do us part' bit."

She couldn't have been more startled if he'd turned green before her eyes. She stared at him. "You can't mean that."

"Why can't I mean it?" he demanded irritably. "This is a hell of a reception for the only marriage proposal I've ever made."

She couldn't help it; she laughed at the anger in his tone, even though she knew inside that he would soon forget her. He was still involved in their intense, isolated therapist-patient relationship, with the added complication of their physical involvement. She'd known that making love with him was a mistake, but she hadn't suspected that he would carry it as far as considering marriage.

"I can't marry you," she said, shaking her head to reinforce her refusal.

"Why not?"

"It wouldn't work."

"Why wouldn't it work? We've been living together for almost half a year, and you can't say that we don't get along. We've had some great times. We fight, sure, but that's half the fun. And you can't say that you don't love me, because I know you do," he finished tightly.

Dione stared at him in silent dismay. She'd tried so hard not to let him know, but he'd seen through her pitiful defenses anyway. He'd demolished every wall that she'd built. She couldn't stay. She'd have to leave immediately, get away from him while she still could. "There's no sense in dragging this out," she said, pulling away from him. "I'll leave today."

Once she was free of his grip she knew that he wouldn't be able to keep up with her. Her conscience twinged at leaving him alone to make his way back to the house—what if he fell? But needs must when the devil drives, and her devil was driving her mercilessly. She went straight to her room and began pulling out her clothes. She was swift and efficient; she had all the clothes lying on the bed in neat stacks when she realized that the new clothes she'd bought made it impossible for her to fit everything into her two suitcases. She'd either have to leave them there, or buy another suitcase. If she bought another suitcase, she'd have to beg a ride from someone… No, where was her brain? She could always call a taxi. She didn't have to beg for anything.

"Dee, you're not leaving," Blake said gently from the doorway. "Put everything back and calm down."

"I have to leave. I don't have any reason to say." It had been a waste of breath for him to tell her to calm down. She was utterly calm, knowing what she had to do.

"I'm not reason enough to stay? You love me. I've known for quite a while. It's in your eyes when you look at me, your touch, your voice, everything about you. You make me feel ten feet tall, darling. And if I still needed proof, I had it when you let me make love to you. You're not a woman to give herself to any man without love. You love me, even if you're too stubborn to tell me the words."

"I told you," she said, her voice muffled with pain. "I always fall in love with my patients. It's practically required."

"You don't go to bed with all of your patients, do you?"

He already knew the answer to that. He didn't need the miserable little shake of her head, or the whispered, "No," to reassure him.

"It's not one-sided," he murmured, coming up behind her to wrap his arms around her middle. "I love you, so much I hurt. You love me, and I love you. It's only natural that we get married."

"But you *don't* love me!" she shouted, driven beyond control at hearing those precious words. It was unfair that she should be punished so much for loving him, but everything had to be paid for in coin. For daring to transgress, she would pay with her heart. She began to struggle against the bonds of flesh that held her, but he merely tightened his hold, not enough to hurt her, but she was securely restrained. After a moment of futile effort she let her head drop back against his shoulder. "You only think you love me," she wept, her voice thick with the tears lodged in her throat. "I've been through it before—a patient becomes so dependent on me, so fixated on me, that he confuses his feelings of need with love. It won't last, Blake, believe me. You don't really love me. It's just that I'm the only toy in your playground right now. When you go back to work you'll be seeing other women and everything will fall back into proportion. It would be awful if I married you and then you found out it had all been a mistake."

"I'm a man," he said slowly. "There have been other women who I wanted, other women who caught my interest, but give me credit for being intelligent enough to know the difference between the way I felt with them and the way I feel about you.

I want to be with you, talk with you, fight with you, watch you laugh, make love with you. If that's not love, honey, no one will ever know the difference."

"I'll know the difference, and so will you."

He sighed impatiently. "You still won't listen to reason, will you? Then let's compromise. Are you willing to compromise?"

She eyed him warily. "It depends."

He smiled even as he shook his head. "You'd think I'm a mass murderer, the way you're looking at me. It's just a simple deal. You say that when I get out more and see other women to compare you to, I'll realize that I've just been infatuated with you. On the other hand, I say that I love you and I'll keep on loving you, regardless of how many other women I see. To settle the issue, all you have to do is stay until I've had a chance to make that comparison. Simple?"

She shrugged. "I see what's in the deal for you—you win, either way. I know that you're planning to sleep with me, and I'm honest enough to know that if I stay, that's exactly how things will work out. If you decide that it was just a passing fancy after all, then you've lost nothing and had a bed partner while you thought about it."

"There's something in it for you, too," he said, grinning.

The wicked gleam in his eyes gave him away. She could have kicked him, but it seemed that he could always make her laugh no matter how upset she was. "I know, I know," she said, beginning to giggle. "*I* get to sleep with *you*."

"That's not such a bad deal," he said with blatant immodesty.

"You talk a good game, Mr. Remington," she said, still laughing despite all she could do to stifle it.

"That's not all I do well," he said, reaching for her and folding her against him. His lips found the slope of her throat and she shivered, her lashes falling to veil her eyes. "Think of it as therapy," he encouraged. "A sort of repayment for your own therapeutic knowledge. You gave me a reason to live, and I'll show you how to live."

"Egotistical."

"Truthful."

"I can't do it."

He shook her, then pulled her back to him and began to lay tender seige to her mouth, storming the barrier of her teeth and taking the treasure that lay beyond. "You will do it," he insisted softly. "Because you love me. Because I need you."

"Past tense—you needed me. That's in the past. You're on your own, and you're doing fine."

"I won't be doing fine if you leave me. I swear I'll put myself back in the wheelchair and not get out again. I won't go to work. I won't eat. I won't sleep. I need you to take care of me."

"Blackmail won't work," she warned him, trying not to laugh again.

"Then I'll have to try another tactic. Please. Stay for me. I love you, and you love me. What if *you're* wrong? What if I'm still as wild for you ten years from now as I am today? Are you going to throw that chance away just because you're afraid to believe it can happen?"

The pain that seared her heart told her that at last he'd hit on the real reason why she wanted to leave. She was afraid to believe in love, because no one had ever loved her. She stared at him intently, aware inside of herself that she had reached a personal milestone. She could play it safe and run but people who played it safe never knew the intoxication of going for it all, of putting their hearts on the line. They never risked anything, so they never won anything. Everything had to be paid for; she reminded herself of that once again. All she could do was try. If she won, if by some miracle she gained the golden apple, her life would be complete. If she lost, would she really be any worse off than she was now? She already loved him.

Would leaving him now make the pain any less than leaving him later?

"All right," she said huskily, aware of the bridges burning behind her. She could feel the heat at her back. "I'll stay with you. Don't ask me to marry you, not yet. Let's see how it works out. An affair is a lot easier to recover from when it goes sour than a marriage is."

He quirked a dark eyebrow at her. "You're not overconfident, are you?"

"I'm…cautious," she admitted. "Marriage was traumatic for me. Let me take one hurdle at a time. If…if everything works out, I'll marry you whenever you want."

"I'll hold you to that," he murmured. "I'd like to marry you now. I'd like to make you pregnant right now, if I could. I was looking forward to our devoting a lot of time to that project, but now I'll have to take precautions. Our children will all come *after* we've been married for at least nine months. No one's going to count their fingers and smirk at our babies."

Her eyes were such wide, huge golden pools of wonder that they eclipsed the rest of her face. The thought of children was so enticing that she was tempted to tell him that she would marry him right then. She'd always wanted children, wanted to be able to pour out the deep reservoir of love that was dammed up inside her. The care and nourishment that she'd never received from her own mother were there, waiting patiently for a child of her own. Blake's child: blue eyes; dark hair; that engaging grin that brought out his hidden dimple.

But a child was the one thing she couldn't gamble with, so she didn't argue with him. Instead she offered quietly, "I'll see a doctor and get a prescription."

"No," he refused, steel lacing his voice. "No pills. You're not taking any risks, however slight, with your body. I can handle it without any risk at all, and that's the way we'll do it."

She didn't mind; the thought that he was willing to take

responsibility for their lovemaking was a warm, melting one. She put her arms around him and nestled against him, drinking in his scent.

"Tell me you love me," he demanded, cupping her chin in his palm and lifting her face to him. "I know you do, but I want to hear it."

A tremulous smile quivered on her lips. "I love you."

"That's what I thought," he said with satisfaction, and kissed her as a reward. "Everything will be all right, darling. Just wait and see."

CHAPTER 11

She didn't dare to hope, but it seemed as if he might be right. He bought a slim black cane that looked more like a sexy prop than something that was actually used as support, and every morning Miguel drove him to work. At first Dione fretted every moment he was gone. She worried that he might fall and hurt himself, that he'd try to do too much and tire himself out. After a week she was forced to admit that he was thriving on the challenge of working again. Far from falling, every day he improved, walking faster and with less effort. Nor did she have to worry that he was pushing himself too hard; he was in excellent shape, thanks to her program.

She almost drove herself mad thinking of all the women he was in contact with every day; she knew herself how attractive he was, especially with that intriguing limp. When he came home the first day she all but held her breath, waiting for him to say cheerfully, "Well, you were right—it was just infatuation. You can leave now."

But he never said it. He returned home as eagerly as he went to work, and they spent the afternoons in the gym, or swimming if the day was warm. December was a pleasant month, with the afternoon temperatures often in the high sixties and low seventies, though at night it sometimes dipped close to freezing. Blake decided to have a heating unit put in the pool so they could swim at night, but he had so much on his mind that he kept putting it off. Dione didn't care if the pool was ever heated or not; why bother with swimming when the nights were better spent in his arms?

Whatever happened, whatever the ending that was eventually written to their particular story, she would always love him for freeing her from the cage of fear. In his arms she forgot about the past and concentrated only on the pleasure he gave her, pleasure which she joyously returned.

He was the lover who she had needed; he was mature enough to understand the rewards of patience, and astute enough to sometimes be impatient. He gave, he demanded, he stroked, he experimented, he laughed, he teased, and he satisfied. He was as happily fascinated with her body as she was with his, and that was the sort of open admiration that she needed. The events that had shaped her had made her wary of repressed emotion, even when that emotion was happiness, and the complete honesty with which Blake treated her gave her a secure springboard from which she launched herself as a woman, secure at last in her own femininity and sexuality.

The days of December were the happiest of her life. She had known peace and contentment, not a small accomplishment after the terror she'd survived, but with Blake she was truly happy. Except for the absence of a ceremony, she might already have been married to him, and each passing day the idea of being his wife became more firmly rooted in her mind, changing from impossible to implausible, then to chancy, then to a half-scared, hopeful "maybe." She refused to let herself progress beyond that, afraid of tempting the fates, but still she began to dream of a long stretch of days, even years, and she found herself thinking up names for babies.

He took her Christmas shopping, something she'd never done before in her life. No one had ever been close enough to her to either give or receive a gift, and when Blake learned this, he embarked on a crusade to make her first real Christmas one that would boggle the imagination. The house was decorated in a unique and not always logical blend of traditional and desert styles; every cactus found itself sporting gaily colored bows or even decorative glass balls, if the spines were large enough. He had holly and mistletoe flown in and kept in the refrigerator until it was time to put them up, and Alberta entered into the spirit of the season by scouring cookbooks for traditional Christmas recipes.

Dione realized that they were all going to so much trouble for her, and she was determined to throw herself into the preparations and the happiness. Suddenly it seemed that the world was full of people who cared, and those she cared for.

She'd been half-fearful that Blake would embarrass her by giving her a lot of expensive gifts, and she was both delighted and relieved when she began opening her gifts to find that they were small, thoughtful and sometimes humorous. A long, flat box that could have held a watch or an expensive bracelet instead yielded an array of tiny charms that made her laugh aloud: a miniature barbell, a track shoe, a sweatband, a Frisbee, a loving cup trophy and a little silver bell that actually gave a tinny little chime when she shook it. Another box held the charm bracelet that the charms were supposed to go on; a third gift was a bestseller that she'd picked up in a bookstore just the week before, then replaced and forgotten to buy in the confusion of shopping. A lacy black mantilla drifted over her head and she looked up to smile at Richard, who was regarding her with an oddly tender look in his cool gray eyes. Serena's gift made her gasp and quickly stuff it back into the box, as Serena rolled with laughter and Blake immediately came over to wrestle the box away from her and hold up the contents: a very intimate garment with heart-shaped cutouts in strategic places.

"This was something you overlooked when you bought all those clothes to wage war in," Serena said innocently, her blue eyes as limpid as a child's.

"Ahh, those clothes." Blake sighed in satisfaction.

Dione snatched the teddy…thing…whatever…away from him and replaced it in the box, her cheeks fiery red. "Why is everyone watching me?" she asked uncomfortably. "Why aren't you opening your own gifts?"

"Because you're so beautiful to watch," Blake replied softly, leaning down so only she could hear him. "Your eyes are shining like a little girl's. I have something else for you to… ah, unwrap later on tonight. Think you might be interested?"

She stared at him, her black pupils dilating until they almost obscured the golden rims. "I'm interested," she murmured, her body already quickening at the thought of the lovemaking they'd share later, when they were laying pressed together in his big bed.

"It's a date," he whispered.

The rest of the gifts were opened amid laughter and thank-yous; then Alberta served hot buttered rum. Dione seldom drank, having an aversion to alcohol that dated back to her earliest childhood, but she drank the rum because she was happy and relaxed and suddenly the old restrictions no longer mattered so much. The rum slid smoothly down her throat, warming her, and when that was finished she drank another.

After Serena and Richard had left, Blake helped Dione up the stairs with a steadying arm around her waist. He was laughing softly, and she leaned into him, letting him take most of her weight. "What's so funny?" she asked sleepily.

"You are. You're half-drunk, and you're beautiful. Did you know that you've had the sweetest, sleepiest smile in the world on your face for the last fifteen minutes? Don't you dare go to sleep on me, at least until after you've kept our date."

She stopped on the stairs and turned fully into his arms, winding herself around him. "You know I wouldn't miss that for the world," she purred.

"I'll see that you don't."

She let him talk her into wearing the scandalous teddy that Serena had given her, and he made love to her while she had it on, then even that scrap of fabric seemed to get in his way and he stripped it off her. "Nothing's as lovely as your skin," he whispered, stringing kisses like popcorn across her stomach.

She felt drugged, her mind a little fuzzy, but her body was throbbing, arching instinctively to meet the rhythmic thrusts that took her to bliss and beyond when he left off kissing her all over and possessed her again. When they were finished she lay weak and trembling on the bed, protesting with a murmur when she felt him leave her side.

"I'll be right back," he reassured her, and he was, his weight pressing the mattress familiarly. She smiled and moved her hand to touch him lightly, all without opening her eyes.

"Don't go to sleep," he warned. "Not yet. You haven't unwrapped your last present."

She propped her lids open. "But I thought that you were… When we made love, I thought that…" she mumbled in confusion.

He chuckled and slid an arm behind her back, urging her into a sitting position. "I'm glad you liked that, but I have something else for you." He placed another long, slim box in her hand.

"But you've already given me so much," she protested, awakening at the feel of the box.

"Not like this. This is special. Go ahead, open it."

He sat with his arm still around her, watching her face and smiling as she fumbled with the elegant gold wrapping, her

agile fingers suddenly clumsy. She lifted the lid off and stared
speechlessly at the simple pendant that lay on satin lining like
a cobweb of gold. A dark red heart, chiseled and planed, was
attached to the chain.

"That's a ruby," she stammered.

"No," he corrected gently, lifting it from the box and placing it around her neck. "That's my heart." The chain was long,
and the ruby heart slid down her chest to nestle between her
breasts, gleaming with dark fire as it lay against her honeyed
skin.

"Wear that forever," he murmured, his eyes on the lush
curves that his gift used as a pillow. "And my heart will always be touching yours."

A single, crystalline tear escaped the confines of her lashes,
and rolled slowly down her cheek. He leaned over and caught
it with his tongue. "An engagement ring wasn't good enough
for you, so I'm giving you an engagement heart. Will you wear
it, darling? Will you marry me?"

She stared at him with eyes so huge and deep that they
drowned the entire world. For a month she'd shared his bed,
trying to prepare herself for the day when she was no longer
able to do so, savoring every moment with him in an attempt
to store up pleasure as a squirrel stores acorns as insurance
against a hard winter. She'd been certain that he would lose
interest in her, but every day he'd turned to her and taken
her in his arms, told her that he loved her. Perhaps the dream
wasn't a dream, after all, but reality. Perhaps she could dare
to believe.

"Yes," she heard herself say shakily as her heart and hungry
yearnings overruled her head, and her head instantly tried to
recover lost ground by adding, "but give me time to get used
to the idea…. It doesn't seem quite real."

"It's real, all right," he muttered, sliding his hand along her
rib cage until a warm, full breast filled his palm. He studied

the sheer perfection of her softly veined flesh, the taut little cherry tip that responded instantly to his lightest touch, and his body began to tighten with the familiar need that he could never quite satisfy. Gently he began to ease her down into a supine position. "I don't mind a long engagement," he said absently. "Two weeks is plenty of time."

"Blake! I was thinking in terms of months, not weeks!"

He looked up sharply; then as he saw the frightened uncertainty in her face, his gaze softened and his mouth eased into a smile. "Then name the day, darling, as long as it's within six months and you don't pick either Groundhog Day or April Fool's Day."

She tried to think, but her mind was suddenly fuzzy, entirely preoccupied by the rough, wonderful rasp of his hard hands over her body. His finger slid between her legs and she gasped aloud, a hot twinge of pleasure shooting through her body. "May Day," she said, no longer really caring.

He was disconcerted, too, his senses caught by the rich beauty of the woman under his hand while he tried to make sense of her words. "Mayday?" he asked, puzzled and a little shocked. "You're asking for help?"

"No...May Day, not mayday," she explained, exaggerating the two words so he could hear the pause between them. "The first of May."

"What about it?" he murmured, dipping his head to taste the straining nipples that had been tempting him. He was rapidly losing all interest in the conversation.

"That's when we're getting married," she gasped, her body beginning a slow, undulating dance.

Those words made sense to him, and he lifted his head. "I can't persuade you to marry me before then?"

"I...don't know," she moaned. Her nails flexed into his shoulders. He could probably talk her into anything he wanted, the way she felt now. Though they had made love only a short while before, the need that was filling her was so urgent that it might have been years since he'd taken her. She turned to him, her sleek, soft body crowding him, and he knew without words what she wanted. He lay back, his hands guiding her as she flowed over him and engulfed him. She was wild when she loved him like that, her long black hair streaming down her back, falling across his face when she leaned forward. She worshipped him with the ancient, carnal dance of love, and the ruby heart lay on her breast like a drop of liquid fire.

For two days nothing intruded on the spell of happiness that held them enthralled. Everyone was pleased with the engagement, from the taciturn Miguel to a bubbling Serena. Alberta was as satisfied as if she'd arranged it all herself, and Angela hummed all day long. Serena passed along Richard's best wishes; evidently a wedding was just what everyone wanted, and Dione almost forgot why she'd been so cautious in the beginning.

On the third day Serena arrived for dinner, alone and pale, though she was composed. "I might as well tell you, before someone else does," she said quietly. "Richard and I are separated."

Dione stifled her gasp of shock. They had been getting along so much better for the past several weeks that she'd stopped being concerned with their situation. She looked swiftly at Blake, and was shocked again at the change in his expression. She had known him as laughing, loving, teasing, angry, even afraid, but never before had she seen him so deadly and intent. Suddenly she realized that she'd never really felt the force of his personality, because he'd always tempered his actions with consideration for her. Now the steel, the sheer power, was showing as he prepared to protect his sister.

"What do you want me to do?" he asked Serena in a calm, lethal tone.

Serena looked at him and even smiled, her eyes full of love. "Nothing," she said simply. "This is something I have to work out with Richard. Blake, please, don't let this interfere with your working relationship with him. This is more my fault than it is his, and it wouldn't be fair for you to take it out on him."

"How is it your fault?" he growled.

"For not growing up and getting my priorities straight until it was almost too late," she replied, a hint of the same steel lacing her sweeter voice. "I'm not giving up on him, not without a fight. Don't ask me any more questions, because I won't answer them. He's my husband, and this is a private matter."

He regarded her silently for a moment, then gave a brief nod. "All right. But you know that I'll do whatever I can, whenever you ask."

"Of course I do," she said, her face relaxing. "It's just that I have to do this on my own. I have to learn how to fight my own battles." As she spoke she flashed Dione a look that said, "See, I'm trying." Dione nodded in acknowledgment, then looked up to find that Blake had witnessed the little exchange and was also staring at her, a steel determination in his expression. Dione met his stare blandly; he could ask, but she didn't have to answer. If Serena wanted her brother to know that she was deliberately trying to put a distance between them, then she would tell him. If not, then he'd have to figure it out for himself. Richard and Serena didn't need any more interference in their marriage, and if Blake discovered that he was the basic cause of their separation, he was fully capable of taking it up with Richard.

Later that night, after he had made love to her with an intensity that left her dazed and sleepy, he said lazily, "What's going on between you and Serena? All those significant glances have to mean something."

It was a sneak attack, she realized, struggling to gather her wits. He'd made love to her as usual, waited until she was almost asleep, and caught her unaware. To make the situation more even, she cuddled against him and slid her hand down his side in a long, slow caress. When she reached his thighs she was rewarded by the clenching of his entire body.

"It was nothing," she murmured, pressing soft, hot kisses on his chest. "Just a conversation we had the day she took me shopping for all those sexy clothes that you liked so much. She must have a secret fetish for indecent underwear. She picked out most of those barely there nightgowns, and then she gave me that teddy for Christmas."

Hard fingers wrapped around her wrist, and he removed her hand from his body. Leaning over, he switched on the lamp and washed them with light. Dione watched him, knowing that he wanted to be able to read the nuances of expression that crossed her face. She tried to shield her thoughts, but an uneasy coldness began to creep over her skin as she stared into his piercing blue eyes.

"Stop trying to change the subject," he ordered sharply. "Was Serena warning you away from Richard?"

That again! She stiffened, both angered and hurt by the way he had continually accused her of seeing Richard on the sly. How could he possibly think that of her? She had agreed to marry him only two days before, but for some reason she couldn't get it out of his mind that she might be involved with another man. She sat up, the sheet falling to her waist, but she was too angry to care if she were nude.

"What's with you?" she demanded furiously. "You sound like a broken record. What is it that makes you so suspicious of me? Why am I always the cause of any trouble between Serena and Richard?"

"Because Richard can never take his eyes off you when you're together," he replied, his mouth a hard line.

"I'm not responsible for Richard's eyes!" The injustice of it made her want to scream.

"Aren't you?" he snapped. "Whenever you look at him, it's as if you're passing secret messages."

"You just accused me of doing the same thing with Serena. Am I having an affair with her, too?" Dione exploded. She clenched her fists in an effort to control the burgeoning fury in her. It would be stupid to lose her temper, so she forcibly sucked in a deep, calming breath and made her muscles relax.

Blake eyed her narrowly. "If you don't have anything to hide, then why won't you tell me what Serena meant by what she said?" he questioned.

Another sneak attack. She registered the hit and realized that again he'd caught her when her control was slipping. "If you're so curious, why don't you ask her?" she said bitingly, and lay down again, turning her back to him and pulling the sheet up to her chin.

She heard his breath hiss through his teeth a split second before the sheet was jerked away from her and thrown to the foot of the bed. An iron hand bit into her shoulder and turned her over, flat on her back. "Don't turn your back on me," he warned softly, and the cold uneasiness in her turned into icy dread.

Silently, her face white and set, she threw his hand off her shoulder. She had never, *never,* been able to passively endure, even when resistance cost her additional pain. She didn't think; she reacted instinctively, the automatic resistance of someone fighting for survival. When he reached for her, angered by her rejection, she eluded his grasp and slid from the bed.

It didn't matter that this was Blake. Somehow, that made it worse. His image blurred with Scott's, and she felt a stabbing pain that threatened to drive her to her knees. She had trusted him, loved him. How could he have turned on her like that, knowing what he did about her? The sense of betrayal almost choked her.

He sprang from the bed and reached her as she stretched her hand out for the doorknob. He grabbed her elbow and spun her around. "You're not going anywhere!" he growled. "Come back to bed."

Dione wrenched herself away from his grip and flattened her body back against the door. Her golden eyes were blind, dilated, as she stared at him. "Don't touch me," she cried hoarsely.

He reached for her again, then stopped abruptly when he looked at her and saw the fixed expression in her eyes. She was white, so pale that he expected her to slide into a faint at any moment, but she held herself tautly upright. "Don't touch me," she said again, and his arms dropped heavily to his sides.

"Calm down," he said soothingly. "It's all right. I'm not going to hurt you, darling. Let's go back to bed."

She didn't move, her eyes still locked on him as she measured every move he made, however slight. Even the expansion of his chest with every breath he took made an impact on her senses. She saw the slight flare of his nostrils, the flexing of his fingers.

"It's all right," he repeated. "Dee, we had an argument, that's all. Just an argument. You know I'm not going to hit you." He extended his hand slowly to her, and she watched as his fingers approached. Without moving her body somehow drew in on itself, shrinking in an effort to avoid his touch. Just before he would have touched her, she slid swiftly to the side, away from the threatening hand.

Inexorably he followed, moving with her but not coming any closer. "Where are you going?" he asked softly.

She didn't answer; her eyes were wary now, instead of blindly staring. Blake held out both his hands to her, palms up in supplication.

"Honey, give me your hands," he whispered, desperation threading through his veins, congealing his blood. "Please believe me—I'll never hurt you. Come back to bed with me and let me hold you."

Dione watched him. She felt odd, as if part of herself were standing back and watching the scene. That had happened before with Scott, as if she somehow had to separate herself from the ugliness of what was happening to her. Her body had reacted mindlessly, trying to protect itself, while her mind had exercised its own means of protection by drawing a veil of unreality over what was happening. Now the same scene was being replayed with Blake, but it was somehow different. Scott had never stalked her, never talked to her in a crooning, husky voice. Blake wanted her to put her hands in his and go with him back to that bed, lie beside him as if nothing had happened. But what *had* happened? He had been angry, and he had grabbed her shoulder, throwing her to her back... no, that had been Scott. Scott had done that once, but they hadn't been in bed.

Her brow knitted, and she brought both hands up, rubbing her forehead. God, would she never be free of Scott, of what he had done to her? Blake's anger had triggered the memory of the other time, and though she hadn't confused their identities, she had been reacting to Scott, not Blake. Blake hadn't hurt her; he had been angry, but he hadn't hurt her.

"Dee? Are you all right?"

His beloved, anxious voice was almost more than she could bear. "No," she said, her voice muffled behind her hands. "I wonder if I'll ever be all right."

Abruptly she felt his touch, his hands on her arms, slowly drawing her to him. She could feel the tension in him as he folded her into his arms. "Of course you will," he reassured her, kissing her temple. "Come back to bed with me. You're cold."

Abruptly she felt the cold, the chill of the night on the bareness of her body. She walked with him to the bed, let him put her between the sheets and draw the comforter up over her. He walked around to the other side, turned out the lamp and got into bed beside her. Carefully, as though he were trying not to startle her, he pulled her into his arms and held her tightly to his side.

"I love you," he said in the darkness, his low tones vibrating over her skin. "I swear, Dee, that I'll never again touch you in anger. I love you too much to put you through that again."

Hot tears burned her lids. How could he apologize for something that was, essentially, a weakness in her? How long would it take before he began to resent the flaw in her nature? He wouldn't be able to act naturally with her, and the strain would tear them apart. Normal couples had arguments, yelled at each other, knowing that their anger didn't harm the love between them. Blake would hold himself back, fearing another scene; would he come to hate her because he felt restricted by her? Blake deserved someone whole, someone free, as he was free.

"It would probably be better if I left," she said, the words trembling despite all she could do to hold her tone level.

The arm under her neck tensed, and he rose up on his elbow, looming over her in the darkness. "No," he said, and he achieved the firmness that she had striven for but failed to obtain. "You're where you belong, and you're going to stay here. We're getting married, remember?"

"That's what I'm trying to say," she protested. "How can we have any sort of life together if you're constantly watching what you say and do, afraid of upsetting me? You'd hate me, and I'd hate myself!"

"You're worrying about nothing," he said shortly. "I'll never hate you, so forget that line."

The edge in his voice cut her like a razor, and she fell silent, wondering why she had ever been fool enough to actually believe that they could have a normal life together. She should have learned by now that love wasn't meant to be a part of her life. Blake didn't love her; hadn't her common sense told her that from the beginning? He was infatuated with her, lured by the challenge of seducing her and the hothouse atmosphere that his intense therapy program had generated. Hothouses produced spectacular blooms, but she should have remembered that those blooms wouldn't flourish in the real world. They had to have that protected atmosphere; they withered and died when exposed to the often unfriendly elements of normal life.

Already the bloom of Blake's infatuation was dying, killed not by the attraction to another woman as she had feared, but by daily exposure to reality.

CHAPTER 12

Knowing that it was happening was one thing, preparing herself for it was another. Every time she glanced up and caught Blake watching her broodingly she had to turn away to hide the pain that twisted inside her. She knew that he was regretting his marriage proposal, but his pride wouldn't allow him to back out of it. Probably he would never ask to be released from the engagement; she would have to do the severing. She sensed that he still wasn't ready to admit that he'd been wrong, so she didn't try to take any action to break their engagement now. When the time came she would know, and she would free him.

New Year's passed, and, as he had planned, he began working full-time. She could tell that he was always eager to leave the house, and he began to bring home a briefcase crammed with papers. Dione wondered if he brought work home so he would have an excuse to shut himself in the study and escape her company; then he mentioned that Richard had taken his suggestion and indulged in a month of vacation, and she felt guilty. He really was buried in paperwork without Richard to take part of the load off him.

One night he came to bed after midnight and groaned wearily as his body relaxed. Dione turned over and touched his cheek, trailing her fingers over his skin and feeling the prickle of his beard. "Do you need a massage to relax?" she asked quietly.

"Would you mind?" He sighed. "My neck and shoulders have a permanent kink in them from leaning over a desk. My God, no wonder Richard and Serena are having problems. He's had two years of this, and that's enough to drive any man crazy."

He rolled over on his stomach, and Dione pulled her nightgown up to her thighs, straddling his back and leaning forward to work her magic on his tight muscles. As her kneading fingers dug into his flesh he made a muffled sound of pain, then sighed blissfully as the tension left him.

"Have you seen Serena lately?" he asked.

Her fingers paused for a moment, then resumed their movement. "No," she replied. "She hasn't even called. Have you talked to her?"

"Not since the night she had dinner here and told us she and Richard had separated. I think I'll call her tomorrow. Ahh, that feels good. Right there. I feel as if I've been beaten."

She rolled her knuckles up and down his spine, paying particular attention to the spot that he had indicated needed extra work. He made little grunting noises every time she touched a tender area, and she began to laugh. "You sound like a pig," she teased.

"Who cares? I'm enjoying this. I've missed the massages. Several times I've started to call you and ask you to come to the plant to give me a rubdown, but it didn't seem like such a smart thing to do in a busy day."

"Why not?" she asked tartly, a little irritated that he considered her to be a traveling massage parlor, and a lot irritated that he hadn't followed through on his idea.

He laughed and rolled over, deftly keeping his body between her thighs. "Because," he murmured, "this is what usually happens to me during one of your massages. Let me tell you, I had a hell of a time keeping you from realizing what was going on when you thought I was impotent and were so sweetly trying to turn me on to prove that I wasn't."

She moved off him like a rocket, her entire body blushing. "What?" she yelled furiously. "You *knew* what I was doing, and you let me go ahead and make a fool of myself?"

He laughed uproariously, reaching out to pull her into his embrace. "It didn't take me long to figure it out," he admitted, still chuckling. "As if you needed sexy clothes to turn me on…but I couldn't let you know what you were doing to me without frightening you away. Honey, you weren't seducing me—*I* was seducing *you,* but I had to let you think it was the other way around."

She burned with embarrassment, thinking of the things she had done, the revealing clothes she had worn. Then she felt his hand on her breast, and the heat intensified, but no longer from shame. He hadn't made love to her for several days; he had been coming to bed late and falling asleep as soon as his head hit the pillow, and she had missed his touch.

"You don't really mind, do you?" he asked softly, pulling the nightgown over her head. "What are you doing with this thing on?"

"I get cold when you aren't in the bed," she explained, stretching her body in his arms, reveling in the rasp of his hair-roughed skin against hers.

With a growl he rolled her to her back and buried his face between her breasts. "I'm here now, so you don't need it," he said, his voice muffled by her flesh. He took her quickly, impatient after the days of abstinence. She held him even after he was asleep, her doubts momentarily eased by the passion of his lovemaking.

★ ★ ★

Serena called the next morning. "I've just talked to Blake," she said, laughing a little. "He practically ordered me to take you out to lunch. He said that you're going a little stir-crazy with him so tied up at work. Does he really think I believe that?"

Dione laughed. "He thinks you're sitting there alone, brooding, and he wants you to get out of the house for a while. Shall we make him happy and go out to lunch?"

"Why not? I'll pick you up at twelve."

"I'm not brooding," Serena said firmly a few hours later as she bit into a crisp radish. "Richard wanted some time to himself, and I gave it to him. We didn't have an argument or anything like that. He's in Aspen. He loves to ski, and I've never learned how. He hasn't been since we were married, because he wouldn't do anything that I couldn't enjoy. I'm not athletic," she explained, grinning.

"You're not upset at all?"

"Of course I'm upset, but I'm borrowing a page from your book and keeping it all under control." She shrugged lightly. "We had a long conversation before he left, got everything out in the open. That's a first for Richard. He's so good at keeping his thoughts to himself that sometimes I want to scream. We decided that he's been under so much stress that the best thing to do was to get away from each other, let him relax and catch up on his sleep, before we did any more talking."

"Have you talked to him since he left?"

"No. That was part of the bargain. When he comes back we'll settle things once and for all."

Serena had changed a lot in the months since they had met, becoming a self-assured woman. Things might not work out for her, but she was facing the future with her chin up; Dione only hoped that she could do the same. While Blake was making love to her, she could forget that he was growing away from her, but they couldn't spend the rest of their lives in bed. The ruby heart rested warmly in the valley between her breasts; he had said that it was his heart, and she wouldn't be selfish. She would give his heart back to him.

"I know what we can do," Serena said firmly. "Let's go shopping! We can look for your wedding dress."

Shopping was Serena's cure-all, and Dione went along with it, though she couldn't work up any enthusiasm for any of the dresses that they looked at. How could she be concerned with a dress for a wedding that would never take place?

Blake was so tired when he came home that night that his limp was more pronounced, but he cross-examined her over dinner, asking for a word-for-word repetition of everything Serena had said, how she had looked, if she had seemed worried. Dione tried to reassure him, but she could tell that he was anxious about his sister.

The passion of the night before wasn't repeated; when he finally came to bed he threw his arm over her and went to sleep before his mumbled "Good night" was out of his mouth. She listened to his steady breathing for a long time, unwilling to sleep and miss a moment of her time with him.

With calm resignation she made plans the next day for her future; she contacted Dr. Norwood and accepted a case, then booked a flight to Milwaukee. Her next patient was still hospitalized, but in three weeks he would be able to begin therapy, so that gave her three weeks to spend with Blake.

Every day he became more distant from her, more involved in his work, needing less from her. In her weak moments she tried to tell herself that it was just because he had so much work to do, but she couldn't believe that for long. She responded by doing as she had always done, shoving her pain and misery into a dark corner of her mind and building a wall around them. If it killed her, she would still leave him with her shoulders straight and not distress him by crying all over him. He wouldn't like that, and she wasn't the weepy type, anyway. She wouldn't just hit him with it; she would tell him that she was having doubts about their marriage, and that she thought it would be a good idea for them to spend some time apart. She would tell him that she'd taken another case, and that when it was finished they would discuss their situation. His conscience wouldn't bother him if she did it that way; he would be relieved that it was her idea.

She learned that Richard was back in town when he called her and asked if he could talk to her privately. She hesitated, and he said wryly, "Serena knows that I'm here. She suggested that I talk to you."

Why would Serena want Richard to talk to Dione? What could she possibly tell him that Serena couldn't say just as well? But a third party could sometimes see more clearly than the ones involved, so she agreed.

He drove over early that afternoon. He looked younger than he had, tanned from his weeks in Aspen in the winter sun, and far more relaxed. The lines of strain that had been in his face were gone, replaced by a smile.

"You're even more beautiful than before," he said, leaning down to kiss her cheek. She didn't shy away from him now; Blake had taught her that not all men were to be feared. She smiled up at him.

"You're pretty great-looking yourself. I gather you've seen Serena?"

"We had dinner together last night. She sent me to you."

"But why?" Dione asked, bewildered. They walked out to the courtyard and sat down in the sun. With the walls of the house keeping any wind away from them, the cool January day was pleasant, and she didn't even need a sweater.

Richard leaned against the concrete back of the bench, crossing his ankle over his knee. She noticed idly that he was wearing jeans, the only time she'd ever seen him dressed so casually, and a blue pullover sweater that made his gray eyes seem blue. "Because she's a smart woman," he mused. "She's known from the beginning that I was attracted to you, and our marriage can't work if you're between us."

Dione's eyes widened. "What?" she asked weakly. "But... but Serena's been so friendly, so open...."

"As I said, she's a smart woman. She knew that you didn't return my interest. You've never been able to see anyone but Blake. How I feel about you is something that I have to work out."

She shook her head. "This is ridiculous. You don't love me. You never have. You're in love with Serena."

"I know," he admitted, and laughed. "But for a while I was pretty confused. Serena didn't seem to care if I was around or not, and there you were, so damned lovely that it hurt to look at you, so strong and sure of yourself. You knew what you wanted and didn't let anything stand in your way. The contrast was striking."

Was that how he had seen her? As strong and confident? Hadn't he realized that she was that way only in her profession, that privately she was crippled, afraid of letting anyone get close to her? It was strange that, as astute as Richard was, he hadn't seen her as she really was.

"And now?" she asked.

"I'll always admire you." He chuckled. "But this visit is just for Serena's peace of mind. You were right all along. I love her, and I've been punishing her because she relied on Blake instead of me. I freely admit to the illogic of it, but people in love aren't logical."

"She wanted you to be certain before you went back to her."

"That's right. And I am certain. I love skiing, but I spent the entire time I was in Aspen wishing that she was with me. You should hang out a shingle as a doctor in psychology," he said, laughing, and put his arm on her shoulder to hug her.

She walked him to the door and sent him on his way, glad that he'd ironed out his problems, but she was also depressed at the thought that she'd been involved in any way at all, however innocently. She walked back out to the courtyard and resumed her seat. She was tired, so tired of these months of emotional strain. She closed her eyes and lifted her face to the winter sun, letting her thoughts drift.

"How long had he been here?"

The harsh voice sliced through the air and she jumped, getting to her feet and whirling to face Blake. "You're early," she stammered.

"I know," he said, his voice as hard and cold as his face. "I haven't been able to spend much time with you lately, and when I managed to get everything cleared for today I decided to surprise you. I didn't mean to interrupt anything," he finished with a sneer.

A sick feeling in her stomach made her swallow before she answered. "You didn't," she said briefly, lifting her chin. Suddenly she knew that this was it, that he would use this as an excuse to break their engagement, and she couldn't bear to listen to him saying things that would break her heart. It would break anyway when she left, but she didn't want to have the memory of hard words between them.

"He hadn't been here over five minutes," she said remotely, lifting her hand to cut him off when he started to speak. "He and Serena have patched up their differences, and he wanted to talk to me. She sent him over, as a matter of fact, but you're welcome to call her if you don't believe me."

His eyes sharpened, and he took a step toward her, his hand reaching out. Dione backed away. It had to be now, before he touched her. He might not love her, but she knew that he desired her, and with them, touching led inevitably to sex. That was another thing she couldn't bear, making love with him and knowing it was the last time.

"Now is as good a time as any to tell you," she said, still in that remote voice, her face an expressionless mask. "I've accepted another case, and I'll be leaving in a few days. At least, those were my original plans, but now I think it would be best if I left tomorrow, don't you?"

His skin tightened over his cheekbones. "What are you saying?" he demanded fiercely.

"That I'm breaking our engagement," she said, fumbling with the delicate clasp at the back of her neck and finally releasing it. She took the ruby heart and held it out to him.

He didn't take it. He was staring at her, his face white. "Why?" he asked, grinding the word out through lips that barely moved.

She sighed wearily, rubbing her forehead. "Haven't you realized by now that you don't love me?"

"If you think that, why did you set a wedding date?" he rasped.

She gave him a thin smile. "You were making love to me," she said gently. "I wasn't in my right mind. I've known all along that you didn't love me," she burst out, desperate to make him understand. She couldn't hold out much longer. "I humored you, but it's time now for it to end. You've changed these past weeks, needing me less and less."

"Humored me!" he shouted, clenching his fists. "Were you also 'humoring me' when we made love? I'll be damned if you were!"

She winced. "No. That was real…and it was a mistake. I've never been involved with a patient before, and I'll never let it happen again. It gets too…complicated."

"Lady, I don't believe you!" he said in disbelief. "You're just going to waltz out of here as if nothing ever happened, aren't you? You're going to mark me down as a mistake and forget about me."

No, he was wrong. She'd never be able to forget him. She

stared at him with pain-glazed eyes, feeling as if she were shattering inside. A sickening headache pounded in her temples, and when she held the necklace out to him again her hand was trembling. "Why are you arguing?" she asked raggedly. "You should be glad. I'm letting you off the hook. Just think how miserable you'd be, married to someone you don't love."

He reached out and took the necklace, letting the tiny gold links drip over his fingers like metal tears. The sun pierced the ruby heart, casting a red shadow that danced over the white bench beside her. Savagely he shoved it into his pocket. "Then what are you waiting for?" he shouted. "Go on, get out! What do you want me to do, break down and beg you to stay?"

She swayed, then steadied herself. "No," she whispered. "I've never wanted you to beg for anything." She moved slowly past him, her legs weak and unwilling to work as they should. She would pack and go to a hotel, and try to get an earlier flight rather than waiting until her original flight was scheduled. She hadn't imagined that it would be so difficult, or that she would feel so battered. This was worse, far worse, than anything Scott had ever done to her. He had hurt her physically and mentally, but he had never been able to touch her heart. It was killing her to leave Blake, but she had to do it.

Her headache was worse; as she stumbled around the bedroom trying to gather her clothing she had to grab at the furniture several times to keep from falling to her knees. Her mind was muddied, her thoughts jumbled, and nothing made much sense except the overpowering need she had to be gone. She had to leave before she was hurt any more, because she didn't think she'd be able to live if anything else happened.

"Stop it," a low voice commanded, and a hand caught her wrist, pulling her fingers away from the lingerie that she had been tossing carelessly into her suitcase. "You can pack later, when you're feeling better. You have a headache, don't you?"

She turned her head to look at him and almost staggered when her vision swayed alarmingly. "Yes," she mumbled.

"I thought so. I watched you practically crawl up the stairs." He put his arm around her waist, a curiously impersonal touch, and led her to the bed where they had shared so many nights. "Come on, you need a nap. You surprise me. I didn't think you were the type who lived on nerves, but this is a tension headache if I've ever seen one." His fingers moved down the front of her blouse, slipping the buttons out of their holes, and he eased the garment off her.

"I'm almost never sick," she apologized. "I'm sorry." She let him unsnap her bra and toss it aside. No, it wasn't a matter of *letting* him do anything. The truth was that she didn't feel capable of struggling with him over who would remove her clothes, and she badly needed the nap he had suggested. It wasn't as if he hadn't already seen every inch of her body. He eased her down on the bed and unfastened her slacks, sliding an arm under her and lifting her so he could pull them down over her hips. Her shoes came off with the slacks; then his hands returned and made short work of the filmy panties that were her last remaining garment.

Gently he turned her on her stomach, and she sighed as he began to rub the tight muscles in her neck. "I'm returning the favor," he murmured. "Just think of all the massages you've given me. Relax and go to sleep. You're tired, too tired to do anything right now. Sleep, darling."

She did sleep, deeply and without dreaming, sedated by his strong fingers as they rubbed the aching tension from her back and shoulders. It was dark when she woke, but her headache was gone. She felt fuzzy and disoriented, and she blinked at the dark form that rose from a chair beside the bed.

"Do you feel better?" he asked.

"Yes," she said, pushing her heavy hair away from her face. He turned on the lamp and sat down on the edge of the bed, surveying her with narrowed eyes, as if gauging for himself how well she was feeling.

"Thank you for taking care of me," she said awkwardly. "I'll pack now, and go to a hotel—"

"It's too late to go anywhere tonight," he interrupted. "You've slept for hours. Alberta left a plate warming for you, if you feel like eating. I think you should try to eat something, or you'll be sick again. I didn't realize what a strain you had been under," he added thoughtfully.

She was hungry, and she sat up, holding the sheet to her. "I feel as if I could eat a cow," she said ruefully.

He chuckled softly. "I hope you'll settle for something less than a whole cow," he said, untangling a nightgown from the jumble of clothing that still littered the bed. He plucked the sheet away from her fingers and settled the nightgown over her head as impersonally as if he were dressing a child. Then he found her robe, and she obediently slid her arms into the sleeves while he held it.

"You don't have to coddle me," she said. "I feel much better. After food, I want a shower, and then I'll be fine."

"I like coddling you," he replied. "Just think of how many times you helped me to dress, how many times you coaxed me to eat, how many times you've picked me up when I lay sprawled on the floor."

He walked downstairs with her and sat beside her while she ate. She could feel his steady gaze on her, but the anger that had been there earlier was gone. Had it been only pride that made him lash out at her; did he now realize that she was right?

When she went back upstairs he was right behind her. She looked at him questioningly when he entered the bedroom with her. "Take your shower," he said, taking her shoulders and turning her in the direction of the bathroom. "I'll wait out here for you. I want to make sure you're okay before I go to bed."

"I'm fine," she protested.

"I'll stay," he said firmly, and that was that. Knowing that he was waiting, she hurried through her shower. When she came out of the bathroom he was sitting in the chair he'd occupied before, and he got to his feet.

"Bedtime." He smiled, pushing the robe off her shoulders. She hadn't fastened it, knowing that she would be taking it right off again, and it slipped to the floor. He leaned down and lifted her off her feet, then deposited her on the bed. She gasped and clutched at his shoulder.

"What was that for?" she asked, looking up at him.

"For this," he answered calmly, and kissed her. It was a deeply intimate kiss, his mouth opening over hers and his tongue moving in to touch hers. She dug her nails into his shoulder in surprise.

"Let me go," she said, pulling her mouth way from his.

"I'll let you go tomorrow," he murmured. "Tonight is mine."

He bent down to her again, and she rolled her head away; denied the sweet bloom of her lips, he found the sensitive slope where her neck met her shoulder and nipped at it with his teeth, making her gasp again. He dipped his hand into the bodice of her nightgown, rubbing his palm over the rich globes that had lured him.

"Blake...don't do this," she pleaded achingly.

"Why? You love me to touch your breasts," he countered.

She turned her head to look at him, and her lips were trembling. "Yes," she admitted. "But I'm leaving tomorrow. This... will only make it more difficult. I've accepted another job, and I have to go."

"I understand," he murmured, still stroking her flesh. "I'll put you on a plane tomorrow, if that's what you want, but we still have tonight together, and I want to spend it making love to you. Don't you like what we do to each other? Don't you like making me go out of my skull? You do. You make me wild, with your body like hot silk on me. One more night, darling. Let us have this last night together."

It was exactly what she hadn't wanted, to make love to him and know that she never would again, but the sensual promise he was making her with his hands and body was a heady lure. One more night, one more memory.

"All right," she whispered, beginning to unbutton his shirt. His hot flesh beckoned her, and she pressed her lips to him, feeling the curling hair under her mouth and the shiver that rippled over him. The intoxicating excitement that always seized her at his touch was taking over again, and she unbuckled his pants, helped him kick them away. He parted her legs and fit himself between them, the fever of feeling so high that no more preparation was needed, no more loving required to make her ready for him.

With a slow, smooth thrust he took her, and she adjusted her body to his weight and motion, letting the excitement well up like a cresting wave and take her away.

One more night. Then it would be finished.

CHAPTER 13

It didn't get any better. She had thought that it would get easier, even if the wound never quite healed, but from the time Blake saw her onto the plane at Sky Harbor Airport, the hurting never peaked, then declined. It stayed with her, eating at her. If she could forget about it during the day while she worked with Kevin, who was her new patient, it returned full force at night when she went to bed and lay there alone.

Milwaukee was at the opposite end of the world from Phoenix, or seemed like it. In a matter of a few hours she had exchanged a dry desert for several feet of snow, and she couldn't seem to get warm. The Colberts were nice, friendly people, anxious to do what they could to help her with Kevin, and Kevin was a darling, but he wasn't Blake. The childish arms that hugged her so spontaneously didn't satisfy the need she felt for strong, masculine ones, nor did the wet, loving kisses that Kevin and his little sister, Amy, gave her every night make her forget the kisses that had drowned her in a sea of sexual pleasure.

She had never thought that she would miss the fights that she and Blake had had, the loud and boisterous arguments, but she did. She missed everything about him, from his early-morning grumpiness to the wicked smile that lit his face when he was teasing her.

With foolish desperation, she hoped that the last night they'd had together would result in a baby; he hadn't taken any precautions that night, and for almost three weeks she was able to dream, to pretend. Then she discovered that it wasn't to be, and her world turned that much darker.

When she received a large check in the mail, forwarded by Dr. Norwood, it was all she could do to keep from screaming aloud in pain when she saw his signature. She wanted to tear it up, but she couldn't. The check was for the agreed-upon money. She traced her fingertip over the bold, angular script. It was just as she had known it would be; once she was away from him, she became only a part of his past. She had done what was best for him, but she hadn't known that she would have to live the rest of her life on the fine edge of agony.

With grim determination she set about rebuilding the defenses that he had torn down. She had to have them, to push the pain and memories behind, to hold the darkness at bay. Someday, she thought, looking at the wintry gray sky, she would find pleasure in living again. Someday the sun would shine again.

She had been with the Colberts exactly one month when she was called to the telephone. Frowning in perplexity, she gave Kevin his coloring book and crayons to keep him occupied until she returned, then went out to the hall to answer the phone.

"It's a man," Francine Colbert whispered, smiling at her in delight; then she left to see what had happened to make Amy suddenly bellow as if she were being scalped.

Dione put the phone to her ear. "Hello," she said cautiously.

"I'm not going to bite you," a deep, rich voice said in

amusement, and she slumped against the wall as her knees threatened to buckle under her.

"Blake!" she whispered.

"You've been there a month," he said. "Has your patient fallen in love with you yet?"

She closed her eyes, fighting down the mingled pain and pleasure that made her throat threaten to close. Hearing his voice made her weak all over, and she didn't know if she wanted to laugh or cry. "Yes," she gulped. "He's madly in love with me."

"What does he look like?" he growled.

"He's a gorgeous blond, with big blue eyes, not as dark as yours. He pouts for hours if he doesn't win when we play Go Fish," she said, and wiped a stray tear from her cheek.

Blake chuckled. "He sounds like real competition. How tall is he?"

"Oh, I don't know. About as tall as your average five-year-old, I suppose," she said.

"Well, that's a relief. I suppose I can leave you alone with him for a few more months."

She almost dropped the phone and had to grab the cord before it got away from her completely. Putting it back to her ear, she heard him say, "Are you still there?"

"Yes," she said, and wiped another tear away.

"I've been doing a lot of thinking," he said casually. "You told me over and over again that I didn't love you. You explained in great detail why I couldn't love you. But one thing that you never said was that you don't love me, and it seems to me that should have been your number-one reason for calling off a wedding. Well?"

What did he want? To reassure himself that she was all right, that she wasn't pining away? She bit her lip, then said weakly, "I don't love you."

"You're lying," he snapped in return, and she could feel his temper rising. "You're so crazy about me that you're standing there crying, aren't you?"

"No," she denied, fiercely dashing the wetness from her face.

"You're lying again. I've got a meeting waiting for me, so I'll let you get back to your patient, but I'm not through with you. If you thought you could end it by getting on a plane, you have a lot to learn about me. I'll be calling you again. Dream about me, honey."

"I will not!" she said fiercely, but she said it to a dial tone, and she *was* lying anyway. She dreamed about him almost every night and woke up with her pillow damp from the tears she'd shed in her sleep.

Thoroughly rattled, she returned to Kevin, and delighted him by losing a game of Go Fish.

Over the next few days her nerves gradually settled down, and she stopped jumping every time the phone rang. A blizzard shut the city down for two days, knocking out phone service and the electricity. The electricity was restored in a matter of hours, keeping them from freezing, but the phone service waited until clear skies had returned. She was out in the snow with Kevin and Amy, building a snowman for them with their inexpert but hilarious help, when Francine called her.

"Dione, you have a call! It's your friend again. Come on in. I'll bring the children in and get them dried off."

"Aww, Mommy," Kevin protested, but Francine was already pushing his little wheelchair inside and Amy followed obediently.

"Hello," Blake said warmly after she stammered out a hesitant greeting. "Are you pregnant?"

This time she was prepared and held on tightly to the receiver. "No. I...I thought about that, too, but everything's all right."

"Good. I didn't mean to get carried away. Serena *is* pregnant. She didn't waste any time when Richard came back. She was so excited at the possibility that she couldn't wait to take one of those early-warning tests, or whatever you call them."

"I'm happy for her. How do you feel about being an uncle?"

"It's okay by me, but I'd rather be a father."

She cautiously leaned against the wall. "What do you mean?"

"I mean that when we get married I'm going to throw away my whole supply of—"

"We're not getting married!" she yelped, then glanced around to see if anyone had heard her. No one was in sight, so she guessed that Francine was still occupied with the children.

"Sure we are," he returned calmly. "On the first of May. You set the date yourself. Don't you remember? I was making love to you."

"I remember," she whispered. "But don't you remember? I broke the engagement. I gave your heart back to you."

"That's what you think," he said. "We're getting married if I have to drag you kicking and screaming back to Phoenix."

Again she was left listening to a dial tone.

She couldn't make any sense out of what he was doing. Sleep got harder and harder to attain, and she lay awake going over the possibilities. Why would he insist that they were getting married? Why couldn't he just let it go?

It was a week before he called her again, and Francine had an amused gleam in her eye when she handed her the phone. "It's that dishy guy again," she said as Dione lifted the receiver to her ear.

"Tell her thank you." Blake chuckled. "How are you, honey?"

"Blake, why are you calling me?" she asked in desperation.

"Why shouldn't I call you? Is it against the law for a man to talk to the woman he's going to marry?"

"I'm not going to marry you!" she said, and this time she

bellowed it. Francine popped her head out of the kitchen and grinned at her.

Blake was laughing. "Sure you are. You already know all my bad habits and love me anyway. What could be better?"

"Would you listen to reason?" she yelled. "It's out of the question for me to marry you!"

"You're the one who's not listening," he countered. "You love me, and I love you. I don't know why you're so convinced that I can't love you, but you're wrong. Just think of the fun we're going to have while I show you how wrong you are."

"This is crazy," she moaned.

"No, this isn't crazy. You've got some crazy ideas, though, and you're going to get rid of them. You've convinced yourself that no one is going to love you, and you walked away from me, knowing that it was tearing me apart and half killing yourself at the same time. Your mother didn't love you, and Scott didn't love you, but they were only two people. How many people since then have loved you, and you pushed them away because you were afraid of getting hurt again? I'm not going to let you push me away, honey. Think about it."

"Some guy," Francine teased when Dione walked into the kitchen. Then she saw Dione's white face and quickly pushed a chair at her, then poured a cup of coffee. "Is something wrong?"

"Yes. No. I don't know." Dazed, she drank the coffee, then raised stunned golden eyes to the other woman. "He wants to marry me."

"So I gathered. What's so surprising about that? I imagine a lot of men have wanted to marry you."

"He won't take no for an answer," she said abstractedly.

"If he looks as great as he sounds, why would you want him to take no for an answer?" Francine asked practically. "Unless he's a bum."

"No, he's not a bum. He's…even greater than he sounds."

"Do you love him?"

Dione buried her face in her hands. "So much that I've been about to die without him."

"Then marry him!" Francine sat down beside her. "Marry him, and whatever problem is keeping you apart will be settled later. You'd be surprised how many problems people can settle when they're sleeping in the same bed every night and they wake up to the same face every morning. Don't be afraid to take the chance. Every marriage is a gamble, but then so is walking across the street. If you didn't take the chance you'd never get to the other side."

Words tumbled around in Dione's mind that night as she lay sleeplessly in bed. Blake had said that she was afraid of getting hurt again, and it was the truth. But was she so afraid of getting hurt that she had deliberately turned her back on a man who loved her?

No one had ever loved her before. No one had worried about her, held her when she cried, comforted her when she was upset....

Except Blake. He had done all those things. Even Richard had thought she was strong and confident, but Blake had seen beneath the act, had realized how vulnerable she was, how easily hurt. Blake had replaced the memories of violence with the memories of love. When she dreamed of a man's touch now it was his touch she dreamed of, and it filled her with aching need.

Blake loved her! It was incredible, but she had to believe it. She had set him free, expecting him to forget her, but it hadn't happened like that. It wasn't a case of "out of sight, out of mind." He had gone to the trouble of finding out where she was, and he had given her time to think about a life without him before he called. He hadn't given up.

As the days passed she went through her routine with Kevin with a smile on her face, humming constantly. He was so willing to do anything she asked that it was a pleasure to work with him, and she knew that soon he wouldn't need her any longer. That automobile accident that had injured him was long forgotten, and all he was concerned with now was if he would be able to play ball by the time summer came.

"How's your patient doing?" Blake asked the next time he called, and Dione smiled at the sound of his voice.

"He's doing great. I'm about ready to graduate him to a walker."

"That's good news, and not just for him. That means you'll be able to take a long honeymoon."

She didn't say anything, just stood there smiling. No, Blake Remington didn't give up. Any other man would have thrown up his hands in disgust, but when Blake decided that he wanted something, he went after it.

"Have you fainted?" he asked warily.

"No," she said, and burst into tears. "It's just that I love you so much, and I miss you."

He drew a long, shuddering breath. "Well, thank God," he muttered. "I was beginning to think I really would have to kidnap you. Lady, it's going to take a lifetime of massages to make up for what you've put me through."

"I'll even sign a contract, if you want," she said, swiping at the tears.

"Oh, I want, all right. An ironclad contract. What day can I fetch you? If I know you, you have Kevin's schedule mapped out to the very day you kiss him goodbye and walk away, and I'm going to be there to meet you when you walk out the door. You're not getting out of my sight until you're Mrs. Remington."

"April twelfth," she said, laughing and crying at the same time.

"I'll be there."

★ ★ ★

He *was* there, leaning on the doorbell at nine o'clock sharp that morning, while a spring snowstorm dumped its white load on his unprotected head. When Francine opened the door he grinned at her. "I've come for Dione," Blake said. "Is she awake yet?"

Francine opened the door wider, smiling at the tall man with the slight limp who entered her house. There was a reckless air about him; he was the sort of man who didn't let the woman he loved walk away from him.

"She's trying to get everything packed, but the children are helping her and it could take a while," Francine explained. "I imagine they're both wrapped around her legs and crying."

"I understand the feeling," he muttered, and at Francine's questioning look he grinned again. "I'm one of her ex-patients," he explained.

"Take good care of her," Francine pleaded. "She's been so good to Kevin, keeping his spirits up, not letting him get bored. She's special."

"I know," he said gently.

Dione came around the turn of the stairs with two tearful children in her arms. She stopped when she saw Blake, and her entire face lit up. "You came," she breathed, as if she hadn't dared to let herself really believe it.

"With bells on," he said, going up the steps in a graceful leap that made a mockery of the remaining limp. There was no way to get his arms around her without including the children, so he pulled all three of them to him and kissed her. Amy stuck her finger between their mouths and giggled.

Blake drew back and gave the little girl a rueful look, which she returned with wide-eyed innocence. "Are you the man who's taking Dee away?" Kevin asked tearfully, lifting his wet face from Dione's neck.

"Yes, I am," Blake replied gravely, "but I promise to take

good care of her if you'll let me have her. I was her patient, too, and I need her a lot. My leg still hurts me at night, and she has to rub it."

Kevin could understand that, and after a moment he nodded. "All right." He sighed. "She's real good at rubbing legs."

"Kevin, let Dione put you down," Francine directed. When both of the children were on the floor, Amy wrapped her plump little arms around Blake's leg and looked up a long, long way to his face. He looked down at her, then lifted his eyes to Dione's face. "At least two," he said. "And maybe even three, if you don't give me a daughter on your first two tries."

"I'm thirty years old, remember," she said cautiously. "Almost thirty-one."

"So? You have the body of an eighteen-year-old, only in better shape. I should know," he murmured, the hot light in his eyes making her cheeks turn pink. In a normal voice he said, "Are you packed?"

"Yes, I'll bring my suitcases down. You wait right here," she said hurriedly, turning and sprinting up the stairs. Her heart was galloping in her chest, and it wasn't from the stairs. Just seeing him again had been like getting kicked, except that it didn't hurt. She felt alive, truly alive; even her fingertips were tingling with joy. In eighteen days she would be getting married!

"Hurry it up!" he called, and she shivered with delight. Picking up her two suitcases she ran down the stairs.

When they were in the car he sat for a long moment just looking at her. Francine and the children had said their last goodbyes in the house, not coming out into the snow, so they were all alone. The snow had already covered the windows of the car, encasing them in a white cocoon.

"I have something for you," he murmured, reaching into his pocket. He withdrew the ruby heart and dangled it before her eyes. "You might as well keep it," he said as he clasped it around her neck. "It never did work right after you tried to give it back, anyway."

Tears burned her eyes as the ruby heart slid down to its resting place between her breasts. "I love you," she said unsteadily.

"I know. I had some bad moments when you first gave the heart back to me, but after I thought about it, I realized how frightened you were. I had to let you go to convince you that I loved you. Lady, that was the hardest thing I've ever done in my life, letting you get on the plane without me. Learning how to walk again was child's play compared to that."

"I'll make it up to you," she whispered, going into his arms. His familiar scent teased her senses, and she inhaled it delightedly. The smell of him brought back hot, sunny days and the echo of laughter.

"Starting tonight," he threatened. "Or better yet, as soon as we can get to the hotel room I've booked for us."

"Aren't we flying back to Phoenix today?" she asked, lifting her head in surprise.

"In case you haven't noticed, we're in the middle of a snowstorm." He grinned. "All flights are grounded until it clears, which could be days and days. How would you like to spend days and days in bed with me?"

"I'll try to bear it." She sighed.

"Do you spell that *b-a-r-e?*" he asked, nuzzling her neck. Then, slowly, as if he had waited as long as he could, he closed his lips over hers. He kissed her for a long time, savoring the taste and feel of her, then pulled himself away with a visible effort.

"I'm able to drive now," he said unnecessarily as he put the car into gear.

"So I see."

"And I'm flying again. I tested a new engine last week—"

"Are you going to keep doing the dangerous stuff?" she interrupted.

He eyed her. "I've been thinking about that. I don't think I'll be taking as many chances as I used to. There's too much excitement going on at home for me to risk missing any of it."

She was swimming laps, the hot May desert sun beating down on her head. The exercise felt good to her body, stretching muscles that had felt cramped. She had missed the pool and the well-equipped little gym where she and Blake had played out so many of their crises. That morning she had gone to a Phoenix hospital and been hired on the spot; she would miss the intensity of a one-on-one therapeutic relationship, but the regular hours would permit her to be with Blake at night and still keep doing the work she loved.

"Hey!" a deep voice called. "Are you in training for the Olympics?"

She began treading water. "What are you doing home so early?" she asked, pushing her hair out of her eyes.

"That's a fine welcome," her husband of two weeks grumbled. He shed his coat and draped it over one of the chairs, then pulled his tie loose. Dione watched as he systematically undressed, dropping his clothes on the chair until he stood as naked as the day he was born. He came into the water in a neat, shallow dive, and reached her with a few powerful strokes of his arms.

"If you get caught like that, don't blame me," she warned.

"It's too hot for clothes," he complained. "Did you get the job?"

"Of course I got the job," she sniffed.

"Conceited." He put his hand on top of her head and dunked her, which didn't bother her at all. She was as good a swimmer underwater as she was on top of it, and she kicked her graceful legs, darting away from him. He caught up with her when she reached the edge.

"You never did say why you're home so early," she said, turning to face him.

"I came home to make love to my wife," he replied. "I couldn't keep my mind on what I was doing. I kept thinking about last night," he said, and watched in fascination as her eyes grew heavy-lidded with memory.

He moved in closer to her and pressed his mouth to hers, his hand going to the back of her head and slanting her mouth across his. Their tongues met in mutual desire, and Dione quivered, letting her body float against his. Her legs twined with his and found them steady.

"You're standing," she said, lifting her mouth away.

"I know." His hand moved purposefully up her back and deftly unclipped her bikini top. He pulled it way from her and tossed it out of the pool. It landed on the tiles with a sodden plop. His fingers touched her breasts, cupping them together as he leaned forward and took another kiss.

With a moan she twined her arms around his neck; then she was wrapped around him like a vine. No matter how often he made love to her, it kept getting better and better as her body learned new ways of responding to him. The cool water lapped around them, but it didn't cool their hot skin. The fires within burned too brightly to be dampened by a little water.

He lifted her out of the water until her breasts were on a level with his mouth; then he feasted on the ripe curves that thrust so beguilingly at him. "I love you," he groaned, pulling at the ties that held the minuscule bikini bottom on her hips.

"Blake! Not here," she protested, but her body lay against his in sweet abandon. "Someone will see. Miguel...Alberta..."

"Miguel isn't here," he whispered, sliding her down the length of his body. "And no one can see what we're doing. The glare of the sun on the water takes care of that. Put your legs around my hips," he directed.

Suddenly she laughed aloud, throwing her head back and

lifting her face to the hot Phoenix sun. "You're still a dare-devil," she crooned, catching her breath as he took her with a long, delicious slide of skin against skin. "You love to take chances."

She clung to his shoulders, her senses dazzled, drenched in the beauty of the day. He watched her face, watched the wonderful play of emotions in her exotic eyes, watched them grow slumbrous, watching her teeth catch that full, passionate lower lip as she quivered with the desire he was carefully building in her. "Lady," he chanted. "Woman. You're all mine, aren't you?"

She laughed again, drunk with pleasure. She lifted her arms to the sun. "For as long as you want me," she promised.

"Then you'll go to your grave as my lady," he said. "And even that won't be the end of it."

★ ★ ★ ★ ★

FATAL JUSTICE
MARIE FORCE

For Cindy, Cheryl, Kendra and Linda—my writing BFFs.
How did we ever survive before the Lair?

And for all the readers who've written to say they LOVE the idea
of a romance series featuring the same couple in every book—
thank you, thank you, THANK YOU! I knew you were out there!

CHAPTER 1

As Sam raised her right hand to take the oath that would make her a lieutenant, every cell phone and pager in the room began to vibrate.

Tearing her eyes off the city clerk, she ventured a glance at her partner, Detective Freddie Cruz, and noted the grim expression on his handsome face as he checked his pager.

The moment Sam said the final words of the oath, several of the other officers in the room bolted for the doors, calling out that they'd see her later at the party. She heard one of them say, "DD, mass cas."

Ugh, Sam thought, *domestic disturbance, multiple casualties— the worst kind of hell for cops.*

"…I have tremendous confidence that she'll continue to serve with honor and distinction in her new role," concluded Chief Farnsworth, a man she'd called Uncle Joe when she was a child. "It's my great personal and professional honor to introduce for the first time, Lieutenant Sam Holland."

Contending with a huge lump in her throat, Sam received the thundering applause from the colleagues who remained in the room. Her sisters, Tracy and Angela, stepped forward, followed by their father in his motorized wheelchair.

As her sisters pinned on the gold bars, Sam marveled at the surreal sensation. Thanks to the dyslexia she'd battled all her life, she hadn't allowed herself to imagine this moment. Tears wet her father's cheeks as he watched from his chair. He loved his three girls passionately, but the special bond he shared with Sam was obvious to everyone who knew them.

Once the bars were in place Tracy and Angela stepped back.

Sam leaned forward to rest her head on her father's shoulder, which was a poor substitute for the hug she'd have given anything to receive from him right then. Two long years had passed since he'd last been able to hug her.

"Congratulations, Lieutenant," he said in a gruff tone.

"Thank you, Chief."

He kissed her cheek.

She turned to shake hands with Chief Farnsworth.

Watching the remaining cops leave the room, Sam had to hold herself back.

"It's okay if you want to go with them," Nick said from behind her.

"No way," she said as she turned to him. "I'm off today."

"Sam."

"Nick."

He leaned in and kissed her square on the lips in front of her father, her sisters, the chief and the mayor. The *mayor,* for God's sake!

"Congratulations, Lieutenant," Nick whispered.

"Thank you," she muttered. She planned to speak to him once again about his inappropriate PDA habit once they were back in that stupid limo he'd insisted on to transport them around the famously congested District of Columbia on their big day.

"The uniform is *h-o-t,*" he whispered in her ear. "I'll need a private viewing later."

"*Stop.*" She pushed at his chest. Even through the suit she could make out the pronounced contours of his muscular pectorals.

His full, sexy mouth lifted into the smile that promised carnal delights, and Sam's panties went damp. That was all it took, and he knew it.

As they partook in the coffee and pastry reception, Sam felt twitchy with anxiety as she waited to hear something—*anything*—from the scene of the domestic disturbance. Sipping her second diet cola of the day, she watched Nick share a laugh with her father and was grateful that the two of them had bonded over their shared concern for her safety. She wished they were a little *less* concerned, but hey, at least her father had stopped trying to intimidate Nick every chance he got—something Skip was still quite good at, even from his wheelchair.

Angela and Tracy materialized out of the crowd and linked their arms through Sam's.

"Ready to move on to part two?" Tracy asked.

"Do I have to?" Sam asked, a shaft of pain through her midsection reminding her of her many worries about Nick's new job. It also reminded her that she'd promised him she would have this annoying stomach situation checked by his doctor once the O'Connor case was closed. She hoped he would forget but knew he wouldn't. "I need to get changed."

"We'll go with you," Angela said.

Sam signaled to Nick that she'd be right back and headed for her new corner office in the detectives' pit where she had stashed a change of clothes earlier. The suit she'd paid way too much for hung on a hook behind the door.

"Come in here and help me, you guys," Sam called to her sisters. "I'm all thumbs."

Angela and Tracy marched through the door and took over, changing Sam out of her uniform and into the black suit with a subtle silver pinstripe. The three-button jacket revealed just a hint of her substantial cleavage, but she worried it was too much. They capped off the outfit with Sam's prized black Jimmy Choo heels and their grandmother's pearls, which Sam hoped lent her an aura of respectability.

Angela helped Sam with the shoes, straightened and then wobbled. "Whoa," she said, reaching for the wall to steady herself.

"What's the matter?" Sam asked.

"Nothing. Just got dizzy for a minute there."

"Did you skip breakfast again?" Tracy asked.

"Maybe," Angela said sheepishly. "I'll grab something on the way to the Capitol." Turning her attention on Sam, she added, "You look fabulous, Sam. Absolutely gorgeous."

Sam tugged at the top button of the suit, willing it up another half inch. But the moment she let it go, it slid back down over breasts she thought were far too big. "It's not conservative enough."

"Well, since Nick is a flaming liberal, that shouldn't be a problem," Ang joked.

"Very funny," Sam said. "The chief justice of the Supreme Court is swearing him in. He isn't going to want to see my boobs."

"Wanna bet?" Tracy said with a smirk.

Sam fought to swallow the lump of panic forming in her throat. "I can't do this, you guys. I'm not cut out to be a senator's whatever I am."

"Love of his life?" Angela said.

The poignant simplicity of her sister's statement nearly undid Sam.

"You look beautiful, classy and elegant." Tracy smoothed

her hands over Sam's lapels. "Nick should be honored to have you by his side today."

"He is," Nick said from the doorway.

Startled, they turned, and the love Sam saw in his gaze chased away all her fears.

Tracy cleared her throat. "We'll, ah, go get Dad and Celia and see you at the Capitol." Grabbing Angela's arm, she steered her younger sister out of the office.

Sam continued to fiddle with the low-cut jacket.

Nick retrieved her hand and brought it to his lips. "You're stunning."

"This suit is all wrong," she said, unaccustomed to wardrobe malfunctions of this magnitude. Fashion was the one area of her life where she was usually one hundred percent confident. "I don't know what I was thinking. It shows too much—"

He put his arms around her. "It's beautiful, you're beautiful and I love you. I was so proud of you in there, watching your sisters pin those gold bars on your collar."

Touched, she worked up a smile for him. "You understand why I asked them and not you, don't you?"

"Of course I do. They stood in your dad's place. It was perfect."

"Thanks," she said, relieved that he understood—that he always seemed to understand. Tall herself, she had to tip her head back to meet his hazel eyes. At six-four, he was one of the few people in her life who towered over her. "Are you ready?"

The slight hitch in the deep breath he released was the only sign of nerves she could detect in his otherwise cool demeanor. "As ready as I'll ever be." He offered her his arm. "Shall we?"

Sam hesitated but only for a second. He was everything. To deny that would not only be foolish, it would be pointless. She hooked her hand through his arm. "Absolutely."

★ ★ ★

An hour later, as Sam stood under the Capitol dome and held the O'Connor family Bible while Nick swore to preserve and protect the Constitution of the United States against all enemies foreign and domestic, it occurred to her that his big day trumped hers by a mile. The president of the United States, a close friend of the O'Connor family, surprised Nick by showing up with the first lady.

It was the second time in a week Sam had seen President and Mrs. Nelson. The first time had been at John O'Connor's funeral, where she'd also met Nick's father, Leo. Today, Leo had brought his pretty young wife and adorable three-year-old twin sons, and Sam was once again struck by Leo's youthfulness. Since he was only fifteen years older than Nick, it made sense that he looked more like Nick's brother than his father.

The entire O'Connor family had come. Sam could only imagine how difficult it must be for them to watch their murdered son and brother's best friend replace him in the Senate. John's father, retired Senator Graham O'Connor, had hand-picked Nick for the job. And while Graham and his wife Laine's eyes shone with pride as they watched the man they thought of as a son take the oath of office, Sam could also see the heartbreak. Their loss was so recent and raw, and was made worse by the fact that John had been taken from them by his own son.

Before Sam knew it, Nick was declared a United States senator, and he had committed the next year to the people of Virginia. As Nick shook hands with the president, Sam hoped her crazy job wouldn't somehow ruin it for him.

CHAPTER 2

Nick received hugs from his father, the O'Connors and the first lady. Amazing. The son of high school-age parents, he'd been raised by his grandmother in a one-bedroom apartment in Lowell, Massachusetts. He'd landed an academic scholarship to Harvard, where he'd met John O'Connor and later, John's family. Over the years, the O'Connors had become Nick's family, too, which was the only reason he was now a United States senator.

From the setting under the Capitol rotunda to the chief justice to the governor of Virginia, this whole thing felt like it was happening in a movie rather than to him. As the president of the United States extended his hand and said, "Congratulations, Senator," it finally became real. He was Senator Nicholas Cappuano, Democrat of Virginia. But when he remembered how he'd gotten here, that his best friend had been murdered, and that he had been tapped to take his place, Nick's heart ached. As if anyone could take John's place.

The crowd moved toward his suite of offices in the Hart Building for the reception the Virginia Democrats were throwing in his honor. Nick went against the flow to find

Sam as he continued to accept congratulations. He saw her at
the end of the line, tagging along behind her father and his
fiancée, Celia, as they headed to the elevator. Reaching for
Sam's hand, Nick held her back.

"We'll be right there," he said to Skip and Celia.

"Take your time, Senator," Skip said, the half of his face
that wasn't paralyzed lifting into a grin.

"That sounds so weird," Nick said to Sam when they were
alone.

She reached up to brush a stray lock of hair off his forehead.
"You'd better get used to it."

Moved by her loving gesture, he still wanted to pinch himself when he realized he could touch her, be with her, sleep
with her and love her every day after six years of dreaming
about her. The one who'd gotten away was back in his life,
and there was nothing he wouldn't do to keep her there. "Are
you all right?"

"Sure," she said. "Why wouldn't I be?"

"You're a little pale."

"Am I?"

"Uh-huh. Are you still worried about all this?"

She looked up at him with those light blue eyes that be-
trayed her every emotion. "No."

"Liar," he said, smiling as he leaned in to kiss her.

She tried to pull back from him, but he resisted. "You can't
do that here," she said. "You're a senator now."

He glanced around at the deserted rotunda. "Who's looking?" Tipping his head, he brushed his lips over hers and was
gratified to feel some of the resistance leave her shoulders.

"Do I have to call you Senator now?" she asked with a
glint in her eye.

"Only in bed."

Her cheeks flamed with color. "Why do you have to say that stuff?"

"Because it flusters you."

"It does not."

"Liar."

She poked his ribs, making him laugh.

A throat was cleared behind them. They turned to find Nick's communications director, Trevor Donnelly, waiting for him. Nick had retained all of John O'Connor's staff, including the perpetually frazzled, mop-topped Donnelly.

"Um, excuse me, Senator, but the media is waiting to have a word with you, and the president and first lady were looking for you in the office. They have to get going."

"I'll be right there."

"Should I, ah, wait?" Trevor asked.

"No, go on ahead."

With an awkward nod, Trevor left them.

"It has to be weird to them," Nick said, watching him go. "Two weeks ago, I was a staffer, too. Now they have to call me Senator."

"There'll be some adjustments, but you'll make it work."

"Thanks for the vote of confidence. I hope you're right."

"You'd better go. The president's waiting for you."

"Before I do," he said, reaching for her hands and bringing them to his lips, "I have to do something about that anticipating-disaster look on your face." When he had her full attention, he said, "I love you, Samantha, and you're the most important thing in my life. More important than my job, my new title and all the perks that'll come with it."

"That's sweet of you to say." She finally cracked a grin as they walked toward the elevator. "Do you know how many police lieutenants there are in this country?"

"Maybe a couple thousand plus one more today?" he said, perplexed by the question.

"That's about right. Guess how many U.S. senators there are?"

"That one I know—exactly one hundred. What's your point?"

"No point. I was just doing the math."

In the elevator, he backed her up against the wall. "Your big day was every bit as big as mine."

"No, it *wasn't*," she said, her hands resting on his chest. "I got the mayor. You got the *president*."

"Big whoop. He came out of respect for John and because he's an old friend of Graham's."

"He came because he wants to court the newest Democratic senator."

Nick shrugged. "None of this is going to change me, Sam. I swear. I'm the same guy you woke up with this morning. I'm the same guy you're going to sleep with tonight. I promise."

"Making a lot of assumptions, aren't you?" She tossed a saucy grin over her shoulder as she stepped off the elevator ahead of him.

"No assumptions." He took her hand and fought her efforts to break free of him as they stepped into his crowded office. "Just stating the facts, Lieutenant."

"You'd better go talk to the president."

"Come with me."

"You go ahead. I'll be right over there." She pointed to where her father, Celia, Tracy, Angela and their families had congregated, outside of what used to be Nick's office.

Ignoring that, he tightened his grip on her hand and moved toward the president. As she reluctantly followed him he could feel her tension, but he refused to allow her to put distance between them. That was *not* going to happen.

"Mr. President," Nick said, extending his free hand. "I can't thank you enough for being here."

"My pleasure, Senator," President Nelson said. Turning his attention to Sam, he added, "And it's nice to see you again, Sergeant."

"Actually," Nick said, sliding an arm around Sam's waist, "it's Lieutenant. As of about two hours ago."

"Well, congratulations to both of you."

"Thank you," Sam said.

"We have to be going," President Nelson said, "but I look forward to working with you. If I can do anything for you, my door's always open."

"Likewise, sir," Nick said.

"We'll be hosting a state dinner for the prime minister of Canada in a couple of weeks," the president added. "I hope you both can make it."

Nick felt Sam stiffen. "We'd be honored," he said.

President and Mrs. Nelson left a few minutes later. While Nick and Sam visited with his father's family, Trevor approached them again.

"I'm sorry to interrupt, Senator, but several reporters are waiting for you in the conference room."

"Would you please excuse me?" Nick said. "I'll be back in a few minutes."

He left Sam with his family and followed Trevor. Over the next thirty minutes, he made it clear to the press that his top priority was ensuring passage of the immigration bill that had been scheduled for a vote by the full Senate on the day John was found murdered.

"Will you be a cosponsor?" a reporter from *The Hill* asked.

"Senator O'Connor's name will remain on the bill as a cosponsor with Senator Martin. My office will work with Senator Martin's staff to get the bill on the floor for a vote."

"Have you been apprised of your committee assignments yet?" asked a reporter from the *Richmond Times-Dispatch*.

"No, but I imagine I'll take Senator O'Connor's assignments since I'm only here for a year."

"Your relationship with Lieutenant Holland has gotten a lot of attention lately—"

"I'm not going to discuss that."

"The public is interested."

"My personal life is of no consequence to my duties as a United States senator. Let's keep the focus on that."

"Do you plan to get married?"

Frustrated, Nick stood up. "I have an office full of guests, so if you'll please excuse me, I'd like to get back to them." He left the conference room and bumped into Christina Billings, whom he had promoted from deputy chief of staff into the job that used to be his—chief of staff.

"What's wrong, Senator?" she asked. "You look pissed."

He ran a hand through his hair, noting the odd sound of his new title coming from his longtime friend and colleague. "The country's at war, the economy's in shambles and all they want to talk about is my love life."

"People are curious. It's to be expected."

"It's annoying."

Nick watched her glance across the room to where Sam was in the midst of an animated conversation with her father and sisters.

"Are you going to be able to get past it, Chris? She matters to me."

"She was a total bitch to me. Treating me like a murderer. As if I could've killed John."

"She was just doing her job."

"Her job sucks."

"On many days, she'd agree with you, but I need you to get over it. She's not going anywhere."

Her eyes clouded as she tucked a strand of short hair behind her ear. "It's only been a couple of weeks."

"I know." Nick's heart went out to Christina, knowing she'd suffered from unrequited love for John O'Connor and had been heartbroken by his death as well as the murder investigation that briefly focused on her. Nick spotted John's brother Terry in the crowd and realized he was heading for the door. "I'll catch up to you," he said to Christina as he set out to stop Terry.

"Hey, Terry!"

At forty-two, John's older brother had settled into middle age after a string of problems added ten extra years to his once-handsome face. With dark hair gone to salt-and-pepper and dark, dead-looking eyes, he bore no resemblance to his late blond-haired, blue-eyed younger brother. Broken capillaries in Terry's face were a testament to his long-running battle with alcohol.

After Terry was caught driving drunk three weeks before he'd been scheduled to announce his candidacy for his father's Senate seat, Graham O'Connor had turned to his younger son John, who reluctantly buckled under enormous pressure to run for the seat that had been in their family for nearly forty years.

"Hey, Nick, er, I mean Senator," Terry said.

Even more than five years later, Nick could still sense the bitterness in Terry. It had kept Terry on Sam's short list of suspects in his brother's murder, especially when Terry had been unable to produce the woman he'd had a drunken encounter with on the night John was killed. "May I have a minute?" Nick gestured to Christina's office since it was closest.

"Sure," Terry said with a shrug.

Nick ushered Terry into the room and closed the door behind them.

"What's up?" Terry asked.

"How've you been?"

"Fine. You know, it's tough."

The brothers hadn't been close, but Nick had no doubt Terry's grief was real. "Yeah. I keep waiting to feel better, but I'm not quite there yet."

"Mother says these things take time."

They shared a smile over their mutual love for Laine O'Connor, a pillar of strength and gentle wisdom, even during the darkest days of her life.

"Listen, the reason I wanted to talk to you is I'm sure you heard I promoted Christina to chief of staff."

"That's a good move," Terry said. "She'll be great."

"I agree. But her promotion leaves me in need of a deputy. I wondered if you might be interested."

If Nick had said Martians were landing on the south lawn of the Capitol, Terry probably wouldn't have looked more surprised. "What?" he whispered.

"Would you like to be my deputy chief of staff?"

Terry stared at him.

"Terry?"

"Why me?" he stammered. "Surely you can find someone who's not dragging a shitload of baggage behind him."

"I want you."

"Why?" he asked again, his face still slack with shock. He had a bullshit job at a lobby firm that his father had gotten for him, but otherwise his prospects had been slim since his once-promising political career flamed out following the DUI.

Nick took a step closer to the other man. "John was my best friend, my brother as much as he was yours."

"No question about that."

"I think he'd approve of you helping to ensure that all his hard work wasn't in vain, that what he started here continues. And I could use someone with your political acumen on my team."

"You mean it?" Terry asked, his expression wary.

"Yes, I mean it, but I have a condition."

"I should've known there'd be strings."

"No strings, just a condition—thirty days in-patient alcohol rehab, followed by daily AA meetings. This is a one-shot deal, Terry. One screwup, and you're out. I may not have any illusions of a career in politics, but I won't stand for anyone disgracing me, John or this office."

Terry jammed his hands into his pockets and appeared to think it over.

"So what do you say?"

"Don't you need someone now?"

"Christina can handle it for a month. We'll hold the job for you if you want it."

Terry was silent for another long moment, during which Nick wondered if he'd asked too much.

"Yes," Terry finally said. "I'd be honored."

"Great. I'm sure your doctor can refer you to some treatment facilities. If that doesn't pan out, let me know, and I'll have someone here look into it for you."

"That won't be necessary. I'll work it out." He extended his hand to Nick. "Thank you."

Nick nodded. "I hope this'll be a whole new start for you, Terry." He paused. "There's one other thing."

"What's that?"

"Sam."

Terry's expression hardened. "What about her?"

"She's in my life to stay. You'll be running into her."

"Yeah, so?"

Nick didn't care for his tone but let it slide. "Can you handle that?"

The woman Terry had been with the night John was murdered eventually come forward to cement Terry's alibi, but not before Sam reduced him to a shell of a man in the interrogation room.

"If I have to."

"I'm going to need better than that," Nick said. "Either you assure me you'll treat her with courtesy and respect, or the deal is off."

"I'll do my best," Terry said.

Nick extended his hand to the other man. "Then I'll see you in a month or so."

"I'll be here." He shook Nick's hand.

Terry opened the door to find his father approaching.

"There you both are!" Graham said, smiling. "You have a special guest, Senator." Graham stepped aside to usher Julian Sinclair into the room.

Nick let out a surprised gasp. "Julian! What're you doing here?" He was shocked to see Graham's close friend. Nick had known Julian since his years on the Harvard hockey team when Julian, a Harvard Law professor, had been one of the team's most ardent supporters.

Grinning, Julian returned Nick's embrace before greeting Terry just as warmly. "I have a meeting in town tomorrow," Julian said, "and I wanted to be among the first to congratulate the newest United States senator."

Nick took a good long look at his friend, noting that his hair had gone entirely to silver since the last time Nick had seen him. The hint of sadness in Julian's brown eyes was also new. John's sudden death had hit them all hard.

"Listen to him being modest," Graham said. He looked

happier than Nick had seen him since John died, which made Nick feel lighter, too. "Tell them who the meeting is *with*."

"Nelson," Julian said with a sheepish grin.

"*Oh!*" Nick said, understanding dawning on him all of a sudden. "The court." Longtime Justice William Jeremiah had recently announced his retirement, giving President Nelson his first opportunity to make a nomination to the Supreme Court.

Graham clapped his hands together. "You said it, Senator. You boys are looking at the next Supreme Court Justice!"

"Wow," Terry said. "Congratulations."

"Thank you, but it's all up to the Senate, of course," Julian said. "I'm told I should prepare for one hell of a dogfight."

Nick couldn't disagree with him. Julian's liberal views on abortion and other hot-button issues made him a polarizing choice on Nelson's part.

"You've got at least one vote sewn up, right, Senator?" Graham said.

"Of course," Nick said. "I'll do anything I can to help. This is one of those times when I'm glad I only have a year in the Senate and can piss off anyone and everyone without a worry."

Julian laughed. "Don't expend all your political capital on me, my friend."

"I can't think of anyone better to spend it on," Nick said sincerely. Julian was one of his favorite people. "How long are you in town?"

Julian shrugged. "For the duration, come what may."

"We'll have dinner at my new place next week," Nick said. "I want you to meet Sam."

"I can't wait to meet this woman who's got our boy's head all turned around—and a cop, no less," Julian said, grinning at Graham.

"When you meet her, you'll see why his head is turned," Graham added with a wink.

"All right, you two. That's enough." Nick was thrilled to see Graham's playful side reemerging after the grim days that followed John's murder. "She's here somewhere."

"I have to take a rain check. I don't have any time right now, and I'd like to be able to really get to know her." Julian checked his watch. "I'm due to meet with Hanigan," he said, referring to the White House chief of staff. "I just wanted to pop in and say congratulations." He extended his hand to Nick. "I'm so very, very proud, and John would be, too. He always said you were the brains behind the entire operation."

"Thank you," Nick said softly. "That means so much coming from you."

"Make us proud."

"I'll do my best."

CHAPTER 3

Nick spent the next half hour working the room, visiting with Judson Knott and Richard Manning, the chair and vice chair of the Virginia Democratic Committee, as well as Virginia Governor Mike Zorn and his wife, Judy. While Nick made polite small talk and sipped a glass of wine someone had pressed into his hand, he scanned the room in search of Sam.

"Would you all excuse me?" Nick asked the others. As he made his escape, he realized he didn't see Sam's family, either. After circling the big room, he finally ducked into John's office. Of course, it was his office now, but Nick would probably always think of it as John's. He found Sam staring out the window at the Washington Monument off in the distance.

"Hey, babe," he said, closing the door. "I was looking for you."

She turned to him with a small smile. "Here I am."

"Everything all right?"

"Uh-huh. You?"

"Yep. Did your dad leave?"

She nodded. "They all said to tell you congratulations and

they'll see you later at the party. Celia wanted my dad to rest up before tonight."

"What're you thinking about?" he asked, as he massaged her shoulders.

She turned to him. "Just about everything that happened to put you in this office."

"We need to put that behind us," Nick said. Touching his lips to hers, he was startled by the charge of desire even though he knew he should be used to it by now. He wondered if it would always be like that between them and suspected it would. Their connection had spanned six years and survived her manipulative ex-husband Peter's efforts to keep them apart. "Everything's new today. It's a new beginning for both of us." His hands shifted from her waist up to cup her face as she ran her tongue over his bottom lip. He gasped. "I wish we could fly away right now, today, to somewhere tropical, where I could do nothing but make love to you for a whole week."

"You'd get tired of me before the week was up."

"No," he whispered, sliding one hand down her back to align her with his erection. "Never."

"Doesn't Congress take a recess around Easter?"

"Yes," he said, nibbling her earlobe.

She trembled. "Let's go then."

"Really? Can you get away?"

"To spend a whole week in bed with you? I think it can be arranged."

He rested his forehead against hers. "But that's months from now."

"We'll both be so busy, the time will fly."

"Once we move into the new place, things will calm down a bit." He'd bought a townhouse three doors from her dad's on Ninth Street so she could be close to her father and to work. "The Realtor is putting my place in Arlington on the market right after the New Year, but we can move into Ninth Street next week."

She shifted out of his embrace and turned back toward the window. "That's good."

He rested his hands on her shoulders. "What's going on inside that head of yours?"

"Nothing."

"Samantha. I know you better than that. What gives?"

"Everything's moving so fast. I'm having trouble catching my breath."

"It's been crazy, I won't deny that, but once we get settled in our place in the city, it'll calm down. And just think, we'll be able to sleep later when we don't have to drive in from Arlington."

"True."

"So then what's the problem?"

With a deep sigh, she turned to face him. "I'm not ready to move in with you yet."

He tried to hide his disappointment from her. "I wanted us to do this together. Set up the house and stuff."

"It'd probably be better if you set things up your way. You're the one who's particular that way."

"How long are we talking? A week? A month?"

"I'm not sure. I just know I'm not ready yet."

A jolt of anger took him by surprise. "Because of Peter." He'd love to get five minutes alone with her asshole ex-husband, but since the guy was in jail for strapping crude bombs to both their cars and nearly killing Sam, that wasn't going to happen.

"Not entirely. More because of me." She rubbed her hand over her belly, a sign that the conversation was stirring up her nervous stomach. "After everything that happened, I'm more cautious than I used to be."

Anxious to stop the stomach thing before it became a full-blown incident, Nick said, "We can talk about it later, babe. Don't let your stomach get going. And by the way, you promised you'd get that checked after you closed the O'Connor case."

"I will. Soon."

He hugged her, loving the way they fit together so perfectly, like two halves of a whole. "I'll hold you to that."

Her cell phone rang, and she pulled back from him to retrieve it from the inside pocket of her suit jacket. "Holland."

Since the phone was on speaker, he heard Freddie Cruz say, "Lieutenant."

"What's going on?"

"Four vics."

Sam winced. "Kids?"

"Three, one a baby."

"Damn."

"Yeah," Freddie said with a weary sigh. "It's bad. The father was seen running from the house covered in blood. But, um, you might want to get over here."

"Why's that?"

"We found a bunch of stuff about your dad's case in the house, newspaper clippings and other stuff about the shooting. I thought you might want to take a look." He rattled off the address.

"I'll be right there." Her eyes became hard and dispassionate, the way they got when she worked a case. She returned the phone to her pocket and looked up at Nick. "You don't mind, do you?"

"Of course not." Nick could see that she had already slipped into her zone. "Do you want me to come with you?"

She shook her head. "You have guests. I'll call you."

Leaning in to kiss her, he said, "Be careful."

"I always am."

★ ★ ★

Sam did her best to stay calm as a taxi ferried her to the southeast corner of the city. They had waited so long for a break in her father's case. Could this be it? After many disappointments, she refused to allow herself to hope.

Just over two years ago, Deputy Chief Skip Holland had been on his way home from work when he pulled over an erratic driver on G Street. The last thing he remembered was reporting in to dispatch and then approaching the car. A bullet lodged between the C3 and C4 vertebrae had left him a quadriplegic with just one slightly functioning finger on his right hand. A week after the shooting, a mild stroke rendered the left side of his face paralyzed.

They hadn't a single clue—no witnesses, no ballistics since the doctors decided removing the bullet could kill him, the car hadn't had a license plate, and they had no description of the driver since Skip was shot before he saw the driver's face. A long time ago Sam and her colleagues concluded that the only way the case would be solved now was if someone bragged about shooting a cop and one of their snitches passed it along. As the case went cold, Sam had learned not to get her hopes up.

If her newfound media notoriety had any upside it was the opportunity to remind the press that her father's case remained unsolved. Someone knew something. If only they'd come forward. They just needed a thread. One thread to pull and the whole thing would unravel. Her sisters and even her father, to some extent, were resigned to the fact that they might never catch the shooter. Sam would neither rest nor retire as long as the case was unsolved.

Skip had been just ninety days shy of retirement at the time of the shooting. The months that followed were filled with fear and frustration as his family and friends did what they could to help him adjust to his new reality—confined to a wheelchair by day, hooked to a respirator by night and reliant upon the specially outfitted van the union bought for him.

When the taxi pulled up to a dilapidated row house on First Avenue in the violent, poverty-stricken neighborhood of Washington Highlands, Sam retrieved her 9 millimeter handgun from her purse, tucked it into the back of her skirt, and clipped her badge to the lapel of her coat.

Ignoring the crowd of onlookers gathered outside the yellow police tape, she tossed a twenty to the driver and wove her way between cop cars, an ambulance and the medical examiner's van on her way to the chain-link front gate. Pushing the rusty gate open, she hurried up the sagging stairs and almost bumped into Freddie as he emerged from the house looking pale and drawn.

Sam ached for her kindhearted, compassionate partner who would suffer more than most over a scene like this. She rested a hand on his trench coat–clad shoulder. "Take a few breaths."

He did what he was told, but his complexion was ashen, and his brown eyes were flat with grief and anger. "I just can't imagine how anyone does that to helpless kids. A dad is supposed to *protect* his kids."

"It's always harder when it's kids." A memory of the child who was killed when she ordered a shootout at a crack house resurfaced suddenly, sending a shudder rippling through her.

"He shot the mother in the kitchen," Freddie said. "Seems like he took her by surprise. No defensive wounds. Point of entry on the back of her left shoulder. McNamara said the bullet probably hit her heart. We found a gun thrown into a box in the back of the bedroom closet. There was another box in the closet that had the clippings about your dad."

Sam watched him struggle with his composure as he proceeded with the rote recitation of the facts.

"The kids were beaten. We found a baseball bat with brain matter on it."

Sam winced. "Do we know him?"

"Clarence Reese, thirty-nine, long list of priors, mostly B&E and drug stuff. Juvie record, too, but nothing violent."

Sam wished she could say she recognized the name. "Next of kin?"

"Gonzo and Arnold found an address for Reese's mother. They left about twenty minutes ago. We've got an APB out for Reese."

The front door opened and Chief Medical Examiner Dr. Lindsey McNamara emerged behind paramedics wheeling a tiny body in a bag out of the house. Known for her stoicism, Lindsey's green eyes were bright with tears. "Unreal," she whispered on her way by.

Sam squeezed the other woman's arm.

"That's the last one," Freddie said, sounding relieved.

Tearing her eyes off the black bag being loaded into the M.E.'s vehicle, Sam returned her attention to Freddie. "Have you found any connection to my dad in any of Reese's priors?"

"After we came across the stuff about the shooting, Captain Malone ordered a more detailed run of Reese's record. He went back to HQ to move that along."

"Show me what you've got."

As if to fortify himself, Freddie took another deep breath of the cold air before he led Sam into hell.

The smell hit her like a fist to the face. Death. Blood. Bodily waste.

Old toys covered the floor of a Spartanly furnished living room dominated by a big-screen TV. Spattered blood coated the screen and the walls behind it. A tan sofa had clearly been ground zero for one of the murders as the cushions were soaked with drying blood.

Crime scene officers sifting through the carnage nodded to her as she entered the room.

"Jesus," Sam whispered, and for once Freddie didn't object to her use of the Lord's name.

He led her past the kitchen where Clarence Reese had shot his wife in the back. They went up a flight of stairs to a second floor with three small bedrooms and a tiny bathroom.

Sam noted disarray throughout the house—dishes piled in the kitchen sink, toys everywhere, scuffed walls, pictures hanging at crooked angles, towels and dirty clothes scattered about the floor of the bathroom and a filthy stained rug lining the hallway. Things had been difficult in this household long before today, long before Clarence Reese lost his mind and butchered his family.

In the master bedroom, a king-size bed took up almost every inch of the room. Freddie pulled a box from the closet floor, set it on the bed and then moved aside so Sam could take a closer look.

She slipped on the latex gloves he handed her before she touched yellowing newspaper articles from the aftermath of her father's shooting, carefully clipped from all the local newspapers, as well as coverage taken from the department's website. Under the clippings were photos, and various other news stories about her father's thirty years on the force that ran after the shooting.

"Was it him?" Sam asked in a small voice, glancing up at the family photo that hung over the bed. Nothing about Clarence Reese was familiar to her. He had the stocky build of a former high school football player, coffee-colored skin, brown eyes and a thick shock of dark hair. He was handsome in a quirky sort of way. His wife was white with a plain face, stringy brown hair, dull eyes and a world-weary expression. "Do you think he shot my dad?"

"We don't know, but we're going to find out. You're not the only one who wants to know, believe me. Farnsworth and Conklin were both here," Freddie said of the chief and deputy chief, both of whom were old friends of her father's. "Farnsworth had fire in his eyes when Malone showed him this stuff."

"Let's bag it all and have the lab work it up. Not that the gun will tell us anything about my dad." How she wished they could get at that bullet lodged inside him.

"Malone said the same thing. I was just waiting for you to see it."

With a nod she stepped out of the room so he could tend to the evidence. Drawing a deep breath in through her nose, she blew it out her mouth, a process she had discovered helped to short-circuit the stomach pains before they could spiral out of control. She made the mistake of glancing into what had been the baby's room and quickly looked away from the gruesome scene.

"I don't want my dad to know we found this stuff until we have more," she said.

"I'll put out the word."

"I'd hate to get his hopes up."

"I understand, and so will everyone else."

"If we can't find a connection from Reese's arrest record, we'll have no choice but to ask my dad."

"We can cross that bridge if we come to it, but you're right—there's no need to tell him until we have something solid. Hopefully, we'll find Reese fast and get him into interrogation."

"What was the wife's name?" she asked.

"Tiffany. Kids were Jorge, Ramon and the baby was Maria."

Sam studied the family photo, zeroing in on the plain-looking mother. "She doesn't look like a Tiffany."

"No." Freddie zipped the plastic evidence bag closed and pulled off his gloves. "Let's get out of here. If there's anything else, crime scene will let us know."

She took another long look at the photo of the shattered family before she followed Freddie out of the house.

CHAPTER 4

Hours later, Sam stood in front of the mirror in her bedroom at her father's house and adjusted the cowl neck of the plum-colored cashmere sweater he'd given her for Christmas. Of course Celia had picked it out, but that didn't matter. It was the thought that counted, and her father had always been a thoughtful gift-giver. A tough, don't-fuck-with-me cop with a soft spot a mile wide for his family, Skip had loved to shop, to find the perfect gift, to hide it away, and then present it with a flourish for a birthday or Christmas or just because it was Tuesday.

Bitterness threatened to consume her as she added another item to the long list of things a nameless, faceless shooter had taken from her father, from all of them. But now when she imagined the person who shot her father, she pictured Clarence Reese. She just wished they could find him. They'd scoured the city all day but had turned up no sign of him either with family members or at any of his usual haunts.

Hands braced against the dresser, Sam let her head hang between her shoulders, rolling off the tension—or attempting to. Hours of sifting and digging had also found no connection between Skip Holland and Clarence Reese. Not an arrest, a traffic stop, a verbal warning, nothing—unless Skip had had some sort of undocumented altercation with Clarence. To find that out, she'd have to ask her father, but she wasn't prepared to do that until they had more. She refused to set him up for yet another disappointment.

Taking a deep breath, she attempted to shut down her mind, to leave the investigation for tomorrow. Tonight was for celebration—at least that was the plan. Sam didn't feel much like celebrating and was almost resentful that her new personal obligations were pulling her away from what she really wanted to be doing right now.

She ran a brush through her long toffee-colored curls and applied a light touch of eye shadow. Maybe she wasn't in the mood to party, but she'd be damned if she'd go out looking like crap.

As she bent to zip high-heeled black boots, Nick stepped into the room and closed the door behind him. From between her legs she saw that he wore a black sweater over well-faded jeans that hugged him in all the right places.

"Mmm, mmm, *mmm,* that's one hell of a view," he said, taking a good long look at her ass.

She shot him an upside-down scowl.

"Uh-oh. What's wrong?"

Righting, she ran her fingers through her hair. "Nothing."

"Something."

"Stop acting like you know me so well," she snapped.

With a slow, sexy smile that she watched unfold in the mirror, he came up behind her and rested his hands on her shoulders. "I do know you so well." He punctuated his words with a brush of his lips over her neck that made her tremble. "See?"

Sam tried—and failed—to shake him off.

"I know you're frustrated, babe—"

"You don't know anything."

"I know I love you, and I hate to see you hurting."

Damn if he didn't always know just how to get to her! The starch left her spine, and she sagged into his embrace.

His chin settled on the top of her head, his arms tightened around her waist. In the mirror, he found her eyes. "Talk to me."

"It makes me so mad!"

"What does?"

"That my dad is stuck forever in that chair, and the person who shot him is walking around, living his life, like nothing ever happened. He took my dad's freedom! He took *everything!* He should have to pay for that." A lump of emotion in her throat reduced her voice to a whisper. "He should have to pay."

"Yes, he should. And I have no doubt that he will, because you won't give up. You'll never give up until you find him." He turned her so they were face-to-face. "And guess what? *He* knows that, too. He *worries* about you. The best detective in this city is on his trail, and he *knows* it, Sam. I'll bet it keeps him awake at night."

She rested her cheek against the hard muscle of Nick's chest. "It makes me mad."

"Mad is good." He held her tight against him. "Mad is motivating."

"Mad is debilitating."

"Only if you let it be. Your dad was so proud of you earlier." Nick's lips brushed through her hair as he spoke softly to her. "He all but radiated with it, Sam. Watching your sisters pin those bars on your collar, he had tears rolling down his face. That was enough for him today. So maybe it can be enough for us, too. Why don't we put Clarence Reese on the back burner until tomorrow so you can enjoy tonight? Every cop on duty in this city is out there looking for him, so why don't you let it go for tonight? You've worked so hard to get to this day. Don't allow anyone to make it less, especially someone who could do what that guy did to his family."

Begrudgingly, Sam looked up at him. "You're good."

His face lifted into the sexy grin that made her bones go weak. "I try."

"You're good for me."

"I want to be." He pressed his lips to hers and sucked the oxygen right out of her lungs with a soul-stirring, mind-altering kiss that cleared her brain of every thought except the urge to tear the clothes off his body.

"I know you're bummed about what I told you earlier, about moving in," she said when they came up for air.

Pressing another kiss to her lips, he said, "I'll be there whenever you're ready to join me."

"It's not you. I hope you know that. It's just that I lived with a man, for four years I *slept* with a man who was capable of trying to blow up both of us, but I never saw that in him. I'm a cop, for Christ's sake, and not once did I imagine he had that in him."

"Sam—"

"I know you're going to say that has nothing to do with you and me, with us."

"It doesn't."

"It *does*, Nick. My ex-husband tried to *murder* us. How do I just put that behind me like it never happened and move in with you? There must be something wrong with me that I didn't see—"

Again, he kissed the words right off her lips. "There's *nothing* wrong with you. You were a victim. We both were. He's headed for prison, Sam. There's no sense in you going with him."

"I need some time to process it all. I need to be sure I've

put the pieces back where they belong before I take the next step with you."

"That's fair enough."

Feeling madly vulnerable, she glanced up to find his hazel eyes hot with emotion and desire. She still had trouble believing that was all for her. "You don't mind waiting?"

"I'd wait forever for you. And in the meantime, I'll be three doors up the street anytime you want to make a late-night booty call."

She laughed. "That'll probably be most nights."

"So you just want me for my body. I see how it is."

She slid her hands under his sweater and up to cup well-defined pectorals. "What are you doing right now, Senator?" she asked with a coy smile.

His jaw tightened with tension as he removed her hands from under his sweater. "Taking you to our party."

"Damn."

He leaned in to catch her earlobe between his teeth. "But later we'll be having our own *private* New Year's party."

Sam shivered with anticipation and marveled at how he had managed to put her in the mood to celebrate. This love stuff definitely came with some major benefits.

"*This* is your idea of a *small* party?" Sam asked an hour later as she took in the mobbed K Street lounge Nick had reserved for the occasion. When she suggested a beer and pizza party at O'Leary's—her favorite cop bar—he'd turned up his senatorial nose, so she'd left it to him to orchestrate this joint celebration.

"I can't help it if you have a hundred cop friends."

"I don't even know most of these people."

"Like who?"

"Her." She pointed to a voluptuous brunette flirting shamelessly with Freddie. "An old girlfriend of yours?"

"Hardly. That's Ginger, one of the legislative aides in my office."

"*Ginger* needs to get her filthy hands off my partner," Sam said, even though she was relieved to see Freddie smiling again after the gruesome day he'd put in.

"I think we've got a bigger problem over there."

Sam's head whipped around. "Where?"

Nick pointed to one of the cozy booths where his chief of staff, Christina Billings, was having an intimate conversation with Detective Tommy "Gonzo" Gonzales.

"Get her off him!"

"Why?" Nick asked, amused. "They're both consenting adults."

"She doesn't like me."

"So she can't talk to your friend?"

"He's not just my friend. He's my subordinate now. She'll turn him against me."

"Honestly, Samantha." Nick led her to the dance floor. "The twists and turns of your mind are a constant source of fascination to me."

"Glad I'm available to entertain you," she grumbled.

"You do." He brought his lips down on hers. "Endlessly."

"Get a room, you two," Sam's sister Tracy said as she danced up next to them with her husband, Mike.

Sam tried to put some space between herself and Nick, but he just tightened his hold on her.

"Great party," Mike said.

"Thanks," Nick replied. "Did your dad get something to eat?"

"Celia's on it," Tracy said. "He's having a great time visiting with all his cop buddies."

They glanced over to find Skip with Celia, Chief Farnsworth, Deputy Chief Conklin and their spouses, as well as

Detective Captain Malone and some of the other department captains.

"He's in his glory," Sam said to her sister.

"It's been a good day for him," Tracy said.

"Yes." Sam thought of Clarence Reese and wished she could share the possibility with her sister, but didn't want to disappoint her, either.

"The O'Connors just got here," Nick said, his eyes on the door. "We need to go say hello." To Mike and Tracy, he added, "You guys have a good time."

"We're kid-free," Tracy said, beaming at her husband. "We're already having a good time, and it's only going to get better."

"I like her," Mike said with a lascivious grin. "I like her *so* much."

Laughing, Nick and Sam left the happy couple on the dance floor.

"They're awfully cute together," Nick said.

"They always have been. I've been envious of how easy they make it look."

He squeezed her shoulder and leaned in to kiss her cheek. "No need to be envious anymore. We'll show them easy."

Heartened by Nick's words, Sam tried not to feel awkward as Senator and Mrs. O'Connor greeted her with warm hugs. Nick thought of them as his adopted family, and Sam knew she needed to get over the resentment she harbored from when they'd lied to her during the investigation into their son's murder. Sam had uncovered John's illegitimate twenty-year-old son who'd been kept hidden from the public in deference to the senior Senator O'Connor's political career and reputation. That son, his mother and that secret turned out to be a motive for murder.

"What a lovely party," Laine O'Connor said to Nick.

"I'm glad you could come," Nick said.

"Oh, we wouldn't miss it. Royce and Lizbeth are right behind us," she said, referring to her son-in-law and daughter. Laine reached for Nick's hand. "And what you're doing for Terry. I just can't thank you enough. *We* can't thank you enough."

"It was a generous move, Senator," Graham added gruffly. "He won't let you down."

"Of course he won't."

"Julian sends his regrets," Graham said. "He'd hoped to be here, but his meeting at the White House ran late."

"I'm sure they've got a *lot* to talk about."

"Gonna be a battle royal," Graham said with a gleeful grin. "The Republicans will flip their lids—especially Stenhouse." Graham O'Connor's bitter relationship with Senate Minority Leader William Stenhouse went back decades, and for a brief time, he, too, had been on Sam's short list of suspects in John's murder.

"Good thing we don't need 'em," Nick said with a grin of his own.

Graham rubbed his hands together. "I love being in the majority."

Sam found his use of the present tense interesting. You could take the man out of the Senate…

"Hopefully, he can find a free night for dinner next week," Nick said. "I want to show you all my new place in the city."

Sam wondered if he had lost his mind. A dinner party for a potential Supreme Court justice at the place he hadn't even moved into yet? Next week? Right. But even as she thought it, she knew he would pull it off the same way he had pulled off their party—effortlessly.

"Sounds like a plan," Graham said.

"I can't wait to see your new house, Nick," Laine said. "I'm sorry. I should call you Senator now."

"You should call me Nick." He kissed her cheek. "Why don't you grab a drink, have something to eat and we'll catch up to you in a bit?"

"Excellent," Graham said, putting his arm around his wife to lead her to the bar.

"They seem better," Nick said to Sam when they were alone.

"What did you do for Terry?"

Nick had his eyes—and obviously his mind—on the O'Connors. "What?"

"Terry. What did you do?"

"I offered him the deputy chief of staff job."

"*What?* Why?"

"Because he knows his stuff, and he's wasting away in that bullshit lobby job. He's also John's brother. It felt like the right thing to do."

"But he hates me, too! Your two most senior staffers hate me!"

"I've made it very clear to both of them that if they can't treat you with courtesy and respect they'll be looking for new jobs."

"You did?" Sam squeaked, her heart pounding in her chest. The emotion could hit hard when she least expected it.

"They can be replaced. You can't."

"You have a way with words, Senator," she said with a sigh. "You really do."

CHAPTER 5

At two minutes to midnight, Nick couldn't find Sam and panic was setting in. A heartbeat away from asking the DJ to page her, he spotted her tucked into a corner, checking text messages on her phone.

Pushing his way through the crowd, he took the phone, stuffed it into his back pocket, reached for her hand and tugged her up.

She resisted. "Hey! What're you doing?"

"Come," he said, leading her out of the room to a stairway.

"Where are we going? Isn't it almost midnight?"

"Yep." Nick charged up the stairs, almost dragging her along with him. At the top of the darkened stairwell, he pushed open the door to the roof. Their city stretched out before them. Above, the clear sky twinkled with stars.

"Oh, *wow,* Nick," she said breathlessly. "Oh, look at this!" She spun on her heel to get the full view of the Capitol, White House and monuments at the far end of the Mall.

Nick drew her into his arms. "You like?"

"Totally. This is amazing!"

"Are you cold?"

"No," she said, gazing up at the stars.

From the sidewalk below, they heard revelers counting down the final ten seconds of the year.

He brought his hands up to frame her face. "I love you. This year, next year, every year."

She reached for him, and as fireworks burst into the sky above them, she kissed him softly, thoroughly, deeply. "I love you, too. Thank you for the best New Year's ever."

"The first of many." He kissed both her cheeks. "I promise."

"Can we do this every year?" Her eyes brimmed with excitement, the way he liked them best. "Can we come back to this very spot to ring in every New Year?"

"It's a date," he said, his throat tight with emotion. He'd had no idea, no idea at all, that it was possible to love someone this much. "Next time, I'll remember the champagne."

"We don't need it."

Even though it was cold, even though their breath came out in puffy clouds, they stayed on the roof to watch the entire fireworks display. Nick kept his arms tight around her from behind, immersed in the jasmine and vanilla fragrance he would recognize anywhere as hers.

"I love the way the colors in the fireworks reflect on the monuments," she said, her hands covering his at her waist.

"Mmm, me, too."

The fireworks ended with a booming finale of color and sound.

Sam sighed. "That was fabulous." She turned to him. "Thank you so much."

"I have a theory."

Her mouth quirked with amusement. "And what's that?"

Unable to resist, he touched his lips to hers. "That how you spend the first minutes of the New Year is how you'll spend the year itself." Adding a light brush of his tongue over her bottom lip, he leaned into the kiss when her arms curled around his neck. The tangle of teeth and tongues took his breath away. Reaching down, he cupped her ass and lifted her right off her feet. She surprised him when she wrapped her long legs around his waist.

"I take it you like my theory," he said when he had no choice but to come up for air. He wanted her desperately, as if he had gone without for years rather than hours.

"It's a great theory—and a great way to spend a year." Grinning, she pressed against his erection. "But I'd hate for my favorite new senator to be caught in such a *compromising* position on his first day in office."

Reluctantly, he let her slide back down. "Let's get the hell out of here."

"We can't leave our own party."

"No one will notice. I guarantee it."

Nick surprised her when he directed the cab to her father's Capitol Hill neighborhood. After the way he'd sprinted her out of the party, she assumed he wanted to be alone with her at his place in Arlington.

"We're going to my dad's?" she asked.

"Nope."

"Then where?"

"You'll see."

She eyed him suspiciously. "What are you up to?"

"Nothing," he said with a smile that said her hunch was dead on.

"Tell me!"

"Patience, Samantha."

"Not my best quality."

"*No,* really?"

She tried pouting, cajoling and even a few dirty tricks, but nothing worked. Except for a couple of heated make-out sessions, he kept his mouth shut until they pulled up to the house he had bought on Ninth Street. "What're we doing here?"

He paid the cabbie and reached for her hand. "Come on, I'll show you."

Puzzled, Sam followed him to the house three doors up the street from her dad's. "Do you even own this place yet?" she asked as he used a key in the lock.

"Not yet, but the owners didn't mind me moving in a few things early."

"What things?"

"God, you're such a pain in the ass!"

"Thank you."

He turned, kissed her nose and took her coat. "You're the only woman I know who would take that as a compliment."

"That's why you love me."

Laughing, he led her into the kitchen. "What do you think?"

"*Oh,*" she said, taking in the large, stylish kitchen where everything was brand-new. "I knew they were renovating this place, but I never imagined this." She ran a hand over the stone countertop. The cabinets were dark wood, the appliances sleek stainless steel. Above the bar that piggybacked the kitchen and living room, teardrop lights hung from the ceiling. "I love it."

"I hoped you would."

She stepped into the living room and gasped at the size of it. At the far end, a marble mantel framed a large fireplace. "What the heck?"

"I take it you didn't know he bought the place next door and knocked out the walls."

"I had no idea! This place is huge! What're you going to do with all this space?"

He shrugged. "Maybe raise a bunch of kids with you?"

Her heart stopped at the mention of kids. He knew she couldn't have them but had made it clear he didn't care and that they'd adopt if and when the time came.

"Sam? Are you all right?"

"Sure," she said, shaking it off. "Show me the rest."

Besides the kitchen and living room, the first floor of the double-sized townhouse boasted an enormous dining room as well as a full bathroom. The floors were a light wood and recently refinished. The second floor had four bedrooms and two more bathrooms.

"I thought for now we could use that one for a guest room, that one for an office and maybe a gym in there," he said of the extra bedrooms.

"You've got it all figured out."

"When I first looked at it, I could see us here together. That's why I bought it."

"It's a really nice place," she conceded. "I've certainly never lived anywhere nicer."

"Neither have I. Come check this out." He led her to the master bedroom where a new king-size bed with an elaborate wrought-iron head- and footboard was the only furniture in the room.

Startled, Sam said, "You bought a bed already?"

"Yep." He sat on the bed and kicked off his shoes. "I wanted to stay here tonight."

"And they just let you truck a bed in here?"

"They, um, they think it's cool that they're selling to a senator."

Seeing him flustered made Sam laugh. "Already taking full advantage, are you?"

"I wouldn't say that—exactly. Take a look at the closet. I figured you'd like that."

"Nice way to change the subject." Sam stepped into the walk-in closet and took a good look at the decent-sized space, deciding that about half her clothes would fit in there.

"Isn't it great?" he asked with a smile.

"Where would you keep your stuff?"

His smile faded. "I figured we'd share it."

"Um, sure. Okay."

"You don't have *that* many shoes."

"What I have at my dad's is about one-tenth of the total. The rest are in storage."

His mouth dropped open in shock. "Are you *serious?*"

"I never joke about shoes."

Scratching at the stubble on his chin, he studied her. "Well, I guess we can put the gym on the third floor and build you a big old closet in one of the extra bedrooms."

She sat down next to him on the bed. "You'd do that for me?"

"Sure, I would. Besides, it's probably better if we don't share a closet. You're not quite as, um, neat as I am."

"Anal you mean."

"I prefer neat."

Laughing, she said, "I'm sure you do." She kissed him and rested her head on his shoulder. "It's a great place."

"I'm glad—and relieved—that you think so. As I was buying it without telling you, I told myself I was probably making a huge mistake."

"It wasn't a mistake. A place like this wouldn't have lasted long on the market."

"That's what the Realtor said, too." He rubbed her back and nuzzled her neck. "I want you here with me, Sam." With his other hand, he produced a key.

Touched, she took it from him and slid it into her back

pocket. "I promise I'll be here so much you'll feel like I live here."

"That's not the same."

"Can it be enough for now?"

"I guess I'll have to settle for what I can get," he said with a dramatic sigh that was offset by the twinkle in his eye.

"I hate to disappoint you."

He brought her hand to his lips. "You're not." Standing up, he tugged her along with him. "There're two more things I want to show you." In the master bathroom, he pointed out the huge Jacuzzi tub.

"Oh, man, *seriously?*"

"Have you got something against Jacuzzis?"

"I *love* them. I've always wanted one in my house." Stomping her foot, she added, "This is so not fair!"

"All this could be yours."

She scowled. "What's the other thing?"

He pointed back the way they'd come. In the bedroom, he went to the fireplace and flipped a switch under the mantel to start the gas fire.

Sam sighed. "So not fair."

"Let me guess—you've always wanted a fireplace in your bedroom, too?"

She nodded, reached for the pillows and throw blanket on the bed and brought them over to the carpet in front of the fire.

"What're we doing?" he asked as he let her draw him down next to her.

"Camping."

"So I could've skipped the bed?"

Tugging the sweater up and over his head, she tossed it aside. "Uh-huh." She urged him onto his back and dropped kisses on his chest in a trail to his belly.

Nick sucked in a sharp deep breath and combed his fingers through her hair. "Am I getting this special treatment because I have a Jacuzzi?"

"No," she said, adding her tongue to the mix.

"Then why?" He gasped when she unzipped his jeans and dragged a finger over his straining erection.

She looked up at him with a mischievous expression on her face. "I've always wanted to screw a senator." Taking him into her mouth, she kept her movements slow and precise.

His laughter faded into a groan. *"Sam."*

"What?" She swirled her tongue, lapping at him like a hungry cat.

Sighing, he sank back into the pillow. "God, you're good at that."

She cracked up. "Can I put it on my resume?"

Shaking his head, he said, "That's only for me." He reached for her and brought her up to rest on top of him. "Kiss me."

Her lips fused to his, she broke the connection only to let him remove her sweater. Helping him get rid of the rest of their clothes, she moved quickly, craving the feel of his skin against hers, the soft brush of his chest hair, the firm muscles, his scent. Everything about him appealed to her—and scared her. To love like this was to risk so much, things she'd sworn to never risk again after her disastrous marriage.

"What?" he asked, his lips coasting over hers.

"I was just thinking that if this is how we're going to spend it, I'm going to like this year."

"That's not what you were thinking," he said, reversing their positions so he was on top. He kissed her softly, his eyes intent on hers, letting her know she could hide nothing from him.

"I was thinking how much I love you and how sad I'd be if—"

"Don't say it." He slid into her. "Don't think it. It's not going to happen."

Sam arched her back to take him in. *"Nick."*

"What, babe?" he asked, his lips soft against her jaw.

"Faster."

"Not tonight."

"Why?"

"I read in the paper today," he said close to her ear, his hips moving with aching slowness, "that sex therapists say intercourse should last between three and thirteen minutes."

How can he talk right now? she wondered. *I'm having trouble breathing!*

"Since we usually work the lower end of the spectrum," he continued, "I thought we'd see what the other side is like."

Burning up from the inside out, she gripped a fistful of his silky brown hair and wrapped her legs around him. Thirteen minutes? She'd be dead in five. But nothing she did, nothing she tried, got him to move any faster.

His mouth descended on hers, his tongue sweeping into her mouth as he cupped her breast. Suddenly, he withdrew from her and kissed a path to her nipple.

Sam could have wept from the loss and the sweet torture of his kisses even as she felt the now-familiar signs of impending climax. It happened so easily with him that she'd almost forgotten how unattainable it had been in past relationships.

His lips were on her belly, his tongue laying a trail to her burning center.

The rosy glow of the fire burnished his skin. Just looking at him took her breath away, but watching him watch her as he made slow love to her was about the sexiest thing she'd ever seen. She reached for him.

He shook his head. "Not yet." His broad shoulders forced her legs farther apart as he settled between them. Touching his tongue to her, he stayed with the slow theme, teasing her until her legs quivered and her heart raced. Leaving her clinging to the precipice, he kissed his way back up to her lips, pushed into her and sent her over the edge with a sharp cry of release that took him with her.

With his lips pressed to her neck, he whispered, "Happy New Year."

CHAPTER 6

While Nick spent New Year's Day packing up his Arlington house, Sam sat hunched over her laptop scrolling through every scrap of information she could find on Clarence Reese. In the meantime, Gonzo and Arnold were leading the manhunt for him on the streets. Through her research, Sam learned he'd grown up blocks away from her Ninth Street childhood home and wondered if perhaps he'd had a neighborhood altercation with her father. A call to Tracy, who was just a year older than Clarence, yielded nothing useful since she had no recollection of being in school with anyone with that name.

By noon, Sam was ready to tear her hair out. The connection had to be there. It *had* to be. Her stomach rumbled, and she decided to venture downstairs on a fishing expedition. She found her father sitting at the kitchen table scanning the reading device propped in front of his wheelchair. Bending to kiss his cheek, she said, "How's it going?"

"All right. What've you been up to all morning?"

"Just catching up on some paperwork."

"Nice party last night."

"That was all Nick."

"No kidding, really?"

His sarcastic eye roll amused her. "Would've been beer at O'Leary's if I'd gotten my way."

"Gives you a run for your money, that boy. I like that about him."

Anxious to change the subject, she nodded to the reader. "What's that?"

"The *Post*."

"What're they saying about the DD yesterday?" she asked in what she hoped was a nonchalant tone as she opened a diet cola and joined him at the table.

"Most of what you already know. They interviewed some neighbors and friends who're shocked. Never would've suspected he'd be capable. The usual. The kids and the wife were well liked, but he kept to himself. Apparently, he just got laid off."

"Something about his name is familiar to me." Sam watched her father intently. "Ring any bells with you?"

"Nope."

She hoped the disappointment didn't show on her face. "I read that he grew up on Seventh."

"I saw that. Who's running the investigation?"

Nothing, Sam thought with dejection. If Skip Holland had ever met Clarence Reese, he didn't remember it. "Gonzo and Arnold."

"Losing his job could've triggered something."

"Maybe. Judging by the condition of the house, things had been rough for some time. But the job thing might've been the final straw."

"Nice article about Nick's swearing in if you want to check it out. The *Post* did a poll in Virginia yesterday, and more than eighty percent of those surveyed approved of the governor choosing him to finish out O'Connor's term. That's a hell of an approval rating to start with."

Sam reached for the front page and almost choked on her soda when she saw the huge picture of her holding the Bible as Nick took the oath of office. "Oh, my *God!* You could've warned me!"

"And miss that reaction? No way."

The caption read, "Metro Police Lieutenant Sam Holland holds the Bible as Chief Justice Byron Riley administers the oath of office to Nicholas Cappuano. A Democrat from Virginia, Cappuano will complete the last year of recently murdered Senator John O'Connor's term. The romance between Cappuano and Holland has captured the attention of the entire capitol region over the last few weeks."

Skip laughed. "It's quite a picture. You look petrified."

Sam dropped her head to the table. "*Why* do they care about us so much? *Why?*"

"You're young and attractive, you have important jobs and people love a good romance."

"Why can't they just mind their own business?"

"Not gonna happen, honey. It's probably going to get worse before they lose interest—*if* they lose interest."

"*Great.*"

Skip's nurse and fiancée Celia emerged from the basement carrying a laundry basket. "Hey, Sam, did you see the paper? What a wonderful picture of you and Nick!"

Skip smiled as Sam scowled.

"Yes, it's *wonderful*," Sam said.

"Sam's not loving her moment in the spotlight," Skip said.

"I think it's so sweet," Celia said with a dreamy expression. "You two are just *adorable* together."

As Skip chortled with laughter, Sam banged her forehead against the table.

★ ★ ★

Detective Freddie Cruz paced the sidewalk in front of Total Fitness on Sixteenth Street. On this first day of the New Year, he was all about resolutions and none of them involved spending more time at the gym. No, this was the year he was finally going to get laid. No matter what it took, no matter what he had to do, no matter what personal ideals he had to sacrifice, he was going to have sex.

Raised a devout Christian by a single mother, he'd done his best for twenty-nine long years to make his mother proud by saving himself for marriage. But since he didn't even have a girlfriend, let alone a potential wife, and with rampaging hormones making his life a living hell, he had decided to give in.

Nick's aide Ginger had practically thrown herself at him at the party last night, but Freddie wasn't interested in her.

Since he and Sam interviewed personal trainer Elin Svendsen during the O'Connor investigation, he found himself fantasizing about her day and night. The way she'd been so free about her sexuality and talked so openly about the kinky sex she'd had with the dead senator. She was all Freddie could think about. She was the one he wanted.

That was why he was lurking outside Total Fitness, wearing one of his trademark trench coats while trying to work up the nerve to step inside to inquire about personal training. She didn't need to know he was interested in personal training of a different sort. At least not right away.

"Detective Cruz?"

Startled, he looked up, and there she was. Tall, blonde—so blonde her eyebrows were almost white—she had dark blue eyes and a smile right out of a toothpaste commercial. Carrying a tray containing four coffees and wearing a light blue down vest and black yoga pants, it was all Freddie could do to keep from drooling. She was even sexier than he remembered—and he remembered every excruciating detail of the night he'd spent protecting her in a hotel room while Thomas O'Connor hunted down his father's ex-girlfriends.

"I thought that was you," she said. "How are you?"

"I'm, um, fine. And you?"

"Crazy today. It's the busiest day of the year for us—all the resolutions."

"Right," Freddie said, remembering his own resolutions.

"Are you working on a case?"

"Me?" *No, idiot,* Freddie thought, *that other guy she's talking to.* "Not today. I was just in the neighborhood and thinking about resolutions."

She smiled.

He went hard as a stone and was thankful for the long coat.

"Do you want to come in? I could show you around and tell you about our program."

"Um, sure, that sounds good." He wondered if she'd think it strange if he kept his coat on inside.

After spending Sunday helping Nick finish packing up his place in Arlington, Sam woke up Monday morning with a stomachache. She lay still in Nick's big new bed and tried to breathe her way through pain that had become predictable. Anytime she was nervous or stressed out, she could count on her stomach to let her know. And judging by the particularly sharp pain, she was some kind of nervous.

Today she would officially take command of the HQ detectives. She had wanted the job for as long as she'd been a detective, but was nervous about all the responsibility that would come with overseeing forty detectives, hundreds of cases each year and all the accompanying personnel matters.

Another stabbing pain made her whimper.

Nick looped an arm around her. "What?"

"Stomach."

"That's it. I'm making you an appointment."

"I'll do it. Today."

"Promise?"

Sam bit her lip and nodded as another sharp pain took her breath away.

"Come here." Arranging her head on his shoulder, he rubbed her back and spoke softly to her.

Sam couldn't help but relax into his embrace. Surrounded by the fragrance of soap and sporty deodorant, the scent of Nick, she focused on breathing her way through it. "Are you nervous?" she asked. "About today?"

"Nah. We're both going to work in the same place with the same people."

"Except we're the bosses now."

"Is that going to change you?"

"I'm not planning to let it," she said.

"Neither am I. So everything will be just fine. Be yourself, be fair and you can't lose. The other detectives love you. They'd do anything for you, and they know you'd do anything for them."

"Some people in the department think I got this promotion because of my father and his connections."

"Which you know isn't true."

Sam swallowed hard and glanced up at him. "It kind of is."

His eyebrows narrowed with confusion. "What do you mean?"

"I had trouble with the exam. I flunked it the first two times—because of the dyslexia. I just barely passed this time."

"But you *did* pass."

"My dad told Farnsworth about the dyslexia. He used his discretion as chief to authorize my promotion. If that ever gets out, people will scream favoritism."

"Is the exam the only qualifying factor?"

"No, there's more to it than that—experience, training, interviews, the graduate degree I worked my ass off to get. It all counts."

"Then it sounds to me as if Farnsworth promoted the most worthy candidate."

Sam smiled and realized her stomach no longer hurt. "And you're not the slightest bit biased."

"Not one bit," he said, tipping her chin up to receive his kiss. "You're going to be the best lieutenant that department has ever had. I have no doubt."

She needed to get up and get moving but couldn't seem to bring herself to leave the warmth of his embrace. "Thanks."

"Anytime." He shifted so he was on top of her.

"What's this?" she asked with a coy smile.

"Just making sure you get a good breakfast on your first day," he said, entering her.

Sam laughed even as she gasped from the impact. "We don't have time…"

"Then we'd better be quick."

"Mmm," she said as she sighed. "I love quick."

CHAPTER 7

Emerging from Nick's house forty-five minutes later, they were blinded by camera flashes.

"What the hell?" Sam muttered, covering her eyes.

With his hand on her elbow, Nick guided her down the stairs. "Let us through," he said in a tone full of controlled fury as he pushed his way through the half-dozen photographers. "Goddamn it," he whispered.

Not wanting to give the photographers any more fodder, Sam tried to shake off his hand, but he just held on tighter.

They reached her car, and Nick took her keys to unlock it. As more flashes exploded around them, she looked up at him with a forced smile. "This is fun."

His face was set in an unreadable expression. "I'll call you. Good luck today."

"You, too." Without the kiss she would've liked to have had, Sam got into the car, and he closed the door. She watched him until he was safely inside his black BMW. Her cell phone rang. "Holland," she said without checking the caller ID.

"Are you okay?" Nick asked.

"Fabulous. You?"

"Terrific," he said with a laugh. "I'm sorry."

"For what?"

"All this attention. It'll die down. Eventually."

"I don't think it's going to."

"You sound pissed," he said.

"I'm more resigned than pissed."

"When are you going to mention that you told me so?"

"I'm saving that for when I *really* need it," she joked. The combination of his sexy voice and their teasing banter helped to restore her good mood.

"I'll look forward to that," he said. "See you later?"

"Yes, you will. Love you."

"Love you, too, babe. Be careful today."

"I always am."

Sam navigated her way through rush-hour traffic and arrived at the public safety building fifteen minutes later. Her good mood once again dissipated when she found Lieutenant Stahl waiting for her in the office that used to be his.

"I need to call maintenance." She flipped on the lights and hung her coat on a hook behind the door. "The rat traps they set in here clearly aren't working."

"You think you're so funny, don't you?"

The revolting wiggle of his double chin made her want to puke.

"Things not working out for you in the rat squad?" she asked, referring to his new post in the department's Internal Affairs Bureau.

"Actually, I'm settling right in." He bit a chunk of skin off his cuticle and spit it onto the floor.

Sam made a mental note to stay away from that corner of the office until it was fumigated.

"And you're my first order of business."

"I'm flattered."

His beady eyes narrowed. "You won't be so mouthy when your sordid affair with a witness gets you busted down to patrol."

She leaned on her desk to look him in the eye. "Three words, Lieutenant—Bring. It. On."

Fuming, he hauled his portly ass out of the chair. "Your wish is my command." He slapped a piece of paper on her desk. "Administrative hearing next week. Be there, and be ready to explain yourself."

"I'll look forward to it," she said, taking a shallow breath to short-circuit the pain grinding in her belly.

"Don't think your precious daddy can get you out of this one, Lieutenant." He stopped at the door and turned to leave her with a greasy smile. "And you'd better enjoy that title while you can. By the time I'm through with you, you'll be thankful for a night security job at a parking garage."

Sam let him have the last word because she couldn't have spoken if she had to. The moment she was alone she lowered herself into her chair and fought to breathe through the pain. This was *not* how she wanted to start her first day.

Freddie came to the door. "Getting settled, Lieutenant?" He took a closer look at her. "What's wrong?"

Sam made a huge effort to shake off the pain and anger. "Nothing. How are you? Good holiday?"

He stepped into the room and closed the door behind him. "You're pale as a ghost. What gives?"

She handed him the paper Stahl had left with her.

As Freddie glanced at it, his brows furrowed. "A summons to an IAB hearing? What the hell?"

"Nick."

"What about him?"

"Stahl's got Internal Affairs investigating me for hooking up with him in the middle of the O'Connor investigation."

"Are you serious? Without Nick's help we'd *still* be looking for O'Connor's killer."

"He was the one who found O'Connor dead, so technically I shagged a witness. Stahl's going to find a way to screw *me* for that."

"You don't have anything to worry about. Farnsworth and Malone will back you."

"They'll be forced to confirm that I became involved with Nick during the investigation." She ran her fingers over the hair she'd corralled into a clip for work. "Goddamned Peter." Just the thought of her ex-husband made her stomach turn, but with disgust rather than pain. In a jealous rage, he'd planted crude bombs on her car and Nick's. When her car had exploded and injured them both, it also blew the lid off their secret relationship. "This is all his fault. Without him dicking with me, no one would've known about me and Nick until Thomas O'Connor was locked up and we were ready for them to know."

"It'll be fine, Sam. Stahl's got a beef with them giving you his command. That's all this is, and everyone will see right through it."

"I hope you're right," she said with zero confidence that he was. "Do me a favor and don't say anything about this to Nick or my dad."

"You aren't going to tell Nick?" Freddie asked, incredulous.

"Not if I can avoid it. He's got enough on his plate right now, and this'll just upset him."

"Won't he be more upset when he finds out you kept it from him?"

Sam's scowl answered for her. She'd handle this her way, and if Nick didn't like it, that was too damned bad. She wasn't about to start telling him how to run his career. "Are Gonzo and Arnold here yet?"

"They caught a sexual assault first thing. They're at the George Washington E.R. taking a statement from the victim."

"Send them in the minute they get here. I want to know what they've got on Clarence Reese so far. I worked his name into conversation with my dad and got zilch. If he had contact with Reese, he doesn't remember it."

"Frustrating."

"To say the least. I just keep asking myself—why would Reese have all that stuff about the shooting if he wasn't involved somehow? Let's see what Gonzo and Arnold found out, and then we'll hit it ourselves this afternoon. I want to talk to Reese's mother and brother."

"You're the boss, L.T."

"It's going to be kind of weird around here until I figure things out. I'd understand if you wanted to partner with someone else—"

He held up his hand to stop her. "I'm all set with the partner I have."

"I'm planning to work some second and third shifts in the next few weeks to touch base with everyone. You don't want to do that."

"I'll work when my partner works."

She eyed him suspiciously. "Are you sucking up?"

"Always."

Taking another long look at him, she sized him up. "What's with you? You're all spiffed up today."

"Nothing," he said, but he blushed.

Sam stood up and walked around the desk for a closer look. Standing almost eye to eye with him, she turned on her most intimidating expression. "Tell me the truth—did you hook up with that Ginger chick from Nick's office?"

"No!"

Sniffing, she realized he was wearing cologne. "Something's up."

"I don't know what you're talking about." He stepped back from her. "Just because you're Little Miss Romance these days doesn't mean the rest of us are, too."

She raised an eyebrow. "Who said anything about romance?"

"I've got work to do," he huffed, his GQ-handsome face turning red again.

Oh, yes, something was *definitely* up.

"Let me know when you're ready to head out," he said as he beat feet to the safety of his cubicle in the detectives' pit.

"You'll be the first to know."

She watched him go, noting the pressed khakis and the untucked striped dress shirt that were wildly out of character for her denim-wearing, T-shirt–clad partner. *Does my little boy have a girlfriend?* Scratching at her chin, she decided to keep a very close eye on young Freddie.

Returning to her desk, she read and re-read the IAB summons. With a sigh, she put her aching head down on folded arms.

"I guess that answers my question about how your first day is going."

Jerking her head up, she found Captain Malone standing in her doorway. Her mentor was almost as tall as Nick with broad shoulders and gray hair. His warm brown eyes crinkled with mirth. Today he wore a crisp white uniform shirt and dark pants. His gold shield was pinned to his chest, his service weapon holstered to his hip.

"Is it time to go home yet?"

"Not even lunchtime, I'm afraid."

She rested her head against the back of the desk chair. "I've never understood the expression 'be careful what you wish for' until today."

He laughed.

"I may not be cut out for this," she confessed. "Not even an hour in the office and I'm already jonesing for the streets."

"No reason you can't do both."

She shot him a skeptical look.

"You're the *boss,* Lieutenant. Set things up the way they best suit you. Delegate, delegate, delegate."

Sam pondered that advice. "I'll go out of my mind if I can't work some cases."

He shrugged. "So pick and choose what you want."

For the first time since she arrived, Sam had reason to smile.

"It's called *command,* Lieutenant. Take command."

"Stahl did all his own admin," she reminded him.

"Stahl sucked, his people hated him and his commanders did, too. Don't take your cues from him. Pave your own path. Just don't let your shit roll uphill to me, and we'll be fine."

She reached for the paper Stahl had left, handed it to the captain and watched his mouth tighten with displeasure.

"Since I'm sure you won't forget what this says, do you mind if I take it to show the chief?"

"Be my guest."

"Try not to worry. Stuff like this tends to blow over more often than not."

"He's got a beef with how I ended up here," she said, gesturing to the office. "He can't prove the promotion was bogus, so he's going after me with the gift-wrapped package I handed him during O'Connor."

"Nick was never a suspect," Malone reminded her. "Worst possible outcome is a disciplinary letter in your jacket."

"It's still a slap."

"Put it out of your mind for now. I'll do what I can on my end."

"Thanks."

"Hope your day improves," Malone said with an encouraging smile as he left her to the piles of paper Stahl had bequeathed to her.

Nick's first order of business was a meeting with Christina and Trevor.

"We need to talk about a deputy," Christina said, pulling a sheet of paper from her binder. "Here're a few people to consider."

Nick scanned the list of staffers. "I've already taken care of that."

Startled, Christina looked up at him. "Who?"

"Terry O'Connor."

She stared at him. "You're kidding, right?"

"Nope."

Her face went slack with shock. "But, I don't understand. Why?"

"Because he was groomed his whole life to hold this office, and I guarantee he'll bring more to the table than anyone on that impressive list of yours."

"This is you being loyal to the O'Connors, isn't it?"

Nick suppressed the burst of anger that shot through him. "This is me doing what I want to do, Christina."

"He's got a lot of baggage," Trevor observed.

"Luckily we're not running for anything," Nick said. "What's next?"

They exchanged glances.

"What?"

Trevor tugged a paper from his pile and held it up for Nick to see.

"Son of a bitch," Nick muttered as he got a look at a print-out of the photos taken that morning outside his house. "They're already online?"

"On the *Post* site and the *Star*'s."

"Great," he said, imagining Sam's reaction to the suggestive photos.

"We've got some new polling data in, too," Trevor said with a nervous look at Christina. "Your approval rating in the Commonwealth is hovering right around seventy-eight percent. Unfortunately, the other twenty-two percent tend to be in the conservative, family-values column, and they don't approve of this." He referred to the picture.

"Well, that's too bad." Nick's jaw felt tight with tension. "Again, I'll remind you that I'm not running for anything."

"No, but that moral minority can make the next year awfully unpleasant for us," Trevor said.

"It'll be a distraction, Nick, er, I mean, Senator," Christina said. "Sorry."

"This subject is off-limits, people," Nick said.

"You could take care of the whole thing," Trevor said hesitantly, "if you, you know, married her."

"I can't even get her to officially move in with me. She's not ready for that, and she's certainly not ready for the *M* word. Not after what she just went through with her ex-husband."

"I know you don't want to hear this, Senator," Trevor said, "but your relationship with her is going to pull the focus off the issues. All I'm saying is if you could convince her to marry you, it'd take the wind out of the media's sails. Even an engagement would make things a lot easier."

"He's right," Christina added. "Once the relationship is legitimate, it loses its appeal."

"Are you guys finished analyzing my personal life?" Nick asked.

They had the good grace to at least squirm a little.

He leaned forward to make sure he had their full attention. "The relationship is *already* legitimate, and I couldn't care less what anyone thinks of it. Is that clear?"

"We get it," Christina said. "All we're asking is that you think about what Trevor said. If you're heading toward marriage, sooner would be better than later."

"You've met Sam," Nick said, amused by the ridiculous conversation. "How do you think she'd take the idea of marriage for political expediency?"

"If I were to guess," Christina said, "I'd say not well."

"Precisely. So can we please drop this and move on to what we're here for?"

Clearing her throat, Christina consulted her notes. "You're set to meet with Senator Martin on the phone at ten to discuss getting O'Connor-Martin back on the floor after the recess. Also, Senator Cook's office called, and he'd like to have lunch with you today if you're free."

"That's fine," Nick said, anxious to meet with the senior senator from Virginia, a fellow Democrat, as soon as possible.

"Finally, we have studio time booked this evening so you can record the welcome message they play in the Virginia airports."

"I remember John doing that years ago," Nick said, smiling at the memory of John fumbling through about fifty takes to get the one-minute message nailed. The pain of his loss resurfaced with surprising ferocity, reminding Nick of how he had gotten there. He took a deep breath and forced himself to focus. "Anything else?"

"You've had a slew of interview requests," Trevor said, handing him a two-page list of reporters.

"I'll take a look," Nick said.

"Trevor, would you give us a minute, please?" Christina asked.

"Sure." Trevor got up and left the room, closing the door behind him.

Nick eyed his aide warily. "If you're going to start in on me about Sam again—"

"No," she said, twisting her hands in a rare show of nerves. "I was going to ask you if you'd mind, or if it would be weird at all or, um…"

Laughing, Nick said, "Spit it out, will you?"

"Sam's friend, Tommy Gonzales, asked me out. I just wondered if you'd have any problem with that."

As he tried to decide whether or not he was in the mood to mess with her, Nick sat back in his chair and studied her. "Why would I mind?"

"Two reasons—one, I'm not exactly Sam's favorite person."

"She has no beef with you, Chris. Yes, she hassled you during the investigation, but nothing about that was personal."

"Felt kind of personal to me."

Since he couldn't argue with that, he didn't try. "What's the second reason?"

"John," she said softly. "It's only been a few weeks. It's too soon for me to be thinking about going out with someone else."

Nick stood up and came around the desk. "You were a loyal and faithful friend to him. I know you had strong feelings for him, but you weren't a couple as much as you might've wished otherwise. I can't see how going out on a date would be inappropriate."

She brightened. "Thanks." With a wicked smile, she added, "Sam's going to flip her lid when she hears I'm going out with Tommy."

"Probably."

"Why does that make it even *more* exciting?"

"You're being nice to her," he reminded her.

"Absolutely," she said, smiling over her shoulder as she left the room. "Always."

CHAPTER 8

At noon, Senator Robert Cook escorted Nick into the Senate dining room. "So glad you could join me today, Nick."

He was nervous in the company of Cook, a senatorial institution. Sure, he had worked closely with Cook's staff for many years but he'd had limited contact with the man himself. Dining alone with him was certainly unprecedented. "Thanks for asking me."

"It's a good chance for us to get better acquainted while we're out of session," Cook said in a deep southern Virginian drawl.

They were shown to a table in the ornate room where only one other table was occupied.

"Southern Comfort, neat, darlin'," Cook said to the waitress.

She smiled. "Sweet tea, Senator?"

"Oh, all right," Cook said with a hangdog expression that made Nick grin.

"Same for me," Nick said.

"Millie's told everyone about my damned blood pressure,"

Cook grumbled about his wife. "Can't get a decent drink anywhere in this town."

Nick smiled at his dismay.

"You've gotta try the Senate bean soup," Cook said.

Nick ached when he remembered how much John had enjoyed the traditional soup. "I've had it before. Senator O'Connor loved it."

"Yes," Cook said. "He did."

When the waitress reappeared with their drinks, they ordered two bowls of the soup along with turkey clubs.

When he shook his head with dismay, Cook's mane of snow-white hair barely moved. "Such a terrible shame what happened to him. I know I don't have to tell you."

"No, sir."

Cook squeezed a lemon into his tea and stirred, his every movement and gesture signaling his utter comfort in his own skin. Nick couldn't help but be a little intimidated. "What's that saying?" Cook asked. "When life gives you lemons, make lemonade?"

"Where I grew up in Massachusetts we say you squeeze them on a lobster."

Cook's lined face lifted into a smile. "I like that. Very good." He took a long drink from his glass. "Life has handed you some lemons lately, Nick. It's time to squeeze them on a lobster."

"That's my plan. In fact, I talked to Senator Martin earlier, and between the two of us, we're going to call every member and try to get O'Connor-Martin back on the floor as the Senate's first order of business after the recess."

Cook nodded his approval. "I hate to say it, but we need to play the grief card and get it done before people move on and forget about O'Connor's untimely death."

Nick was quite certain he would never forget John O'Connor's untimely death but chose not to say so, knowing the older man was speaking from decades of political experience—and that he was right. It wouldn't take long for official Washington to forget that John had once graced the halls of power. The time to act on the landmark immigration legislation he had cosponsored was right now.

Leaning in, Cook lowered his voice and seemed to choose his words carefully. "You've only got a year, Nick. I'd like to help you make it count."

"I'd appreciate that, Senator."

"Call me Bob. But as I was saying, the time will go quickly, and I'm sure you're interested in making as big an impact as possible."

Nick ate the flavorful soup and nodded in agreement. "Of course."

"I think it would be best if you just followed my lead, son. Let me blaze the path, make it easier for you."

Nick rested his spoon in the bowl and wiped his mouth with the white cloth napkin. He might be younger and he might be green, but he recognized condescension when he heard it and wondered if Cook had tried to pull the same thing on John. If so, Nick hadn't heard about it. "I'm afraid I don't follow you, Bob," he said, deciding to play dumb in case he was reading it wrong.

"Well, let's face it, you don't have time to strike out on some independent path all your own. We're both serving the same constituency. If you let me call the shots, you come out looking good, the people are taken care of and the party gets what it needs from both of us."

Nope. Not reading it wrong. Swallowing his anger, Nick forced himself to stay quiet and let the other man continue to dig the hole.

"Take this nomination of Julian Sinclair, for instance."

"What about it?"

"He's a poor choice for the high court. Way too far out to the left. I don't know what Nelson was thinking." Cook scowled. "He's put us in a terrible spot—what choice do we have but to confirm him? After all, we can't hand the Republicans that kind of easy victory."

"Sinclair's a respected jurist. I think it's a wise choice."

"He's a divisive and inflammatory son of a bitch," Cook snapped, his amiable expression hardening as it seemed to dawn on him all of a sudden that Nick had a mind of his own and fully intended to use it. "Surely you can't tell me you support this nomination."

"I more than support it. In addition to being a good friend of mine, Julian is a respected attorney, and I have nothing but the utmost regard for him."

Cook scowled. "Wait 'til the protestors get ahold of him. I hope he's watching his back. Someone might take a shot at him."

"Is that a threat?" Nick asked, appalled by the implication.

"Don't be ridiculous. Of course it isn't a threat." Cook took a long drink of his tea before turning hard eyes on Nick. "Son, you haven't been around long enough to know how much damage a nomination like this can do to the Senate. It'll split us right down the middle, and the ill will could infect the entire session."

Nick could tell he startled the older man when he stood up and dropped his napkin on the table next to his half-eaten bowl of soup. "I appreciate you laying out the ground rules for me, Senator, but I'm fairly certain I've been around just long enough to know how to get the most out of my year in office." He took a step away from the table before he turned back. "Oh, and you can feel free to call me Nick or Senator, but I'm not your son. You have a good day now."

★ ★ ★

Sam stood in Clarence Reese's bedroom, staring at the photo of him with his wife and children. They had scoured the city and found no sign of the man who'd slaughtered his family. If Reese's mother or brother knew where he was hiding out, they weren't talking. Until they located him, Sam could only wonder what involvement Reese had in her father's shooting.

"Are we done here?" Freddie asked from the doorway. "This place gives me the creeps."

Taking another long last look at the man in the picture, Sam turned to her partner. "We're missing something."

"Crime scene took this place apart." The disheveled condition of the house backed up the statement. "There's nothing else here."

She rested her hand over her gut, her most trusted ally when it came to situations like this. "There's something. I know it."

"What do you want me to do? Where should I look?"

"That I *don't* know," she said, feeling defeated. "I wish I did."

"Sam, listen, maybe it's just a coincidence that Reese had those clippings—"

"You don't believe that any more than I do."

The clatter of metal in the alley behind the house caught their attention.

"What was that?" Freddie whispered.

Sam drew her weapon and gestured for him to do the same. She pointed him toward the front door and headed for the back of the house.

Moving slowly, her gun leading the way, Sam crept toward the back door. Another clatter rang through the alley, announcing the presence of a cat, a raccoon or a foolish perp returning to the scene of a crime. Sam hoped and prayed it was the latter. The door swung open.

"Freeze!" Sam caught a brief glimpse of Reese's startled face before he turned and bolted. "Freeze, police!" She took off after him, down the back steps and through a fetid alley stacked three feet deep on both sides with trash. Normally, she might've taken a shot at him, but he was no good to her dead. He had information she desperately needed. Hoping Freddie would cut Reese off at the other end of the alley, Sam chased after him, her thighs burning from the exertion, her lungs tight from the cold air pumping in and out.

Reese looked back, saw she was gaining on him and fired an erratic shot over his shoulder. The bullet whizzed past Sam's right ear, fueling her rage and her desire to catch him. *That might've worked on my dad, you son of a bitch, but it's going to take more than a cheap shot to take me down.* Running on adrenaline, she jumped over the bag of trash he threw in her path, came down on a patch of black ice and went flying.

Her chin took the full brunt of the fall. Sam howled with pain and tried to get her unarmed hand down to break the second half of the fall. Elbows and knees connected with hard pavement. She looked up in time to see Reese round the corner at the end of the alley. Freddie was nowhere in sight.

For a long moment, Sam lay there assessing her injuries and trying to catch her breath. The cold air made breathing painful, but that pain was nothing compared to the burn in her chin, knees and elbows. Forcing herself to move, she got up and called for backup to start a canvas of the neighborhood. Clearly, Reese hadn't gone far after butchering his family.

With each step more agonizing than the last, she made her way slowly to the end of the alley. Not seeing Freddie, she moved around to the front of the house to find him slapping cuffs on the arms of a stocky, dark-haired man. Her heart began to race. Had he gotten Reese after all? But when he turned the cuffed man around, Sam could see that it wasn't Reese but his brother, Hector, whom they'd interviewed the day before.

"What've you got?" Sam asked Freddie as she limped up to them.

"What happened to you? You're hurt."

"I'm okay. I fell on some ice chasing Reese. No biggie. What's up with him?"

"You have blood pouring from your chin, and you say no biggie?"

Sam wiped away the blood with an impatient sweep of her hand and gave him a look that said he'd better start spilling on Reese's brother.

"Caught this guy coming in the front. He said he needed to get a few things, and he has every right to go into his brother's house."

"It's a crime scene," Sam reminded Hector Reese. "You were told to stay out of there."

"My mama wanted some of the kids' things," he said in a surly tone, glaring at her. "This is hard on her."

"If that's so, why'd you bring your brother with you? The same brother you told us earlier today you couldn't find? The same brother who killed those kids your mama is grieving over."

"I didn't bring him here," Hector retorted. "And he didn't kill no one."

"Oh, so we're supposed to believe it's a coincidence that you and your brother were sneaking into the house at the same time?" Glancing at Freddie, Sam added, "You buying that, Cruz?"

"Not for one second, Lieutenant."

"Got anything you want to tell us, Reese?"

Hector looked down at the ground, his posture tight with hostility.

"I'll take that as a no." Sam gestured to one of the newly arrived officers. "Take Mr. Reese to HQ and book him."

"On what?" Hector cried. "This is my brother's house!"

"Tampering with a crime scene, aiding and abetting a fugitive from justice."

"I told you! I *don't know* where he is!"

Sam got right up in his face. *"I* told *you.* I don't believe you."

"Cunt cop," he muttered under his breath.

"What's that, Hector? I didn't hear you."

He glared at her.

"Add a disorderly conduct charge to that list," Sam said to the officer leading Hector to a cruiser. "Oh, and if you want to tell us where your brother's hiding out, I'd be happy to talk to the U.S. Attorney about lesser charges for you."

"Fuck you."

"I try to be nice and it just gets thrown back in my face," Sam said to Freddie. "That hurts my feelings."

"If you had feelings, I'd be sorry for you."

Sam snorted. "Good one, Cruz. You're getting better."

"I work on it in my spare time." He glanced at Sam. "We should hit the E.R. and get that looked at."

"I've got bandages at home." Or at least she hoped Nick did. She took a long look around. "Reese is hiding out close by."

"Wonder what he left behind in the house that was important enough for him to risk coming back."

"I want twenty-four-hour surveillance. Tomorrow, we're getting crime scene back here to find out what he was after. And then we'll take down the tape and set a trap. He came back once. Whatever he's after, he'll be back for it again. Next time, we'll be ready."

★ ★ ★

Much later that night, after what seemed like at *least* sixty takes to nail the recording that welcomed visitors to Virginia airports, Nick let himself into the Capitol Hill house he was due to close on the next day. He was greeted by throbbing music coming from the second floor. Smiling, he leaned back against the front door. He had learned in the past few weeks that Sam had a passion for all things Bon Jovi, and volume was key to her relationship with the band.

Tilting his head, he listened intently and recognized the song "Make a Memory," a particular favorite of hers. Even though Nick was anxious to see her, he took a moment to look around at the vast emptiness of the first floor, realizing he felt more at home in this house he didn't even officially own yet than he ever had anywhere else.

Doesn't take a rocket scientist to figure out why, he thought, as he dumped his coat, work bag and keys in the kitchen and headed upstairs to her. The music grew louder the closer he got to the bedroom. Jon Bon Jovi's distinctive voice soared through the melodic chorus. In the doorway, Nick stopped to study the scene. Sam was asleep in bed, a book folded over her chest, every light in the room on and the music set to ear-splitting.

Shaking his head with amusement and the ongoing delight at finding her in his bed each night, he bent to turn off the combination alarm clock and iPod docking station she had shown up with a few days ago. He'd been encouraged by her moving something of hers into the new house until it dawned on him that, other than a toothbrush, it was the only thing she had brought.

He took a closer look at her and noticed the bandage on her chin and the bruises surrounding it. Hurt again. His heart ached and his mind raced when he allowed himself to think about the many ways she risked herself every day. The idea

that she could one day be taken from him without any warning chilled him to his bones, and suddenly he needed to be
close to her.

Draping his suit over the footboard, he shut off every light
but one, hit the bathroom and crawled into bed. When he
saw what she'd been reading, he laughed softly: *Congress for
Dummies.* Gently, he attempted to lift the book off her chest.

She stirred and studied him with sleepy eyes.

He leaned over to kiss her. "Sorry, babe," he said, brushing the hair off her forehead.

"You're late," she said, her voice hoarse and sexy from sleep.

"I tried to call, but I guess you couldn't hear the phone
over Bon Jovi."

She flashed him a sheepish grin. "Sorry."

Trailing a finger lightly over the bandage on her chin, he
studied her face. "What happened?"

"Me versus black ice. The ice won."

He winced.

She tugged two badly bruised and scraped elbows out from
underneath the comforter.

"Ouch." Dropping soft kisses on each elbow, he said, "Did
you have X-rays?"

"Nah. Nothing broken." She made a brave attempt to bend
each arm to prove her point.

"Stop. That's making me hurt just watching it. Anything
else?"

"Knees. Same as the elbows."

"Samantha, my poor baby." He brushed a soft kiss over her
lips. "Did you put something on the road rash?"

"Celia fixed me up."

"So this was really just you and some ice?"

"Uh-huh," she said, looking away.

"You can either tell me the truth or I'll tickle it out of you, which, in light of your injuries, might not be as fun as usual."

"You wouldn't do that to an officer wounded in the line of duty."

He raised his fingers in a menacing claw over her ribs. "Try me."

"Fine! I was chasing Reese. He came back to his house when Freddie and I were doing another walk-through."

"Without backup?" Nick asked, alarmed.

"I had Freddie. Do you want to hear this or not?"

He gestured for her to go ahead, and she told him the rest.

"He *fired* at you?"

"It was a wild shot. Missed by a mile."

Nick put his head down face-first into his pillow and groaned.

"I heard that, and you made me tell you."

Turning on his side, he faced her. "You wouldn't have, though, would you?"

Her eyebrows knitted with confusion. "What?"

"You wouldn't have told me if I hadn't forced it out of you."

"I don't like to upset you, and my job can be upsetting. I'm fine, so what's the point in dumping it on you and getting you all wound up?"

Reaching for her hand, he laced his fingers through hers. "The point is I want to know. If you get shot at or hurt in any way, I want to know. Deal?"

"You promise not to freak? That was kind of an issue with Peter. I never told him anything because he always freaked out. But then he would find out from someone else, and that was always worse."

"I can't promise not to be upset, but I won't freak. At least not at you."

"Or anyone else from the MPD."

He hesitated.

"Nick…"

"Or anyone else from the MPD, unless—"

She silenced him with a kiss. "No unless. We have a deal."

"Where'd you get this?" He held up the book she'd been reading and couldn't believe it when his brave, competent cop blushed.

"You weren't supposed to see that." She took the book from him and dropped it to the floor.

Careful to avoid her injured chin, he gently turned her face to force her to look at him and raised an eyebrow in question.

Sighing in defeat, she said, "I've lived in this city all my life, just a mile from the Capitol, but I don't really know what goes on there."

"I could tell you."

"I wanted to be able to talk to you about it," she said with a shy glance that staggered him. "I wanted to know what your day would be like."

His heart galloped in his chest as he brushed his lips over hers. "I love you," he whispered and was thrilled when her mouth opened under his to welcome him in. Her injured arms encircled his neck, and Nick sank into the kiss. "So what did you learn?" he asked many minutes later as he sprinkled kisses over her face.

"That a filibuster is a technique used to prolong debate in order to stop or postpone a vote," she said with a proud smile. "I've always wondered what that was." Her smile transformed into the coy grin he loved so much. "Do you think you'll ever get to filibuster?"

"I don't know," he said, laughing. "I suppose if desperate times call for desperate measures…"

With an exaggerated shudder, she said, "Oh, that's *so* sexy,

imagining my man hijacking the Senate floor with his elo-
quent rhetoric. But you know what's *not* sexy?"

Reveling in being referred to as her man, he nuzzled her
neck. "What's that?"

Shifting onto her side to face him, she rested her hand on
his chest. "Seersucker Thursday," she said, wrinkling her nose.

"What?" He feigned offense. "You don't think I'll look hot
in my seersucker suit?"

The hand caressing his chest stilled. "You aren't serious."

"I want the full experience, babe. Besides, it's a tradition,
a harbinger of spring."

"Seersucker is seriously *not* sexy."

"It will be on me."

"A little full of yourself, aren't you?"

"I'm just saying." He hooked his leg over her hip to tug
her in close to him.

"I won't be seen with you."

Cupping her breast, he rolled her nipple between his fingers. "Yes, you will."

"No way."

"Other than getting shot at, how was your first day, Lieutenant?"

As he toyed with her nipple, her eyes fluttered closed. "Fine.
Nothing special. And don't try to change the subject."

"You want to talk about Congress some more?"

"Just one more thing." She rolled onto her back and brought
him with her.

"What?" he asked, breathless with wanting her as he hovered over her, mindful of her injuries.

With a big grin, she raised her hips and pressed against his
erection. "Fill her, buster."

Laughing, he did as she asked.

CHAPTER 9

Late on Friday night, Freddie brought his battered Mustang to a stop at the curb in front of Elin's apartment building and cut the engine. His heart beat fast with nerves and desire. All he had to do was send the signal and he could spend the night in her bed. But now that "the moment" had arrived, he was filled with uncertainty. The decision that had seemed so clear a few days ago was back in play. Twenty-nine years of celibacy had come down to this.

She turned to him and rested her hand on his arm. "Do you want to come in?"

Studying her, thoughts and images of all kinds spiraled through his mind and landed in his lap in a surge of lust.

"Freddie?"

"Can I take a rain check?" He couldn't believe the words were coming out of his mouth. "Sam's got us working funky shifts so she can touch base with everyone. I'm wiped, and I have to work again at seven."

"I've been reading about her and the senator in the paper."

"She *loves* all the attention they're getting," he said, rolling his eyes.

"I can imagine."

Freddie hadn't expected to enjoy being with Elin as much as he did. He found her easy to talk to, engaging and funny. She had caught on right away that he had come around the gym looking for more than personal training, and when he suggested dinner, she enthusiastically agreed. He'd spent most of the night trying to rein in his raging hormones. He hadn't even kissed her yet despite the signals that she'd be receptive.

He knew if he touched her he wouldn't stop until he had all of her.

"Freddie?"

"Hmm?" He glanced at her and found her watching him. In that moment, he remembered learning during the O'Connor investigation that she had a heart with a Cupid's arrow tattooed on her left breast and her nipples were pierced. His cock twitched, and he shifted to ease the ache.

She reached for him and crushed her lips to his.

Startled, his eyes flew open to find hers closed as she ran her tongue over his bottom lip. He sank his hand into her hair to tug her closer. Her fingers danced over his chest, unbuttoning his shirt and tunneling in until skin reached skin. When she scraped her fingernail over his nipple, he almost came in his pants.

Tearing his lips free of hers, he caught her hand. "Elin."

"Yes?" she asked with a sexy grin as she ran her free hand up over his thigh to cup his straining erection.

Freddie swallowed hard and fought to keep his mind off the fire burning in his lap. He had never been with a woman who was so brazen, but that was what had attracted him to her in the first place.

She stroked him through his jeans.

He let his head fall back against the seat in surrender.

"Are you *sure* you can't come in?" she asked, sliding her tongue along his neck.

"Got to work," he said through clenched teeth. Locked in a haze of desire and temptation, he was unaware of her freeing him from his pants until the cold air hitting his fevered skin jolted him out of his reverie. "Whoa."

The words died on his lips when she bent to take him into her mouth. Oh, *God.* He figured he should at least try to stop her, but couldn't seem to get the neurons in his brain to form the words he needed. This was going to be fast. And *damn* if the woman didn't know exactly where to squeeze, to lick, to suck.

"Elin, honey," he said, his voice full of warning.

As if he hadn't spoken, she took him even deeper, and he climaxed with a roar that surprised him. His breath came out in puffy white clouds as he fought to recover from the intense orgasm.

She sat up and licked her lips, looking quite pleased with herself. "Too bad you have to work so early," she said with a playful pout.

"Yeah," he gasped. "Too bad."

"Next time?"

"Sure," he said, still having trouble catching his breath. He glanced at her and rested his hand on her leg. "What about you?"

She smiled. "I can take care of myself. Don't worry."

Something about the way she said that stirred his recently satisfied libido back to life as he imagined her "taking care of herself." He released a ragged deep breath, feeling like he was in *way* over his head here. "I should go."

Leaning over, she touched her lips to his. "I had fun tonight. Thanks for dinner."

He caressed her baby-soft cheek. "My pleasure."

"Call me?"

Freddie nodded, knowing he should walk her in but not sure his legs would follow his directions. He watched her until she was safely inside and then zipped up his pants and started the car. For a long time, he sat there trying to collect himself before he shifted the car into gear and drove home.

With the media clamoring for justice for the murdered family and Sam pursuing her own personal agenda, they tore apart the Reese home the next day. Hours later, the house lay in tatters, and the only interesting thing they'd found was ten thousand dollars in a metal box in the basement.

"At least we know now what he was after," Freddie said, referring to the fat wad of hundred-dollar bills.

"He's desperate and on the run," Sam said. "He needs money to get out of the city, and this is probably all he has. I'd bet my badge that he'll be back for it."

"I talked to Gonzo. They've scoured the neighborhood, but no one's seen him."

"Or they're protecting him."

"Why would they protect a guy who did what he did to his family?"

"Who knows? Neighborhood dynamics and loyalties run deep."

Freddie's handsome face shifted into a scowl. "I guess no one was loyal to Tiffany and her kids."

"She didn't grow up here. I read that she moved here from Pennsylvania seven years ago."

"Then she had the good fortune to meet Reese."

"Yeah."

"There's not much more we can do here, Lieutenant."

Sam took a hard look around the messy living room. "I know."

"You want to split?"

"I'm going to hang for a while. See if he comes back."

"You can't stay here by yourself," he protested.

She rested her hand on the weapon holstered to her hip. "I won't be by myself."

"I'm not leaving until you do." He plopped down in a chair and crossed his arms defiantly.

"Suit yourself." She took another chair and put her feet up on the dilapidated coffee table. After a long period of silence, she fixed her eyes on her partner, noticing once again his above-average attire. "Since we have some time to kill, why don't you tell me about your girlfriend?"

"What girlfriend?" he sputtered, his blush giving him away. "I don't know what you're talking about."

"Uh-huh." Sam settled into the chair, warming up to bust his chops. "How about we examine the evidence?"

"Here's a big idea—let's not."

Nick rushed through a quick shower and shave while reviewing his mental checklist for the dinner party one final time. The past week had been beyond chaotic. He'd closed on the new place, moved in and focused all his energy on getting the downstairs portion of the house ready for tonight's gathering—on top of contacting half the senate to rally support for John's immigration bill.

The second floor was a maze of boxes and unassembled furniture. He expected Laine would want to see the upstairs, but she'd understand about the mess.

Nick hated disorder. He hated chaos, and more than anything, he hated that Sam seemed to be avoiding him. While pursuing Clarence Reese with relentless determination, she'd also been working crazy shifts as she attempted to connect with all the HQ detectives who now answered to her. Other than a few rushed phone calls, Nick hadn't had any time with her since the night he discovered her reading *Congress for Dummies* in his bed a week ago. She had been sleeping at her dad's house because, as she said, she didn't want to disturb him with her middle-of-the-night comings and goings. He hadn't succeeded in convincing her that he *wanted* to be disturbed by her.

"Maybe I'm the dummy," he muttered to his reflection.

He knew she was uncomfortable about acting as his cohost at the dinner party for Julian, which was why he'd limited the guest list to Julian, Graham and Laine, and refrained from discussing it with her during their brief conversations. Caterers had handled the food, a florist had taken care of the flowers and he had set what he considered to be a rather elegant table for the five of them. All she had to do was show up. He glanced at his watch, dismayed by how close she was cutting it.

That he had to wonder if she was going to show up at all flat out pissed him off. It wasn't like he asked so much of her. *No, you've only asked just about everything of her, and you're unhappy because she's not ready to give it to you.*

As he tugged a burgundy cashmere V-neck sweater over his head, Sam came flying into the room, her cheeks red from cold and exertion. "Sorry, sorry, sorry."

"For what?" he asked, working to keep the frustration out of his tone.

"I'm running late. Today was the funeral for Reese's family, and the day got away from me."

He turned to her and was wowed by the beaded top she wore over formfitting black dress pants. "How was the funeral?"

"A total horror show," she said with a sigh as she used the mirror on his dresser to fix her hair, which she had left down the way he liked it best. "We interviewed brothers, sisters, friends, cousins. No one ever heard Reese talk about my dad. And no sign of him, either."

"I'm sorry, Sam."

She shrugged. "Another dead end." Rolling her head on her shoulders, she added, "The longer he's in the wind the less likely we are to find him."

"You should talk to your dad about what you found at Reese's house. He's stronger than you think, and he might be able to shed some light."

"You're right. I was thinking the same thing earlier." She turned from the mirror to face him. "The house looks great. I can't believe how fast you got it done. You've even got pictures on the walls!"

"Any of it can be changed if you don't like it."

"What's not to like?"

He bit his tongue to keep from telling her he didn't like the way she was avoiding him. Instead, he said, "You look gorgeous."

"Thank you." She reached up to adjust the collar of his shirt. "You're not looking too bad yourself." Going up on tiptoes, she planted a kiss on him. "I've missed you."

Because he couldn't help himself, he looped his arms around her waist and brought her in close to him. "Me, too."

"What's wrong?"

"Nothing."

"Something," she said, stealing his usual line.

He shook his head. "Thanks for coming tonight."

She looked up at him, studying him. "Of course I came tonight. It's important to you, but I wish you'd tell me what's wrong. Are you mad because we haven't seen much of each other—"

Bending his head, he captured her mouth in a deep, passionate kiss.

"—the last few days," she muttered against his lips, her eyes closed, her cheeks flushed anew with color that had nothing to do with cold or exertion.

"If you lived here with me, we'd see more of each other."

"Nick."

He rested his forehead on hers. "I know. You don't want to talk about that." Releasing her, he went to find his shoes.

"You're pissed. I knew it."

"I'm not pissed." He shoved his feet into loafers. "I'm frustrated."

Sam nibbled on her bottom lip. "I'm sorry."

"Stop apologizing to me," he snapped, his tone sharper than he'd intended.

She came to him and slid her hands up over his chest. "Why? It's my fault. You've offered me so much, and I'm holding back. I know that bothers you."

"I want this to work so damned bad," he said, surprised by the urgency he heard in his own voice. "I want it more than anything."

"I do, too." Her eyes implored him to believe her. "We knew it was going to be crazy."

"I don't want to go days without seeing you. I can't stand that. I need you, Samantha."

"Do you think it's *not* working?" She massaged his shoulders. "Is that why you're so tense?"

"It's working," he said but hardly managed to convince himself.

Her hands fell from his shoulders. She wrapped her arms around herself protectively, a gesture that tugged at his heart. "Wow. You're really wound up. I'm sorry I had to work so much this week."

"You're apologizing again."

Her eyes flashed with anger and what might've been panic.

"Then tell me what I'm supposed to say, Nick! What do you need to hear? That I love you? You know I do. If you're doubting that—"

"I'm not."

"Ugh!" She threw her hands into the air. "This is exactly why I haven't gotten involved with anyone since I split with Peter. I can't deal with this!"

A blast of fear charged through Nick, leaving him staggered in its wake. "I'm the one who should be sorry. I've been burning the candle this week, and I'm fried." He ran a hand through hair still damp from the shower. "I don't know why I'm taking it out on you."

"Do I need to be worried?" she asked, her face a study in vulnerability, which was in sharp contrast to her usual confident, cocky demeanor. He hated that he had given her reason to question him—to question *them*.

He went to her and hugged her fiercely. "No, babe. No worries. I just need some time with you."

She clung to him. "I'm off until tomorrow night at eleven. I'm all yours."

"Good," he said, his voice husky with emotion and relief as he held her close to him. How had this even happened? How had he managed to give them both reason to doubt the only thing in his life that truly mattered?

The doorbell rang downstairs.

He released her reluctantly. "Ready?"

"As ready as I'll ever be."

"I love you," he said, kissing her hand, "and I'm really glad you're here."

"So am I."

CHAPTER 10

Rattled by the odd conversation with Nick, Sam did her best to put on her party face as they greeted the O'Connors and Julian Sinclair, who arrived at the same time. She was still getting used to the warmth the O'Connors directed her way simply because she was with Nick.

He slipped a possessive arm around her and introduced her to Julian, who held her hand between both of his. "It's such a pleasure to meet you, Sam. I've read all about you in the paper."

She rolled her eyes. "Oh, joy."

"What did today's article say? 'Not since Jack and Jackie has Washington been so riveted by a political couple'?"

"Thanks, Julian." Nick shook hands with him. "She really needed to hear that again."

Julian laughed. "You're looking good, Senator. Power becomes you."

Sam was amused by Nick's befuddled reaction to the compliment. Julian was shorter than he appeared on television, his forehead barely reaching Nick's shoulder. He had smooth skin, silver hair and a warm smile. *Erudite* was the word that came to mind as she watched him interact with the others. Classy, elegant and right at home with Nick and the O'Connors—so at home, in fact, that Sam felt like an outsider looking in at a family reunion.

In the kitchen, Graham opened a bottle of merlot. "It's so great to have you in town for a while, Julian."

"I was so sorry I couldn't be here for John's service," Julian said. "I was in Sacramento for a wedding the day before the funeral. If I hadn't been the best man, I'd have been on the first plane."

"We got your lovely note." Laine patted his arm. "And the flowers, too. You were there in spirit."

"What's the latest with Thomas's case?" Julian asked as he accepted a glass of wine from Graham and followed the others into the living room.

Sam opened a bottle of pinot grigio and poured herself a glass before she joined them.

"They're exploring an insanity plea," Graham said.

"Not a bad idea," Julian said.

Graham's face tightened with grief. "It was my fault for keeping Patricia and Thomas hidden away for all those years. I forced John to live a double life and to lie to them. When Thomas found out there'd been other women in his father's life, he just snapped."

"You did what you thought was right, Graham," Julian said. "Those were different times. You would've taken a hard political hit if people found out that your teenage son had fathered a child—not to mention what it would've done to John's future."

"Did you know?" Nick asked Julian. "About Thomas?"

Julian glanced at Graham. "I did."

Expelling a long deep breath, Nick sat back against the sofa. Sam knew Nick was still dealing with leftover shock and disbelief that John had kept his son hidden from even his closest friend and most trusted aide.

"He was one of the few," Graham said quickly, tuning in to Nick's dismay. "I didn't know what to do, so I asked a couple of close friends for their advice."

"I agreed with what you did, so that makes me partly culpable, I suppose," Julian said, swirling the wine around in his glass, a rueful expression on his face.

"There's no point in second-guessing," Laine said, sending the message to the others that she had heard enough about the circumstances of her youngest child's death.

"You're absolutely right, Laine," Julian said, turning his attention to Sam. "So you're a detective."

"And a recently promoted lieutenant," Nick added with a proud smile.

"Congratulations," Julian said. "A wonderful accomplishment."

"Thank you."

"How's the new job, Sam?" Laine asked with what appeared to be genuine interest.

"Chaotic."

"She did a first-class job on John's case," Graham said. "First-class."

With a small smile to acknowledge the compliment, she said, "Thanks."

"So your sister-in-law is getting as many headlines as you are lately," Laine said to Julian.

"Indeed," Julian replied with a chagrined expression. "She does have her opinions."

"I never knew she was so hateful," Graham said. "To say what she does about homosexuals, Jews and African-Americans, and on television, no less. I heard they're giving her a prime-time show. A whole hour of hate and venom."

"It's shameful," Julian said. "I never have understood what my brother sees in her. From the day he met her, he's been completely besotted. Did you hear the latest?"

"About her book?" Graham asked.

Julian nodded. "It'll be out in two weeks. An update on a book her minister father did years ago on how homosexuals will be the downfall of the republic."

Nick released a low whistle. "Wow."

"She's on a roll, lately," Julian said.

"Do you ever hear from them?" Laine asked.

Julian shook his head. "I haven't spoken to either of them in years."

"Were you surprised to be nominated to the Court?" Sam asked, sensing they were all anxious to change the subject.

"Well, since David warned me I'd be at the top of his list the first chance he got, I can't say I was all that surprised to get the call."

"David did, did he?" Sam wasn't sure where this edge to her voice was coming from. She chalked it up to the mood Nick had put her in with his odd behavior earlier.

Nick directed a raised eyebrow her way.

"I'm sorry," she said in a more conciliatory tone. "I'm still getting used to being around people who call the president of the United States by his first name."

"I call him Mr. President when I'm with him," Julian clarified.

"I've seen your face on the front page as much as I've seen my own lately," Sam said.

"We knew the nomination would generate some controversy," Julian acknowledged.

"Protestors will be descending on this town in the next few days," Graham added.

"We had a meeting yesterday about crowd control," Sam said. "They're expecting up to a million people."

"That many?" Julian said, seeming taken aback.

"You're surprised?" Sam asked.

Nick's face was set in a stony, unreadable expression Sam hadn't seen before.

"I knew there'd be some protests," Julian said quietly. "But a million. Wow."

"People feel very strongly about this," Sam said. "After all, your confirmation would tip the court firmly to the left."

"Are you opposed to that, Sam?" Laine asked. Her question seemed to contain only interest and not judgment.

"I'm a cop."

"With no beliefs?" Graham asked, arching a white eyebrow with what might have been delight at her sauciness.

A quick glance at Nick told her he was anything but delighted.

"I have a few. Usually, I keep them to myself."

"Please," Nick said. "Enlighten us."

Something in his tightly spoken words sent a trickle of discomfort through her. "I'm sure you all have other things you'd rather talk about."

"Actually, you've got us riveted," Nick replied, his eyes boring a hole in her.

Her stomach churned with anxiety. "I'd like to see the abortion issue resolved definitively," she ventured.

"And you don't think it was with Roe v. Wade?" Julian asked.

"If it had been, we wouldn't still be talking about it more than thirty years later."

"That's a good point," Laine said.

"So if you were Julian," Nick said, "and a case came before the court that would overturn Roe, how would you vote?"

Sam squirmed under the heat of his gaze. "I don't know. Don't ask me that."

Clearly flabbergasted, Nick stared at her. "You don't believe in a woman's right to choose?"

"I never said that."

"You don't know if you'd vote to overturn Roe? That doesn't make you much of a supporter of women's rights."

"No," Sam shot back, "it makes me a supporter of those who can't speak for themselves."

"I never would've guessed," Nick said, incredulous.

After a long period of uncomfortable silence during which Nick stared at her, Sam cleared her throat. "I think I smell something burning. I'll go check." Getting up quickly, she went into the kitchen and leaned against the counter, trying to stop the pounding in her chest. How had she let the conversation get so heated and out of control?

"What the hell was that?" Nick fumed as he followed her into the kitchen.

"What?" Sam asked, opening the oven and peering inside— more for something to do than anything.

"Were you baiting him?" he asked in an exaggerated whisper.

"*You* were baiting *me!*"

Ignoring that, he said, "Have you forgotten he's our guest?"

"*Your* guest."

"Right." He stormed around the kitchen, adding dressing to a tossed salad and retrieving dishes warming in the oven. "It's not like we're a couple who'd do something so *committed* as entertain together or anything."

Sam folded her arms, her back rigid with tension. "Maybe I should just go."

"Fine. Run away. That's what you do, isn't it?"

"No," she said softly, "usually I stay, which is how I ended up unhappily married for four long years to a man who tried to control my every thought and action."

Nick's expression shifted from anger to regret.

The anger, she decided, was easier to handle.

"Sam—"

She held up a hand to stop him from approaching her. "I'm going to go so you can visit with your friends in peace. I don't belong here."

"That's not true. You know it isn't."

"Tell them I got called in to work," she said, desperate to get out of there before she embarrassed herself by getting emotional. "I'm sorry." With a last glance at his unreadable face, she darted from the kitchen, grabbed her coat and headed out the door while contending with a huge knot in her throat.

CHAPTER 11

The lobster had been flown in from Maine, but to Nick, it might as well have been cardboard. The meal he had planned down to the garnish received rave reviews from his guests. He couldn't have cared less. Oblivious to his dismay, the other three laughed and talked and told old stories. Even though he participated in the conversation, Nick wished they would leave so he could go after Sam and nip this thing growing between them before it couldn't be fixed.

They lingered over dessert and coffee and then asked to see the rest of the house.

He took them through the three floors, answered their questions about his plans for the place, and withstood their good-natured ribbing about his oh-so-public romance with the pretty lieutenant.

By the time they finally left at eleven, Nick was on the verge of a nervous breakdown. He grabbed his coat, rushed down the street and up the ramp to Skip's house. After a month of being in and out of there, it didn't occur to him to knock. Bursting into the darkened living room, he found Skip and Celia on the sofa locked in a passionate embrace.

"Oh, shit," Nick muttered through his mortification. "Sorry."

Like a teenager who'd just been caught in a clutch with her boyfriend, Celia scrambled off Skip's lap and pressed her hand to her swollen lips. Skip's empty wheelchair sat next to the sofa where he was propped into the corner with pillows under his arms. Clearly, they had given this arrangement some serious thought, and Nick was horrified to have interrupted them.

"I'll, ah, just go up to see Sam."

"She's not here," Celia said. "We thought she was with you. At your dinner party for the justice."

"She was. Earlier. But we had an, um, a thing."

"A fight," Skip said, his sharp eyes trained on Nick.

"Sort of." Nick pushed a frustrated hand through his hair. "Where do you think she'd be?"

"How upset was she?" Skip asked.

"Pretty upset."

"Lincoln."

"Excuse me?"

"She goes to see Lincoln when she's upset or needs to think."

"As in the *monument?*"

"One and the same."

"At eleven at night?" Nick asked, incredulous.

"She carries a gun. The dark doesn't faze her."

"All right. I'll check there. Thanks for the info."

"What did you do to her?"

"Nothing!"

"It wasn't nothing if she's gone to see Mr. Lincoln."

"It's nothing we can't work out," he said with more confidence than he felt.

"Go find her, Nick," Celia said, sending a pointed glance at Skip.

"Sorry again for the interruption," Nick said on his way out the door. He jogged down Ninth Street, cut through Eastern Market and hailed a cab on East Capitol.

"Lincoln Memorial," he told the cabbie.

"Not much happening there this time of night," the driver said, no doubt thinking he'd picked up a misguided tourist.

"I know," Nick replied in a clipped tone that discouraged further conversation. They arrived ten minutes later. Nick paid the driver, emerged from the car and took off jogging toward the lighted memorial.

"Help you, sir?" a park ranger said as Nick headed for the marble stairs.

He could've said no. The monument, like all the others, was open twenty-four hours a day, and he didn't need permission to be there. But for the first time in the two weeks since he was sworn in, Nick decided to take advantage of his newfound rank. "I'm Senator Nick Cappuano. I'm meeting someone here."

"Pleased to make your acquaintance, Senator." The ranger shook Nick's hand. "I believe your friend is on that side," he said, pointing, "under the Gettysburg Address."

Nick still found it hard to believe that he was half of a couple everyone in the capital region recognized. "Thank you." Over his shoulder, he caught the ranger's grin as he watched Nick take the stairs two at a time. He found Sam right where the ranger had told him she'd be. Sitting on the floor, she had her knees pulled up to her chest, her arms tight around them and her face tucked into the valley formed by her knees.

"Samantha."

Her head shot up, a shocked expression on her tear-streaked face. "What're you doing here?"

"Your dad told me I might find you here." Undone by her ravaged expression and wondering if he was responsible for it, he glanced at Lincoln. "Is it a coincidence that you flee to the first Republican president when you want to be alone?"

"I don't come because he was a Republican."

Nick sat down next to her on the cold floor. "Then why?"

She shrugged. "It's so peaceful here. I've always loved it."

"I'm drawn to Jefferson myself."

"Naturally. The original Democrat."

"One of them." He studied her for a long moment before he said, "Are you a Republican, Samantha Holland?"

"Will you love me less if I say I am?"

He shook his head and reached for her hand. "Nothing could make me love you less."

Her face tightened with strain that confused and scared him as he rubbed some warmth into her chilled hand. "Don't be so sure."

"That doesn't answer my question."

"Like I told Graham before—I'm a cop. I'm not affiliated with either party."

"But if you *could* be, which one would it be?"

She glanced up at Lincoln. "Neither, really. I'm more of an issues kind of gal."

Nick released a long deep breath.

"Are you disappointed I didn't say I'm a Democrat?"

"Of course not."

"I may not always agree with your position on issues that really matter to you."

"I don't expect you to."

"Are you sure of that? Politics is such a big part of who you are, Nick. Now more than ever. I'd understand if some differences were too big for you to deal with. After all, we rushed into this. We didn't really know each other—"

He stopped her with two fingers over her lips. "I know you. Do I know everything there is to know? Nope. Do I want to?

Absolutely. Will there be other surprises? I sure as hell hope so. But don't tell me I don't know you. I know your heart, Samantha. I know what matters." He didn't expect her to break down into gulping sobs. Sliding his arm around her, he brought her head to rest on his chest. "What's going on, babe?"

"I'm sorry for the way I acted with Julian," she said when she could speak again. "I was way out of line. You were right. He was our guest, and I *was* baiting him."

"He's used to people with strong opinions. You can't have beliefs like his without generating some controversy."

"But you weren't expecting that from me, and I embarrassed you."

"No, you surprised me."

"I surprised myself. I had no plans to get into that with him."

"So why did you?" he asked, more curious than anything.

"All the coverage about him coming to town, about his nomination, knowing I was going to meet him. It's stirred up some stuff for me."

"What kind of stuff?"

"It's kind of a long story," she said with a wary glance at him.

He sat back against the marble wall and brought her in close to him to keep them warm. "Mr. Lincoln and I aren't going anywhere."

She was quiet for a long time—so long that he wondered if she was going to tell him what was causing her such dismay. "I've never told anyone this," she finally said. "Other than my sisters, that is."

Bracing himself for whatever he was about to hear, Nick linked their fingers and held her hand between both of his.

With a deep sigh, she said, "When I was a junior in college, I dated a French exchange student named Jean Paul for a couple of months toward the end of the school year. You probably don't want to hear this, but it was one of those relationships that was long on sex and short on relating, if you know what I mean."

He knew exactly what she meant and hated the idea of her with anyone else, but he kept his mouth shut so she'd continue.

"Jean Paul had already gone home to France when I discovered I was pregnant."

Sensing where this was going, Nick fought to retain his composure.

"Tracy had just had Brooke," she said of her fifteen-year-old niece. "I told you about Brooke's father leaving Tracy to raise her alone, right?"

Nick nodded, recalling how Tracy's husband, Mike, was raising Brooke as his own child.

"After watching what Tracy was going through, I totally panicked. I had one more year of school to finish and had my sights set on the police academy. With the dyslexia, school was a huge struggle, but I was determined to get that degree because I knew it would help me get promoted. How in the world was I going to fit a baby into that picture? And I had no one who could help me. My mother had run off to Florida with that guy she'd hooked up with, my dad was a mess over what my mother had put him through, Angela had a new job and was dating Spencer. Tracy was struggling to take care of Brooke. I can honestly say it was the only time in my life when I had no idea what to do."

Nick wiped the tears from her cheeks. "You couldn't have put the baby up for adoption?"

"My dad was so upset and disappointed with Tracy. Not that he ever expressed that to her, but he talked to me about it. No one even thinks about that anymore because we love Brooke so much, but at the time, it was a big deal."

"You didn't want to disappoint him, too."

"No," she said, sounding so utterly defeated. "I couldn't have taken that on top of everything else I was dealing with."

"So what did you do?"

After a long pause, she said, "I made an appointment at a clinic," in a voice so soft it was almost a whisper. "I couldn't see any other way out. I was awake the entire night before with what I thought were stomach pains, but when they examined me before the procedure, they discovered I was miscarrying."

"You didn't do anything wrong, Sam."

"I was going to *kill* my baby!" The hysteria he heard in her voice alarmed him. "How can you say I didn't do anything wrong? My periods were never the same afterward, and then the endometriosis set in a year or so later. It was like my body was punishing me for this awful thing I almost did." Her voice caught on a sob. "I'm so ashamed, Nick. Even all these years later, I'm still so ashamed."

Because he didn't know what else to do, he held her tight against him and let her get it out.

"I cried for two weeks afterward. My sisters took care of me, saw me through the worst of it, but I've never told another living soul about that day until right now. I know it's why I miscarried twice more, and it's why I can't have others."

"How do you figure?"

"I'm being punished for being so willing to toss away the one I didn't want."

"Sam, honey, how can you think that?"

"Because! Look at what's happened! When I *wanted* to get pregnant, I couldn't, and then when I finally did, I couldn't *stay* pregnant. How else am I supposed to see it?"

"As an awful coincidence. How would you have supported that child as a twenty-year-old college dropout?"

"I would've found a way."

"But you never would've been a cop. Think of the lives you've saved and the murders you've prevented by getting all those killers off the streets. Doesn't that in any way compensate?"

She shook her head. "Nothing can compensate for not wanting my own child."

"You were a kid yourself. You felt trapped and alone. It wasn't about *wanting* your child. It was about knowing you couldn't care for him properly."

"Sometimes I wonder if he knew I didn't want him, and that's why I miscarried."

"I'm sorry this happened to you. That you were put in this position and had to make such an awful choice."

"I know you must think less of me."

"I don't, Sam. I swear I don't. I support a woman's right to choose—any woman. Even you."

As if he hadn't spoken, she said, "Your own mother was only fifteen when she had you, and you turned out fine."

"No thanks to her."

"But still." Sam took a deep shuddering breath. "At the crowd-control meeting we had at work the other day, they showed us some of the propaganda so we'd be prepared for what to expect from the protestors. They had pictures of aborted fetuses. I hit the recall button on my pager to get myself out of there. I got so sick in the bathroom. I thought it would never stop."

"I'm sorry, babe," he whispered. "I'm so sorry you had to see those pictures. I'm sorry you had to go through this whole ordeal and that you carry such a heavy burden."

"In some twisted way, I think maybe I baited Julian because I wanted to tell you. I just couldn't figure out how. But I wanted you to know."

"I'm glad you told me."

Resting her head on her knees, she turned her face so she could see him. "This is why we won't have kids."

"You can't know that for sure. You may have ended up with endometriosis anyway, even if you hadn't had that miscarriage. Maybe you already had it, didn't know it, and that caused the miscarriage."

Startled, she looked up at him. "You really think that's possible?"

"Anything is possible. The point is you'll never really know so why assume the worst? Have you tried to have kids with anyone other than Peter?"

"Of course not."

"How much you wanna bet he was the problem, not you?" Nick waggled his eyebrows at her. "We've already proven *he* was the problem in another important area, right? You've never tried to have *my* kids. And remember what I told you—when we're ready, we'll have them. If we can't have them the usual way, we'll adopt, we'll hire a surrogate, whatever it takes. We'll have them."

"I don't know if I deserve them—or you."

He got up and reached out a hand to her. "Sure you do."

She took his hand and let him help her up.

Because he needed it as much as she did, he hugged her close to him.

Under his coat, her fingers clutched his back. "I love you," she whispered. "I love you so much."

"And I love you even more than I did earlier, if that's possible." With his arm around her shoulders, he led her to the stairs. "Let's go home. I saved you a lobster."

She glanced up at him, a hint of a smile on her face. "Thanks."

He knew she wasn't talking about lobster. "Anytime, babe."

CHAPTER 12

This was it, Freddie decided, as he let Elin drag him through her dark apartment. He wasn't going to back out, he wasn't going to think of his mother, his faith or the promises he made to himself years ago before he'd become a man with man-sized urges. In his right mind, he would've preferred some romance, some candles maybe. Love would've been nice, too.

But that hadn't happened, and this was going to. And it was going to be over before it started unless he could find a way to slow things down.

He reached for her hands, which were at work on his shirt buttons. "Hey."

She nuzzled his chest hair. "What?"

"How about we take our time?"

Rolling his nipple between her teeth, she said, "We *have* taken our time. We've been out three times, Freddie."

"Three whole times," he said more to himself than to her.

"What's wrong with you? Don't you want this?"

Did he? Did he really want it this way? Then he remembered his resolution. This was the year. He had chosen this woman, knowing she would be easy and uncomplicated. It wasn't her fault that uncomplicated had turned out to be empty and unsatisfying. "Yeah," he said, pulling off his coat.

She took it from him and with a saucy glance over her shoulder, she said, "Get comfortable. I'll be right back."

Freddie sat on the bed and looked around at the surprisingly feminine room. He wasn't sure what he'd been expecting, but pink and frilly wasn't it. Maybe she'd surprise him in other ways, too.

"Freddie."

He looked up and almost swallowed his tongue. Stark naked, she stood in the doorway. Zeroing in on the cupid tattoo on her left breast, he watched in stunned fascination as her pierced nipples sprang to life.

"See anything you like?"

"Uh-huh," he managed to say. "Come here."

She sashayed over to him and stepped between his parted legs. With her hands on his shoulders, she offered her breasts to him.

Flipping his tongue back and forth over one of her nipples, he cupped her firm ass and brought her in closer to him. Every toned inch of her was proof of the hours she spent at the gym. "Did it hurt?"

"What?" she asked breathlessly.

"Having them pierced."

"Like a sonofabitch."

"Then why do it?"

"Because it makes what you're doing right now even more intense, and they make me feel sexy."

"I can't believe you need any help feeling sexy."

She glanced down at him, a vulnerable expression on her usually confident face, and shrugged. Pushing the shirt off his shoulders, she tossed it to the floor and urged him to lie back.

He watched her as she divested him of his pants and underwear. And with that, with both of them naked and needy, he had already gone further than ever before.

Elin kissed her way down the front of him, and Freddie let her, knowing he needed to take the edge off if he was going to get through the main event without embarrassing himself. No doubt a woman like her had some pretty significant expectations. Over and done with in under thirty seconds probably wasn't one of them.

Wrapping her hand around his erection, she stroked him until he was harder than he could ever recall being.

"Mmm," she said as she wrapped her lips around him.

He had heard his friends and coworkers talk about women who actually liked giving blow jobs versus those who did it just to please their partner. If the enthusiastic way in which she stroked, licked and sucked was any indication, he had found one who seemed to like it as much as he did. Clutching her hair, Freddie discovered that watching her make love to him with her mouth was every bit as hot as the act itself.

When she cupped his balls and took him deep into her throat, Freddie cried out as a powerful orgasm gripped him. On the way back down to earth, he realized he still had a firm grip on her hair and loosened his hold.

She lapped at him, cleaning him up. "How can you come like that and still be so hard?" she asked, stroking him.

He reached for her, bringing her up to rest on top of him. "Stamina." And lack of use, he wanted to say but didn't.

"We need a condom," she said.

"In a minute." He captured her mouth in a hot, penetrating kiss, and suddenly it didn't matter that he didn't love her or that he'd been taught this was wrong outside of marriage. It didn't feel wrong. It felt good, and he wanted more. He wanted everything. "Let me grab that condom."

"Oh, no, let me," she said with a sexy glint in her eye.

Just as he was about to tell her about the condoms he'd been carrying around in his back pocket—just in case—she reached for her bedside table and produced a black foil packet.

"Ribbed, to enhance *my* pleasure." With her eyes fixed on his, she used her teeth to tear off the wrapper and rolled it on.

Freddie bit his lip to keep from losing it as she moved her hand slowly over his straining length.

When she was finished, she straddled him and leaned forward to touch her lips to his.

He filled his hands with her breasts and had to remind himself to breathe. This was really happening. Finally.

"How do you like it?" she whispered.

"Any way you like it."

"In that case, it's a good thing we have all night."

Using her hand, she led him to her slick channel and sank down on him.

Buried to the hilt in her heat, Freddie gasped.

"Does that hurt?" she asked, looking down at him with concern.

Unable to breathe let alone speak, he shook his head and gripped her hips.

She leaned back and took him even deeper.

Freddie wasn't sure if he should move or let her ride him, but his hips seemed to have a mind of their own as they surged up to meet her thrusts. *Oh, God, why had he waited so long to do this? Why?*

As if a wild beast had been unleashed inside him, he sat up, wrapped his arms around her and turned them over so he was on top. Bringing her to the edge of the bed, he kept his feet on the floor to gain maximum leverage and pounded into her. Sweat pooled at the base of his spine, burned his eyes and wet his forehead, but he felt nothing beyond the velvet heat surrounding his cock.

She sank her fingers into his ass, holding him deep inside her when she came with a sharp cry.

Somehow, Freddie managed to hold on to his control long enough to take her up and over once more. When he finally gave himself permission to join her, the relief that he'd managed to get through this without embarrassing himself tempered the mind-blowing release. Panting on top of her, still joined with her, he wondered how long he had to wait before he'd be able to do it again.

Sam rested her head on Nick's chest and listened to the soft cadence of his breathing. They had shared the leftover lobster and a bottle of wine, inaugurated the new Jacuzzi and done some serious power snuggling. He hadn't tried to make love to her, and she had been relieved that he seemed to know she needed something else tonight: a shoulder to lean on. His shoulder.

Touching her lips to his chest, she sighed with contentment. An odd sense of peace had come over her after she shared her deepest, darkest secret with him. That he knew the worst of her and loved her anyway was such a special gift in the midst of everything else he had brought to her life.

"Why are you awake at four a.m.?" he whispered, startling her.

"Why are you?"

"Insomnia."

"How come I don't know that after a month of sleeping with you?"

"Because you're usually sawing logs when I'm awake."

"I do not 'saw logs,'" she said indignantly.

"Um, yeah, you do."

"Want me to rub your back?" she asked.

"Really?"

"Turn over."

They shifted into position so she could caress his back.

He released a long deep breath. "Feels good."

"What's the deal with the insomnia?"

"It comes and goes, usually depending on the stress level at the moment."

"And you thought being a senator would be good for that?"

He laughed into his pillow. "It was a concern. One of many."

"You should see a doctor about it."

"As soon as you see Harry about your stomach." He referred to his friend, the internist, who'd agreed to sneak her in.

"I have an appointment on Friday."

"Good. Want me to go with you?"

"You'll be knee-deep in nomination hearings on Friday."

"I can be there if you need me."

"I'll be fine." She kissed his shoulder. "Go to sleep."

He put his arm around her and drew her in close to him. "Only if you do."

"Deal."

They were both on their way when the phone rang.

"It's mine." She reached for her cell on the bedside table. "Holland."

"I'm sorry to disturb you, Lieutenant," Detective Jeannie McBride said. "We've got a homicide, and you asked us to let you know."

"Where?"

"Lincoln Park."

"I'm on my way." She got up and reached for the clothes she'd worn the night before and realized they were inappropriate for a middle-of-the-night winter crime scene. "Crap. I'll have to go to my dad's to change."

"You know, if you lived here, your clothes would, too," Nick muttered.

"Ha-ha."

He got out of bed.

"What're you doing?" she asked.

"Saving you some time." He stepped into his closet and emerged with a sweater of his that he tossed to her. In his other hand, he held up a pair of running shoes. "You left these here last week."

"Excellent," she said, as she pushed her arms into the sweater. "Mmm, smells like you."

"Do you need socks?"

Pulling on her black dress pants, she flashed him a sheepish grin. "Um, yeah."

He handed her a pair.

"Thanks." Wrapping her arms around his warm, naked body, she went up on tiptoes to kiss him. "Try to get some sleep."

"Be careful out there, babe."

"I always am."

Sam raised the yellow crime scene tape and stepped into Lincoln Park. The blustery winter wind smacked at her face as she worked to shake off the stupor of a sleepless night. She shivered, yearning for Nick and the warmth of his bed.

The first hint of sunrise graced the horizon. Across the park, under the glare of lights that had been brought in, two patrol officers stood watch over the victim.

"What've we got?" she asked Detective Jeannie McBride.

McBride consulted her notebook. "Victim is male, Caucasian, late sixties. Killed with a single gunshot wound to the back of the head. His hands and feet were bound."

"Execution style?"

"Yes, ma'am."

"ID?"

"None on him, but he's well dressed."

"Start a log of everyone who's here now or comes in later."

"Got it."

"Where's Cruz?"

"Not answering his phone or pager."

Startled, Sam glanced at Jeannie. "That's odd."

"Yes, Lieutenant."

Wondering where in the hell her partner was, she jammed her hands into her coat pockets. "Try him again." Sam's long-legged stride ate up the distance to where the victim lay crumpled on the ground.

Nodding to the patrol officers, she tugged on latex gloves and squatted down to examine the twine that had been used to bind his hands and feet. His shoes, she noted, were missing. Blood pooled at the site of the gunshot wound. With her hand on his shoulder, she turned him and gasped as she looked down at the dead face of the man they'd dined with the night before.

"Oh, God," she whispered. "Oh, poor Nick." Standing over the lifeless body of Supreme Court nominee Julian Sinclair, all Sam could think about was the day she and Nick had gone to Leesburg to tell the O'Connors their son had been murdered. And now their longtime friend was dead, too. She couldn't imagine how any of them would withstand this new blow on top of the one they'd so recently sustained.

"Lieutenant?" Detective McBride said from behind her.

"It's Julian Sinclair."

McBride gasped. "The Supreme Court nominee?"

Sam nodded. "Contact Malone and Farnsworth. Let them know that Senator Cappuano, Senator and Mrs. Graham

O'Connor, and myself were among the last people to see him alive."

McBride stared at her for a long moment.

"Make the calls, Jeannie."

"Yes, ma'am."

Jeannie walked away, and Sam returned her attention to the victim. "What happened, Julian?" she whispered, feeling horrible about the odd confrontation she'd had with him the night before. She checked his hands and found no defensive wounds. Whoever grabbed him had caught him off guard. "What happened after you left Nick's house?"

"Lieutenant," McBride said a few minutes later, "the medical examiner is here. The chief and the captain are on their way. No luck reaching Cruz."

"Thank you." She took another long last look at Sinclair before she stood up and tugged off the gloves. "Who found him?"

"A drunk tripped over him. The guy is freaking out." She pointed to an ambulance parked at the curb. "Paramedics are with him now."

"Let me brief the brass, and then I want to talk to him. Canvass?"

"Tyrone and a couple of uniforms are on it," she said, referring to her partner.

"Good job, McBride. Thanks."

"So, um, you met him? The vic?"

"He had dinner with us at Nick's new place on Capitol Hill. They were friends."

"Jeez, and he just lost his other friend."

Her lips tight with tension, Sam said, "Yes."

Captain Malone and Chief Farnsworth arrived minutes apart, and Sam filled them in. "I left before dinner, so I need to talk to Nick about what time it ended and how Sinclair got back to the hotel."

"Get to it," the chief said, his expression grim as he studied the gunshot wound to Sinclair's head.

"I'm waiting on crime scene to get here," Sam said.

"I'll wait for them," Malone replied. "You go on ahead."

"Gonna be another hot one, Lieutenant," Farnsworth said.

"And the spotlight will once again be on me and my personal life," she grumbled.

"Will it be too much of a distraction?" Farnsworth asked.

"No, sir. McBride, you're with me." She gestured for the other woman to follow her.

Jeannie trotted along behind Sam as she stalked across the park to talk to the wino who'd found Sinclair. He was all but incoherent, adding nothing to the investigation.

Furious, she took off for her car, again with Jeannie in hot pursuit.

"Do you want me to try Cruz again for you?"

"No." Sam struggled to find the words she would need to break the devastating news to Nick. The very thought of it broke her heart, but there was no room for her emotions in the midst of what needed to be done in the next few hours. "He'll have to catch up when he resurfaces."

CHAPTER 13

Sam parallel parked on Ninth Street and stared at the front door to Nick's house.

"How do you want to do this?" Jeannie asked.

"He's still asleep," Sam said, glancing up at the dark window on the second floor. "I'll wake him up and have him come down. I want you to witness the conversation."

"Right." McBride twisted her fingers in her lap.

"I know this'll be uncomfortable for you, Detective, but I need you there to record and witness the conversation. Everything about this has to be by the book. He's a potential witness."

"I understand."

Sam concentrated on breathing her way through the pain that circulated in her gut.

"Are you all right, Lieutenant?"

"Yeah." In a cold sweat brought on by the pain, she reached for the door handle. "Let's get this over with."

Jeannie followed Sam up the stairs and waited while she used her key in the door.

Inside, Sam flipped on a light.

Jeannie released a low whistle. "Wow, nice place."

"Uh-huh. Have a seat. I'll be right back." With a deep breath to calm her nerves and her stomach, Sam started up the stairs. Turning on a light in the hallway, she went to the bedroom doorway and stood there for a long moment watching him sleep and wishing with all her heart that she could spare him from what she was about to do to him.

Moving to the bedside, she leaned down to kiss his cheek. "Nick." She shook his shoulder. *"Nick."*

"Mmm, hey, babe. Back already?"

"I need to talk to you."

"'K." He gave her hand a tug to bring her into bed with him.

Sam resisted. "Nick."

His eyes fluttered open.

"I *need* to talk to you."

"What's wrong?"

"Can you come downstairs?"

Running his fingers through his hair, he looked up at her. "Why not right here?"

She swallowed hard. "I need it on the record."

"What the hell, Sam?" he asked, sitting up.

"Please."

"Fine." He tossed back the covers and reached for his sweats. "Am I allowed to take a leak first?"

"Yes, but hurry. Detective McBride is downstairs waiting for us."

He shot her a furious scowl but thankfully didn't ask any more questions as he headed into the bathroom and closed the door.

Sam went downstairs to find Jeannie wandering around. "He'll be right down."

"This place is huge!"

"The guy who lived here before bought the place next door and knocked out walls."

"Are you living here, too?"

"No. I'm still at my dad's three doors down."

"Why?"

"Because—"

"Because she's not ready," Nick said, now wearing a T-shirt with his sweats, as he came down the stairs to join them. He slipped an arm around Sam and kissed the top of her head.

She shook him off.

Startled and possibly hurt, Nick stared at her.

"This is Detective Jeannie McBride."

Nick extended his hand. "Yes, I remember from the party."

"Nice to see you again, Senator."

"Please, call me Nick." He turned to Sam. "Are you going to tell me what's going on?"

"Sit," Sam said, gesturing toward the sofa.

"I'd rather stand. Thanks."

Hands on her hips, Sam said, "Detective McBride, please record this conversation."

Nick stared at her. "Sam—"

Sam nodded to Jeannie, who set the pocket-sized recorder on the coffee table. "I'm sorry to have to inform you that Julian Sinclair was found murdered early this morning in Lincoln Park."

Nick took a step back, shook his head and whispered, "No." He shook his head again and then dropped into a chair when his legs seemed to give out beneath him.

"I'm very sorry," Jeannie said.

"But he was just here." Nick looked up at Sam, his eyes shiny with tears. "How?"

"He was shot," Sam said, deciding quick and dirty was the best strategy. "His hands and feet were bound."

Nick buried his face in his hands and wept, all the while continuing to shake his head.

Jeannie shot a nervous glance at Sam and tipped her head, silently imploring Sam to go to him.

Desperate to maintain her professional edge but aching for him, she moved over to perch on the arm of the chair. She put her arm around his shoulders.

He turned into her embrace and shook with sobs. "How could this have happened? First John, and now this. Oh, God, Graham and Laine. This'll kill them."

"I know it's a terrible shock for you, but I need to ask you a few things."

Wiping his face, he nodded. "Whatever I can do."

"What time did Julian leave here last night?"

"It was just after eleven," he said, quickly adding, "I was watching the clock, because I wanted them to leave so I could go find you."

Sam glanced at Jeannie, who hung on their every word. "Did he say or do anything to indicate he was worried about something or had been threatened by anyone?"

"No, nothing like that. He was anxious about the confirmation hearings, but he didn't mention anything else."

"Would he have? If he was anxious or worried, would he have said something?"

"I think so. Especially after you left and it was just the four of us. He and Graham are the best of friends, and he knew he could trust me, too."

"How did he get back to the hotel?"

"Since he had taken a cab over here, Graham and Laine dropped him off."

She glanced at Jeannie. "I need to talk to them."

"I'll go with you," Nick said, standing up.

"You don't have to," Sam said. "We can take care of it."

His eyes narrowed. "Don't ask me to sit here while you're in Leesburg crushing them—again. Don't ask that of me, Sam."

They stared each other down in a fierce battle of wills.

"I could have Tyrone pick me up here," Jeannie interjected. "We can go to Sinclair's hotel, interview the doorman, get the security tapes and go through his room."

When Sam realized it wasn't necessary to win this stand-off, she glanced at Jeannie. "Do it." She turned back to Nick. "Why don't you go get dressed?"

With a long, hard look at her, he turned and went back upstairs.

The stony silence in the car worked on Sam's nerves. She had no idea what she should say or if she should reach out to him. Something told her he wouldn't welcome anything from her just then. What she didn't know was why. Was he blaming her for this latest wave of devastating news? She'd just been doing her job.

She glanced over and found him staring out the window, lost in his own thoughts, far, far away from her. The distance frightened her.

"Nick."

He didn't answer, didn't blink, didn't seem to even know or care she was there.

Reaching over, she curled her hand around his. "Talk to me."

"Nothing to say."

"I'm sorry this has happened to your friend. And to you."

"Thank you."

"Are you mad at me?"

His eyes finally shifted from the window to focus on her. "Why didn't you tell me when we were upstairs? When we were alone?"

"Because I couldn't."

"Right."

"I did it that way to protect you! So your statement and your reaction would be witnessed and on the record. You were one of the last people to see him alive. I was trying to ensure that you'd be cleared of any suspicion."

Sagging into his seat, he said, "I didn't think of it that way."

"I hated having to tell you that, and I hate that we're once again on our way to deliver devastating news to two people who don't deserve it."

"No," he said softly. "They really don't."

"Neither do you."

"I don't have a lot of close friends," he said, once again looking straight ahead. "There're not a lot of people I feel completely comfortable with. Julian was one of them."

Her heart aching for him, she tightened her grip on his hand. "You have me now," she said. "I'm right here with you."

He replied with a small nod.

As Sam drove, she kept one eye on him. The combination of the two murders had plunged him into such deep despair that she had no idea how to reach him.

At the O'Connors' country home in Leesburg, Laine greeted them with a warm smile and hugs.

"Nick! Sam! How nice to see you again so soon." She ushered them into the foyer. "What brings you out this way?"

Nick fell into Laine's embrace and broke down.

Alarmed, Laine held him close. "Sweetheart, what is it?"

Sam had never seen Nick quite this undone, even after John died, and was unnerved by it. She was also struck by the odd sensation of once again being on the outside looking in. That he'd waited to get here, to his adopted mother, before he gave into the full depths of his devastation hurt Sam.

"You're frightening me, Nick," Laine said, reaching up to

brush the tears from his face. "Will one of you please tell me what's wrong?"

"It's Julian," Nick said softly.

Laine gasped and took a step back from him. With her hand over her heart, she stared at him. "No."

"Is Senator O'Connor at home?" Sam asked.

"He's in his study."

"I'll get him," Nick said, wiping his face as he left the room.

"How?" Laine asked with the steely, patrician strength Sam had grown to admire in the weeks she had known her.

Sam told her what she knew.

"This'll demolish Graham," Laine whispered.

"I said the same thing about Nick."

Their eyes met and held, two women united in their worries about the men they loved.

A ravaged howl came from a room off the living room.

Laine rushed off in the direction of the study.

Sam followed her. They found the two men sitting on the sofa, Nick's arm around Graham's shoulders.

Laine went to her husband.

"I just can't believe this," Graham said through his tears. He reached for his wife's hand. "He was fine. We just saw him."

Sam stepped into a room made cozy by the heat coming from the fireplace. "I'm sorry for your loss," she said.

Laine gestured her over to join them.

Sam took the seat next to Nick.

Graham turned his grief-stricken eyes on Sam. "Will you find out who did this? I need to know who could've done this."

Grateful for the opening, she said, "I know this is a terrible shock, but you were among the last people to see him alive. Can you tell me about taking him back to the hotel?"

Graham wiped his face with the back of his hand. "He was staying at the Willard, so we said we'd drop him off."

"What time was that?"

He glanced at his wife. "About eleven-fifteen or so?"

She nodded.

"Did you watch him enter the hotel?"

Laine thought about that. "I can't say that I did."

"I didn't, either," Graham said.

"Were there any other people around?"

Laine paused for a moment. "I believe one of the hotel staff was working the door."

"Yes," Graham said. "I saw someone in a uniform."

"How about other cars?" Nick asked.

"We were the only ones in front of the hotel," Graham said. "I remember commenting to Laine that the middle of the night was the only time Washington isn't gridlocked."

"During your visit with him," Sam said, now addressing the three of them, "did he talk about anything or anyone he was having a problem with? A friend, girlfriend, acquaintance?"

They exchanged glances.

"What?" Sam asked.

"Julian was gay," Nick said.

Processing the information, Sam sagged into the leather chair. "Did people know?"

"Those closest to him, but he was discreet," Nick said. "The media hadn't zeroed in on his orientation yet."

"But he knew they would," Laine said. "He suspected it would come up during the confirmation hearings."

"Was he concerned about that?"

"Not particularly," Graham replied in a soft voice. The devastation wrought by the double-whammy of losing his son and now his close friend seemed to have diminished him. "His mother died several years ago without ever knowing he was gay. Her death liberated him in many ways. He didn't care quite as much if people found out."

"Was he in a relationship?"

"Not anymore," Laine said, looking to Nick when she added, "How long ago did he and Duncan break up?"

"More than a year."

Graham nodded in agreement.

"Were they together a long time?" Sam asked.

"Had to be twenty years," Graham said.

"Was Duncan out of the closet?"

"Only to the people closest to him. Duncan wanted to retire and move to Florida," Nick said. "Julian wasn't ready to stop working, which is what broke them up. Julian loved teaching at Harvard, and when Nelson was elected, he knew the Supreme Court nomination was likely." His voice faltered. "I just can't believe he's gone."

"Is it possible," Sam ventured, "that Duncan was worried about unwanted attention during the nomination hearings?"

"Worried enough to tie Julian up and shoot him in the back of the head?" Nick asked.

Laine gasped. "Oh, God. *God*."

"I'm sorry," Nick said. "I didn't mean to just blurt that out."

"Duncan loved Julian," Graham said. "I've never really understood how two guys, you know… But seeing them together…"

Laine dabbed at tears. "They were a lovely couple. We adored them both."

"I'll need to talk to Duncan," Sam said. "Do you know where I can find him?"

"He lives in South Beach." Laine rose and crossed the room to the smaller of the two desks. Returning, she handed Sam a piece of paper. "Here's his address."

Sam tucked the address into her back pocket and checked

her watch. Almost nine o'clock. "I need to get back to the city," she said to Nick. "Do you want to stay here?"

He glanced at Graham.

"You need to be at the Capitol for the start of the new session," Graham said.

"Are you sure?" Nick asked. "I don't mind staying."

"Go to work, Senator. Get John's bill passed."

Nick clutched the older man's hand and leaned into his embrace.

"We'll get through this," Graham said gruffly. "Somehow, we'll get through it."

Nick nodded and stood to hug Laine.

Sam followed suit.

"You'll be gentle when you tell Duncan?" Laine said.

"I promise."

Laine reached up to caress Sam's face. "I don't envy you your job, but I have full confidence that you'll find the person who did this to Julian."

Taken aback by the loving gesture, Sam said, "I'll do my best."

CHAPTER 14

After another quiet ride, Sam was even more alarmed by Nick's withdrawal. Her attempts to lure him into conversation failed, and he passed most of the ride staring out the passenger window. As she pulled into a parking space on Ninth Street, her stomach began to ache. She desperately needed to get to HQ, but how could she leave him like this?

"Nick?"

He stared unseeing out the window.

Reaching out to him, she rested her hand on his arm. "Nick, honey, come on. We're home."

All at once, he seemed to snap out of the stupor he had sunk into. "You must need to get to work."

"I'll walk you in." She got out of the car and went around to open his door. Following him up the stairs and into the house, Sam watched him lower himself into the first chair he encountered and drop his head into his hands.

In her pocket, her pager vibrated for the sixth time in the past ten minutes. Her cell phone rang, but as much as it pained her to let it ring, she ignored it—again. She went into the kitchen to make him some coffee and found his cell phone on the counter. Debating for a moment, she reached for it and scrolled through his list of contacts. Second to her on his speed dial list was Christina. Sam pressed send.

"Senator," Christina said. "I just heard about Julian Sinclair. I'm so sorry."

"Um, it's Sam."

"Oh. Hi. Is he—"

"He's a mess. I need to go to work, but I can't leave him like this."

"I'll be right there."

"Do you mind?" Sam asked, cringing at how foolish she sounded.

"Of course not. I care about him, too, you know."

"I know you do."

"I'm sorry. I just can't believe this has happened."

"No one can."

"I'll be there as soon as I can."

"Thank you."

Sam was astounded when she opened the front door twenty minutes later to find Christina *and* Gonzo.

"What're you doing here?" she asked Gonzo as she stepped aside to let them in.

Right before Sam's eyes, the formidable Tommy "Gonzo" Gonzales blushed. "I was, uh, with her when she got the call about Sinclair. I thought maybe I could help."

Sam looked from Gonzo to Christina, who had gone straight to Nick on the sofa, back to Gonzo. "Define *with* her."

He squirmed. "You know, *with* her." Nodding to Nick, he added, "The way you're *with* him."

"Are you freaking kidding me?"

"What? We're both consenting adults."

Before she could reply, Sam's cell phone and pager rang si-

multaneously. She checked both LCDs and took the call from
Captain Malone.

"Lieutenant. I've been trying to reach you for an hour."

"I was interviewing Senator and Mrs. O'Connor, probably
the last people to see Sinclair alive."

"What've you got?"

She recited the O'Connors' version of the routine drop off
at the hotel. "I sent McBride and Tyrone to the Willard to
get the security tapes and interview the staff."

"She's back with the tapes. They're viewing them now. The
bellman who was working the door is coming in at noon."

"Good, tell her to let me know what he has to say. I need
you to authorize travel to Miami for myself and Detective
Gonzales."

"Where's Cruz?"

"Good question."

"What's in Miami?"

Sam checked the sofa and saw Nick speaking softly to Christina. She tried not to be bothered by the fact that he had been
unable to talk to her but was having no problem unloading
on his chief of staff.

"Lieutenant?" Malone said.

Tearing her eyes off the scene on the sofa, Sam said, "Sinclair's longtime lover. Duncan Quick."

"He was gay?"

"Yes. He ended a twenty-year relationship with Quick a
year ago, and apparently, Quick is still partially in the closet."

"The confirmation hearings would've blown the lid off
that."

"Your thinking parallels mine. I want to see Quick's reaction to the news that Sinclair's dead."

"Approved."

"We'll be back tonight."

"Do we need to be worried about Cruz?"

"Hang on a sec." She did a quick scroll through her missed calls and pages, but found nothing from Freddie. "No word from him at all this morning. That's not like him."

"I'll send patrol by his apartment."

"Let me know." She ended the call and turned to Gonzo. "I'll meet you outside."

"Got it."

Sam approached the duo on the sofa. "Ah, would you mind giving us a minute?" she said to Christina.

"Sure." She released Nick's hand and got up.

Sam sat next to him and lifted her hand to brush the hair from his forehead. "I'm going to Florida to talk to Duncan."

"Okay."

"I don't feel right about going. About leaving you." She rested her forehead on his shoulder.

"I want you to find out who did this."

"Are you going to work?"

"Yeah. Christina told me the Senate is going to take up John's bill as its first order of business in the new session."

"Oh, Nick. That's great news."

That he seemed to barely care only added to her growing list of worries.

She pressed a kiss to his cheek. "I'll be back. As soon as I can."

"I know."

Reluctantly, she got up and went into the kitchen where Christina was pouring coffee. "You'll be with him?" Sam asked.

"Every minute."

Sam glanced at Nick staring off into space in the next room. "This is worse than after John."

"Yes."

Running her fingers over hair that she'd corralled into a clip, Sam considered taking a pass on the case. It was up to her, after all. She could put Gonzo in charge, send him to Florida and stay in D.C. with Nick. But he'd rebuffed all her efforts to comfort him.

"Sam."

She turned to find Christina studying her intently. "He'll understand if you go. He knows it's your job, and he has to go do his today. We need his vote."

Sam nodded. "Don't leave him alone." And then she remembered Christina wasn't one of her detectives. "Please."

"You have my word."

"Thank you." She went into the living room and bent to kiss Nick's forehead. "I'll see you tonight."

If he heard her, he gave no indication.

Only when she was outside did she realize he hadn't told her to be careful.

Sam approached the car where Gonzo waited for her. With every step she took away from Nick, she became more conflicted. Pacing the sidewalk, she tried to figure out what to do. Unused to being paralyzed by indecision, she examined every angle and kept coming back to the same conclusion. Before this, before Nick, there'd never been a decision. The job came first. Always. Now it wasn't quite so simple.

Gonzo waited patiently, watching her as she moved back and forth.

Finally, Sam stopped and turned to him. "Go to Florida." From her pocket, she withdrew the slip of paper Laine had given her, handed it to him and filled him in on what she knew about Duncan Quick. "He was with Sinclair for twenty years, so be gentle in how you deliver the news. I want to know where Quick has been for the last twenty-four hours. I want confirmation from anyone he names as an alibi."

"You aren't coming?"

Sam glanced at the front door to Nick's house. "No."

Gonzo's eyes widened with surprise.

"Don't say it," she growled.

His expression one of total innocence, he said, "Say what?"

"Call me the minute you have anything."

"I'm on it."

She watched him walk to his car and drive away, and then she kicked the living shit out of one of the tires on her own car.

"Sam?"

Looking up, she found her father and Celia watching her.

"What's wrong?" her father asked, directing his chair around a patch of ice on the sidewalk as he came toward her.

"Did you hear about Sinclair?"

"The chief called your father," Celia said. "We're stunned. How's Nick?"

"Horrible."

"Is that why you're abusing your car?" Skip asked.

"I need to go to Florida to interview Sinclair's ex-lover, but how do I do that when he's practically catatonic?" Sam asked, gesturing to Nick's house.

"Is anyone with him?" Celia asked.

"Christina, his chief of staff," Sam said. She should be the one offering comfort to Nick, but for some reason he didn't want it from her.

Nick's front door swung open, and they watched as Christina held the storm door open, urging him out ahead of her. He had changed into a suit, but hadn't bothered to shave.

Sam, Skip and Celia watched them come down the stone stairs.

"What are you still doing here?" Nick asked Sam in a dull, flat tone.

"I sent Gonzo to Florida."

"Oh."

"We're going to the Capitol so he can be there for the opening of the new session and to vote on O'Connor-Martin," Christina said.

"I'll catch up to you after," Sam said.

"Talk to Senator Cook," Nick said, still wearing a faraway expression on his face.

"Why?" Sam asked.

"He made a comment to me about Julian," Nick said. "That he should watch his back because someone might take a shot at him."

"I'll talk to Cook." Sam went up on tiptoes to kiss his cheek. "That helps. Thank you."

Christina ushered Nick into her car, and they drove off.

"Wow," Skip said. "You weren't kidding."

"What do I do?" Sam said. "I don't know how to help him through this."

"You love him," Celia said. "You just love him. That's all you can do."

Freddie awakened from a deep sleep, his body languid and replete after an all-night sex fest. With his hand tucked into the soft lushness of Elin's breasts, he wondered if there was any special morning-after stuff he should say or do.

As he pondered that question, she stirred, her muscular ass brushing against his groin.

His dick actually ached from what he'd put it through during the night. It was a good thing he had to work this morning. Otherwise, he might be expected to perform again, and he wasn't sure he could.

Stretching his stiff muscles he raised his arm to check his watch to see how much time he had before his cell phone alarm would tell him it was time to get up. "Shit!" He sat up so fast that Elin almost fell off her side of the bed.

"What?"

Freddie bolted from the bed and ran for his coat, which Elin had put in the living room the night before. Rifling through the pocket, he found his cell phone and stared at it in stunned disbelief. It was off. He never shut off that phone. Ever. "Did you shut my phone off?" Returning to the bedroom, he powered up the phone.

Still half-asleep, she muttered, "Hmm?"

"Elin! *Did you shut off my phone?*" It went crazy beeping with messages. *"Sonofabitch."*

"You were off duty," she said without opening her eyes. "I wanted you to relax."

"Are you *serious?* I'm a homicide detective! I'm never off duty!" Multiple calls from Jeannie McBride, Sam and Captain Malone popped up on the list of missed calls. "Shit, shit, *shit,*" he whispered, tugging on his clothes as fast as he could, his heart racing with anxiety and dread. What had he missed?

Elin watched him from the bed, the sheet pulled up snug against her ample breasts. "Are you mad?" she asked in a small voice.

He was so far beyond mad he was afraid to say anything for fear he'd totally lose it with her. Pushing his feet into the hiking boots he favored in the winter, he headed for the door without tying them.

She got up, donned a robe and followed him into the living room. "I'm sorry, Freddie. I wasn't thinking about your work."

Without a single look back, he stalked out the door and let it slam behind him.

On his way to HQ, Freddie fought back surge after surge

of nausea. He had no one to blame but himself. This was his punishment for abandoning his morals for a night of mindless sex. If he hadn't given into his base urges, he'd be at work right now where he belonged rather than desperately trying to come up with an excuse that Sam would buy.

"Play that back again." Sam watched the screen with intense focus. "There. Freeze that." She pointed. "Is that him talking to the doorman? The height is about right."

Jeannie consulted her notes. "The doorman said he didn't remember Sinclair talking to him."

"It's kind of fuzzy, Lieutenant," Malone said from behind her. "Could be anyone."

"No one recalled talking to him," Jeannie said. "We interviewed the entire shift."

"Take it to the lab," Sam said. "See if they can enhance that frame for us."

Freddie came bursting into the room.

"Cruz," Sam said. "Nice of you to join us."

"I'm sorry, Lieutenant," he said, breathing hard. "I overslept. My phone died."

"Which is it, Detective?" Sam said, studying his disheveled appearance.

Freddie took a deep breath. "My phone died and the alarm didn't go off so I overslept. I apologize. It won't happen again. What did I miss?"

"A homicide," Sam said, filling him in on the details.

"Isn't that Nick's friend?"

"Yes."

"Oh, man," Freddie said.

He turned his head, and Sam zeroed in on the hickey on his neck.

"What can I do?" he asked. "Give me something to do."

Still eyeing him suspiciously, Sam handed him the tape and repeated the instructions to have the lab zero in on the frame in question. "I'll be partnering with Detective McBride on this one."

"*Why?*" Freddie cried. "Because I was late *one* time?"

"No." Sam leveled him with a cold stare. "Because you lied to me."

"I told you what happened! I've never been late before. Ever."

"Take the tape to the lab, Detective, and then go relieve the officers watching Reese's house."

Freddie's mouth fell open. "For real?"

"You heard me."

He stalked out of the conference room, slamming the door behind him.

"I'm, um, going to check on the canvas," McBride said, scooting out after him.

Malone studied Sam.

"What?" she snapped.

"Being kind of hard on Cruz, aren't you?"

"You told me to run my command any way I see fit. That's what I'm doing."

"How do you know he lied?"

"I know him."

"Very well," Malone said. "I'll leave you to it. You know where I am if you need me."

When she was alone, Sam paced the small room. The frustration threatened to boil over. Where was Clarence Reese? Who had killed Julian Sinclair? How would she deal with Nick and his devastation in the midst of two homicide investigations? And last, who had been chewing on her partner's neck?

CHAPTER 15

Gonzo sat on the floor outside Duncan Quick's apartment for more than an hour. A window at one end of the hall looked out over South Beach, eleven stories below. The boredom gave him far too much time to think about the incredible night he had spent with Christina Billings.

She had surprised him with her willingness to sleep with him after just two dates. He'd expected to have to work harder to win over a sharp, successful woman like her. Not that he was complaining. No way. The woman was h-o-t. It was just that not too many people surprised him anymore after ten years as a cop.

Not only did she surprise him, she intrigued him. He wasn't used to being intrigued by women. Entertained, yes. Intrigued? Not so much. He'd expected her to be like most of the women who passed through his life as transients. They were on their way to something more lasting, something they knew they wouldn't find with him. So he had a reputation for being a bit of a player. So what?

"I think I might keep this one around for a while," he muttered to himself. "See what transpires." Of course the fact

that Sam had freaked when she saw them together only added
to Christina's appeal. "A smart man wouldn't antagonize his
boss." Laughing to himself, Gonzo combed his fingers through
jet-black hair. "I guess I'm not that smart."

He checked his watch again. Where the hell was Quick?
The neighbors hadn't been able to shed any light on his whereabouts. In fact, no one had seen him since the previous morning. Gonzo had already checked all the neighborhood haunts
he'd been told Quick frequented to no avail.

His cell phone rang. "Gonzales."

"What've you got?" Sam asked.

"Nothing yet. No sign of Quick anywhere."

"Interesting."

"How long do you want me to wait?"

"As long as it takes. He has to come home eventually."

"I was afraid you'd say that. What's happening there?"

"We've got jack. No one at the hotel remembers seeing Sinclair after the O'Connors dropped him off. We've got some
grainy film that seems to show him talking to someone, but
the image isn't clear enough to be of any help."

"Is it possible he was meeting someone?"

"We're looking at that. His estranged brother lives here in
town. McBride and I are on our way to talk to him now."

"Keep me posted. Any sign of Cruz?"

"He rolled in about an hour ago with a hickey on his neck
and a boatload of excuses about his phone dying."

Gonzo howled with laughter. "Aw, our little boy is finally
growing up."

"He needs to grow up on his own time."

"It's the first time he's ever been late. Lighten up, Lieutenant."

"I wish everyone would stop saying that to me!"

"Would you ride anyone else this hard?" Gonzo asked, bracing himself for her retort.

"What're you saying? That I favor him?"

"He's your partner. Of course you favor him. But maybe you expect more of him, too." Again he braced himself. "Because you trained him."

"Hmm. I hadn't thought of it that way."

"So he had a big night out. It's high time, don't you think?"

"Maybe," she conceded. "I should probably partner up with you or someone more experienced so I don't have to deal with this crap."

"You'd break his heart, Sam. He's totally devoted to you."

"Christ," she muttered. "All these entanglements. When did I get so *entangled?*"

Gonzo laughed. "It's such a bitch having people care about you, isn't it?"

"Seriously! Call me when you find Quick."

"Will do." Gonzo stashed the phone in his pocket and got up to wander to the window again. Looking out at the palm trees, sugar-white sand and crystal-blue water, he wished he were here on vacation. *When was the last time I had a vacation?* he wondered. His grandparents had lived here when they first came from Cuba, but the family later moved north. Maybe after they closed this case, he'd bring Christina here for a week on the beach.

"Whoa," he said. "Where'd that come from?" He wasn't the kind of guy who took a woman on a vacation. Hell, he rarely saw them again after he slept with them. The ding of the elevator arriving at the other end of the hallway jarred him out of his disturbing thoughts. Turning, he found an older man coming down the hallway at a determined clip. Only when he drew closer did Gonzo spot the bruises on the man's face

and the drying blood on his lip. He carried a small duffel bag and was dressed in khakis and an untucked button-down shirt.

"Mr. Quick?"

The other man jolted, clearly startled by Gonzo's unexpected appearance.

"I'm sorry to scare you. Are you Duncan Quick?"

"Who wants to know?"

Gonzo flashed his badge. "Detective Tommy Gonzales, Metro Washington, D.C. Police."

Quick ran a trembling hand through thinning gray hair. "I'm Duncan Quick. What can I do for you?"

"What happened to your face?"

"I had an accident."

Gonzo didn't believe him but decided not to push it—yet. "Do you mind if we go inside?"

"What's this about?"

"Let's go in, and I'll tell you."

Warily, Quick opened his apartment door and gestured Gonzo into a stylish, contemporary space.

"Nice place."

"Thank you. Now what can I do for you, Detective?"

"I'm sorry to have to tell you that Julian Sinclair has been murdered in Washington." Gonzo had learned to cut to the chase in these instances.

Quick gasped and took a step back, his face ashen with shock. The bruises stood out against the sudden pallor. "That's not possible," Quick stammered. "He's going to be on the Supreme Court. I saw the news."

"He was murdered last night."

"How?" he whispered.

"He was shot. His body was found early this morning in a Washington, D.C., park."

"That just can't be," Quick said, sinking to the sofa as if his bones had liquefied. He dissolved into deep gulping sobs.

Gonzo found himself looking out at the water view, anything to avoid watching the raw display of grief. "Can I get you something?" he asked a few minutes later.

Without looking up, Quick shook his head.

Gonzo gave him another couple of minutes. "Mr. Quick, I'm sorry to have to do this, but I need to know where you've been for the last twenty-four hours."

Quick released a harsh laugh. "Where have I been? I was getting the shit beat out of me by a guy I met in a bar." His voice caught on a sob, and he buried his face in his hands. "Julian, oh, God, this is all my fault."

Gonzo sat down across from Quick. "What do you mean?"

"I forced the issue." He wiped tears from his face. "I wanted him to retire and move down here with me, but he wasn't ready. If I had stayed with him, if I had been with him, maybe…"

"I'm going to need the name of the man you were with last night."

Quick raised his anguished face, his eyes connecting with Gonzo's. "You suspect *me?*"

"I need to rule you out." Gonzo nodded toward the duffel Quick had dropped inside the door. "What's in the bag?"

"Gym clothes."

"Mind if I have a look?"

With the weary wave of his hand, Quick granted permission.

Gonzo went over to squat down next to the bag. Unzipping it, he pulled out a bloody T-shirt and turned to Quick.

"What I was wearing when this happened," he said, pointing to his lip.

Studying the older man's battered face, Gonzo believed

him. According to Sam's report, Sinclair's body had shown no sign of a struggle the likes of which Quick had obviously endured. "Who were you with, Duncan?"

Quick ran a weary hand though his hair. "You really have to talk to him?"

"I really do."

"I'd appreciate it if you didn't mention all of this," he said, gesturing to his face.

"Why would you want him to get away with that?"

"I've been so lost without Julian, Detective." The statement and the grief behind it touched Gonzo. "I took a risk and paid the price." He shrugged. "Not the first time, probably won't be the last."

"When did you last speak to Julian?"

"A couple of months ago. He called to tell me the nomination was imminent and to assure me he would do his best to keep my name out of the proceedings."

"And that was important to you?"

"There are people in my life who aren't aware."

"What was at stake for you if they found out?"

"Plain old bigotry." He paused, gathering his thoughts. "Julian has a brother who stopped speaking to him after he found out about us. They hadn't spoken in thirteen years." Sadness radiated from him. "Can you imagine? Not speaking to your brother simply because of who he loves?"

"No, sir. I can't."

"That's how it is for people of our generation." He got up, went to a bar set up by the windows overlooking the beach, and poured himself a shot. "We often have to hide who we are from even those closest to us."

Gonzo shook his head at the offer of a drink.

"We were very discreet. Always. For the first seven years we were together, only a small circle of close friends knew that we were more than the best of friends. We even maintained separate residences, at least on paper. Then his sister-in-law found out about us and went ballistic. We were much more careful after that." Duncan poured another drink. "But I reached a point where I couldn't live a lie for one more day. Twenty years is a long time, you know?"

Gonzo nodded.

"Julian's mother died. His brother was out of the picture. My family hardly would've been surprised if I officially came out. I couldn't understand what was standing in our way."

"So what was?"

Duncan smiled, but it didn't reach his eyes. "Ambition." He returned to the sofa and sat down hard. "Julian wanted the court more than he wanted me."

"That must've angered you."

"It hurt me. I'd planned to grow old with him." His voice hitched on a sob. "I loved him. More than anyone else in this world. I *loved* him. After he was nominated, I kept hoping the press would find out."

Gonzo waited for him to continue.

"I figured if it got out, it might derail the nomination. As far as we've come, I don't know if America is ready for a gay Supreme Court justice. I'm ashamed to say I even considered leaking it. But I discovered I couldn't do that to him. That's how much I loved him. So when I heard he was in Washington for the hearings, I went out, got drunk, met a thug named Ron and went home with him. You know the rest."

"Ron's last name and address?"

Grimacing, Duncan rattled off the information.

Thirty minutes later, Gonzo stood at the door to Ron Spaulding's apartment, accompanied by two South Beach police officers. Obviously, they had gotten Ron out of bed, and

Gonzo was gratified to note that his bottom lip was split and swollen. Duncan had gotten off at least one good shot in self-defense.

"Waddya want?" Ron mumbled. He was blond and handsome in a cocky sort of way with a pierced ear and perfect pecs. Gonzo wanted to smack him around for roughing up Duncan, a man thirty years older.

"Ron Spaulding?"

"What's it to you?" he grumbled, scratching his belly above the waistband of gym shorts.

Gonzo flashed his badge. "Detective Tommy Gonzales, Metro Washington, D.C. Police. Did you spend last night with a man named Duncan?"

"Yeah, so?"

"What time did you two hook up?"

"I don't know. Nine maybe?"

Sinclair was still alive at eleven-fifteen when the O'Connors dropped him off at the hotel. "Were you with him all night?"

"Uh-huh."

Whereas Duncan had seemed ashamed of hooking up with a stranger, this guy was so matter-of-fact about it that Gonzo suspected it was a regular occurrence in his life. He turned to the cops he'd brought with him. "He's all yours."

"You're under arrest for the assault of Duncan Quick," one of them said.

"What the *fuck?*" Spaulding said. "Get your fucking hands off me!"

Gonzo left them to fight it out. He had what he needed.

CHAPTER 16

"What do we know about Preston Sinclair?" Sam asked Jeannie McBride as she drove to Sinclair's place in Georgetown.

Reading from her notes, Jeannie recited what she'd uncovered when she ran his name. "History professor at Catholic University. Grew up in Massachusetts, one of two sons. Went to Princeton for undergrad, Harvard for graduate school. Has a Ph.D. in American history. He's lived in the District for twenty-three years. Estranged from his brother, Julian, for the last thirteen years. Married with two grown sons, one an accountant, the other an attorney. His wife, Diandra, is a conservative commentator on the Capital News Network."

"Yes, the hatemonger. We talked about her the other night at dinner. Julian was horrified by her."

"I can see why, but she has a huge following."

"Good work, McBride." Pulling onto Sinclair's street, she found a parking space and turned to Jeannie. "I appreciate your help with this one."

"No problem. Have you spoken with the senator? Since we saw him earlier?"

"No."

"I feel sorry for him."

"I do, too." Sam was trying her best not to think about how crushed Nick had been earlier. Lately, she had grown so accustomed to leaning on his quiet strength that she had no idea how to help him. "I'm sure he'll be fine. He's strong." But even as she said it, Sam wasn't entirely sure that he'd be okay. "Let's see what Mr. Sinclair has to say about the murder of his brother."

Located in one of Washington's more affluent neighborhoods, Sinclair's brick-front townhouse was well tended. His wife, a striking blonde, answered the door.

"Mrs. Sinclair?" Sam showed her badge. "Lieutenant Holland, Metro Police. My partner, Detective McBride. May we have a moment of your time?"

"What's this about?"

Nonplussed by the other woman's curtness, Sam said, "We need to speak to you and your husband. May we come in?"

Resigned, Diandra Sinclair stepped aside to allow them in. No doubt decorated by a high-price interior designer, the house was furnished with an eclectic mix of antiques and contemporary pieces.

"Is your husband at home?"

"He's very busy. It'd be better if you came back at another time."

"We need to see him now." Sam held the other woman's furious gaze until Diandra turned away.

"I'll get him."

"Chilly," Jeannie whispered.

"Seriously."

She returned five minutes later with a man who bore a resemblance to his late brother but was several inches taller and a couple of years older.

Sam introduced herself and Jeannie to him.

"I've seen you in the paper," Preston said.

"Mr. Sinclair, I'm very sorry to have to tell you your brother was murdered early this morning."

Preston gasped. "What?"

Diandra reached out to her husband.

Sam gave them the few details she knew.

He moved to a sofa. His wife followed, sitting next to him and taking his hand.

"I'm sorry for your loss," Sam said.

"Thank you," he said, his voice little more than a whisper.

"I understand you and your brother were estranged."

"That's right," he said, looking pained. "Thirteen years."

"And why was that?"

"A difference of opinion that got out of hand. You know how these things happen."

"Actually, I don't. It wouldn't occur to me to not speak to my sisters for thirteen years."

"You have no right to judge him," Diandra snapped.

"No judgment," Sam said. "Just stating the facts, ma'am." Turning back to Preston, she said, "You've had no contact with him since he was nominated for the Supreme Court?"

Preston glanced at his wife and then back at Sam. "No." He cleared his throat. "Well, except for an email I sent to congratulate him."

Diandra stared at her husband, shocked. "When?"

"The other day." He seemed chagrined. "I wanted him to know I was happy for him."

"Did you get a reply?" Sam asked.

Preston shook his head. "I know he must've been so busy. He would've written back when he could."

"Have you communicated with him by email before this?" Diandra asked, stealing Sam's next question.

"Once or twice."

Diandra's eyes flashed with anger. "I can't believe this!"

"He was my *brother,* Di. My only sibling."

"He was a liar and a fraud."

"He was my brother," Preston whispered, wiping a tear from his face.

"Stop it," she snapped, seeming appalled that he was crying over Julian's death.

As Preston obediently mopped up his tears, Sam and Jeannie exchanged glances. This was one twisted relationship.

"Did you expect to see him while he was in town?" Sam asked.

"I'd hoped to. In the email, I offered to meet him, but like I said, I never heard back from him."

"Unbelievable," Diandra muttered, glaring at her husband.

Preston looked down at the floor like a chastened child whose mother was angry with him.

"Mrs. Sinclair, can you tell me how your husband and his brother came to be estranged?" Sam said.

"Why don't you ask him?"

"Because I'm asking you."

"Fine. I saw them—Julian and that fag he referred to as his 'friend.' They were kissing! Right out in public! And I'd allowed my children—my *sons*—to sleep at his home. He'd exposed them to his immoral lifestyle, and God knows what else." She shuddered.

"He adored those boys," Preston snapped. "You know he did! And they adored him." To Sam he said, "They'll be crushed by his death. They'd reestablished contact with him and saw him regularly."

"They did not!" Diandra said, her face flat with shock.

"Yes, they did," Preston retorted defiantly. "Once they were out of your house, they made their own decisions."

Diandra sent him a venomous glare, and once again he wilted.

"Where were the two of you last night?" Sam asked, imagining the chewing out Preston was in for after they left.

Taken aback by the question, Preston said, "We had dinner out and went to bed early. Around ten or so, I guess."

Her lips tight with fury, Diandra nodded in agreement.

"And neither of you left the house again after you returned from dinner?"

"No," he said.

"Of course not," she said.

"Do either of you require medication in order to sleep?"

"What kind of question is that?" Diandra asked.

"It's a simple yes or no kind of question. Do you require medication to sleep?"

"I take a sleeping pill every now and then," Preston said.

"Did you take one last night?"

He nodded. "I've been having trouble sleeping since Julian was nominated."

"Why's that?" Sam asked.

"I've had some concerns," Preston said haltingly, "about his nomination stirring up old hurts. Things that are better left in the past."

Sam turned to Diandra. "Do you take sleeping medication?"

"I do not."

"Tell me, Mrs. Sinclair, what does it do to a 'career' like yours if your brother-in-law comes out as a gay man to all of America during his confirmation hearings?"

"I have no idea," she said, spitting the words at Sam. "I guess we'll never know."

Sam stared her down for several long seconds. "I'd like to speak to your sons. Are they local?"

"What for?" Diandra asked.

"This is a homicide investigation. I can talk to anyone I want."

"I'll write down their information," Preston said with a pointed look at his wife. "They're both here in the city."

Sam and Jeannie left after requesting that the Sinclairs stay local until the investigation was completed.

"Wow," Jeannie said when they were in the car. "That woman was tightly wound, huh?"

"And a total homophobe. You don't see that kind of hatred very often these days."

"No question she's the reason the brothers were estranged."

"She didn't approve of Julian," Sam said. "I want to know what kind of problems it would've caused her 'career' if Julian's orientation became public."

"Definitely worth looking into."

"Yeah, she knew damned well that it would be a disaster for her if he came out just as her book was released. I also want to talk to their sons. I'm willing to bet they were his heirs."

"Probably. Why'd you ask about the sleeping medicine?"

"A hunch," Sam said. "They're each other's alibi, but if one of them was drugged up, the other could've snuck out."

"I never would've thought to ask that," Jeannie said, her voice tinged with admiration.

"Shit," Sam muttered. "Now you're starting to sound like Cruz." A pang of guilt struck her as she thought of him sitting in the cold watching Reese's place. Then she got over it. One shift spent on surveillance wouldn't kill him, and it was the least of what he deserved for lying to her.

"Let's go have a chat with Senator Robert Cook," Sam said.

At the Capitol, Sam and Jeannie were told that Senator Cook was in a meeting and couldn't be disturbed.

Sam narrowed her eyes into her most intimidating stare and

watched the administrative assistant shrivel before her. Excellent. "Either you can go in there and get him, or I'm going to. Your choice."

"Please wait right here," the admin said, scurrying away.

"Can you teach me that look?" Jeannie asked.

"It's a gift. You have to be born with it."

Jeannie laughed. "I should've known you'd say something like that."

The admin returned. "Right this way, please."

"See that?" Sam said to Jeannie, loud enough for the admin to hear her. "I love when the citizenry cooperates with their law enforcement professionals."

"It's critical to maintaining law and order," Jeannie replied, playing along.

The admin probably would've scowled at them if she had dared.

Cook's spacious office, Sam noted, was easily four times the size of Nick's. Seniority had its perks.

"What can I do for you?" Cook growled. "I'm very busy."

"Then we won't take much of your time," Sam said. "You told Senator Cappuano that Supreme Court nominee Julian Sinclair should watch his back. That someone might take a shot at him. Can you tell me what you meant by that?"

"It was a figure of speech," Cook said, visibly ruffled by the question. "What does he do—run home and tell the little woman everything that transpires around here?"

"No, just comments that factor into murder investigations."

"Murder investigation? What're you talking about?"

"Julian Sinclair was murdered last night."

Cook's portly face turned an unbecoming shade of purple. "You aren't *possibly* insinuating that I had anything to do with it."

"Do you know of anyone who might've had something to do with it?"

"Of course I don't. I hardly associate with murderers."

Sam consulted her notebook. "Weren't you once associated with Robert 'Junior' Despositio, who's doing time in federal prison for attempted murder and racketeering?"

Cook's face twisted with rage. "He was a high school class-mate of mine who made poor choices. I haven't been 'associated' with him in thirty years."

"Had you ever met Mr. Sinclair?"

"I had not. I believe we had a meeting on the schedule for sometime in the next week. Meeting with the senators who'll be voting for them is part of the routine for Supreme Court nominees."

"Where were you last night after eleven?"

"Home in bed."

"Can anyone confirm that?"

"My wife."

Sam held out her notebook to the senator. "A number where I can reach her?"

Cook stared at her for a long moment. "I'm a United States senator. My word should be more than good enough."

"It isn't," Sam said. "The number please?"

He snatched the notebook from her hand. "Your superiors will be hearing about this."

"They enjoy getting complaints about me doing my job. Should I give you the best number to reach them?"

Cook thrust the notebook back at her. "Tell your *boyfriend* he needs to learn to keep his mouth shut if he plans to make any friends around here."

"You aren't threatening him, are you, Senator?"

"Of course not," Cook huffed. "I'm just pointing out that blabbing to cops is no way to make friends."

"I'm sure that making friends around here is of far less concern to him than finding the person who killed his *real* friend. Detective?"

Jeannie followed Sam from the room. "That was *ill.*"

"Is that good or bad?" Sam asked, baffled.

"Good," Jeannie said. "Very *good.*"

"Ill. I like that." Sam filed it away for future use.

Freddie shivered in the icy cold, his eyes fixed on Reese's house. He'd turned on the car and heater half an hour before, but the warm air had made him too sleepy. Even though he was freezing, he burned with anger directed at Sam, Elin and mostly himself. This was his own fault. If he had remained true to his faith and his beliefs, he'd be working a homicide with his partner right now rather than sitting in a frigid time-out. The day grew dark early as heavy clouds hung over the city, and Freddie fought to stay awake.

He should've known Sam would zero in on the lie. "Stupid," he muttered, his breath coming out in puffy clouds. Shrinking deeper into his coat, he wanted to smack the crap out of Elin. Except, of course, he never would. But it sure was nice to fantasize about spanking that perfect ass. When his body reacted with infuriating predictability to that image, Freddie roared with frustration, aggravation and shame.

Since he hadn't gotten to take a shower, her essence clung to his skin. Images from their erotic night together tortured him like a movie he couldn't seem to escape. As much as he wanted to throttle her, he feared that if she appeared beside the car right now, throttling wouldn't be the first thing he'd do to her.

Freddie checked the clock on the dashboard. "Three more hours. I'll die before then." He wanted a shower, a warm bed and eight uninterrupted hours of sleep so bad he was tempted to sell his well-protected soul to the devil to get them. With a mighty yawn, he reached for his cell phone wishing he could call Sam to find out what was going on with the Sinclair case.

He hated that he'd let her down. After his mother, Sam was the most important woman in his life—not that he'd ever admit that to her. Tomorrow, he would find a way to fix this. They worked too well together and meant too much to each other to let this fester.

He stared intently at Reese's house. He'd give everything he had to be the one to snag the guy who shot Skip Holland. Freddie loved the hell out of Skip and wanted to close his case almost as much as Sam did.

Another hour passed in frigid silence, until Freddie thought he'd lose his mind if he had to stare at the dark house for one more minute. Suddenly, he saw a narrow beam of light moving through the house. Were his tired eyes playing tricks on him? No, someone was definitely walking through the house with a flashlight.

Reaching for his radio, he started to call for backup but stopped himself. How much would it mean to Sam if he arrested Reese? It would certainly go a long way toward repairing the rift between them. But going in without backup went against all his training. Regardless, Freddie kept his eyes on the beam of light as he got out of the car and crossed the deserted street.

Cutting through the alley behind the house, he drew his weapon and approached the back door, his heart pounding with adrenaline and excitement. An arrest like this would make him a hero at HQ, and even though his better judgment urged him once again to call for backup before he went in, he didn't.

His heart beat like a bass drum in his ears. The back door was unlocked. He eased it open and stepped into the kitchen.

Down the hallway, he could see the flashlight moving around and headed in that direction, his gun leading the way. Just as he was about to take the intruder by surprise, Freddie's cell phone rang, alerting the other man to his presence. Cursing himself for being so stupid, he grabbed the phone and flipped it open to stop the ringing.

The man, dressed all in black, spun around and fired.

The bullet hit Freddie in the shoulder, the force propelling him back against the wall. As he sank to the floor, his gun and phone fell from his hands. The last thing he saw before he lost consciousness was a gun pointed at his chest.

CHAPTER 17

In the HQ conference room, Sam labored over the murder board. Starting to the left with grainy images retrieved from the hotel security to photos of Julian Sinclair dead in Lincoln Park to autopsy photos, Sam laid it out in chronological order. Each piece to the puzzle would eventually add up to the whole. So many threads to this one—the secret sexual orientation, the family rift, the extreme views on hot-button issues—his and his sister-in-law's—and the connection to the O'Connors.

Sam thought about the man she'd dined with two nights prior and was surprised by a wave of sadness over his loss. He'd come to town, to *her* town, expecting to be confirmed as a Supreme Court justice and would leave in a body bag. As someone charged with ensuring the safety of visitors and residents alike, the loss of his life offended her on a deep, personal level.

"I'll get him, Julian," she promised the deceased face in the photo. "I promise you, I'll get him."

The conference room door flew open.

"Shots fired at Reese's house," Jeannie McBride said, her eyes wide with dismay.

Sam's heart contracted. "Cruz?"

"Not answering his radio, and his cell just rings."

Sam ran from the room, grabbed her coat and headed for the door. "Tyrone, McBride." Sam's throat contracted, robbing her of air and speech.

The two detectives scurried after her and sprinted with her to the parking lot.

"He's fine," McBride said. "He's got Reese, and he'll be calling it in any minute."

"Make sure rescue is on the way," Sam ordered, feeling considerably less optimistic.

"His mother called dispatch," Tyrone said. "She had reached his cell and heard gunfire. She's freaking out."

"And there's no word from Cruz?" Sam asked.

His face grim, Tyrone shook his head as the radio crackled with reports of a possible officer down.

Sam couldn't seem to get oxygen to her lungs. Flying across the city with sirens and flashing lights, she tried to take a deep breath but couldn't get air past the huge knot of fear in her throat. She sent him there as punishment and now… *Please don't let him be dead.*

"Lieutenant," Jeannie said.

Startled out of her thoughts, Sam glanced over at her.

"Patrol is on the scene. They want to know if they should go in ahead of us."

Sam's mind raced. If the shooter was still in the house, she'd be risking additional people by sending them in. But if Freddie was in there and wounded, time could be critical. "Do they have vests?"

Jeannie conveyed the question. "They do."

"With vests, two in the back, two in the front. Go in together."

Jeannie relayed Sam's order.

They waited in tense silence as they wove through traffic on their way to the scene.

When the code for an officer down came over the airwaves a few minutes later, Sam wanted to wail. *"Shit,"* she whispered, pressing the accelerator to the floor.

They arrived just as paramedics wheeled Freddie out of the house.

"Oh," Jeannie gasped, taking a step back.

Freddie's face was sheet-white, and the paramedics running alongside the gurney were working frantically to stop the blood streaming from his shoulder.

"Jesus," Tyrone muttered, slipping a supporting arm around Jeannie's shoulders.

"What've we got?" Sam asked one of the officers in an effort to keep from shrieking at the sight of Freddie's lifeless form.

The rattled officer took a deep breath. "Gunshot wound to the shoulder. Significant blood loss. We found a flashlight, still lit, in the hallway. It's possible Cruz took the shooter by surprise."

"No sign of the shooter?"

"No, ma'am."

"Where're they taking him?"

"GW Trauma." He reached into his pocket. "Cruz's cell phone has been ringing like crazy."

Sam took the phone from him and checked the missed calls. "His mother," she said, watching the ambulance pull away. "I'll take care of it." She gestured for Jeannie and Tyrone to follow her inside. They assessed the first floor and found the still-lit flashlight as well as the large pool of Cruz's blood. Fixated on the blood, Sam said, "You two are in charge here. I want a full sweep of this entire neighborhood. First shift is retained. Recall third shift. Let's find this scumbag."

"Yes, Lieutenant," Tyrone said, his eyes hot with fury. "Will you let us know about Cruz?"

She bit her lip and nodded.

Jeannie squeezed her arm. "He's going to be fine. He's young and strong."

"Yeah." Before she could embarrass herself by breaking down in front of her detectives, she left them and headed back to HQ. Her heart beat fast from the rage that overtook her, and her fingers were so tight around the steering wheel that her knuckles turned white.

Freddie's cell phone rang again, and bracing herself, Sam answered it. "Mrs. Cruz, this is Lieutenant Holland."

"Sam! Tell me what's happening! I heard a gunshot! *Freddie.*"

"He was shot in the shoulder."

"Oh, no. Oh, *God.*"

"They're taking him to GW Trauma. Do you want me to send a car to take you there?"

"Is he going to live, Lieutenant? Please. Tell me the truth."

"I don't know, ma'am. He lost a lot of blood."

The other woman's wretched wails rattled Sam's already frayed nerves. "I'll send a car. Sit tight. They'll be there in a few minutes, and I'll meet you at GW, okay?"

"Thank you."

Sam called in the order for Mrs. Cruz's ride as she tore into the HQ parking lot, slammed the car into Park and took off running. At the city jail, she ordered the flustered officer at the desk to put Hector Reese in an interrogation room.

Reese smirked when he saw her coming five minutes later. "They told me the cunt cop—"

She ripped him out of his chair and hurled him back into the wall.

"What the fuck?"

Sam slapped his face as hard as she could. "Shut the fuck up."

"You can't hit me—"

Her fist slammed into his midsection. "Your word against mine, you useless piece of shit. Who's going to believe you?"

Gasping for air, Hector winced when she tightened her grip on his shirt collar. "What'd you want?" he choked out.

"Where's your scumbag brother? And do *not* tell me you don't know."

"I don't—"

Sam gut punched him again.

He sank to his knees. "I swear to God. I don't know."

"He shot my partner."

Startled, Hector looked up at her.

"Every cop in this city is looking for him. They won't hesitate to shoot if they find him. He's already suspected in the shooting of one cop—"

"What cop did he shoot? He didn't shoot no cop."

"My father, you asshole." She hauled him back up. "So don't fuck with me. Tell me where he's hiding out."

"I'm not telling you shit," he said. "You want him, you find him."

"He's gonna wind up dead. You could stop that."

"He can take care of himself, and so can I."

Sam jammed her knee into his groin, dropping him once again to his knees.

He howled in pain. *"You fucking bitch!"*

Gripping a fistful of his hair, she forced him to look at her. "You can sit in here and rot for all I care. But if you decide to cooperate, I might be willing to deal. You think about that." She released him and headed for the door.

"Cunt cop," he muttered from the floor.

Sweating, frustrated and infuriated, Sam left the room and found Captain Malone waiting for her.

"Anything?" he asked, his face tight with stress.

Sam wiped the moisture from her forehead with a hand that was sore from repeatedly connecting with Hector's ribs. "No." She signaled to the officers guarding the door to return Hector to his cell and looked up at the captain. "I roughed him up pretty good."

"Okay," he said, even though they both knew it wasn't. When one of their own went down, many of the usual rules were overlooked.

"Any word on Cruz?"

"He's in surgery. The blood loss is a big concern."

"I need to get over there."

"I'll go with you."

Sam used the lights and siren to expedite their trip to the hospital.

"President Nelson called the chief earlier," Malone said. "He wants to know what's being done to find Sinclair's killer. They were good friends. He's beside himself."

"We're working the case," Sam said. "But I've directed all available resources toward the search for Reese. For the time being anyway."

Malone nodded his approval. "We'll give that everything for a couple of hours, and then we've got to get back to Sinclair."

They encountered a media circus outside the hospital entrance.

"Lieutenant, who was shot?"

"Is the shooter Reese?"

"What's being done to find him?"

"How close are you to an arrest in the Sinclair case?"

Malone gestured for her to go ahead into the hospital while he dealt with the media.

Thankful for his assistance, Sam entered the hospital and was directed to the surgical waiting room where she found

Freddie's mother and extended family engaged in a prayer circle. With her hands jammed into her coat pockets, Sam waited
for them to finish. Thinking about her handsome, sensitive,
energetic, junk-food-loving partner, Sam's throat closed and
she feared tears might be next. She fought back the rush of
emotion to focus on Freddie's mother.

Juliette Cruz wiped her face and turned to Sam. "Oh, Lieutenant."

"It's Sam." She hugged the attractive, youthful woman she
had met a few times. "What've you heard?"

"Nothing more since they took him into surgery."

Sam led Freddie's mother to a chair and encouraged her
to sit.

"It's good of you to be here," Juliette said.

"I wouldn't be anywhere else."

"He's all I have," Juliette whispered. "I don't know what
I'll do if—"

Sam's stomach clenched with pain as she gripped Juliette's
hand. "He's going to be just fine."

The alternative was unimaginable.

Nick sat in his office, staring out the window. John's bill
had passed by ten votes—nine more than they would've gotten before he was killed. The O'Connor name was now forever linked to sweeping immigration reform. After more than
a year of hard work on that bill, Nick knew he should be eu-
phoric, but all he felt was numb.

In its opening session, the Senate paid glowing tribute to
John and held a moment of silence for Julian—two of Nick's
closest friends, both murdered in the scope of a month.

Christina rushed into the room. "Trevor just got word that
a cop was shot in the house where that guy killed his family last week."

Her words cut straight through the numbness, the panic snapping him out of the stupor he'd sunk into after learning of Julian's death. Nick was out of his chair before she finished the sentence. "Who?" He resisted the urge to grab her shoulders and shake the information out of her. *"Who is it?"*

"They haven't released a name. Trevor said they took the injured officer to GW."

Running, Nick skipped the elevator and took the stairs on his way to the car, aware that numbness had been replaced by bone-crushing fear. Sam was obsessed with finding Reese. It had to be her. If he lost her, too… He stopped running when his legs threatened to buckle under him.

Christina caught up to him and guided him into her car.

On the way, Nick focused on breathing. His chest ached under the weight of the dread. No one could have this much bad luck. He kept telling himself that, over and over. Breathe in. Breathe out.

"You don't know it's her," Christina said tentatively. "It could be Tommy or someone else."

Nick shook his head. "Sam's been after Reese. She thinks he had something to do with her father's shooting."

"Try not to think the worst."

"Why would I do that?"

They drove the rest of the way in uncomfortable silence, every minute feeling like a year.

At the hospital, Nick once again made use of his new-found clout to learn that the injured officer was in surgery on the seventh floor. With Christina trailing behind him, Nick emerged from the seventh floor elevator and ran down the hallway to the waiting room at the end. He came to a stop when he saw Sam talking to a pretty dark-haired woman. Taking a step back, all the stress of the last palf hour came out as an anguished moan that caught Sam's attention.

She got up and rushed over to him. "I'm so glad to see you."

Christina was right behind him.

"What happened?" he managed to ask, still trying to catch his breath and slow his racing heart.

"It's Freddie," Sam said in a small voice, her arms curling around him, her head resting on his chest. In a rush of words, she continued, "I sent him to watch the house because I was mad at him. He went in there alone, and Reese shot him. It's bad, Nick. He lost a lot of blood."

Christina stepped around them into the waiting room.

Nick knew he should comfort Sam but couldn't seem to move his arms. All at once, fear became anger. "I can't." He shook her off.

"What?" she asked, startled.

"I can't be here. I'm sorry." Spinning around, he started back down the long corridor to the elevator.

She followed him. "Where're you going?"

He walked faster, needing to get out of there. Immediately. "I don't know. Home. I can't do this, Sam. I thought I could, but I can't."

"What can't you do?" She grabbed his arm, forcing him to look at her. "What're you saying?"

"I thought it was you." His heart breaking, he studied her one-in-a-million face. "I thought you'd been shot."

"But I wasn't, Nick." She rested her hands on his chest, beseeching him with her eyes. "I'm right here. I'm fine."

"This time."

"You're upset about Julian. Let's talk about this later. When I get home."

He shook his head. "I can't spend my whole life waiting for it to be you. I'm sorry, Sam."

The elevator doors opened and Skip and Celia emerged. "Sam!" Celia cried. "How's Freddie?"

Nick got into the elevator and punched the button for the lobby. As the doors closed, he caught a last glance of Sam's stunned expression.

CHAPTER 18

"Sam?" her father said. "What is it? Is Freddie worse?"

Fixated on the elevator doors, she shook her head. "I think Nick just broke up with me." She couldn't believe how much it hurt to say those words.

"No, honey." Celia slipped an arm around Sam's shoulders. "He'd never break up with you. He's upset."

"This was more than that."

"Once things calm down, he'll come around," Skip said.

In that moment, Sam realized things would never calm down, not with two all-consuming jobs sitting at the center of their relationship. "I don't know, Dad. He sounded pretty sure."

"Look at me."

Startled by his sharp tone, Sam let her eyes drop down to meet his. "He's upset about Sinclair. You can't take anything he says or does right now to heart. Give him some space. He'll come around."

"Sam," Captain Malone called from the waiting room, waving at her to come.

With her father and Celia in tow, Sam headed down the

hall. She couldn't think about what'd just happened with Nick. Right now she needed to stay focused on Freddie, the search for Reese and the Sinclair case. She'd do what she always did when life became too much for her—she'd work until she dropped from exhaustion. Nick loved her. Of that she had no doubt and in that she would have faith until she could be with him again.

An O.R. nurse had been sent to inform them that Freddie was out of surgery and in recovery. The surgeon would be down to speak with them shortly.

Upon hearing that news, Sam sagged into a chair and closed her eyes to say a silent prayer of thanks. She reached for her cell to call Gonzo, who had texted her to let her know he was back in town and at Reese's house. "He's out of surgery," she said when he answered.

"And?"

"That's all I know right now. What's up out there?"

"No sign of Reese anywhere," Gonzo said, his voice tight with strain. "That bastard had better hope I'm not the one to find him."

"I want him alive," Sam said. "Put out the word. I know he had something to do with my dad's shooting. He's no good to us dead."

"You got it, L.T."

She checked her watch. Ten after midnight. She'd been up almost twenty-four hours and was starting to feel muzzy around the edges. "Release first shift now. Let second shift go at four. Get everyone back to HQ by eight to regroup. We'll divide the resources—half on Reese, the other half on Sinclair. Everything else is back burner for now. Any sign of Reese, I want a call."

"I'll put out the word, and I'll be over there as soon as I can. Everyone wants to come."

"I'd rather you went home and got some sleep." She glanced at Christina across the waiting room and wondered why she was still there since Nick had left. And then it dawned on her—Christina was hoping Gonzo would show up. Sam wasn't about to tell him his "girlfriend" was waiting for him.

"I'm not sleeping until Cruz is out of the woods."

Knowing there was no point in arguing since she agreed with him, she said, "I'll see you when you get here."

She closed the phone and found her father watching her.

"What does Reese have to do with my case?"

Her stomach clenched with pain. "Let's go out in the hall-way."

Leaving Celia to comfort Freddie's mother, Skip followed her out of the room.

Sam willed herself to stay calm, to take deep breaths, and to keep her stomach out of the equation.

Skip looked up at her expectantly. "Tell me."

"We found stuff in his house. Newspaper articles, pic-tures—"

"About the shooting?"

She nodded.

"And when were you planning to tell me this?"

"When I knew more. I didn't want to get your hopes up until I was sure."

"It's a good thing I can't throttle you right now."

"*For what?* Wanting to protect you from more disappoint-ment?"

"I want him caught, Sam. I really do. But once he's be-hind bars, I'll still be in this chair. Nothing's going to change for me."

"How can you stand knowing he's out there living his life when you're trapped in hell? How can you *stand* it?"

"What choice do I have? I've got the best detective in this

city looking for the guy. I know she's going to get him one of these days. Beyond that, I don't give it much thought, to be honest with you."

She stared at him. What was *with* the men in her life tonight? "You don't give it much thought?" Tossing up her hands, she said, "It's *all* I think about."

"That's because you have the ability to actually *do* something about it. I don't."

Fixating on the wall behind him, she recalled all the near misses and dead ends she'd pursued over the past two years. "Every time I think we're getting close, it turns into nothing. I constantly feel like I'm letting you down. I hate that."

"Sam, you've never let me down. Not once in your whole life. I know you'll get him. And when you do, we'll have the biggest party to celebrate. The biggest party ever."

Back in the day, Skip Holland's parties had been the stuff of legend.

Sam bent to rest her head on his shoulder. "I'll look forward to that. Might be sooner than we think if we can just find that bastard Reese. He's got two cops to account for now, not to mention his family."

"You'll keep me posted?"

"Yeah." She raised her head to meet his eyes. "I'm sorry I kept it from you."

"And you won't do it again?"

"No."

"No matter what happens?"

She squeezed the finger that retained sensation. "I promise." The elevator at the far end of the hall opened, and Sam blinked, certain her eyes had to be deceiving her. "No way," she muttered. "No fucking way."

"What?" Skip asked.

A woman with light hair and eyes red from crying approached them.

"I'm not sure if you remember me, Lieutenant—"

"I do. What're you doing here?"

"I heard about Freddie," she stammered. "On the radio. He's... We're friends."

At least Sam now knew who'd been chewing on her partner's neck.

"Are you the reason his phone was off last night?"

"He was tired—"

"He's a *homicide detective!* He's in here because I punished him for being late! I sent him over there, and he got shot!"

Elin broke down into sobs. "I'm so sorry. It's my fault."

Suddenly, a lot of Freddie's recent behavior made sense—the snappier clothes, the cologne, the befuddlement. The minute he was out of the hospital, Sam was going to beat the hell out of him for this.

"I just wanted to know if he's going to be okay," Elin said between sobs.

"We don't know yet. He got through the surgery."

"I don't want to upset you any more than you already are, so I'll go."

"Wait." Later, Sam would blame exhaustion for the weak moment. "Would he want you here?"

"I don't know." Elin wiped her face. "He was so mad this morning. About the phone. I've never seen him like that before."

Sam smiled to herself. She could only imagine. If someone turned off her phone, they wouldn't still be walking around. "Have you met his mother?"

Elin blanched, which made Sam want to laugh for the first time in hours. "No."

"Allow me to do the honors," she said, sending her father a shit-eating grin.

Skip rolled his eyes, but she could tell he was enjoying the show.

Thirty minutes later, the waiting room was overrun with HQ detectives who had left the search for Reese in the hands of second and third shift so they could check on Cruz. In the hallway, Gonzo huddled with Christina, speaking quietly to her while keeping a firm grip on her hand. Sam couldn't say why the idea of the two of them together bugged her so much. It just did. She didn't like her worlds overlapping. And then she remembered that Nick had stepped out of her world earlier.

Her stomach clenched with dread. This was exactly what she'd been so afraid of—that the moment she allowed him to become essential to her, something would happen to drive them apart. Well, she couldn't let that happen. She *wouldn't* let that happen.

An hour later, Freddie was delivered to a room in ICU. His mother rushed in to see him the moment he was settled. She emerged fifteen minutes later, visibly rattled. "He's asking for you, Lieutenant."

Sam swallowed the huge lump in her throat and went into the darkened room where the beep of machines was the only sound. Venturing a glance at Freddie, she bit back a gasp at how pale and sick he looked. *God.* She rested her hand over his.

His eyes fluttered open. "Hey," he croaked, fighting to keep his eyes open. "I almost had him. If my phone hadn't rang—"

"*That's* what happened?" She struggled to keep her voice down. "How many times have we talked about that?"

He closed his eyes and swallowed. "Too many for me to forget so easily."

"And to go in without backup? What the *hell* were you thinking?"

"I wasn't thinking." He kept his eyes closed. "I wanted to get him. For you."

Sam's own eyes burned. "Stupid. Totally and completely insane. You're lucky he only hit you in the shoulder."

"I know. I'm sorry."

"You're sure it was him?"

"Yeah."

"Has Elin Svendsen been chewing on your neck?"

His eyes flew open. "What're you talking about?"

"Don't screw with me, Cruz," she said, glaring at him.

He released a resigned sigh. "How do you know?"

"I'm the best detective in this city. I know everything."

"Whatever," he said with a grimace that had nothing to do with his injuries.

"She's here."

"She is? Really?"

Thrilled and relieved to have her partner back, she said, "Would I lie to you?"

"Ah, *yeah.*"

"I would not! She's in the waiting room with your mother."

He swallowed hard at that news. "You let her stay? You didn't make her feel like shit and chase her out?"

"I started to," Sam said, a bit disturbed to realize he knew her so well. "But I was too tired to chase."

"I'm sorry I lied to you. I figured you'd freak."

"You figured right, and I plan to beat the crap out of you as soon as you're out of here."

He laughed and then winced. "Thanks for the warning."

"You have a right to a life outside the job," she said begrudgingly. "But don't ever let anyone shut off your phone again, do you hear me?"

"Don't worry. Lesson learned the hard way."

"So, you want to see her or what?"

"Yeah," he said. "I really do."

"*Oy vey*," Sam muttered on her way out the door to get Elin.

Sam pulled onto Ninth Street at three-thirty in the morning, nearly twenty-four hours after she'd received the call about Sinclair. Parking between her father's house and Nick's she debated as to whether she should wait until the morning to confront Nick. Then she looked up and saw the light on in his bedroom.

"Now," she whispered, her breath a cloudy puff in the cold air. "I won't sleep if I don't."

She used her key in his door and dropped her coat on the sofa on the way to the stairs. In his bedroom, she found him sitting up in bed asleep, a whiskey bottle on the bedside table, his hair a tousled mess and his jaw sprinkled with whiskers. She'd never been so happy to see him.

She contemplated whether she should wake him and hated not knowing if she'd be welcome. She decided to let him sleep. After a quick shower, she shut the light off and slipped into bed.

Lying there next to him, Sam felt lonely for the first time since they'd been together. More than anything, she wanted his strong arms around her. She wanted him to tell her that everything was going to be all right the way he always did. It was unsettling to realize how much she had come to depend on his steady presence. How would she ever go back to living without that? Without him?

She snuggled up to him, dropping soft kisses on his chest.

He came to slowly, and his whole body stiffened. "What're you doing?" he asked, trying to get away.

She held him tighter, knowing if she let him escape now he might never come back. "I need you, Nick."

"I told you. This isn't going to work."

"Yes, it is. It works on every possible level." She caressed his chest. "I know you were scared earlier, and I'm sorry about that." His silence grated on her already frazzled nerves. "Talk to me," she said, punctuating her words with kisses. "Tell me what you're thinking about."

He was silent for a long time, so long that Sam wondered if he was going to say anything. "Every time I hear that something's happened to a cop in this city," he said in a halting staccato, "I'm going to think it's you. I don't want to live like that. I *can't* live like that."

"You'd rather live without me?" Her lips left a trail from his collarbone to his jaw. "Without what we have?" When he trembled, she began to feel hopeful that she was getting through to him. "I love you so much, Nick. So, so much. If you take that away from me, I'll never get over it." She sprinkled kisses on his face and encountered dampness on his cheek. "I know you're sad about Julian. I am, too. I only met him once, but I could see what a special person he was. Let me help you, Nick. Let me love you."

His lips found hers in a hungry, desperate kiss as he rolled her under him.

Sam clung to him, meeting the thrusts of his tongue with her own, tasting whiskey and Nick.

He tore his lips free. "Things happen in threes. My grandmother always said that."

"You thought I was the third thing."

Nodding, he rested his forehead against hers. "I knew you were chasing Reese. I was so sure it was you."

"Freddie getting shot was the third thing."

"How is he?"

"He'll be fine in a few weeks."

"Did they get Reese?"

"Not yet. But we will."

"What if he shoots you next time?"

"He might," she said, knowing this was a time for honesty. "Every time I step foot out the door, it can happen. It's a risk we all take, but I don't spend even one minute of my day worrying about it."

"I can't bear it, Sam," he said, his voice hoarse with emotion. "I thought I could, but I found out today that I can't."

"Do you know," she said, tilting her hips against his erection, "that my dad and now Freddie are the only cops I know personally who've been shot on the job? And I've known a lot of cops in my life."

"Don't try to tell me it can't happen to you. Just since we've been together, you've been nearly blown up, shot at—twice—you scraped the skin off your chin, arms and knees, took an elbow to the face, got your throat squeezed by your ex-husband, who wanted you dead, and your partner got shot. Have I forgotten anything?"

Running her hands over his ribs, she fought the urge to giggle at the ridiculous inventory. "That about covers it."

Exasperated, he flopped onto his back. "And that's only our first month."

Sam straddled him and bent to kiss him. "At least it'll never be boring." She teased him by sliding her slick heat over his erection before taking him deep.

He reached for her hips to stop her from moving. "I'm trying to talk to you, Sam."

"And I'm listening," she said as she rode him slowly.

"I can't when you're doing that."

She took his hands and moved them from her hips to her breasts. "What am I doing?"

"Samantha."

"Were you really going to break up with me?"

"Yes."

Filled with overwhelming sadness, she stopped moving. "You told me there was nothing that would make you not want to be with me. You said that." When he didn't answer, she ran her hands over his chest. "More than once."

"That's what I thought, but then, what happened today…"

"Can I ask you something?"

His hands traveled from her breasts to encircle her. "Yeah."

"Isn't it better to have this, for how ever long it lasts, than to let fear drive us apart?"

He turned them over and withdrew from her. "That's not fair. You don't have to worry every day that I'm going to get shot or blown up or run over."

"No one's tried to run me over. Yet."

"You're not taking me seriously."

"You don't think so? I haven't been able to take a deep breath since you walked away from me at the hospital. Just when I was finally starting to have some faith in this, in *us,* you went and changed the rules on me."

"I didn't take a deep breath myself from the second I heard a cop had been shot in Reese's house until I saw you in the waiting room."

"So then we're even. Can we get back to normal?"

He caressed her face. "I don't know what I'd do if something happened to you. If I lost you that way."

"Then don't lose me. Keep me. Take a chance that maybe it'll all be fine."

"I don't ever again want to feel the way I did today."

"I can't promise that you won't."

He ran his fingers through her long hair, a gesture so familiar, so totally his, that her heart fluttered in her chest. "I know."

"So where does that leave us?" she asked.

"I need some time."

A prickle of fear worked its way down her spine. "To do what?"

"Losing Julian has messed me up, Sam. I don't want to say or do anything right now that I'll regret later."

"Okay," she said, suddenly finding it hard to swallow.

"I was unprepared for how it would feel to be certain you were injured or worse."

"Take all the time you need." As she said the words, she wondered where this new, evolved Sam Holland was coming from. With any other guy she would've shown him the door. However, *this* guy, this one was different. "But I do have one condition."

"What's that?"

"If you decide to give us a chance, you can't do this to me again. I can't be worried every time something goes wrong at work that I'm going to have to come home and fight for us, too. Either we're going to do this or we're not."

"Fair enough."

"How much time are we talking?"

He reached for her, brought her in close to him and kissed her forehead. "I don't know. The only thing I know for sure is that I love you. I found out today just how much."

Closing her eyes tight against the rush of emotion, she slipped her arm around him and burrowed into his embrace, painfully aware that sometimes love—even this kind of love—wasn't enough. "I'm sorry you were so scared. If anything like that ever happens again, I'll call you as soon as I possibly can so you'll know it's not me."

He replied by tightening his hold on her.

She nibbled on his neck. "You want to finish what we started?" she asked, forcing a lighter tone.

"Do you?"

She curled her hand around his arousal. "Mmm."

His lips found hers for a soft, sensual kiss that was all about gentle seduction. The usual fire simmered just below the surface as he worked his way from her lips to her neck.

Sam buried her fingers in his hair and closed her eyes, floating on a cloud of sensation despite the nagging worry that this could be their last time. If he walked away. No. He wouldn't. Hadn't he just said how much he loved her?

He cupped her breasts and tended to each nipple, his tongue darting in teasing circles.

Sam arched her back seeking him, wanting him desperately. "Nick."

"What, baby?" he whispered against her breast.

"Now."

He moved up to capture her mouth in a deep, carnal kiss and entered her in one smooth thrust.

Steeped in sensation, Sam rode the wave, knowing deep in her soul that no one else would ever make her feel this way. She wrapped her arms around him, holding him close and slowing the pace to make it last as long as possible.

Their eyes met in the inky darkness.

"I love you," she whispered. "Only you. Always."

"Samantha."

She could tell by the tight set of his jaw that he was close. Her body tingled and surged, trying to meet him at the top.

Breaking free of her embrace, he gave it to her hard and fast, the way she liked it best, but nothing he did could melt the cold knot of fear that remained in her belly.

"Sam," he said, begging her to join him.

For the first time since they'd been together, she closed her eyes and faked an explosive finish.

CHAPTER 19

She'd faked it! Did she think he wouldn't be able to tell the difference? After all the times they'd made love, did she think he wouldn't know? Curled up to him, she snored softly while he lay awake churning.

The insomnia that plagued him during times of stress had kicked into high gear lately, and he had almost no hope of going back to sleep that night. He would've gotten up, gone downstairs and attempted to review the files Christina had sent home with him if he didn't so love having Sam sleeping all over him. Plus, he didn't want to disturb her when she had so little time to sleep.

He hated that she'd felt the need to fake it with him. He knew she'd had trouble in that regard with her ex-husband, but never once with him. Of course it was because he'd scared her with their conversation, and he hated that his worries had that effect on her. But he couldn't help the way he felt. If he let his mind wander back to the sheer terror, the absolute certainty that she'd been shot... No, he couldn't go there again. He'd already relived it a thousand times.

He stewed for what seemed like hours. A week ago he

would've been unable to imagine a scenario whereby he would walk away from her. And now he had good reason to wonder if he had the stomach to be the significant other of a homicide detective. Turning on his side, he brought her in closer to him and breathed in the scent he'd come to crave. His tired eyes burned shut, but he had no expectation that sleep would come.

However, it must have because he startled awake in the gray predawn and reached for Sam. He encountered cold sheets where hot woman should've been and realized she was long gone. Wide awake, he knew it was pointless to try to go back to sleep so he got up to get ready for work. In the shower, he thought of John and Julian and relived the horrible fear that followed Freddie's shooting. Nick's nerves and emotions were raw and close to the surface, an unsettling state for a man used to being in control at all times.

As he was drinking a cup of coffee in the kitchen, he noticed a pile of mail on the counter that Sam must've brought in. Nick flipped through the stack of mostly junk before finding a registered mail envelope Sam had signed for bearing the name of an insurance company. He opened it and sucked in a sharp deep breath when it registered that he was looking at a check for two million dollars. Made out to him. John's life insurance payout. After staring at the check for several long minutes, he tossed it on the counter with the rest of the mail and reached for his suit coat, not wanting to think about the money just now. He had enough on his mind.

Sam rushed down the ramp from her father's house, attempting to juggle her cell phone, half a bagel and the bottle of diet cola tucked under her arm. "So we're no closer than we were last night?" she asked Gonzo.

"We're scouring this city. Every square inch." His voice was full of frustration. "No sign of the bastard anywhere."

"I've got that meeting at eight, and then I'll be out there with you."

"You don't need me at the meeting do you? I'd rather stay out here. I'm working a couple of angles on Sinclair, too."

She slid into the car without dropping the bagel and secured her soda in the cup holder. "No, don't bother coming in. I'll call to see where you need me when I'm leaving HQ."

"Any word on Cruz?"

"I called the hospital an hour ago, and he had a good night. They're thinking he can go home tomorrow or the next day."

"That's good. I'll see you soon."

As Sam slid the key into the ignition, the back door to her car slammed shut. She spun around to find Clarence Reese pointing a gun at her.

"Give me the phone," he growled, "and drive."

Scanning the empty street, Sam swallowed hard, handed him the phone and reached for her own weapon.

"Don't even think about it." The cold metal of Reese's gun pressed against her neck. "Hand it over."

Sam gave him the gun.

"Clutch, too."

Reaching under the cuff of the jeans she had worn to work the streets, she released the second smaller gun strapped to her leg and passed it back to him.

"Now drive. And no funny business."

Sam cleared the panic from her throat. "Where are we going?"

"Head north. Out of the city."

She glanced at the clock. Seven forty-five. In fifteen minutes, they'd be looking for her. On the way past Nick's house, she fixed her eyes on his door, willing him to hear her silent cries for help.

"Is that your senator's place?" Reese asked.

"Yes," Sam mumbled.

"Maybe we should pick him up and take him on our little ride, too."

Sam hit the gas to get out of there before Reese could make good on his threat to drag Nick into whatever nightmare he had planned for her. "What do you want?"

"I want the money you took from my house."

"I don't have it. It's been seized as evidence."

"I want it. Until I get it, I'll be keeping you."

Her cell phone rang. "If I don't answer that, they'll know something's up."

"Don't try to pull no shit."

Sam held out her hand, and Reese gave her the phone. "Holland."

"Lieutenant," Captain Malone said. "Everyone's here for the meeting you called. Where're you?"

"Hi, honey," she said, her heart pounding. She checked the rearview mirror to find Reese's cold eyes monitoring her every move. "No, I'm sorry. I didn't get a chance to pick up the dry cleaning."

"Holland, what the hell are you talking about?"

"You don't have *any* shirts?"

"Is something, wrong?" Malone asked, his voice suddenly tense.

"Yes, honey. I know I promised. I just left the house, otherwise I'd come back to find something for you to wear."

"You're still on Capitol Hill?"

"That's right. You might have to break out the iron."

"Is it Reese?"

"Uh-huh. You can do it."

"Stay calm," Malone said. "We're coming."

"I love you, too. Have a good day."

"Barf," Reese said from the backseat as he reached out to

snatch the phone from her hand. "He's already got you picking up his dry cleaning? I didn't figure you for the domestic
type. You disappoint me."

Relieved that he had bought her side of the phone call,
Sam looked at him in the mirror. "I take care of him. He
takes care of me."

"I'll bet he does." Reese reached forward to run his finger
down the slope of her neck, left bare by her clipped-up hair.
"I'll bet he takes *good* care of you."

Sam worked at not flinching.

"A woman like you needs a real man. Not one who treats
you like his little wife."

"Is that how you treated your wife?" she asked him in the
mirror.

His eyes narrowed. "She was a nag. Nothing was ever
enough for her. She always had to have more."

"So she deserved to be killed?"

"She needed to shut up."

"What about your kids? What did they do to deserve what
they got?"

"None of your business! Just shut the fuck up and drive."

Sam did as she was told while keeping a watchful eye out
for backup. She took Massachusetts Avenue, a main artery
that headed northeast. Another five minutes passed in tense
silence before Sam became aware of an unmarked Metro Police car behind them.

A bead of sweat slid down her back. All she could think
about was Reese being killed before she could ask him the
most important question. Her mouth felt pasty and dry so she
reached for her soda and took a long swig. Of course her stomach reacted with annoying predictability. Taking a couple of
deep, calming breaths, she said, "Did you shoot my father?"

"*What?* What the hell are you talking about?"

"My father, Metro Police Deputy Chief Skip Holland." She watched him in the mirror, waiting for any indication that he recognized the name and got none. "He was shot on G Street two years ago."

Baffled, Reese said, "I didn't shoot no cop on G Street."

Sam gritted her teeth against the urge to scream. "There were newspaper clippings and reports in your house."

"That stuff in the closet? It ain't mine. Belongs to the guy who lived there before me. He was supposed to come get it, but he never did."

"You lived there for more than a year and never got rid of the crap the previous people left behind?"

He shrugged. "We were busy."

For whatever reason, Sam believed him and her heart sank with disappointment. Another dead end. "Who lived there before you?"

"How the hell am I supposed to know? I ain't the freaking landlord."

"Why'd you shoot my partner?"

"Who's your partner?"

Keep him talking, Sam. Get as much as you can out of him before this goes bad. "Yesterday? In your house?"

"*He was a cop?*"

Gratified to see Reese's complexion go pale at that news, she said, "Yeah."

"I didn't mean to shoot no cop. He snuck up on me. I thought he was trying to rob the place. Man's got a right to be in his own house, to protect his property."

Thrilled to have at least gotten his confession on Freddie's shooting, she released a long deep breath, satisfied with the partial victory. "Not after he kills his family in that house he doesn't."

The gun pressed hard into her neck. "Shut the fuck up and drive."

Nick arrived at his office to find the staff huddled around the television in the conference room. "What's up?"

"That guy Reese who killed his family and shot the Lieutenant's partner?" Trevor said.

His heart slowing to a crawl, Nick nodded. "What about him?"

Trevor swallowed hard. "He's taken a Metro cop hostage. They're showing it live. A helicopter is following them on Mass Ave."

Nick moved closer for a better look. At the sight of the dark blue sedan, he gasped. And then he told himself the department had hundreds of those cars assigned to their detectives and high-ranking officers. It could be anyone. "They haven't said who it is?"

Trevor shook his head.

Nick reminded himself of Sam's promise to call him the minute she could to let him know it wasn't her. He retrieved his cell phone from his coat pocket and checked for missed calls. None. Staring at the phone, he willed it to ring.

"What's that?" Reese asked, bending to look out the back window.

"Sounds like a chopper."

"What the fuck? Are they *following* us? How do they even know?"

As he grew more agitated, Sam could think only of Nick and the conversation they'd had the night before. If he knew what was going on—and he probably did by now—he was waiting to hear from her. She ached when she remembered how upset he'd been after the shooting, and now this. Two days in a row, and this time she was actually in danger. No way would he stick around after this. The thought made her unbearably sad.

"They're following us!" He threw the phone at her. "Call them. Tell them to back off."

Her hands shaking, Sam reached for the phone and flipped it open. With only a moment's hesitation, she called Nick.

"Sam!" He sounded as if he had pounced on the phone. "Are you okay?"

Gauging Reese through the mirror, she worked at keeping the hysteria out of her voice. "He wants you to call off the chopper."

"I'll tell Malone. I came over to HQ as soon as I heard the news. He's right here. Do you want to talk to him?"

"Yes." Then, realizing she might never get to talk to Nick again, she said, "Wait. No. You."

"Babe," he said, the single word full of agony. "I love you. I love you so much."

"Me, too."

Reese grabbed the phone from her hand and closed it.

Sam wanted to weep. She had so many other things she needed to say to Nick. If she had a lifetime, she'd never get to say them all.

"What the hell is taking so long?" Reese roared, his eyes fixed on the chopper.

Sam startled at his loud tone. "It could be the press."

"Motherfucker," he muttered.

In the mirror, Sam watched his eyes dart from one side of Massachusetts Avenue to the other.

"There." He pointed with the gun. "Pull in there."

Using the signal to alert the unmarked car behind them, she turned into the parking lot in front of a diner.

"Nice and slow," Reese growled. "Get out and come to the back door." He gripped the clip holding her hair.

Sam winced as he pulled her close enough to whisper in her ear.

"One wrong move and you're dead. You got me?"

"Yeah."

"Hurry up."

Sam hoped her legs would hold up under her as she got out of the car and moved to the back door. Out of the corner of her eye, she watched her colleagues move into position. If she could somehow give them enough room, if they could get off a shot...

But Reese had thought of that. When she opened the back door, he grabbed her and brought her down close to him. Hooking his arm around her neck and pressing the gun to her temple, he whispered, "Get out. Slowly."

Sam took her time standing up.

He half walked, half dragged her into the diner. "Listen up," Reese yelled, keeping the gun pressed to her head. "I want everyone out of here in one minute or this bitch cop is dead and so is anyone left."

Eyeing the gun, customers scrambled for the doors.

"You." Reese nodded to a paunchy middle-aged man who appeared to be in charge of the diner. "Over here."

The man's eyes almost popped out of his doughy face.

Now that they were out of the car, Sam waited for her opportunity to call upon her years of training to immobilize Reese. But not while there were still civilians in the diner.

One of the waitresses escorted the last elderly customer to the door, casting a panic-stricken glance at her boss on her way out.

"Go out there and tell them I want my money." Reese pointed the gun at the petrified manager. "I want every cent of the ten grand they took from my house. They got one hour. *She's* got one hour. Go."

The manager didn't have to be told twice.

Sam checked the clock on the wall. Eight twenty, only thirty-five minutes since Reese grabbed her. It felt like hours. Maybe if he kept her long enough, she'd get out of appearing at Lieutenant Stahl's internal affairs hearing this afternoon. That thought almost made her giggle. As if. Stahl would probably write her up for missing the hearing. Would he care that she'd been taken hostage by a man who'd killed his entire family and had nothing to lose by killing her, too? Probably not.

"Sit," Reese said, ordering her into a booth at the far end of the diner.

Pissed that she'd missed her chance to overtake him, she did as she was told and watched him move from one end of the long, narrow restaurant to the other, closing the blinds as he went.

Sam felt claustrophobic as she imagined what was no doubt happening outside. Her cell phone rang.

Reese groped for it in his pocket.

"They'll want to establish contact with you," she said.

He handed her the phone. "Answer it. Put it on speaker."

She kept her eyes fixed on Reese. "Holland."

"Lieutenant," Malone said. "You're all right?"

"I'm fine."

"Mr. Reese, this is Detective Captain Malone. We want to help you."

"Sure you do. I want my money."

"We're working on getting it for you."

"You'll bring it here?"

"As soon as we recover it from the evidence locker."

"I don't want no games. You give me my money, I'll let her go."

"If Lieutenant Holland is hurt in any way, there's no money. Do you understand?"

Reese ended the call and put the phone back in his pocket.

CHAPTER 20

Sam figured SWAT probably had the place surrounded by now. She wondered if Nick was outside, too. Her mind wandered back to what he'd said the night before. *No, I can't go there. I'll go crazy if I think about that.*

She noticed Reese talking to himself and strained to hear him.

"It's her fault I had to do the babies, too," he muttered. "I never wanted to hurt them."

Sam swallowed hard. "So then why did you?"

He stared at her. "What did you say?"

"Why did you hurt the babies?"

"I didn't mean to. She was screaming at me again. We had no money for groceries."

"Where'd you get the ten grand?"

Reese seemed almost ashamed. "I got a second job, and it still wasn't enough. So I started selling drugs. Didn't mean to get into that, but no matter how much I brought home, it wasn't enough for her. She said she hated me and was going to take the babies and leave me. I didn't want her to know I had the money. If she got her hands on it, she would've left me."

Sam hung on his every word, forcing herself to stay still and let him get it out before she made her move.

"I couldn't let her take my kids. That wasn't going to happen." He didn't seem to notice the tears that tumbled down his face. "I went to get my gun. Just to scare her into shutting up, but she didn't care. She just kept spewing shit at me."

"Why'd you shoot her?"

Clarence's eyes met hers. "She called me a loser. Said she never should've married me." He shook his head. "After everything I'd done for her."

"What happened with the kids?"

"Jorge started screaming. I told him to shut up so I could think. He wouldn't shut up." Clarence's voice caught on a sob. "I didn't mean to hit him. I loved him. I loved all of them, but nothing I did was enough."

Sam wanted to go to him, but was mindful of the gun in his hand. "I can help you," she said. "We can walk out of here with no one getting hurt. If you let me help, this doesn't have to end badly for you."

"It already has," he said in a tone devoid of hope.

"Your life isn't over. I'll talk to the U.S. Attorney. I'll tell them your wife emotionally abused you. I'll make sure you get a good attorney who'll enter a temporary insanity plea. You'll do some time, but in a hospital not a prison. Let me help you."

Reese shook his head. "You can't bring my family back."

Sam stood up. "But I can—"

"Stop!" He aimed the gun at her. "Just stop talking. I want my money. If I get the money, I won't need your help. I won't need anyone."

Moving past the fear, Sam took a step toward him. "They've got this place surrounded by now. SWAT is making a plan. They'll come in and take you out. They won't care about you." She took another step, reaching outside herself for the fortitude. "All they care about right now is saving me. I'm the only one who cares about you, Clarence."

"You don't care about me. I shot your partner."

"He startled you. You thought he was robbing your house."

"I never meant to shoot him."

"I know." She took another step. Three feet to go. "Give me the gun. I'll call them. I'll tell them you're unarmed. No one has to get hurt."

He eyed her warily. "Why do you want to help me? I took you hostage."

"You were desperate. I understand that." She thought of Nick, of what he'd said the night before, and forced herself to concentrate. "I don't want you to get hurt. Think of your mother. She just lost Tiffany and the children. She doesn't want to lose you, too."

His shoulders sagged, a sob hiccupping through him. "Why couldn't Tiffany be happy with me?"

"I don't know, Clarence, but maybe you'll have a chance to make someone else happy. I can help you. I promise I'll help you." She had him. She could see it in his eyes as she took yet another step toward him.

The door to the diner burst open, startling them both. "Freeze, police!" Two SWAT officers dressed in black riot gear aimed their weapons at Reese.

He spun toward them, waving the gun.

"No!" Sam screamed to the officers. "Hold your fire." She held out her hand to Reese. "Give me the gun. I can still get you out of here alive."

He shook his head, his eyes focused on the two officers at the door.

"Drop the gun, Reese," one of them ordered.

"Clarence, I can help," Sam pleaded.

"No, you can't." His eyes shifted to her. "No one can." He put the gun to his temple and pulled the trigger.

The gunshot rang through the diner's parking lot.

"Oh, my God!" one of the reporters cried.

Nick couldn't have said it better himself. Four people were inside—three cops and Reese. Nick's money was on the cops. "Come on," he whispered, watching the door so intently his eyes watered from the need to blink.

Christina squeezed his arm.

Five long minutes passed before one of the SWAT officers escorted Sam out of the building.

A cheer erupted from the crowd gathered in the parking lot.

Nick's legs went weak with relief as he watched her talk to Captain Malone. A few minutes later, Malone gestured behind him to point Nick out in the crowd.

"Thanks for waiting with me," Nick said to Christina. "I'll check in later." He moved toward Sam. The crowd between them parted, their eyes met, and nothing mattered more to Nick than getting to her as fast as he could—not the worries he'd expressed the night before, not the media watching their every move. Nothing mattered but her.

He put his arms around her and brought her in close to him, attempting to shield her from the blinding blur of camera flashes.

"We'll be on every front page in the city tomorrow," she said.

"That's okay."

He held her for a long time before he pulled back to study her pale face.

"I had him," she said. "I just needed one more minute…"

"All that matters is that you're safe."

"I called you. The minute I could. Just like I said I would."

"I know, babe. I know." He noticed there was something gray all over her. "Let me drive you home so you can change."

She brushed at the lapels of his coat. "You'll need to have this cleaned."

"What is that?"

"Clarence Reese's brain."

Nick shuddered. "Jesus, Sam." Ignoring the media clamoring for a word from her, he ushered her to her car and held the passenger door for her. He took off his overcoat, rolled it into a ball and tossed it into the backseat.

"I had him," she said again as they pulled out of the diner.

"I'm sure you did everything you could."

Looking over at him, she said, "He didn't shoot my dad."

"But the stuff in his place…"

"Previous tenant."

"Shit."

"Yeah. Back to square one—again. But at least I have a lead to work with."

"I hope Malone gave you the rest of the day off."

"He tried to, but as soon as I get a shower, I'm back on Sinclair."

"You should take the day, Sam. This was a traumatic thing."

"I'm fine. I need to work."

Nick knew it was pointless to argue with her.

"I was surprised to see you when I came out," she said after a long period of silence. "I wasn't sure if you'd be there."

"Of course I was there."

"I thought you were 'taking some time.'"

Nick's jaw tightened with tension. "I needed to know you were all right."

"Will you still need to know I'm all right if we break up?"

"Sam…"

"I'm just wondering."

"I'll always worry about you, no matter what."

"If that's the case, then it seems kind of stupid to break up. What if I'm with someone else and I get taken hostage? You won't be able to show up like you did today. It won't be your place."

The idea of her with someone else tore at him, which of course was her goal. "I know what you're trying to do."

"I'm trying to show you how dumb you're being."

"Gee, thanks." He was so damned glad to be arguing with her that the barb didn't bother him in the least. On Ninth Street, he parallel parked between his house and her dad's.

"Thanks for driving me," she said. "You must need to get back to work."

"I've got some time. Let's go in. I'm sure your dad is anxious to see you."

He followed her up the ramp to her father's house where Skip, Celia, Angela and Tracy waited for them.

When her sisters started to rush over to Sam, Nick held up a hand to stop them. He shook his head, and they seemed to get the message that Sam needed someone else just then.

She went straight to her dad and rested her forehead on his shoulder. "It wasn't him," she said. "He didn't shoot you."

"That's the least of my concerns right now. How are you?"

"I'm fine," she said, straightening. "I need a shower, though. Reese offed himself right next to me."

Angela winced. "God, that must've been horrible."

Sam shrugged off her sister's sympathy. "I'd almost talked him out of the gun."

Nick's heart ached as he watched her attempt at stoicism. He could see the truth in her eyes. No doubt her family could, too.

"I'm sure you did everything you could," Tracy said. "Just like you always do."

"That's right," Celia said.

"Go on up to the shower," Skip said. "You'll feel better once you get cleaned up."

After Sam went upstairs, Sam's sisters followed Celia into the kitchen.

Skip turned his gaze on Nick. "Takes a special kind."

"Sir?"

"It's not easy loving a cop. You get to do all the worrying."

Hands on his hips, Nick struggled to contain the surge of emotion that hovered just below the surface. "Yeah."

"She needs you," Skip said. "She'd die before she admitted it, but she does."

Nick marveled at how Skip saw right through him.

"I'm, ah, going up to check on her."

"You do that."

Sam scrubbed her skin until it burned. She washed her hair and then washed it again. The horror was harder to get rid of than Reese's brain matter. Standing under the hot water, she relived the whole thing, from the moment he got into her car until the fatal shot. She'd done all she could to bring about a positive conclusion. Of that she was confident. But that didn't change the fact that a man had died a foot from her. All her training and time on the job only went so far on days like this.

She leaned against the shower wall and closed her eyes. All she could see was Clarence's face in the moment she knew she had gotten through to him. And then she saw the gun at his temple. Sometimes the waste, the sheer destruction she witnessed on the job was too much to bear.

The shower door opened, and Nick stepped in.

He reached for her, but she shook him off. "Don't."

He lifted her into his embrace anyway.

Sam fought him. "You can't come in here and do this. Not after what you said last night. You don't have any right."

"I have every right."

"I can't allow myself to rely on you if you're not going to be here next time."

"I'll be here next time. Every time."

"Because you want to be?"

"Because I wouldn't know how not to be." He left a trail of hot kisses from her neck to her shoulder. "I'm not sure why, but for some reason I wasn't as afraid today as I was yesterday. You were in real danger this time, but I knew you'd find a way out of it." Brushing his lips over hers, he added, "You're so smart and resourceful. I had faith, Sam. I *have* faith. In you."

"So what happens the next time someone takes a shot at me? Or if I actually get shot? Will I have to worry about you freaking out and hitting the road?"

He shook his head. "We have a deal, remember? I can't ever do this again."

"I need there to be *one thing,* Nick. I need one thing in my life I can be sure of."

"You can be sure of me, babe. I'm here, and I'm not going anywhere."

"Promise?"

"I promise."

"So this is a forever kind of thing?"

"Absolutely." His lips came down hard on hers for a deep, devouring kiss.

When she came up for air, Sam said, "I need to get to work, and so do you."

"Another couple of minutes won't matter." He pressed her back against the wall, hooked her legs over his hips and thrust into her.

"Only a couple of minutes?" she asked with a coy smile.

"However long it takes." He tipped her chin up so he could see her eyes. "But there'll be no more faking."

Her heart skipped a beat. "How did you know?"

"After experiencing the real thing, there's no mistaking a fake."

"I'm sorry."

"I'm sorry I filled your head with doubts." Cupping her breast, he said, "The way I see it, I owe you two."

Eyes fluttering shut, Sam floated on a cloud of sensation. "Must. Go. To. Work."

He kissed his way down her neck. "You'll get there. Eventually."

CHAPTER 21

Sam and Jeannie pulled up in front of Devon Sinclair's swanky Dupont Circle townhouse just after one o'clock. She had two hours before the Internal Affairs hearing and intended to put the time to good use. Through a call to Devon's law firm, she had learned that he was on bereavement leave.

"Nice digs for an associate," she said.

"You're sure you're up for this, Lieutenant?" Jeannie asked as they climbed the stone stairs. "Tyrone and I could take the lead on this one." She referred to her usual partner.

"I keep telling everyone I'm fine," Sam said, exasperated.

"Just asking."

She turned to Jeannie. "What would you do? If it'd happened to you, would you go home and take to your bed?"

"I'd probably do what you're doing."

"Good, so maybe we can drop it now?" She missed Cruz, who was a lot more fun to abuse than McBride.

"You're the boss."

"Lieutenant Holland!"

Sam spun around and groaned when she saw Darren Tabor,

her least favorite reporter from the *Washington Star,* and several other reporters chasing after her. "Not now, Darren."

"Just a couple of questions about what happened with Reese."

"Not now." She pushed past them and went up the stairs to Devon Sinclair's townhouse.

"You're so popular," Jeannie muttered under her breath.

Sam made a face at her and rang the bell.

Devon Sinclair came to the door. An interesting mix of his parents, he was tall and handsome with close-cropped brown hair and devastated, red-rimmed eyes.

"Mr. Sinclair?"

"Yes."

"Lieutenant Holland and Detective McBride." Sam held out her badge for his inspection. "May we have a few minutes of your time?"

He ushered them into a stylish, contemporary living room where another young man was stretched out on the sofa. "My brother, Austin," Devon said, introducing them. "I assume this is about Julian."

"Yes," Sam replied. "Would you mind if we tape our conversation?"

With a weary gesture, Devon granted permission.

"We're sorry for your loss," Sam said.

"Thank you." Devon took a seat next to his brother, who sat up to make room. Austin was blond and favored their mother.

"You were close to your uncle?"

"Very. This is just the most horrible thing." Devon's eyes filled. "I'm sorry. We're still in shock."

"I'm sure you are. Had you seen him recently?"

"We had lunch with him the day he got to town. He was so excited about the nomination—nervous about the hearings, of course, but mostly excited. We said later that he seemed truly happy for the first time in a long time."

"Did either of your parents know you had seen him?"

"We told our dad," Austin said.

"Did you know Julian's friend, Duncan Quick?" Sam asked.

"Yes, we knew him quite well. Julian had been really down since they broke up, but the nomination seemed to have lifted his spirits."

"I understand from talking to your parents that your father and uncle had been estranged for a number of years," Sam said.

"Since we were young," Austin said. "We'd always been very close with him, spent a lot of time at his house, went on trips. But that all ended after my mother saw him with Duncan."

"She totally freaked," Devon added. "We didn't see him again for years—until we were adults and could make our own decisions."

"Did you know the reason for the estrangement?" Jeannie asked.

Austin glanced at his brother. "We had our suspicions. We knew Julian was gay and that our mother didn't approve. It's not that she's a bad person."

"She has strong views," Devon said. "She's worked really hard for the career she has."

"And an openly gay brother-in-law on the Supreme Court might not help her ambitions," Sam said.

"While we don't necessarily agree with her, we admire her tenacity," Devon said, sounding more like a sound bite than a son.

"Was your mother ambitious enough to kill your uncle to keep the family's dirty little secret in the closet?" she asked.

Both men blanched.

"*Kill* him?" Austin asked, his eyes wide. "She's a deeply spiritual person. She could never harm anyone."

"Were her ambitions more important than the two of you or your father?"

"Of course not," Devon said, but Sam detected a note of hesitation. "She's very devoted to her family."

"How would you describe your parents' marriage?" Sam asked.

"Loving," Austin said. "They're the best of friends."

"Would you say that your mother is in charge, though?"

"What does this have to do with Julian?" Devon asked.

"We're trying to determine what role, if any, the estrangement with your parents might've played in your uncle's death," Jeannie said. "This information helps us to paint a picture."

After a long pause, Austin said, "My mom was in charge when we were at home. I can't really say how it is between them now. She's pursued the goal of writing her book and having her own show for many years. It's taken a lot of her time."

"Is she a conservative Christian?" Jeannie asked.

"Yes," Devon said. "In recent years when Julian's name came up, she was fond of quoting Leviticus, who preached that it's an 'abomination' punishable by death for men to have sex with other men the way they would with women."

"Do either of you believe that?" Jeannie asked.

"We came of age in a different time," Austin said. "A more tolerant time."

"So that's a no?" Jeannie asked.

"That's a no," Austin replied. "We loved our uncle and supported him the same way he supported us."

"But you did that behind your mother's back," Sam said.

"We love them both," Devon said. "We were in an awkward position. Our goal was to keep the peace. It was better that she didn't know."

"Can you think of anyone who might want to harm him? Any enemies or rivals?"

Devon shook his head. "We've been wracking our brains trying to think of who could've done this to him. He had strong opinions and ideals, but he had respect for other people's beliefs, too. That kept him from attracting a lot of overt enemies."

Unlike your mother, Sam thought, *who has no respect for others' beliefs and has attracted an army of enemies.*

"You said he was nervous about the hearings," Jeannie said, "but did he express any worries about his safety or the controversy surrounding his nomination?"

"Not about his safety so much," Austin said.

"He'd declined Secret Service protection," Devon added.

"It was offered?"

Devon nodded. "He had some reservations about the protestors. He was afraid they'd be disruptive, but I'm sure he never suspected someone would want to kill him."

"Where were you both the night before last?" Sam asked.

"*We're* suspects?" Devon asked.

"We need to rule you out," Sam said.

Austin sat up a little straighter at the talk of alibis. "I was with my girlfriend at her place."

"We'll need her name and number." Sam turned to Devon. "And you?"

"I was here."

"Alone?"

"Most of the night. My roommate got home from work around one. He's a waiter."

"And did you see him? Talk to him?"

Devon's eyes darted to his brother. "Yes."

Sam's radar went on alert. "Is there something else, Mr. Sinclair? If so, this would be the time to tell us."

Devon's entire body went rigid with tension.

"Tell them, Dev," Austin said softly.

"Shut up," Devon snapped. "It's got no bearing on what happened to Julian."

"Mr. Sinclair, anything you tell us will remain confidential unless it directly affects the case."

"We've told you everything we know," Devon said, sounding more desperate.

Sam stared him down. "Except?"

Devon glared at his brother. "My roommate, Tucker. He's my... We're involved."

"And I take it your parents are unaware of this?"

"Yes," Devon said through gritted teeth. "And so are his. We'd like to keep it that way."

"How long have you been aware of your brother's orientation?" Jeannie asked Austin.

"Always."

"And your parents have no clue?" Jeannie asked.

"I've gone to great lengths to keep my private life private," Devon said.

"Did your uncle know?" Sam asked.

"Yes," Devon said softly. "He was the only one in my life who understood. In a lot of ways, other than my brother, Julian was my best friend."

Austin rested a comforting hand on his brother's shoulder, the two of them united in their grief.

Sam stood up, and Jeannie followed suit. "Is your roommate home at the moment?"

Panic-stricken, Devon looked up at her. "No, why?"

"We need to confirm your alibi. A formality. Can we get his name and number?"

Reluctantly, Devon got up and wrote down the information. Handing the piece of paper to Sam, he said, "You don't need to tell him I told you about us, do you?"

"I don't see any need to mention it."

"Thank you," he said, relieved.

Austin handed her a sticky note with his girlfriend's name and number.

"One other question," Sam said. "Were you Julian's heirs?"

"Yes," Austin said. "We'll each inherit half his estate."

"I know I speak for my brother when I say we'd give up every dime we stand to gain to have him back," Devon said.

After witnessing their devastation, Sam believed him.

Outside, Sam released a long deep breath. "Wow. I don't envy that kid the road he has ahead of him."

"Me, either. That mother is a piece of work."

"I'd like to dig a little deeper into Diandra Sinclair's background. We also need to take a closer look at Julian's cell phone and email records. He had arranged a late-night meeting with someone. I want to know who it was."

"The cell records didn't show any activity after he arrived at the senator's house for dinner, so whatever he was up to, it was planned before he went to dinner."

"Let's find out what it was. I also want to know why the Secret Service saw fit to offer him protection." Sam checked her watch. "Damn it. I don't have time to do much of anything before that stupid hearing. I guess I'll run by and check on Cruz real quick."

"I'll go with you." When they were in the car, Jeannie looked over at her. "I hope you know everyone thinks this thing with IAB is totally bogus, Lieutenant. Stahl is out for revenge because they gave you his command."

Sam's stomach kicked into gear when she thought about the hearing. "He's had it in for me long before now. And let's face it, I handed him a gift by hooking up with Nick in the middle of O'Connor."

"It's going to be fine."

Sam wished she could be so confident.

"What does Nick say about it?"

"I haven't told him."

"Why not?"

Sam shrugged. "He's got enough going on without having to worry about me getting in trouble because of him. There's no need for him to know about it."

"If you say so. Besides, you're probably right. He's been through an awful lot lately."

"Exactly." But recalling their conversation in the shower, Sam couldn't help but feel guilty for keeping it from him.

CHAPTER 22

Sam waited outside the Internal Affairs hearing room. They were running late, which had sent her stomach into a spiral. She focused on breathing: in through the nose, out through the mouth. It wouldn't have been so bad if she knew she'd done nothing wrong and could chalk this up to a witch hunt by Stahl.

But that wasn't the case.

She had screwed up by getting involved with Nick during the O'Connor investigation. He'd found the body, which made him a material witness. She should've stayed as far away from him as she could get until the case was closed. That he had been instrumental to her successfully closing the case might not matter to the board.

Though she had participated in many IAB hearings during her career, she'd never been the subject of one, even after the fiasco with the Johnson case. An internal investigation had cleared her of any wrongdoing in the death of young Quentin Johnson in the crack house shooting, but the department psychologist had recommended a thirty-day administrative leave. The penalty this time could be much stiffer.

Deputy Chief Conklin, Sam's delegate to the three-person panel, came out to get her. "Lieutenant? We're ready for you."

"Oh. Okay."

Inside the room, Conklin joined Stahl and Captain Andrews from the bomb squad at the head table. The three of them would determine her fate. Chief Farnsworth and Captain Malone were also in attendance. A stenographer was set to record the proceedings.

"Before we begin," said Stahl, who was clearly enjoying this, "I'd like to once again protest the appointment of Deputy Chief Conklin to this panel. He maintains a close personal relationship with the lieutenant's father, and his participation here is a conflict of interest."

"As I've told you before, Lieutenant," Conklin said, "find me anyone in this department—besides yourself of course—who doesn't hold retired Deputy Chief Holland in the highest regard. Per the officer bill of rights, Lieutenant Holland can choose anyone she wishes to act as her delegate to this panel. You're wasting everyone's time with this protest."

"I agree," Andrews said. "Let's move on."

Stahl levied a hateful stare in Sam's direction. "Very well, Lieutenant Holland, raise your right hand." He swore her in and gestured for her to be seated. "You've waived your right to representation?"

"I have." She saw no need to suck someone else off real police work when she was more than capable of defending herself.

"And you're aware of why you're here today?"

"You believe I exercised poor judgment in becoming romantically involved with Nicholas Cappuano during the O'Connor investigation."

Stahl stared at her. Clearly, he hadn't expected her to be so forthcoming. "That's correct," he stammered.

Sam noticed that Captain Malone had a hand over his mouth as if trying to hide a smile.

Stahl cleared his throat. "And to that you say?"

"I can't deny that I become close to Mr. Cappuano during the investigation, or that he was enormously helpful to me and Detective Cruz as we worked to close that case," Sam said, thrilled to realize she was ruffling Stahl.

"Did you know Mr. Cappuano before the O'Connor investigation?"

Ignoring the grind in her stomach, Sam said, "Yes."

"Please elaborate."

"We met six years ago at a party. We spent one night together and didn't see each other again until Senator O'Connor was found murdered."

"And why did you never see him again?"

"A series of misunderstandings."

"Did you disclose this prior relationship with the witness to your superior officers?"

"I did not."

"Why not?"

"It wasn't relevant. It was one night six years ago."

"Did it occur to you at the time that your failure to disclose the relationship might endanger the investigation?"

"No."

"At no time did you think, maybe I ought to tell someone that I know this guy? That I slept with this guy?"

"As I said, since the relationship spanned one night six years earlier, I didn't see how it was relevant to the investigation. Mr. Cappuano was a tremendous asset and saved us a lot of time we would've wasted figuring out who the players were."

"When did you clear Mr. Cappuano of any possible culpability in the senator's murder?"

"Right away. He had an airtight alibi, no motive and his

heartbreak over the loss of his friend and boss was genuine. At no time was he a suspect."

"Even after you learned that he was the beneficiary of a two-million-dollar life insurance policy left by Senator O'Connor?"

"Mr. Cappuano was never a suspect."

"At what point during the investigation did your relationship with Mr. Cappuano become personal again?"

"The first night."

Stahl's eyes lit up with glee.

Sam worked to keep her tone calm and even. "He called me when he realized someone had been in his house."

"So the first night of the O'Connor investigation, you went to Mr. Cappuano's home?"

"That's correct."

"Located where?"

"At that time it was in Arlington, Virginia."

"Which is well outside your jurisdiction."

"I had given him my card with instructions to call if he thought of anything that might help the investigation. When he arrived home and discovered disarray, he did as I asked by calling me. After I got to his house and confirmed that someone had entered the home, I called Arlington police."

"And your relationship took a personal turn that night?"

"I waited with him while Arlington investigated. During that time, he provided more background on the O'Connor family relationships. After the police left, we discussed our personal relationship, which he wished to resume. I told him it would have to wait until the investigation concluded."

"Did it?"

A sharp pain in her stomach stole her breath. This is where things got dicey. "Despite my intentions, the relationship later became serious."

"Did you disclose that to your superiors?"

"I did not. It still had no bearing on the investigation."

"How did your relationship with Mr. Cappuano become public?"

"When my ex-husband planted crude bombs on both our cars. The bomb on my car exploded, injuring both Mr. Cappuano and myself."

"This occurred where?"

"In front of Mr. Cappuano's Arlington home."

"You were there for what reason?"

Sam swallowed the ball of panic forming in her throat. "I had spent the night there."

"How many days into the O'Connor investigation was this?"

"Three."

"That didn't take long."

"Can the editorializing, Lieutenant Stahl," Conklin said.

With a smarmy smile, Stahl said, "Lieutenant Holland, did your superiors confront you about the relationship after the bombing?"

"I discussed it with both Captain Malone and Chief Farnsworth, both of whom accepted my explanation of how the relationship transpired and how helpful Mr. Cappuano had been to the investigation."

"What is your relationship today with Mr. Cappuano?"

"*Senator* Cappuano and I are in a committed relationship as you and everyone in Washington knows."

"Do you think the very public nature of your relationship with the senator could be seen as a detriment to your duties as a police officer?"

"In a perfect world, the media would have no interest in us. Unfortunately, I don't live in that world."

"Do either of you have any questions?" Stahl asked Conklin

and Andrews. Both declined. "In light of Lieutenant Holland's testimony and her inappropriate relationship with a material witness, I recommend two weeks unpaid suspension and reduction in rank to detective."

Sam suppressed a gasp. Two ranks! That couldn't happen. But she refused to give Stahl the satisfaction of an emotional outburst.

"The panel will consider the recommendation in executive session," Conklin said. "Lieutenant Holland, we appreciate your candor. You'll be informed of our decision."

"Thank you, Deputy Chief Conklin. If I may, I'd like to say one more thing—obviously, I don't wish to lose my current rank, but I want you to know that if I had the O'Connor investigation to do over again, I wouldn't change a single thing. That's all."

She got up and left the room. It was out of her hands.

Nick and Christina returned to his office after a marathon meeting of the Senate Homeland Security and Governmental Affairs Committee. Once they had gone over their notes and made a to-do list, she got up to leave.

"Thanks again for going with me earlier," he said. "And yesterday, too."

"Lots of drama lately."

"Yes."

She looked at him as if there was something else she wanted to say but had thought better of it.

"What's on your mind, Chris?"

She studied him for a long moment. "Are you going to, you know, go running out of here every time something happens with her?"

"I don't know," he said, caught off guard by the question. "Maybe. Do you have a problem with that?"

"No, it's just that you might not always be able to. You have so many commitments and obligations now. It's different than before."

"I'm well aware that my role has changed. We're just going through a period of transition. On multiple fronts." He paused before he added, "I know you've had a lot on your plate doing two jobs over the last month, but Terry will be starting soon. It should get better then."

"I guess we'll see how that works out. You have a nice evening, Senator."

"You, too."

For a long time after she left, he sat and stared at the painting of the Capitol that Sam had given him for Christmas. He thought about what Christina had said and acknowledged that she made a good point. It wouldn't always be possible for him to go running when Sam was in trouble—not that she expected him to. But he couldn't imagine sitting through a committee meeting, for instance, if he knew someone was holding her hostage.

They were definitely navigating uncharted waters here, and everyone was going to have to make some adjustments. He finally had time to pick up that day's *Washington Post,* which had devoted much of the front page to Julian's murder. At least they had taken a break from reporting about his romance with Sam. As Nick read the coverage about Julian, he was once again filled with sadness over the loss of his friend.

Suddenly, he remembered an op-ed piece that had run the week before in which Tony Sanducci, a leading abortion protestor, had spouted off about Julian's nomination and the setback it could represent to the rights of the unborn. He had urged his followers to take any steps necessary to stop the nomination. Nick wondered if Sam had thought to talk

to Sanducci. Nick reached for the phone to call her, but got
voice mail.

"Hey, babe, it's me. Listen, I was thinking you ought to
check out an editorial that ran in the *Post* a week or so ago.
Tony Sanducci went off about Julian. Might be a good lead.
I'll send a link to your email. I'll be home in an hour or so.
Maybe we can take another shower or something." The mem-
ory of their earlier shower made him smile. "Love you."

Sam emerged from the hearing and went straight to the
restroom. The pain in her stomach bent her in half. In a cold
sweat, she closed the stall door and rested against it, fighting
for every breath.

She'd meant it when she told the board she wouldn't change
a thing about the O'Connor investigation. Nick was, without a doubt, the best thing to ever happen to her. How could
she regret falling in love with him? How could she regret the
magic his love had brought to her life? But to be busted down
to detective, just as she achieved her longtime goal of making lieutenant…

"God," she whispered, the enormity of it almost too much
to bear.

She took another ten minutes to pull herself together. Determined to get out of there on time for once, she returned to
the detectives' pit, where a crowd waited for her.

Gonzo pounced first. "Lieutenant, how did it go?"

"Are you all right?" Jeannie asked.

"Stahl's an asshole," Arnold chimed in. "This is all about
you getting his command."

Sam held up her hand to stop them. "I appreciate the support, Arnold, but this is about me hooking up with a witness
during a homicide investigation. While Lieutenant Stahl may

have ulterior motives, he's entirely within his rights to call for an IAB inquiry."

"It's so *fucked up*," Gonzo said, his face tight with dismay. "The senator was instrumental in you closing O'Connor as fast as you did. That should count for something."

"We'll see if it does," Sam said, resigned now to whatever fate awaited her. "In the meantime, where are we with Sinclair?"

"I'm digging around in Diandra's background like we discussed," Jeannie said. "I should have a report for you in a couple of hours."

"We aren't authorized any O.T. on this one," Sam reminded her.

"I'll do it on my own time," Jeannie said.

Sam sent her a grateful smile, knowing Jeannie had been moved by Nick's devastation after hearing about Sinclair. The brotherhood—or in this case sisterhood—among her fellow officers had always been Sam's favorite part of the job. Luckily, there were a lot more like Jeannie and Gonzo and Cruz than there were like Stahl.

"I'm going to head home," Sam said. "Shoot your report to my email. I'll be working later."

"Will do, Lieutenant," Jeannie said. "Try not to worry too much. Conklin and Andrews know you're a great cop and a gifted detective. It's going to be fine. I'm sure of it."

"It'd better be," Gonzo added.

"Watch your blood pressure, Gonzo," Sam said, amused by his anger on her behalf. "I appreciate the support, you guys. Let's not allow it to be too much of a distraction. If you need me I'll be on the radio or call my cell."

She left them talking about the injustice of the IAB hearing. Their overwhelming support helped to boost her spirits. On the drive home, she listened to the voice mail from Nick and decided to stop at the store so she could surprise him with a home-cooked meal. After she stashed the makings for linguine and clam sauce in his refrigerator, she went over to check on her dad.

"Anyone home?" she called.

"In here," Skip replied from the kitchen. "Is that my wayward daughter who used to live here?"

"Very funny." Sam bent to kiss his cheek. "I still live here."

"I've been wondering why that is when you've gotten a much better offer from the handsome guy down the street."

"I'm thinking about the handsome guy's better offer."

"Are you now?"

She shrugged. "It is a pretty good offer. And he does have a Jacuzzi."

"You're so easy," Skip said, laughing. "I hope you're not holding out because of me. I'm in good hands with Celia. There's no need for you to be here if you'd rather be somewhere else."

"I'm just trying to take it slow," Sam said. "I don't want to rush into anything."

"Understandable. After all, if you were to rush in, you might end up on the front page of the *Post* every other day, and that would kind of suck."

"You're very funny tonight, Skippy." Sam reached for a soda in the fridge. "What's the occasion?"

"You gonna tell me about it?"

She paused in the midst of opening the bottle. "What?"

He shot her a "you know" look.

Swallowing hard, she said, "How did you hear about it?"

"The question is, why didn't I hear about it from you?"

"I've been in major denial mode."

"What did Stahl recommend?"

"Two weeks unpaid suspension, reduction to detective."

Skip winced. "No way Conklin will let that happen."

"Nothing I can do about it now. I was straight up with them in the hearing, told them exactly how it went down."

"That's the best strategy, which I would've told you if you hadn't kept me in the dark—again. Becoming kind of a disturbing pattern between us."

The comment went straight to her heart because he was right. They'd always been in sync with each other, and she hadn't been holding up her end of the deal lately.

"If you treat me like an invalid, that's how I feel, Sam. I don't want you thinking you have to protect me from this crap. It doesn't get much more crappy than living like this."

"I'm sorry." She dropped into one of the kitchen chairs. "I don't mean to keep stuff from you. I was hoping this was gonna go away before it got this far."

"Should've known better with Stahl involved."

"I know."

"Did you tell Nick?"

Sam looked up at him with a rueful expression.

"Sam! Are you *kidding me?* You've got IAB poking into your relationship with him and you don't think he needs to know that?"

"He's been so down about John and now Julian and wound up about what happened to Cruz. And then the whole mess with Reese today. I was afraid it might be one thing too many, you know?"

"You're playing with fire, baby girl. That man is one to be reckoned with. If you think he's going to put up with you keeping things from him, you're deluding yourself."

Sam knew he was right. "I'll tell him tonight. It'll be fine." She got up and kissed him. "I've got to go. I'm making dinner."

"You? *Cooking?*"

"You really ought to consider a career in stand-up comedy—without the stand-up part of course."

"Now who's being funny? Let me know the minute you hear."

"I will. Try not to worry too much. Whatever happens, Nick was worth it."

"That's a good way to look at it."

"It's the *only* way to look at it. I'll see you in the morning."

After she packed a bag of clothes for the next day, she walked back over to Nick's, thinking about what her father had said. At this point, Nick would probably be furious that she'd waited so long to tell him about the IAB hearing. She'd have to see how the evening unfolded to determine if there'd be a good time to tell him. In the meantime, after dinner she would look into Sanducci.

CHAPTER 23

By the time Nick got home an hour later, Sam was ready for him. She had enjoyed playing house in his primo kitchen and had even indulged in a little fantasizing about what it might be like to really live there rather than just spending most nights in his bed. Her trip down fantasy lane had also helped to keep her mind off the outcome of the hearing. Shouldn't she have heard something by now?

"Hey, babe," Nick called when he came in. "Sorry I'm so late. I got sucked into a Democratic Caucus planning meeting." He stopped short at the kitchen door. "Did you *cook?*"

"Yep," she said, standing at the stove. "You don't need to sound *that* surprised."

He slid his arms around her from behind and kissed her neck. "I didn't think you knew how to turn on the stove."

She pushed her butt into him. "I know how to turn on a lot of things."

Laughing, he tightened his hold on her. "You sure do." He buried his face in her hair. "I'm so damned glad to see you, Samantha. After everything today with Reese. I can't stop thinking about it."

She turned to face him and curled her arms around his neck. This would be a great time to tell him about the IAB hearing, except that he looked like himself again for the first time in days. Was it such a crime to want him to relax and enjoy the evening? "Everything's fine."

He dipped his head to kiss her. "It is now that I'm with you. I love finding you here when I come home."

She divested him of his tie and released his top buttons. "I decided to leave work on time for once."

"What's the occasion?"

Another golden opportunity. "No occasion. I just felt like cooking." She reached for the check she'd found on the counter earlier and waved it at him. "Got anything you want to tell me?"

Staring at the check, his face became unreadable. "You knew about that. You signed for it."

"What're you going to do with it?"

"Part of me wants to give it all away."

Her heart went out to him. The pain of John's loss was still so present. "What would John want you to do with it?"

"He'd want me to enjoy being a millionaire for a while," he said without hesitation.

"Then that's what you ought to do."

"How can I enjoy it when he had to die for it to happen? How do I do that?"

Sam reached up to run her fingers through his hair. "He loved you, Nick. He'd want you to be happy."

"I talked to Graham today, told him I'd gotten the money. He said he'd invest it for me if I wanted him to."

"Why don't you do that? Give it to him and forget about it."

"I guess I will. We have everything we need, right?"

"And then some."

He surprised her when he lifted her onto the center island and stepped between her legs. "Do we have to eat right now?"

"You're turning into a regular sex fiend, Senator," she said, relieved by the return of his playful mood.

"It's your influence." He zeroed in on her neck.

She tilted her head to give him better access. "I need to go back to work after dinner."

"Always with the work," he said, exasperated. "I'm proposing a bill requiring one night a week with no work, no commitments, no obligations, just you and me. We'll call it the Cappuano-Holland To Hell With Work Law." He kissed her. "All those in favor?"

"Mmm," she said against his lips. "Me. Definitely in favor. Holland-Cappuano has a better ring, though."

He smiled. "Passed. Unanimously." Framing her face with his hands, he delved deeper, teasing with his tongue. "Speaking of rings, you know what sounds even better? Cappuano-Cappuano."

Taken aback, Sam stared at him.

"Someday?" he asked with a hopeful, sheepish grin that made her melt.

"Maybe," she stammered. "Someday. But I'm not changing my name."

"Mmm. Progress." His pleasure came through in a deep, passionate kiss.

Her cell phone interrupted them.

She pulled back from him to reach for it.

"We have a law!"

"Sorry," she said. "I really need to take this. Holland."

"Hey, it's Conklin."

Sam held her breath. "What's up?"

"I just now got out of the deliberations."

"Wow."

"Yeah, to call it heated would be an understatement. The suspension was reduced to two days unpaid, effective immediately. That was the best I could do."

She could live with that. Swallowing hard, she said, "And the other?"

"We're meeting again in the morning to discuss it."

Her heart sank. "What's the hang-up?"

"Andrews wanted to think on it overnight."

Sam kept an eye on Nick as he checked the pots on the stove. "That doesn't sound good."

"I'm sure it'll be fine. He's a reasonable guy. You're going to need to watch out for Stahl, though. He really has it in for you. The two-day suspension infuriated him."

"Well, thanks for letting me know."

"I'll call you as soon as I have more."

Sam ended the call and clutched the phone to her chest. Her heart raced with anxiety. And then Nick turned and smiled, chasing away her worries.

"Everything okay, babe?"

"Everything's just fine," she said, surprised to realize it was true. Everything was fine as long as she had him. He was indeed so totally worth it. She sent him a saucy grin. "You know that bill we passed before?"

He popped a bite of carrot from the salad into his mouth. "Yep."

"Can we make it effective as of tonight?"

"Absolutely."

She held out her arms to him. "To hell with work."

Sam woke up the next morning to the feel of Nick's lips laying a path up her back. Keeping her eyes closed, she wallowed in the sensation until she remembered the suspension.

"Why'd you just get all tense on me?"

"No reason," she said, not ready to leave the bubble they'd been in since the night before.

"You need to get going. You're going to be late."

"I'm working from home today."

"How come?"

She bit back the guilt. "I want to dig into that lead you gave me yesterday, and I need to get to some other research that's easier to do at my dad's than at HQ. Plus I want to bounce a few things off him."

"Sounds like a good plan." He kissed her and got up. "Graham told me yesterday that Julian's funeral is Saturday in Cambridge. He's chartering a plane to take the family. He asked if we'd like to join them. I told him I'd check with you."

"That'd be good. If we haven't closed the case by then, I'll need to go to the funeral anyway."

"And if you have?"

"Then I'll go to be there for you." She studied his fine naked form. "I wish you didn't have to go to work."

He emerged from the closet with a suit and dress shirt. "Why?" he asked with a salacious grin. "What would you do with me if you had me to yourself all day?"

"It sure would be nice to find out. We haven't had a whole day off since we've been together."

Leaning over to kiss her once more, he said, "We'll have to fix that. Soon. But today, I have two hundred Girl Scouts coming from Norfolk to tour the Capitol and have lunch with me."

"I'm jealous," she said with a pout.

"Don't be. You're the only girl I love." He left her with a smile and went to take a shower.

Only Nick could've made her forget, even for a few minutes, that she'd been suspended from her job and faced a possible reduction in rank. Even one level would be a bitter pill to swallow. But two. *Ugh, I can't even think about it.* She reached for her cell phone to call Gonzo. "Hey," she said when he answered. "How are you?"

"Better question is how are *you?* I heard about the suspension."

"Could've been worse. Between us, I'm working from my dad's today. Can you put out the word that I'm looking for help with Sinclair?"

"Sure, no problem. The press is clamoring for info on the investigation. Rumor has it the chief is on the warpath. Wants an arrest and wants it now."

"Well, let's get him one. Do me a favor—do a run on a Tony Sanducci. He's a big-time abortion protestor. Meet me at my dad's around ten?"

"You got it. I'll round up the cavalry."

"Keep it on the down low." They both knew she'd be royally screwed if she got caught conducting department business while on suspension.

"Will do."

An hour later, Nick was signing a stack of letters to constituents when Christina came in bearing coffee. He noticed she looked tired. "Late night?"

"Sort of. Tommy was in rare form last night."

"Please," Nick said. "Spare me the details."

"How's Sam?"

"Fine," he said, pleased that she'd asked. That, too, was progress. "She's seen a lot over the years, so she bounces back from something traumatic like what happened yesterday a lot faster than most people would."

"She must be pissed, though. Tommy was enraged over it."

Not sure what Christina was getting at, he said, "I think she was more disappointed that she wasn't able to talk Reese out of the gun in time. Apparently, she almost had him when SWAT showed up."

Christina looked at him like he was speaking Greek. "I mean over the suspension. Tommy said it was totally bogus. You helped them close the O'Connor case and now to have Internal Affairs investigating your relationship! Let's just hope the media doesn't catch wind of it."

Nick felt like she had punched him. "Yeah," he said. "Let's hope not." He stood up and reached for his new overcoat. "What time do the Girl Scouts get here?"

"At noon. Why?"

"I'll be back before then."

"Where're you going?" she asked, baffled.

"I'll be back."

"Tony Sanducci," Gonzo said, "age thirty-nine, native of Cleveland, Ohio. He's been actively protesting abortion for the last decade. Suspected in several violent altercations at abortion clinics, but none of the charges stuck. His rich parents apparently hire a team of high-priced lawyers who always get him off.

"Married, four children, lives outside Cleveland but opened a storefront in the District, on New York Avenue, three weeks ago and has been operating out of there since then. Has a legion of loyal followers who read his daily blog by the thousands and take their orders directly from him. Works outside the boundaries of the mainstream movement, which says it disapproves of his tactics but doesn't do anything to stop him."

"Passive approval," Sam said.

"Exactly," Gonzo said. "His editorial in the *Washington Post* was a thinly veiled hate rant. It was clear that he'd do anything to keep Sinclair off the court."

"We need to talk to him," Sam said. "Let's figure out who

his most faithful followers are, too. Those who inspire legions of zealots have people in their ranks who'd do anything for the leader. He may not have put out the word he wanted Sinclair killed, but reading that editorial, it'd be hard not to get that message."

"I can't believe the *Post* even printed it," Jeannie said.

"Freedom of speech," Skip said.

"I'd also like to know why the Secret Service offered protection," Sam said. "Did they know of specific threats?"

"When you have a million people descending on the city to protest a specific nominee, that warrants protection," Skip said.

"You gotta wonder if Sinclair had all the info about the threats when he turned down protection," Gonzo said. He held up a printout of the *Post* article. "Did he see this?"

"Good question," Sam concurred.

A knock on the front door interrupted them. She got up to get it and found Cruz on the porch.

"Hey," he said. "I hear we're working from the home office today."

"What're you doing here?" He was pale and drawn, and his arm was in a sling. "You're still on medical leave."

"Nothing wrong with my brain."

"Come in," Sam said.

He turned and waved to the driver of a car idling in the street.

Sam looked closer and saw that Elin had driven him. "Still seeing the phone-shutter-offer, huh?"

"I told you it's not going to happen again," he said through gritted teeth. "Can we drop it?"

"Eventually," she said with a grin, delighted to see him back on his feet.

"You okay after everything with Reese?" he asked.

"You know how it goes. Shit happens. He didn't shoot my dad."

"I heard that, too. We'll dig into the prior tenants the minute we close Sinclair."

She nodded, grateful for his unwavering support. "Let's get you up to speed."

The others greeted Cruz warmly and updated him on the case.

"Moving on to Diandra," Sam said. "What'd you find out, Jeannie?"

"She's fifty-six, grew up in Missouri. The dad was a fundamentalist Christian minister, the mother a homemaker. Diandra went to Princeton, studied English literature. Met Preston there thirty years ago. Two sons, Devon and Austin. Began spewing her special brand of hatred as a newspaper columnist seventeen years ago. Moved to TV thirteen years ago."

"Right around the same time as the rift formed with her husband's homosexual brother," Sam said. "Interesting timing."

Jeannie nodded. "I thought the same thing."

"I'd like to get her downtown for a more in-depth interview," Sam said. "I keep going back to the irrational hatred she had for Julian over his sexual orientation. It just seems so over the top to me."

"Conservative Christians are very clear on homosexuality," Jeannie said. "And growing up as she did with a minister father, this stuff was probably pounded into her head all her life. I looked into her father's background. He wrote a book twenty years ago about how homosexuality was going to unravel the fabric of our country. It made quite a stir at the time. Apparently, her book is an update of his."

"So she comes by her hatred naturally," Sam said, feeling the buzz that came from uncovering a juicy lead. "We definitely need to have another conversation with her." She growled with frustration. "Freaking suspension! I want to go at her myself."

"We can handle it," Gonzo said, looking to Jeannie, who nodded in agreement. "We can also talk to Sanducci."

"I can research his closest aides," Cruz said.

"With only one good arm?" Sam asked.

"Don't worry about it."

The front door swung open. Sam looked up and was startled to see Nick. "What're you doing here?"

"May I have a word with you?" He gestured to the porch.

She looked closer, and this time she saw anger. *Uh oh. What now?* "Sure." She got up and reached for her coat. To the others she said, "I'll be back in a minute."

Outside, Nick vibrated with tension as he paced the length of the porch.

Her stomach took a nasty nosedive. "What's up?"

He turned to her, hands on his hips, clearly furious. "Were you going to tell me?"

"Tell you what?" she asked, even though she suspected. How had he heard?

Running a hand through his hair in frustration, he said, "I thought we were past this shit, Sam! I thought we were past the point where we kept stuff from each other."

"I was going to tell you—"

"When?" The single word reverberated through the quiet morning. *"When were you going to tell me?"*

"You've been so upset," she stammered. "About John and Julian, what happened to Cruz, and then the thing with Reese. There just wasn't a good time."

"That's bullshit and you know it. We were together all last night, after you'd been *suspended* for hooking up with me, and *you didn't think I needed to know that?"*

"Can you keep it down?" she whispered. "The people in there work for me."

"I don't care who's listening! How do you think it made me feel to have my chief of staff tell me that my girlfriend, or whatever you are, was *suspended* from her job because of me? How do you think that felt, Samantha?"

"I'm sorry." She silently cursed Gonzo and Christina and Stahl. Goddamned Stahl. This was all his fault. "I just wanted to make it go away without letting it touch us. I was trying to avoid this very scene."

"If you'd have told me about it when it first happened, there might not have been a scene." He took a deep rattling breath, clearly trying to control the impulse to beat the crap out of something—most likely her. "I want to know how this happened. I want every detail, and I want it right now."

So she told him—about receiving the summons from Stahl to the hearing the day before to the phone call from Conklin. She left nothing out.

"This happened on your *first day* as lieutenant? That was before Julian was killed."

"You were still dealing with losing John and your own new job. I was thinking of you, Nick. I didn't set out to deceive you. I was trying to protect you." She took a deep breath to contend with the pain in her gut. "Remember when we talked about you becoming a senator, when I said I was worried about my shit landing all over you and making you look bad just as you got this great opportunity? This is exactly what I was talking about. I was thinking of you."

At that, some of his steam seemed to dissipate. "I don't expect you to protect me. I never asked you to do that."

"Can't help it," she said with a shrug. "I love you. I don't want to be responsible for causing you problems at work or anywhere else."

"And I'm not supposed to feel the same way? You're in trouble at work because of *me*. That kills me, Sam."

She reached for him, brought him close to her and rested her head on his chest. "I'll tell you the same thing I told my dad last night." Glancing up at his handsome, earnest face, her heart ached with love. "You're worth it. No matter what happens, you're so, so, *so* worth it."

Even though he seemed moved by her words, he shook his head. "We should've waited until the case was closed. You knew this could happen. You tried to tell me, but I wanted you so much. I didn't listen to you—"

"Don't." She rested her fingers on his lips. "I wouldn't change one thing about the way we fell in love. It's the best thing that's ever happened to me. *You* are the best thing. How could I regret that?"

"But if you lose your rank. I can't believe they're even considering that."

"It might be for the best."

He stared at her, incredulous. "How in the world can you say that?"

"Less responsibility, fewer hours, fewer demands." She made a huge effort to keep her tone light. "More time for you. Might be just what we need."

"No, it isn't. It can't happen. I'd never forgive myself if I caused that to happen to you."

"Let's not worry about it until it happens. Captain Andrews is known for being logical. He'll do the right thing."

"What if he doesn't?"

"We'll cross that bridge when we come to it." She forced a teasing grin. "You've got Girl Scouts coming to visit. You can't keep them waiting."

"Will you call me? The minute you hear anything?"

"I will."

"And no more keeping stuff from me?"

"No more keeping stuff from you. I promise."

CHAPTER 24

The conversation with Nick stayed with Sam long after he went back to work. She was still getting used to the rules of a real relationship. When she was married to Peter, she'd made an art form out of keeping things from him. His propensity to overreact and overanalyze every little thing made him the last person she wanted to share anything with. Nick was nothing like Peter, but old habits were hard to break.

Chewing on her pen as she stared at the computer screen, Sam thought about Nick leaving the Capitol to come have it out with her when he no doubt had a million other things to do. That was another way he wasn't like Peter, who had loved to give her the silent treatment—sometimes for weeks on end—rather than taking the initiative to talk about whatever was on his mind.

The two men were so diametrically different it was pointless to compare them. Then why, she wondered, was she holding out on moving in with Nick? If she already knew he was nothing like Peter, and since he had proven as much—many times over—what was the hang-up? "Hmm," she said. "Definitely something to think about."

"Talking to yourself, boss?" Freddie asked, returning from the coffee shop on the corner with a tray containing two tall cups.

Sam stood up and reached for the tray. "I'm going to send you home if you keep pushing it."

"I went to get coffee." He flashed the smile that made even the strongest of women go weak in the knees. "Relax, will ya?"

Sam took a sip of her coffee and was surprised by an unexpected surge of emotion. "You scared me," she said, her voice hoarse as she glanced over at him.

"I'm sorry."

"If you ever do anything that stupid again, I'll kill you with my own hands, do you hear me?"

"If I ever do anything that stupid again, I'll deserve it."

"At least you know you're stupid," she muttered. "That's something."

"Hey!"

"And what's the cell phone rule?"

"Believe me, I'm never going to forget that, either."

"Humor me."

"Shut the freaking phone off before you sneak up on a perp."

"Here I was thinking you were coming along so nicely, and then you go and screw up so monumentally. And to go in without backup! Don't even get me started on that!"

"Okay, I won't."

"I appreciate what you were trying to do and why you were trying to do it, but don't risk yourself like that again. You're no good to me dead."

"Gee, I'm really feeling the love, Lieutenant."

"Good." She met his chocolate-brown eyes with an intense

stare. It was as close as she would ever come to telling him how she felt about him.

Freddie cleared the emotion from his throat. "So what happened with Nick before? I've never seen him so pissed."

"He heard about the IAB hearing—through the grapevine."

"Ouch," Freddie said with a wince. "I hate to say I told you so, but, I told you so."

"Shut up."

"You should've told him the day Stahl gave you the summons."

"While I appreciate your sage relationship advice, I'd much rather talk about you and your fuck buddy."

His face turned bright red.

"Ahh, *now* we're getting somewhere."

"That's not what she is," he stammered.

Sam raised a skeptical eyebrow. "Oh, no?"

He shook his head. "I like her."

"You like *banging* her."

"Do you have to be so crude?" he huffed.

Sam pretended to give that some serious thought. "Um, yeah. I do."

"Can you try to be serious for just a minute?"

She could see there was something he wanted to say so she did her best to wipe the smug grin off her face.

"I wasn't expecting to like her so much," he said haltingly. "It wasn't supposed to be about that."

"Oh, for Christ's sake, Cruz, you can't fall for the first chick you ever bang—"

His face lit up once again. "I've asked you not to use the Lord's name in vain, and she's not the first."

Sam shot him a look intended to remind him of who he was dealing with. "Whatever you say, stud. I just hope you're being careful. Women like her aren't looking for forever."

"Neither am I."

"If you say so."

"Why do you have to be so cynical? Isn't it possible that maybe she's the one for me?"

"No, it's not possible. Life doesn't work that way. You can have some fun with her but be prepared for her to get bored and move on. That's how it goes."

"Are you prepared for Nick to get bored and move on?"

The barb shot straight to her heart. "That's different. We're older and ready for a serious relationship." God, at least she hoped so. "You need to test the waters a little more before you start thinking permanent."

"I tested the waters and ended up getting shot."

Snickering, Sam said, "That could really only happen to you."

"Glad to amuse you."

"Oh, you do. That you do." She laughed at the tortured expression on his face. "Thanks for the laugh, Cruz. I really needed that."

His scowl answered for him.

"Now let's figure out who Sanducci's disciples are."

Gonzo parallel parked on New York Avenue, in one of the rougher neighborhoods along a main artery into and out of the city. Since McBride had been working the case, Sam had asked him to partner up with Jeannie for the duration of the Sinclair investigation. He studied the storefront and then looked over at her. "Nice digs."

"I guess his parents are only willing to pony up for bail and lawyers, not real estate." Jeannie reached for the car door handle. "What time did you ask Diandra to meet us at HQ?"

"In an hour, so let's see what Sanducci has to say and get out of there."

"I'm with ya."

The office had the temporary feel of a campaign headquarters, but with the unpleasant decor of posters featuring aborted fetuses. Packing boxes were scattered about, the floor littered with Styrofoam noodles.

Gonzo turned away from the images when his stomach turned with disgust.

A blonde woman who seemed barely old enough to be out of high school greeted them. "May I help you?"

They flashed their badges. "Tony Sanducci, please."

"Um, sure. Just a minute." She returned five minutes later with an aging preppy who seemed better suited to the Yale campus than this squalid storefront. He flashed the matinee idol grin that guys like him used to skirt the rules. Gonzo hated him on sight. "Tony Sanducci?"

"That's right." He extended a hand.

Gonzo flashed his badge. "Detectives Gonzales and Mc-Bride."

Sanducci's hand fell to his side. "What can I do for you?"

"Going somewhere?" Gonzo asked, gesturing to the boxes.

"We don't have much of a cause here anymore. We're just waiting to see who Nelson comes up with next."

"Must've broken your heart to hear that Sinclair had been killed."

"I didn't want him to be on the Supreme Court, Detective, but that doesn't mean I wanted him dead."

"Didn't you?"

The amiable smile faded. "I'm afraid I don't understand."

Gonzo read him some of the more inflammatory passages from the *Post* article.

"So?"

"Where were you the night Sinclair was killed?"

Taken aback, Sanducci said, "I was here all night. I have

a cot in the back where I stay when I'm in the city. Helps to keep the expenses down."

"By yourself?"

Sanducci cast a quick glance at the teenybopper who ran the office. It was fleeting, but Gonzo saw it.

"That's right."

"Would you like to continue this conversation downtown, Mr. Sanducci?"

He ran his hand through well-coifed dark hair. "Listen," he said in a low voice. "I have a wife, four children. It's a fling. Means nothing."

Gonzo wondered if it meant nothing to the child he was sleeping with. "What's her name?"

"Does she really have to be brought into this?"

"Yeah, she really does."

With a deep sigh, he said, "Cindy, can you come over here for a minute, please?"

As if God himself had summoned her, Cindy came scurrying across the big open room.

Gonzo wanted to barf at the worshipful gaze she directed at Sanducci.

"Yes, Tony?"

"Honey, would you mind telling these fine police officers where you were the night Julian Sinclair was killed?"

Her eyes bugged, and for a moment she seemed too stunned to speak.

"It's okay," he said. "Go ahead."

"We were… I was…here."

"You were together all night?"

Humiliation radiated from her. "Yes."

"And your full name?" Gonzo asked.

"Cynthia Kaine." She spelled her last name.

Glancing at Sanducci, Gonzo said, "And how old are you, Cindy?"

"Eighteen."

"And how old are you, Mr. Sanducci?"

"How is that relevant?"

"Answer the question."

"Forty-four."

Gonzo made sure the disgust showed on his face. "I see."

Jeannie had Cindy write down her address and phone number before dismissing her.

Sanducci gave Gonzo a "guys will be guys" smile that Gonzo wanted to punch off his smug face. "We can keep this between us, right?"

"I'll need a list of your employees, members, followers, whatever you call them."

"That list is private," Sanducci sputtered.

"Then we'll get a subpoena. Until it comes through, we'll put you up downtown. Your choice."

Sanducci fumed for a long moment. "Cindy," he said through gritted teeth. "Print out the A list."

She stared at him.

"While you're at it," Gonzo said, "print out the B, C and D lists, too."

Sanducci's lips turned white and his cheeks flamed with color. "Do it."

Cindy got busy at her workstation.

"Must've been a letdown," Gonzo said, nodding to the posters and pickets lining the wall, "to make all these plans and then have nothing to protest."

Sanducci shrugged. "There're others on Nelson's short list who we don't want on the court any more than we wanted Sinclair. That's why we're still here."

"Will you have them killed, too?"

"I don't know what you're talking about!"

"Don't you?"

"I didn't kill anyone!"

"Maybe you suggested to one of your followers that it would be better if Sinclair was dead?"

"I told you," Sanducci said, his preppy veneer crumbling. "We didn't want him on the court. That was it."

Gonzo took the lists Cindy handed to him. "Stay local," he said to Sanducci on his way out the door.

On the sidewalk, Jeannie took a deep breath of fresh air. "I need a shower," she said, shuddering.

"Me, too."

"But he didn't kill Sinclair."

"No, but maybe someone on these lists did." He checked his watch. "We have just enough time to drop them off to the lieutenant and Cruz before our meeting with Diandra Sinclair."

"You read my mind, Detective."

"This is such bullshit," Sam said as she paced the length of her father's living room, gripping the lists Gonzo had brought her. "I'm stuck here when we're finally getting somewhere on Sinclair."

"Want me to make a phone call?" Skip asked.

"No," she said with an emphatic glare. "Don't even think about it. That won't help."

"You could make the call," Gonzo suggested. "Farnsworth is the only one who can override IAB. Tell him you'll serve out the suspension when we close Sinclair."

"Stahl would accuse me of using my connections."

"So what?" Freddie said. "If it'll get you back on the streets when we need you, why not do it?"

"Perhaps," Jeannie said with a mischievous grin, "you could

lead Farnsworth to believe that it was *his* idea to defer the suspension."

"Oh." Sam snapped her fingers. "I like how you think." She reached for her cell phone to call the chief and put the phone on speaker so the others could hear.

"Lieutenant," Chief Farnsworth said when his assistant put Sam right through. "I believe you're on vacation today."

"Is that what we're calling it?"

"What can I do for you?"

"You can get me back on the streets. Sinclair is hot right now. It's not doing the department any good to have me stuck at home."

"While I agree with you, IAB—"

"Screw IAB! I'm in the middle of a case! I'll serve out the suspension after we close Sinclair. Hell, I'll give you four days unpaid at the end. We've got all kinds of leads I could be following, suspects to interview."

"You have plenty of qualified people working for you, Lieutenant. Delegate."

"They need me, Chief. Let me finish this case, and then I'll serve my sentence in silence. You won't hear a word from me."

"That'll be the day," he muttered. After a long moment of silence during which Sam's stomach pinged with pain, he said, "You'll have trouble with Stahl."

"I already have trouble with Stahl, but if you were to say *you* called *me* and ordered me back to work to close Sinclair, well then, there's not much he can say."

"You think you're very clever, don't you?"

"Actually, in this instance, Detective McBride is the clever one."

"Whose idea was it to allow women on the force?"

She smiled. "Is that a yes?"

"I'm ordering you back to work until Sinclair is closed, at

which time you'll serve a *three*-day suspension. The extra day is for manipulating your favorite Uncle Joe."

Sam smiled. "You're the best." She swallowed hard before she added, "Any word from the deliberations this morning?"

"Not yet. I'm sure you'll hear from Conklin the minute he has any news."

What was taking so long? "Yeah."

"Get me an arrest, Lieutenant. The press is on me like white on rice."

"I'm all over it." She ended the call and turned to the others. "Let's go."

CHAPTER 25

"You're invited to Governor Zorn's sixtieth birthday," Christina said to Nick. "They'd also like you to say a few words."

"I promised the governor's wife I'd do that. Tell them yes."

"Just you?"

Nick thought of Sam and the possible outcome of the IAB proceedings. If he didn't hear something soon, he might just lose his mind. "I don't know if Sam can make it or not. Depends on her schedule."

"So what do I tell them?"

"I guess the standard answer going forward will be one for sure, two maybe."

"Allrighty," Christina said, even though her disapproval was apparent. "President Nelson sent you an invite to the state dinner with the Canadian prime minister. You can't be vague on that one. Either she's going or she isn't."

Nick tried to imagine Sam at a White House function. The idea of it made him smile. "I'll see if I can talk her into it."

"We have to let them know by next week. The next thing is this slew of interview requests we've received. Trevor and I agree that you probably need to pick one and do it. You can't just ignore them all." She handed him the list. "But there's one thing."

"What's that?"

"They want both of you."

"Both of who?"

"You and Sam."

"Are you serious?"

Christina nodded. "I know you're painfully aware that the media is enthralled by the two of you. They're clamoring for the first joint interview."

"She'd never do it in a million years."

"Even if you asked her to?"

"She's up to her eyeballs in the Sinclair case." *Not to mention the IAB situation,* he thought to himself. "I can't imagine asking her to sit down for an interview."

"Maybe if you do it," Christina said, "they'll move on to something else and leave the two of you alone."

"You really think so?" Nick asked, skeptical.

"Not really, but it's worth a shot."

"I'll think about it," Nick said, trying to imagine broaching the subject with Sam.

One of the receptionists came to the door. "Senator, Judson Knott is here. He wonders if he might have a few minutes."

Nick glanced at Christina who shrugged. "Not on the schedule."

"Sure," he said. "Show him in."

The chairman of the Virginia Democratic Party stepped into the office, full of apologies for showing up without an appointment.

"It's no problem, Judson," Nick said. "My door's always open for you." To Christina, Nick added, "Would you mind giving us a minute?"

When they were alone, Nick asked if he could get Judson some coffee.

"No, thank you, Senator. I'm fine. I've just come from breakfast with Richard and the rest of the party leadership. I wonder if your ears were ringing."

"Sir?"

Judson flashed a big smile. "You were the hot topic of conversation. The way you've come in and hit the ground running, getting O'Connor-Martin passed. Your approval ratings are higher than anything we've ever seen. You don't see numbers like yours. Ever."

"I'm sure it's just the sentimental bump from Senator O'Connor's loyal base."

"It's much more than that, Senator. You've struck a chord with people in the Old Dominion, and your romance with the pretty police officer hasn't hurt anything."

Nick scowled. He'd never understand why people were so interested in them.

"That leads me to the reason I'm here." Judson shifted in his seat, seeming uncomfortable all of a sudden. "I know we said we needed you for a year and that we'd run Cooper in the election."

"I hope his wife is doing better," Nick said.

"We heard just yesterday that her cancer is in remission."

"Well, that's a great relief."

"Indeed. However, the party is no longer interested in him as our candidate for your seat."

"Why not?"

Judson gave him a "come on, Senator, you're a smart guy" look.

"Wait a minute. You said one year and out. We had a deal."

"Why in the world would we go looking for another candidate when we have the perfect guy already in office? You're our man, Senator. You're the one the party wants. The *only* one."

All Nick could think of in that moment was the far more important deal he had made with Sam when he accepted the position in the first place—one year in the Senate. "I, ah, I don't know what to say."

"Say yes. You're a natural and the very best thing that's happened to our state in years. We're invested in you for the long haul."

"I appreciate that, Judson. I really do. But I need to give this some thought."

"We'll need a decision in the next week or two. Campaign season is right around the corner."

The idea was so overwhelming that Nick couldn't begin to process it. A lengthy campaign, the prospect of a six-year term that he won on his own merits. "Have you talked to Graham about this?"

Judson shook his head. "He wasn't at the meeting today. He's taking Sinclair's death real hard. Such a tragedy, and right on top of losing his son. Well, I guess I don't need to tell you."

"No, sir."

"I have no doubt, however, that Graham will fully support your candidacy. You know he's your staunchest supporter." Judson got up. "You'll think about it?"

Nodding, Nick stood and offered his hand. "I'll be in touch."

"Mrs. Sinclair, how long have you harbored a hatred for homosexuals?"

Diandra blanched at Sam's question. "I don't *hate* anyone, Lieutenant."

"All right then, how about you tell me your views on homosexuality."

"I find it to be an abhorrent lifestyle. However, I have no ill will for people who choose this way of life."

"What about it do you find so abhorrent?"

"Leviticus 20:13, states, 'If a man lies with a male, as with a woman, both of them have committed an abomination: they shall surely be put to death; their blood shall be upon them.' I tend to agree with him, and I was under the impression that as an American, I'm free to pursue my own beliefs."

"He was a hell of a guy that Leviticus, wasn't he Detective Cruz?" Sam said.

"In our time, he'd be considered a bigot," Freddie said with a pointed look at Diandra.

"I'm not a bigot, Detective. My beliefs are grounded in scripture."

"Your friend Leviticus also recommends stoning for married couples who engage in intercourse during the woman's period," Freddie said. "I sure hope you've never done *that*."

"It's not the same thing," Diandra snapped. "A woman's period is a *natural* event."

"How do you reconcile the unnatural 'abomination' with the commandment to love thy neighbor?" Freddie asked. "And Jesus himself said, 'If the world hates you, keep in mind that it hated me first.'"

Diandra glared at him.

Fascinated by the debate, Sam was reluctant to interrupt but needed to get back to the investigation. "Do either you or your husband own a gun?"

Diandra was clearly caught off guard by the change in direction. "We have a gun we keep locked in the house for protection. I've attracted my share of detractors."

"You say that you have no hatred for homosexuals, but would you say you hated your brother-in-law Julian?"

Diandra's posture lost some of its rigidity. "I was once very close to Julian. We lived for many years in Boston while Preston completed graduate studies at Harvard. We spent a lot of time with Julian."

"Yet you never had any idea that Julian was gay?"

She shook her head. "It came as a total shock to me. Like I said the other day, we'd allowed our young, impressionable sons to spend time in his home, to sleep there." She shuddered. "God only knows what they were subjected to."

"Did you suspect that he abused them?"

Diandra's eyes flashed with anger. "Of course not! He would never harm them. He loved those boys. I never doubted that."

"Did Duncan spend the night with Julian when the boys were there?"

"Not that I was ever aware of."

"So your brother-in-law, who was clearly devoted to your sons and who seemed to go to some lengths to keep his orientation hidden from them, was none-the-less banished from their lives?"

"You don't understand, Lieutenant."

"Then make me."

Diandra folded her hands on the table and focused on them. "Times were different then. People were less accepting of alternative lifestyles. Preston and I were building our careers, pursuing our goals—"

"And there was no room for his gay brother in the midst of all that ambition?"

"We didn't want our sons to be influenced."

"You're aware that you can't 'catch' homosexuality, aren't you?"

"That's a matter of opinion."

"Actually," Freddie said, "there's quite a lot of science to support that sexual orientation is something we're born with."

"I don't believe that."

"Mrs. Sinclair, if one of your sons happened to be gay—"

"Don't be outrageous, Lieutenant! My sons are normal, well-adjusted young men."

Oh, how Sam wished she could pop this woman's sanctimonious bubble. But since she had promised discretion to Devon, she bit her tongue. "Let's just speculate for the sake of argument that one of them is gay, would you exile him from your family and your life?"

"There's no point in speculating on something that could never happen."

"Humor me."

"I love my sons," Diandra said, her hand trembling ever so slightly.

"Unconditionally?"

"Yes," she stammered. "Of course."

"So if Devon or Austin came home one day and said, 'I love you, Mom, but I'm gay,' you'd be okay with that?"

"I'd be very disappointed—and shocked after the number of girlfriends my boys have had."

Devon has done a hell of a job hiding who he is, Sam thought. "What would it have meant to your book deal if Julian's orientation became public during the nomination hearings?"

Flustered, Diandra said, "It would've had no bearing."

"Embarrassing?"

"Somewhat. Who wants their family members' sexual predilections discussed publicly?"

"Were you under any pressure to avoid scandal in these final weeks before your book is published?"

"Do I need a lawyer, Lieutenant?"

"As I advised you at the outset, you can request an attorney at any time. However, you're not currently under arrest. We've asked you to cooperate with our investigation."

Diandra took a long sip from the glass of water Sam had

provided at the beginning of their interview. "It's understood that I am to stay above any scandal."

A knock on the door interrupted them.

Sam nodded at Freddie to get it.

He came back in a minute later and gestured for her to join him and Captain Malone in the hallway. "A pizza delivery guy just found Devon Sinclair and his roommate shot in their home."

"Oh, shit." Sam glanced over her shoulder at Diandra in the interrogation room. "DOA?"

"Both were shot," Malone said. "One was DOA. We don't know yet which one."

"At least we can confirm she didn't do this one," Sam said.

"Right," Freddie said. "That was my first thought, too."

Steeling herself, she returned to the interrogation room. "Mrs. Sinclair, I'm sorry to have to tell you this, but there's been a shooting at your son Devon's home."

Gasping, Diandra stood up. "Dev."

"We only know there were two victims, one of them a fatality," Sam said.

Diandra sagged into the chair. "Oh, God, please. Not my Devon. Not my baby."

"If you'll wait here, I'll see if I can find out more."

Diandra nodded.

With Freddie following her, Sam emerged from the interrogation room and ran smack into Lieutenant Stahl.

"Lieutenant," Stahl said, his fat face shifting to a sneer at the sight of her.

Since he used her rank, Sam assumed she still had it.

"You've been suspended," Stahl said. "You have no business here."

"The chief called me back to close Sinclair," Sam said with a satisfied smirk.

Stahl's cheeks turned an unhealthy shade of purple. "You may think you've won this round, Holland, but you mark my words—I'll get rid of you if it's the last thing I ever do."

"Detective Cruz, did you hear Lieutenant Stahl threaten me?" Sam asked, her eyes fixed on Stahl.

"Yes, ma'am. I sure did."

"So if anything suspicious ever happens to me, you'll know just where to begin your investigation, right?"

"Yes, ma'am."

"This is not over," Stahl said, his spit hitting Sam's face.

She wiped it away. "Do you mind getting out of my way? I'm working a homicide here." Shoving past him, she signaled for Freddie to come with her.

"You might want to consider your allegiances, Detective," Stahl said to their backs. "I'd hate to see such a promising young career derailed."

Freddie spun around. "My allegiances, Lieutenant, are with my partner, the best cop on this force, so don't bother wasting your bad breath on me."

Stahl's eyes almost popped out of his fat head.

Sam took hold of Freddie's good arm and half led, half dragged him back to the detectives' pit. "You shouldn't have done that. He was baiting you."

"I knew that."

"It's bad enough he has it in for me. I don't want you sucked into it, too."

"Too late."

Captain Malone joined them. "You've heard the news? No reduction in rank?"

"Not officially until right now," Sam said, the relief almost as overwhelming as the worry.

"Apparently, Stahl about had an apoplexy when Andrews

sided with Conklin," Malone said. "You've got a very significant enemy there, Lieutenant."

"I'm not worried about him." Sam grabbed her radio off
her desk. "I've got another shooting in the Sinclair case to
contend with."

"Word is the roommate, Tucker Farrell, was DOA on the
scene," Malone said. "Devon Sinclair is being taken to GW
Trauma."

Sam watched Freddie struggle into a coat. "Cruz, you're
done for today. Arrange transport to GW for Mrs. Sinclair,
and then call your ride to pick you up."

"But I'm fine!" he sputtered. "I'm good for a couple more
hours."

"Call your ride," Sam said. "You did enough for the first
day back."

"Oh, *come on,* Lieutenant!"

"Detective," Malone said in his quiet but effective way. "I
believe your lieutenant has given you an order."

"Yes, sir," he mumbled, stalking off to his cubicle.

"Thanks for the assist," Sam said to Malone. Viewing the
empty pit, she looked up at him. "I could use a partner. You
game?"

His eyes lit up. "On a real case? Me?"

"If you can stand leaving your desk for an hour or two."

"I'm in. Meet you outside in ten."

"Make it five. Crime scene is waiting on us." On the way
to the parking lot, Sam called Nick. "Hey," she said when he
answered, "no reduction in rank."

"Oh, good," he said, releasing a long deep breath. "That's
good."

He sounded so relieved that she laughed. "Yes, it is."

"I don't know if I could've lived with being responsible for
you getting busted down to detective."

"We would've coped."

"I'm glad we don't have to."

"So am I. What're you doing?"

"Reading committee reports. That seems to be all I've done since I took office."

"Ah, the exciting life of a U.S. senator."

"Nonstop glamour. What's up over there?"

"I'm on my way to investigate a shooting at Julian's nephew's house."

"Oh, no. Which one?"

"Devon."

"Jesus. Is he dead?"

"No, but his roommate is. Devon's on the way to GW."

"I hope he's okay. Julian adored him. He was so thrilled when Dev decided to go to law school."

"Did you know Devon?"

"I never met either of his nephews. Because of Julian's rift with their parents, he kept his relationship with them quiet."

"But you knew he saw them?"

"He talked about them all the time, so I just assumed he did. This is all so unbelievable."

"I'm sorry. I know you're still upset about losing him."

"And now this. Do you think the two shootings are related?"

"I'm working under the assumption that they are."

"Which eliminates a lot of other suspects."

"Not entirely. This could be intended to throw us off the trail."

"True. I guess this means you'll be working late again."

"Right you are. I'll see you when I see you."

He paused, as if there was something else he wanted to say.

"Everything all right?" she asked.

"Yeah. We can talk later."

"Or not," she said, her tone rife with suggestion.

He laughed. "Be careful out there, Lieutenant."

"I always am."

CHAPTER 26

Furious at being exiled, Freddie paced the sidewalk and waited for Elin to arrive. He hated being helpless and at the mercy of others. But since his car had a standard transmission, he couldn't drive until his shoulder healed. Right now, it hurt like a bastard, which meant he was due for another pain pill.

Elin pulled up in her sleek black Acura and leaned over to open the door for him.

"I can get it myself," he snapped.

"Yeah, nice to see you, too."

Freddie slammed the door and did his best to situate his injured arm. The pain left him feeling sweaty and sick.

"You look like shit."

"Thanks."

"The doctor told you to take it easy. It's too soon to be back at work."

"I've already got my mother and Sam bitching at me. I don't need it from you, too."

She abruptly pulled over. "Then why don't you get one of them to drive you home?"

Startled, he ventured a glance at her and was surprised to see that she was genuinely pissed.

"Yeah, I shut your phone off. Yeah, it's my fault you got shot. I get it. Now maybe you can get over it. If you can't, you'll have to find someone else to be your bitch. I've had enough."

"I don't blame getting shot on you," he said haltingly, stunned and unnerved by her outburst.

"Right."

"I *don't*."

"You could've fooled me. I put up with your crankiness when you were in the hospital and when you got home because I blamed myself. But I figure my debt is about paid up at this point."

Suddenly, Freddie didn't want to lose her. He wasn't ready for this—whatever it was—to be over. "You're right. I've been a shit to you, and I'm sorry." He brushed at imaginary lint on his jeans. "I wasn't prepared for this to be more than just…"

"Sex?"

Shrugging, he said, "I thought we'd have some fun, and then go our separate ways."

"No reason we can't."

"I don't want that," he said, reaching for her hand. "We haven't had nearly enough fun yet."

"So you want more sex, and then you'll cut me loose?"

"I don't know what you want me to say, Elin. I like you. I like being with you. That's the part I wasn't expecting."

She stared out the windshield. "I like being with you, too."

"You sound surprised."

"I was in it for the sex, too," she confessed.

"So you're using me," he joked. "I see how it is."

"You were using me, too!"

His eyes met hers. "All I know is that from the first time I met you during the O'Connor investigation, I wanted you. I thought about you, and I wanted you."

"I wanted you, too. Just as much."

"So what do we do now?"

"You're really done being a shit?"

Freddie winced. "I'm done."

She replied with a coy grin. "Then you wanna go home and have some fun?"

He hesitated.

"What?"

"The last time I had that kind of fun, it didn't work out so well."

"It worked out *great* until you got pissed and left."

"Yeah. I guess."

"So what's the problem?"

"I want to tell you, but you might think I'm weird or something."

"Don't worry. I already do."

"Very funny. I'm trying to be serious."

She made a poor attempt at a solemn face. "Please. Proceed."

"You met my mom." His heart raced with nerves and anxiety. When Elin nodded, he said, "It was just the two of us when I was growing up. Our church and our faith were important." He let his eyes wander over to her, petrified by what he'd find. "They still are."

"Okay. That's no big deal to me."

"When I was fifteen, I took a vow of celibacy."

"Oh."

"It was voluntary, and I stuck to it for a long time—a really long time. In fact, I only just recently—"

"Oh, my God! *You're not saying what I think you're saying!*"

He looked down at his good hand, which had rolled into a fist in his lap. "That's what I'm saying."

"Why didn't you tell me?"

"I *am* telling you."

"I mean before."

"What difference would it have made?"

"It just would've been nice to know." She studied him for a long time before her eyes widened. "You sought me out with that in mind, didn't you? You figured I'd be easy."

"No," he said quickly. "I figured you'd be fun. And you were. We had a lot of fun before we ever had sex."

"That's true."

"Are you mad?"

"I never would've guessed," she said with a shy smile.

"Really?"

"It was amazing."

"Yeah." He shifted to accommodate his instant erection. "It was."

"Why do you think I've put up with your crap the last couple of days?"

Clearing his throat, he said, "Because you want more?"

She bit her lip and nodded.

A hot ball of lust surged through Freddie and landed in his lap. "Your place or mine?"

Sam and Malone arrived at Devon's Dupont Circle townhouse at the same time as the medical examiner.

"We meet again," Dr. Lindsey McNamara said. "What've you got?"

Sam filled her in on what they knew. "I'm looking for a connection between Julian Sinclair's shooting and this one."

"If there's a connection," Lindsey said, "I'll find it."

"That's what I'm counting on."

Inside, the place smelled of pizza and death. Sam nodded to the officers who had arrived first on the scene.

"Called in by the pizza delivery guy, Mac Healy, age twenty-three." The patrolman gestured to the living room sofa where Healy sat with his head in his hands. "Shook up."

"We'll talk to him," Sam said.

"Tucker Farrell, age twenty-seven, shacked up with Sinclair, who owns the place," the patrolman continued. "Farrell's next of kin are his parents in Wilmington, Delaware." He handed her a slip of paper with their phone number.

"I'll call them," Sam said, her stomach knotting. She hated making those phone calls. "What about Sinclair?"

"Bullet wound to the back of the head. Paramedics left with him about ten minutes ago. He was found over there." He pointed to a puddle of blood just short of the doorway to the kitchen. "They said his condition is grave."

"The shooter took out Farrell first," Malone observed. "Sinclair was running away when he was hit."

"That's how I see it, too," Sam said. To the officer who'd briefed them, she added, "Thanks, Peterson. Good work." She crouched down to take a closer look at Farrell's chest wound. "Looks like a direct hit to the heart."

Lindsey nodded in agreement. "He bled out fast."

"Might've confronted the shooter," Malone said.

"It was close range," Lindsey concurred.

Sam stood up and went over to talk to the pizza guy. "Mr. Healy, I'm Detective Lieutenant Holland, my partner, Detective Captain Malone. Can you tell us what happened?"

Healy's eyes, flat with shock, were rimmed with red. "I already told them."

"Do me a favor, and run through it one more time," Sam said.

"I brought the pie they ordered." Healy gestured to the

red thermal bag sitting at his feet. "A large sausage and onion. Their usual."

"So they were frequent flyers?" Sam asked.

"Yeah, at least once, maybe twice a week. Anyway, I got here and the front door was wide-open, which was weird this time of year. I rang the bell a couple of times, but no one answered. I stuck my head in and saw a foot on the floor." He zeroed in on Tucker's body. "I started to run away, but then I thought he might need help so I came in. That's when I saw the other guy, on the floor over there." Shaking his head, he took a couple of deep breaths. "I kinda freaked and went outside to call 911."

"When you arrived, did you see anyone leaving or running on the street?"

"No. I didn't think anything was weird until I noticed the door open."

Sam took down his contact info and released him.

"What's next, Lieutenant?" Malone asked as they watched Lindsey follow Tucker's body out of the house.

"A bit rusty, are you, sir?" she said, smiling at his scowl. "Now we knock on doors to see if we can narrow down when the shots were fired and whether anyone saw someone fleeing the scene."

"What're you thinking?"

Sam studied the two bloody areas on the wood floor. "Not sure yet. We've got an uncle and nephew, both of them gay, one still in the closet, shot in the span of a few days. If I hadn't had Diandra in interrogation when this went down, I'd be getting a warrant for her arrest."

"Who else is there?"

"Preston and Austin Sinclair, father and brother of Devon, brother and nephew of Julian."

"Any chance this is unrelated to Julian?"

"Sure, there's a chance." She took a good look around the latest crime scene. "But this doesn't feel random. It doesn't feel random at all."

"Not to me, either."

"We'll have to dig into Farrell's life to rule out anything there, but until we can talk to Devon Sinclair, we knock on doors."

"I'm following you," Malone said.

"I just don't get it," Freddie said, his heart racing. "This has never happened. Ever." He looked down at his limp penis and willed it to life. Not that he'd had much experience, but getting an erection had never been a problem. In fact, having too many of them in his sexually frustrated state had been more of an issue. He had no idea what the hell was wrong with him.

"Don't worry about it." Elin kissed and caressed his chest. "We can do other stuff."

"It's probably the pain drugs." However, it occurred to him that he'd been hard as stone in the car just a short time ago. Now here he was, naked and in a bed with the equally naked Elin, the subject of his most lurid fantasies, and *nothing* was happening? *How could that be?*

"I'm sure that's all it is."

But in the back of his mind, Freddie suspected the guilt had gotten to him. It had eaten away at him until even his manhood was guilty.

Elin sat up, straddled him and ran her hands from his belly to his pecs. "Don't think. Just feel. Close your eyes."

He did what she said, trying to clear his mind of everything except for what was happening right in front of him—and on top of him. Imagining Elin's pierced nipples and the heart-shaped tattoo, Freddie felt a surge of desire.

"That's it," she whispered, her lips cruising from neck to chest to belly. "Just feel. No thinking."

"No thinking."

She massaged his thighs, first with her hands and then with her lips.

Freddie moaned.

Dragging her breasts over his penis, she continued to whisper soft words of encouragement.

He concentrated on putting aside the guilt and the conflict. Even the throbbing in his shoulder couldn't dampen the surge of lust. "Elin." With his good hand, he reached for a handful of soft breast and ran his thumb over her nipple.

She gasped. "Now we're getting somewhere," she said, stroking him until he was hard and throbbing.

"I'm glad it's not broken."

Laughing, she bent to take him into her mouth. "Definitely not broken."

His hips seemed to have a mind of their own. "Mmm." He sighed. "That's so good." The sweep of her tongue, the heat of her mouth, the tightness of her throat had him teetering on the brink in no time. She continued to stroke him until he was so hard he was afraid if he moved, even the slightest bit, he'd lose it. Then she squeezed his balls, just enough to make him surge off the bed. Wincing, he shifted to accommodate his injured shoulder.

"Sorry." She sat up. "We need to make you more comfortable for what I have in mind." Piling up pillows behind him, she arranged him the way she wanted him.

Freddie's heart slammed around in his chest, anxiety battling overwhelming curiosity.

She straddled him and took him into her moist heat.

They hadn't gotten to this position the other night, even though he'd wanted to try it. God, it was even better this way, if that was possible. As she rode him, she kept her gaze fixed on his face.

"Like it?" she asked.

"Oh, yeah." As he climbed toward what would no doubt be another explosive climax, it occurred to him that he could very easily become addicted to this—and to her.

CHAPTER 27

Sam and Malone worked the street for an hour but found no one who had seen or heard anything that could help them.

"I hate middle-of-the-day shit that happens when everyone is at work," she said, rubbing the back of her neck as she tried to regroup.

"Devon Sinclair and his roommate would've been at work, too, if his uncle hadn't been murdered," Malone observed.

"True. So who knew he'd be at home?"

"His family, friends, the pizza guy, coworkers, the roommate's coworkers. What'd he do?"

"He was a chef," she said, her stomach pinging when she remembered she still had to call Tucker's parents.

"Worth looking into."

"Let's see what ballistics gets us. I'd bet all the dough I have that it's going to be the same gun that did Julian, which rules out anything random." Sam's cell phone rang, but she didn't recognize the ring tone. "What the hell?" She glanced at the LCD. "Goddamn it."

"What now?" Malone asked, grinning at the expression on her face.

"I forgot about this freaking doctor's appointment. Nick programmed a reminder alarm into my cell. What a pain in the ass he is!"

"Sneaky bastard."

"I know!" Jamming the phone into her pocket, she took a long measuring look at the deserted neighborhood. "I'll have to reschedule. I need to get over to GW to check on Devon's condition. Hopefully, he'll wake up and tell us who the shooter is. That'd save a whole lot of time."

"I'll go to GW. You're going to the doctor. You can meet me there after."

She stared at him. "You can't make me go!"

He raised an eyebrow, daring her to defy him.

"You can't! It's my personal business."

Scratching at the gray stubble on his chin, he sized her up. "I could take you off Sinclair if I wanted to."

"You wouldn't do that."

"Bet?"

"I can't believe this! We've got two homicides going here, and you're gonna pull rank on me over a doctor's appointment?"

"Whatever is taking you to the doctor must be significant enough for Nick to program a reminder into your phone. So you're keeping the appointment, and you can rejoin the investigation when you're done." He checked his watch. "You'd better get going."

"I should've left you where you belong—on desk duty." With one last furious glance at his laughing face, she stormed off to her car, leaving him to find his own way to GW. "God-damned bossy men," she muttered. "Why can't they mind their own freaking business? It's my stomach. They don't need to be all up in my grill about it." Her cell phone rang again, and this time it was Nick. *"What?"*

"Hello to you, too, babe. Where are you?"

"In the car."

"On the way to?"

"I'm going! For Christ's sake, will you back off and leave me alone?" He laughed, and she saw red. "What the hell is so funny?"

"You are."

"I'm too busy for this shit. I've got two bodies to contend with and no time for doctors."

"You'd better keep that appointment, Samantha. I mean it. You've put this off long enough."

"Stop bugging me! I don't need a freaking keeper!"

"Clearly you do or you would've taken care of this a long time ago."

"It doesn't bother me. It only bothers you."

"Yeah, you're right. It does bother me to see the woman I love crippled with pain on a regular basis."

"It's not that often," she said, ignoring the ache circulating in her gut as the conversation escalated into a fight.

"It's often enough. Now, stop bitching and drive. Call me when you're done. I want to know what he says. Oh, and tell Harry I said hi."

"Screw you. Tell him yourself."

"Love you, too, babe."

Harry made her wait thirty minutes in a cold exam room wearing nothing more than the stupid paper gown they'd made her put on—with *nothing* under it. God, she hated doctors. Due to all the crap she'd been through trying to get pregnant and then the miscarriages, one of them an ectopic pregnancy that had nearly killed her, she had stayed far away from doctors the past few years. And for good reason: they kept you waiting when you had more important stuff to do. Like hunting down murderers.

Maybe she'd send good old Harry a bill for *her* time. She smiled. Yes, that would make her feel much better, and it would piss Nick off, too. Sam loved a plan that killed two birds with one stone.

After a brisk knock on the door, Harry came in a few minutes later, full of apologies for keeping her waiting. Of course he was totally hot. Wasn't that just her luck? Why couldn't he have been homely? Then she wouldn't have cared about him poking around in her parts. That he was also Nick's good friend made this even more uncomfortable and embarrassing. Why in the world had she agreed to this? *Because Nick asked you to,* she reminded herself. *Yeah, well, right now I hate him.*

"It's so great to meet you." Harry shook her hand, his brown eyes sparkling with warmth. "I was sorry I couldn't make it to your New Year's party, but Nick's told me all about you."

"Oh, really?"

"Yep, and of course I've read about you two in the paper."

Sam scowled. "Hasn't everyone?"

He laughed, and she realized he had dimples. Cute dimples. *Great.*

Harry sobered, but his eyes continued to dance with delight. "I suppose I should call him 'Senator' now."

"If you do, I'll shoot you. I'm trying to keep him humble."

"Nick said I would like you, and he was right." He washed his hands and pulled up a stool. "So what brings you here today?"

"Just this deal with my stomach," she said as the organ in question took a nasty dive.

"What kind of deal?"

She took a deep breath to counteract the surge of pain. "It, well, it kind of runs my life. Whenever I get nervous or anxious about something, it acts up."

"Are we talking reflux or heartburn or pain?"

"Pain."

"On a scale of one to ten, where's it at?"

"Um, twenty?"

"Huh. Well, that's no fun."

Sam laughed. "Not so much. Nick's all freaked out by it."

"With good cause, I'd say."

"Figures you'd side with him. You guys all stick together."

"We have to. It's us against you. Let's go over your history, and then we'll take a look."

Despite her best intentions to hate him as much as she hated Nick at the moment, Sam liked him, so she decided to level with him about everything—from the miscarriages to the endometriosis that had stolen her fertility, she laid it all out there.

"Huh," he said again. "How long ago did you hear that you were unlikely to conceive again?"

"Three years."

"And have you been seen since then?"

"No."

His eyes widened. "For *anything?*"

She shook her head. "I basically swore off doctors after that last episode."

"I don't have to tell you that's kind of dumb, do I?"

"It's not like I planned it or anything. It's just that one year became two and then two became three…and here we are."

"Well, I'm glad Nick made you come see me. We'll fix you right up. You might be glad to know that since you began boycotting me and my kind, they've made some great strides in treating endometriosis-related infertility. Women who were told exactly what you were are now having healthy babies after some minor laser surgery."

Sam refused to allow her hopes to rise for even one second. "I think that ship has sailed for me. I'm happy with my life the way it is."

"What're you doing for birth control?"

She looked at him, wondering if he'd heard her say she was infertile. "Nothing. There's no need."

"As long as you still have all your parts, there's always a chance of conception."

Sam pondered that, feeling a surge of hope for the first time in years. But then reality returned, and she pushed the idea from her mind. "It's not something I worry about. I've resigned myself to remaining childless."

"You don't have to decide anything today about the surgery. It's just something to consider." He stood up and encouraged her to lie back on the table. "Since you've been so neglectful of your health," he said with a teasing scowl, "I'm going to treat you to the full deal."

"That's what I was afraid of," she said, swallowing hard. "You're not *that* kind of doctor, so you don't need to worry about the 'down there' stuff."

He replied with a charming smile as he very unobtrusively gave her a breast exam. "I'm a general internist, so I can worry about *all* your stuff."

"Fabulous."

"Do you want a nurse in the room for the pelvic exam?"

She swallowed hard, again. "No, that's okay. I guess if you're Nick's friend, I can trust you." Grimacing her way through a thorough check of her abdomen, she added, "Isn't it weird to be poking and prodding your friend's girlfriend?"

"Nah. It's just like a mechanic looking at a car engine— you've seen one, you've seen 'em all."

Sam's mouth fell open. "Surely some are better than others."

"Oh, yeah, definitely. Now be quiet so I can listen to your heart."

He kept up a steady stream of chatter as he poked and prodded *everything*. She learned that Nick was a menace on the racquetball court, that he still played hockey whenever he could and that he was a regular chick magnet in the bars. She'd have to discuss that with him after she punished him for making her go through this exam in the first place.

"It's not the same since you took him off the market," Harry lamented, as he performed a Pap smear and pelvic exam. "The rest of us have to work a lot harder to get the women to notice us without him there."

She stared at the ceiling and prayed for mercy as he prodded her in places no man had ever gone before. "Sorry to interfere in your conquests," she said through gritted teeth. She was going to beat the living daylights out of Nick for this.

"He seems really happy, though. After his friend John was murdered, we were so worried about him, but then he started seeing you and things seemed better."

"It's been a tough month for him," she managed to say. "Julian Sinclair was a close friend of his, too."

"I know," he said, probing deeper.

How was it possible to go *deeper*? First, she planned to punch Nick square in the face. Then she would kick him right where he lived. Next she would stab him in the heart with a rusty steak knife.

Harry *finally* finished prodding, took off his gloves and told her she could sit up. "Everything checks out well, Sam, so let's talk lifestyle and diet. Are you getting enough sleep?"

She thought of the long hours she kept at work and the late nights she'd had recently with Nick. "Sometimes."

He frowned. "Diet?"

"I try to eat healthy, but it's hard sometimes with my job."

"How do you manage the stress?"

"I focus on breathing. In through the nose, out through the mouth."

"Well, that's one way to cope." Running through a checklist on his clipboard, he asked a bunch of questions. "Caffeine intake?"

"Some," she said tentatively. Her last doctor had freaked out about her diet cola addiction.

"What's some?"

"A few diet sodas every day. No biggie."

"How many is a few?"

"I don't know. I don't keep count."

"Guesstimate—two, three, six, ten? What do you think?"

"Six maybe."

His eyes widened. "Six cans or bottles?"

"Um, bottles usually."

"You drink six twenty-ounce bottles of diet soda a day? *Every day?*"

Sam squirmed under the heat of his stare. This was worse than when he'd had his hands in her unmentionables. "I don't always finish them."

"Six twenty-ounce bottles is one hundred twenty ounces of soda. In other words, a gallon."

"Wow, all this and you can multiply, too."

"I'd say we've found our culprit. The acid in the soda is no doubt eating away at the lining of your stomach. If you don't already have an ulcer, you're probably well on your way to one."

"I need the boost. I can't function without it."

"Sure you can. You've just convinced yourself you can't. It's all psychological."

So now he was calling her crazy? Nick would get another punch for that.

"Here's the deal—I can do a series of invasive tests to rule out anything sinister, or you can give up the soda for a couple of weeks and see if that solves the problem."

"Define *invasive*," she said, swallowing a gulp.

"Down the gullet, up the kazoo—we'd come at you from both ends."

Sam narrowed her eyes, using her best cop stare to intimidate him.

He never even blinked, the bastard.

"I can see why you and Nick are such good friends."

Laughing, he said, "I take that as a compliment. So what do you say?"

"Fine! I'll give it up! But when Nick calls begging you to assist in his suicide, you'll have only yourself to blame. I'm a total gorilla without my caffeine."

"You'll just have to replace it with something equally stimulating, such as exercise or more sex."

"Not possible," she grumbled.

Harry flashed her a dirty grin as he typed something in to the computer. "No wonder why my buddy is looking so... what's the word? *Satisfied* lately."

Sam glared at him. "I hate you. Almost as much as I hate him—and that's a lot."

"You'll thank us both when you stop having crippling stomach pain." Before he left the room, he handed her his card. "If you want some more information on the endometriosis treatment, call me. Otherwise, come back in a month so we can see how the soda famine works out. If you have any problems in the meantime, or if the stomach pain continues to be bad, call me. You'll get the Pap results in the mail."

"Thank you. I think."

He left her with one last charming smile. "I can see why Nick loves you."

Now that wasn't fair! Just when she was starting to seriously hate him he went and said that! She got dressed while pondering life without soda.

This was not going to be pretty. Not one bit.

CHAPTER 28

Gasping for air, Freddie used his good arm to reach up to see if the top of his head had blown off. Everything was still where it belonged, but nothing would ever be the same. He'd had no idea it was possible to come that hard and live through it.

"So," Elin said, peppering his chest and neck with kisses, "did you like it?"

He tried to form the words, but there were none.

She laughed. "I'll take that as a yes." Her hand traveled from his chest to his waist, heading south.

Freddie stopped her.

"What's wrong?"

"Nothing." It took every ounce of energy he could muster to sit up and look for his clothes. If he stayed, he had no doubt they'd be going at it again in no time. He was more than a little appalled by how ferociously he wanted her—he wanted her in every way it was possible to want a woman. Would he ever get enough? Probably not and that was the problem. It hadn't occurred to him that once he did this for the first time, he'd discover an insatiable appetite for more. He was in danger of becoming someone he barely recognized.

"Where're you going?" she asked.

"I need to go home. I'm working tomorrow."

"You're still on medical leave."

"I feel good enough to work." He didn't add that he was anxious to follow up on the people who used to live in Clarence Reese's house. If he couldn't do anything else to help Sam right now, he could do that.

Struggling into his shirt, he attempted to close a few buttons over the bulky sling that held his injured arm.

"Why don't you just stay?" Elin asked, her voice full of petulance.

"I need clothes for the morning, and I've got some stuff I have to do at home."

"Did I do something wrong again?"

"Of course not," he said, but his protest fell flat even to him. "It was amazing." And that, he thought, was the problem. It was just too damned good.

Freddie pushed his second leg into his jeans and tugged up the zipper. Doing things with one hand definitely sucked.

"I wish you wouldn't go," Elin said softly.

He glanced over and was stunned and unnerved to find her big eyes swimming with tears. Reaching for her hand, he brought it to his lips. "I had a good time tonight."

She took back her hand and started to get up. "I'll drive you home."

"No need. I'll grab a cab."

"Oh. Okay. Whatever."

"Elin…"

"Don't. Don't bother giving me the whole 'it's been fun, but it's over' speech."

"Who said anything's over?"

"The handwriting's on the wall."

"Well, it's not my handwriting. I'm going home because

I have bills I need to pay and laundry to do. On top of that, my pain pills are there, and my shoulder's killing me." Making sure he had her full attention, he added, "I'm *not* going home because you rocked my world."

A hint of a smile graced her pretty pink mouth. "I did?"

He bit his lip and nodded. "Totally."

"So you might want to do it again sometime?" she asked, her smile now coy.

Leaning in to kiss her, he captured her bottom lip between his teeth. "Definitely. I'll call you."

Her smile faded.

"What?"

"Guys always say they'll call when they have no intention of calling."

"They do?" Freddie asked, genuinely surprised.

She nodded. "Universal code for a blow off."

Clearly, he still had a lot to learn about such things. "Well, that's not how *I* intended it. I *will* call you." He pulled the covers up over her and kissed her once more. "Get some sleep."

"You, too."

Freddie moved through the dark apartment, collected his coat and locked the door behind him. Once outside, he took several long deep breaths of cold air before glancing up at her window. He'd wanted exactly what he'd gotten from Elin. So why was it that he couldn't shake the feeling that he was in *way* over his head with her?

Sam left Harry's office and went straight to the trauma unit at George Washington University Hospital, where she learned that Devon Sinclair was in surgery, and the outlook was grim. Of course it would've been too simple for him to be awake and alert and able to tell her who'd shot him and his lover. That kind of luck was apparently restricted to TV cops.

In the waiting room, Devon's brother, Austin, tried to comfort his inconsolable mother while weeping bitterly himself. "How could this have happened?" Austin asked. "Who would shoot Dev? Or Tucker?" He looked up at Sam. "God, I can't believe Tucker's dead."

Diandra's shoulders shook with sobs.

"You have no idea who might want to harm either of them?" Sam asked Austin.

"No. No one. They both had tons of friends. Everyone liked them."

"We can't…" Diandra couldn't seem to form the words she needed. "We can't find Preston."

Sam straightened, her spine tingling. "What do you mean?"

Diandra wiped her face with a tissue Austin handed her. "He's not answering his cell, his colleagues haven't seen him all day. I can't imagine where he could be. He needs to know about his son."

"I'll see what I can do to locate him."

"We'd appreciate that," Austin said.

Sam handed him her card. "When your brother wakes up, will you please call me?"

He nodded.

"I'll, um, hope for the best for Devon," she said, hating the way she sounded. She never knew what to say in these situations.

"Thank you," Austin said.

As Sam walked to the car, her sister Angela called. "Hey, Ang. What's up?"

"Are you anywhere close to heading home?"

"Getting there."

"Can you stop by on your way?"

"What's going on?"

"I just want to see you and so does Jack," Angela said, referring to her son.

"Sure, okay. I'll be there as soon as I can." Wondering what was going on with her sister, Sam spent the next hour looking for Preston Sinclair at his office and home. She confirmed Diandra's assertion that no one had seen him all day. When she ran out of places to look, she called in an APB to dispatch, ensuring that every cop in the city would be looking for him with orders to contact her the moment he turned up. Before she could chicken out, she also made the horrible, unimaginable call to Tucker Farrell's parents.

Afterward, her hands were sweaty, her stomach growled and her caffeine level had plummeted. Under normal circumstances, she'd be stopping for a diet cola right now. Her stomach might be benefiting from the soda famine, but her blood pressure was soaring. When she got her hands on Nick...

The cell rang again. Sam took her eyes off the road to glance at the caller ID. "Speak of the devil." She flipped the cell phone to speaker mode. "What?"

"Hello to you, too."

"I'm working here."

"You're in a fine mood. What time will you be home?"

Home? Where was that these days? "An hour or so. I have to stop at Angela's on the way."

"How's Devon?"

"In surgery. Doesn't look good and now his father has gone missing. I'll need to go back to work tonight."

"No problem. I'll feed you and send you on your way."

"Fine."

"Are you going to tell me what Harry said?"

"Nope."

"I'll get it out of you."

"Give it your best shot."

"Oh, I will. You can count on that."

Closing the phone, she tossed it into the passenger seat and headed for Angela's house, where she was greeted by five-year-old Spider-Man.

"Spidey!" Sam scooped him up and swung him around. Jack squealed with delight.

"Where's your mama?"

"In the house." Jack kissed her noisily on the mouth. "Where ya been, Sam?"

"Oh, here, there, everywhere."

"Did you shoot anyone?"

Sam poked his ribs as she carried him inside. "No, silly."

He touched the bandage on her chin. "Didja get beat up?"

Laughing, Sam said, "Not this week."

"Boring."

"*So* boring." She put him down and kissed her sister's cheek, noting that Angela looked pale and drawn.

"Jack, go get changed for dinner and *wash* your hands with real soap, not just water."

"But, Mom! Sam just got here."

Angela narrowed her eyes and pointed to the stairs. "Go."

Jack stomped off, grumbling under his breath.

"He's killing me." Angela sagged into a kitchen chair. "He never runs out of gas."

"You look like you have."

"I'm exhausted."

"What's wrong, Ang? You're scaring me."

After a long pause, Angela said, "I'm pregnant."

Sam took a moment to absorb the instantaneous burst of jealousy. "Really? How far along?"

"Almost three months."

"And you haven't told me?"

"It's hard, Sam. With all you've been through and everything."

"That doesn't mean I can't be happy for you. Who loves Jack more than me?"

"Only me and Spence."

Sam hugged her. "And I'll love this one just as much. I promise."

Angela's eyes went bright with tears. "Fucking out-of-control hormones."

Sam laughed and reached for her sister's hand. "Are you going to find out what you're having this time?"

"I want to, but Spence doesn't."

"Well, find out and tell me!"

Angela's pretty face softened into a smile. "You're sure you're okay?"

"I'm happy for you. You know that." Sam pushed around a toy car Jack had left on the table. "I saw a doctor friend of Nick's today. He told me about some new laser treatment that's working wonders for women who've had endometriosis. But I don't know."

Angela gasped. "What don't you know? You have to do it!"

"It's not that simple. I don't think I could go through that again."

"You have to! You have to at least try!"

"I shouldn't have told you."

"What did Nick say?"

"I haven't talked to him about it. I don't want to get his hopes up."

"Or yours."

"Or mine."

"Sam, if there's a chance, even the *slightest* chance, how can you *not* try?"

"I just heard about it a couple of hours ago. I haven't had time to even process it yet."

"Will you tell Nick?"

Sam shrugged. "I'm mad at him right now."

"Why?" Angela asked, alarmed. "What'd he do?"

"He made me go see his doctor friend Harry, who poked and prodded me in ways and places I've never been poked or prodded before."

Angela howled with laughter. "Oh, the nerve of him! You have to dump him. Immediately!"

Sam shot her a dirty look. "Harry says I have to give up soda. Entirely. Because of my stomach."

Angela stared at her sister. "Shut up. No way."

"Yes way. I'm already going through withdrawal. And it's all Nick's fault."

"Seriously. He must be punished."

Sam stood up. "I'm glad you agree. I've got to get on that. Tell Jack I'll see him this weekend."

"I predict you'll be horizontal under Nick in—" she consulted her watch "—twenty minutes."

Rolling her eyes, Sam headed for the front door. "Whatever," she called over her shoulder. "I'm not the one who's knocked up."

"Yet," her sister shot back.

Sam headed for her car, refusing to even entertain the possibility. She couldn't go through that again. She just couldn't.

Sam parked behind Nick's car on Ninth Street and headed for her dad's.

"Lieutenant!"

She spun around and groaned when she saw Darren Tabor from the *Washington Star* rushing down the sidewalk. "What do you want, Darren?"

"A few minutes of your time."

She kept her back to him. "I'm busy."

"How close are you to an arrest on Sinclair?"

"Which one?"

"Both."

"Not as close as I'd like to be."

"Any suspects?"

Sam stopped and turned to him. "If I was giving out exclusives, what makes you think you'd get one?"

He flashed a smarmy smile. "In other words, you got dick, right?"

"In other words, I'm not telling you."

"How's the senator?"

She rolled her eyes. "Go home, Darren, and get a life."

"Rumor has it you've got some interesting skeletons in your closet, Lieutenant. But that doesn't surprise me."

"What the hell is that supposed to mean?"

He shrugged. "Just rumors."

"I work in facts, not rumors. I'm going home. I'd suggest you do the same."

"Have a nice evening, Lieutenant."

Anxious to get away from the pesky reporter, she dashed up the ramp to her father's house and opened the door to a dark, empty house. Unaccustomed to her father being out when she wanted to see him sent her even further out of sorts.

So many details and thoughts and ideas were bouncing around in her mind that she couldn't make sense of or process any of them. And what the hell had Tabor been spewing about? Rumors? What did he have on her? She probably didn't want to know.

The case was stalled, her body craved caffeine and despite what she'd told Angela, all she could think about was the possibility of being pregnant again. Now she also had to ponder what Tabor had been talking about. He'd been particularly harsh in his reporting about her after a child had been killed in a crack house during a raid she'd supervised. He was the last reporter in town she wanted poking into her business.

Sam decided she needed some time to herself before she saw Nick. Upstairs in her room, she unclipped her hair, stretched out on the bed and stared up at the ceiling, hoping to quiet the chaos in her mind so she could think. Beginning with the discovery of Julian Sinclair's body, she worked her way through each aspect of the case. The shooting of his nephew had to be related. How could it not be? But why? What possible connection existed between the two men that would generate a motive for shooting both of them? Both were attorneys, both were gay, both were successful men. Where was the motive?

Going on the assumption that the two shootings were related, her most promising suspect had vaporized that afternoon when Devon Sinclair had been shot while his mother was being interviewed.

Sam combed her fingers through her hair and wondered where Preston Sinclair had gone. Could there be a third Sinclair victim waiting to be discovered dead or injured? Sam's gut told her it was all related to Diandra and the rift that had festered for years in their family. But how? Where was the connection? As far as Sam could tell, Diandra hadn't seen her brother-in-law in more than thirteen years. How would she know his schedule or his whereabouts?

If she had wanted him dead, wouldn't she have killed him years ago when she discovered his closet homosexuality after her sons had spent time alone with him? Her sons had confirmed her rage at learning that their uncle was gay.

Sam sighed, her head aching from the strain and the caffeine withdrawal. She dug her cell phone out of her pocket and called Jeannie McBride.

"Hi, Lieutenant. What's up?"

"Are you at HQ?"

"Yes, ma'am."

"Do me a favor and re-run the financials of Preston and Diandra Sinclair, only this time go back more than a year."

"Sure thing."

"While you're at it, get me both their sons, too. Devon and Austin Sinclair."

"Will do. Am I looking for anything in particular?"

"A large payment or transfer. Anything that stands out." Sam knew Diandra hadn't pulled the trigger on her son but couldn't rule out her hiring someone else to do it. But why would she have done that?

"I'll get right on it," Jeannie said.

Sam checked her watch and winced when she realized Jeannie's shift was long over. "Thanks. I hope I'm not screwing with your plans."

"No worries. My boyfriend's working late tonight, too."

Sam knew she should ask, that she should show some interest. "What, ah, what does he do?"

"Finance stuff. Investments, portfolio management. Nothing I really understand and nothing quite as exciting as dating a United States senator."

"That's funny, Jeannie. Really. Very funny."

Jeannie laughed. "Just speaking the truth, Lieutenant."

"Call me if you get any hits on the financials."

"Will do."

Sam hung up and continued to stare at the ceiling. Her thoughts wandered to what Harry had said about the endometriosis treatment. Half of her wished she'd never been told it was even possible. She knew herself well enough to accept that she would obsess about it endlessly until she decided whether or not to pursue it.

"There you are."

Startled out of her thoughts, Sam looked up to find Nick leaning against the door frame. As her eyes met his, she was overcome by a sense of rightness and absolute truth. He would make one hell of a father.

CHAPTER 29

Nick came into the room and stretched out next to her. "Everything okay?"

It is now, she thought. *The second I saw you, I felt better. How was that possible?* She worked up a smile for him and laced her fingers through his. "Yeah."

He brought their joined hands to his lips. "Will you do something for me?"

Anything. Anything at all. "Sure."

"I get that you're planning to torture me about how it went with Harry, but will you tell me if there's anything seriously wrong—"

Seeing the worry etched into his face she leaned over to kiss the words off his lips. "There's nothing to worry about."

"You swear?"

"What is this? Fifth grade?"

He released a long deep breath that sounded full of relief. "All day today, I just kept thinking, what if it's something really bad and all this time she's been ignoring it?"

"Your caring concern is ruining my plans to stab you with a rusty steak knife for subjecting me to the most thorough poking and prodding of my life—and as someone who's been through infertility testing, that's saying something."

He winced. "A rusty steak knife, huh?"

"That was just one of my many plans for you."

Shifting so he was on top of her, he pinned her hands to the pillows and kissed her. "What were some of your other plans?" he asked with a lascivious smile.

All at once, she remembered Angela's prediction. Here she was, horizontal under Nick exactly twenty minutes after she left Ang's house. Sam laughed at the accuracy of her sister's statement.

His eyebrows knitted with confusion. "What's so funny?"

She got him to release her hands and looped her arms around his neck. "We are."

Between kisses, he said, "How so?"

"One minute I'm stabbing you with a rusty steak knife and the next you've got me right where you want me."

"Mmm," he said against her lips, delving deeper in sweeping thrusts of his tongue that drove her crazy.

Sam curled her legs around his and pushed hard against his erection, drawing a deep groan from him. She drank him in, the scent of soap and cologne that was all Nick, the corded muscles pressing against her, the heavy weight of his arousal.

He tore his lips free and focused on her neck. "Are you going to tell me why you're over here contemplating the ceiling when you could be home with me eating the chicken I made you?"

Sam closed her eyes and gave herself over to the sensation of his lips on her neck. His softly spoken words sent a shiver of desire all the way through her. "I just needed some time to think."

"I was waiting for you. I looked out and saw your car on the street."

He was hurt that she hadn't gone to him first. She could hear it in his voice. "Make love to me, Nick."

Surprised, he raised his head to meet her eyes. "Let's go home," he said, starting to get up.

She stopped him. "No. Here. Right now."

Wincing, he said, "You know I hate having sex in your father's house."

"At least he's not here this time."

"I still say he's got this room wired. He'll know."

Unbuttoning his shirt, she fastened her teeth on his nipple. He gasped. "Sam! The door's wide-open."

"So? No one's here." She slipped her hand inside his pants and wrapped her fingers around him.

"God," he whispered, shuddering in surrender to her stroking hand.

"I want you. Hurry."

In their haste, they pushed clothes aside rather than removing them.

"Now," Sam said, her eyes closed as she guided him to where she needed him more than the next breath.

"Look at me."

She glanced up to find the hazel eyes she loved so much hot with desire and love. Tightening her hold on him she urged him on and released a long, satisfied sigh when he finally filled her. Without breaking the intense eye contact, she wrapped her legs around his hips to keep him still. Watching him, she reveled in the battle he fought with his control. A bead of sweat formed on his forehead, a muscle in his cheek twitched with tension.

"*Sam.* Come on."

When she released him, he seemed to go a little crazy, driving them both to a fast, explosive finish that left her feeling both drained and energized.

"Jesus," he muttered into her neck several minutes of heavy breathing later. "Are you trying to kill me?"

Aftershocks rippled through her as she tried to catch her breath, the weight of him on top of her filling her more than the physical act ever could with a sense of safety and security. "I was planning to kill you, but now I'm thinking I'll keep you around."

Rolling off her, he laughed. "Gee, thanks."

Sam reached for the blanket at the foot of the bed and covered them. Nuzzling his soft chest hair, she said, "I'm supposed to be working tonight."

"Well, don't blame me for getting sidetracked. I just came over to tell you dinner's ready, and then suddenly your hand was in my pants. What was I supposed to do?"

"Exactly what you did."

"What's wrong, Sam?"

"Nothing."

"Something."

He knew. He always knew. "The case. It's got me stumped. I can't seem to find my usual mojo on this one. Too many distractions."

"After what happened with Reese, I can see why you'd feel off."

"It's not that. I'm okay with that."

"How can you be okay with being kidnapped, held hostage at gunpoint, threatened? Not to mention watching him kill himself right in front of you."

She shrugged. "I'm a cop. Shit happens. You roll with it or you can't get up the next day and do the job."

"Still, it has to have *some* impact."

"It's not what's screwing me up on Sinclair. None of the pieces fit. I keep trying to make them fit, but they don't. Now Julian's brother Preston has gone missing, too."

"That's weird."

"Tell me about it! First Julian is shot and it looks like it's connected to the Supreme Court nomination, but then when his nephew and the nephew's roommate are shot, too, where's the connection? No matter how I spin it, I can't see how anyone would have a beef with both of them."

"So you don't think Julian's murder is related to the nomination?"

"Not if the same shooter did his nephew."

"How soon will you know that?"

"We've put a rush on the ballistics report. In the next day or two, I hope."

"Did you hear that the family postponed Julian's service?"

"No, but I figured they would."

"The nephews were planning it. Graham called earlier to let me know that Austin wants to wait until Devon recovers."

"*If* he recovers. It sounded pretty bad when I was at the hospital." She paused, contemplating how this changed her plans for the weekend.

He massaged her shoulder. "Since you're waiting on ballistics and now we don't have to go to Boston, maybe you could take some down time to recharge?"

She smiled up at him. "I thought that's what I was doing."

"I mean *real* down time. An actual night off with a full eight hours of sleep and everything."

"I need to get in some computer time after dinner."

"That can be arranged."

Pressing her lips to the soft skin under his jaw, she said, "How was your day?" She didn't see so much as feel the change in him, the tensing of previously relaxed muscles.

"Fine."

"And?"

"And what?"

"And what else?"

Laughing softly, he hugged her even closer to him. "I should be freaked out by how well you read me."

"Likewise. Spill it."

"Let's talk about it after dinner." He helped her to sit up and located her bra under the blanket. Handing it to her, he watched her put it on.

Her cheeks heated under the intensity of his stare. "Stop looking at me like that."

"Why?"

"Because. It leads to trouble."

One minute she was attempting to hook her bra, the next she was once again spread out beneath him.

"I love your brand of trouble," he said, capturing her mouth in a deep, sensual kiss that started her motor running all over again.

She sighed against his lips. "At this rate, I'll never get anything done tonight."

"You'll get me done."

Sam laughed. "I thought I'd already checked you off my to-do list."

Smiling, he kissed her nose and then her lips. "Consider this an encore."

"So what gives?" she asked as they lingered over a second glass of wine after dinner. The sex, the food, the wine, *him.* The combination had mellowed her after the crazy day, even if the tabloid reporters positioned outside his house had rattled her on the way in. This is what had been missing from her life before he'd come into it. Balance. In the past, she would've been too focused on the case to take a moment for herself in the midst of it.

He sat back in his chair, suddenly interested in the play of his fingers over the stem of his wineglass.

"Uh-oh," Sam said, watching him. "This doesn't sound good."

"I haven't said anything yet."

"Exactly." She noticed the tension had returned to his face, and her stomach twisted with fear.

"They want me to run."

"For?"

"The Senate. In the general election in November."

Sam sat perfectly still, processing what he had said. She didn't allow an ounce of emotion to show on her face.

After a long moment of silence, he glanced at her. "Say something, will you?"

"You said a year. You said we can do anything for a year."

"I know what I said. It was the truth at the time."

"And what's the truth now?"

"I don't know yet. I guess that depends on you."

"On *me?* Why on me?"

He reached for her hand, linked their fingers. "Because I promised you a year, and this would obviously be much more. Seven in fact. Much of this year campaigning and then six years in office if I win."

"You'd win," she said in a dull, flat tone. "That's why they want you to run. No one can beat you."

"So they said." He scooted his chair closer to hers and brought their joined hands to his lips, a gesture so totally his that Sam's heart ached with love. "Has it been so bad?" he asked with a cajoling smile. "This last month?"

"It hasn't even really started yet. And the press. They're outside your house and chasing me down the street."

"I know they're a pain, and you hate the intrusion. I do, too. But they'll lose interest in us. Eventually."

She pulled her hand free of his and got up to pace the kitchen. "They won't, Nick. It's only going to get worse."

"I don't have to do it. I can say no to them. There's plenty of other stuff I can do that would simplify things for us."

The statement stopped her in her tracks and served to clarify the debate—at least for her. She turned to him and studied the handsome, earnest face she loved more than anything. "Is that who we're going to be?"

His eyebrows knitted with confusion. "What do you mean?"

"Are we going to be people who do what's easy? Or are we going to be people who take a chance to be more than we thought we'd ever be?"

He stood up and held out his hands to stop her from pacing. "What are you saying?"

She smiled as a sense of peace came over her. "Run, Nick. This is your destiny. It's who you were meant to be."

Perplexed by her sudden change of heart, he tilted his head with inquisition.

"You don't see it, do you?" she asked.

"See what?"

"The way you've changed in the last month. How you carry yourself, the confidence."

He released a choppy laugh. "Yeah, right. I feel like a total fraud. As if I'm playing the part until the real guy gets back."

"No," she said, shaking her head. "You *are* the real guy. You're a United States senator, Nicholas Cappuano. That's who you are now."

"But, Sam, the press…"

"We can handle them. We'll toss them an occasional bone to keep them off our backs."

His hands landed on her shoulders. "Are you sure, babe? We don't have to decide anything tonight."

"I've never been more sure of anything in my life, except

that I was meant to spend it with you. Run. Win big. Make me proud. Just don't expect me to make any speeches."

"I wouldn't dream of it." His grin lit up his face. "You never cease to surprise me, Samantha. Just when I think you're going to freak, you go all Zen on me."

Flashing her most dazzling smile, she went up on tiptoes to kiss him. "It's my goal in life to keep you guessing."

"So far, you're succeeding brilliantly."

When he tried to kiss her with more serious intent, she dodged him. "No way, buster. I have to get back to work."

"All right," he said with a dejected sigh. "Be that way. I cooked *and* I get stuck with the dishes. I see how this is going to be."

"Such is the glamorous life of a United States senator. And by the way, no one said we were running a democracy at home, too."

"She giveth and she taketh away."

Laughing, she refilled her wineglass and took it with her. Over her shoulder, she said, "Come visit me when you finish kitchen duty."

"Yeah, yeah."

CHAPTER 30

Sam wandered into the cozy study that Nick had put together with his unique blend of style and practicality. She marveled at how quickly he had made this big empty house into a warm, inviting home. His outstanding taste and sense of style were just two more reasons to love him. Sam had to admit that it no longer seemed preposterous to imagine living here with him.

"Huh," she said, resting her chin on her fist as she absorbed the astounding revelation. "Wonder when that happened?" Over time. That's when it had happened. He hadn't pushed. Instead, he'd allowed her to come to her own conclusion in her own time. "Crafty of him." She decided to wait until she closed Sinclair to act on the decision she seemed to have made at some point over the past few weeks. "Wonder what he'd say if I just show up with all my crap and say, 'Hi, honey, I'm home.'" The idea of disrupting his finely tuned sense of order had her chortling with laughter.

Scooting the leather chair up to the desk, she checked things out. Of course, Nick being Nick, everything was exactly where it belonged, which all but dared her to mess with it. Feeling a little reckless after the conversation they'd just had, she moved a few items around on his impeccable desk while waiting for the computer to boot up.

Delighted with her handiwork, she tried to focus on the computer and the long list of names she needed to run. But rather than log into the police department system, she opened the internet browser and did a search for endometriosis treatment.

That's where Nick found her fifteen minutes later. "What're you looking at?" he asked, massaging her shoulders from behind. "And *why* do you have to screw around every time you sit at my desk?"

Startled, Sam attempted to minimize the window but clicked the wrong button and made it larger.

Nick leaned in for a closer look. "'Laser surgery offers revolutionary hope to endometriosis sufferers,'" he read from the screen.

She closed the window and attempted to shake him off.

"Hey! I was reading that."

"And now you're not."

"What did it say?"

Sam could hear the excitement in his voice, which is exactly why she hadn't mentioned it earlier. She couldn't bear to get his hopes up only to see them dashed the way hers had been by two miscarriages when she was married to Peter. "Nothing. It's nothing."

"It's not nothing." He spun the office chair around, forcing her to look at him. "Talk. Now."

"There's nothing to say."

He raised an eyebrow to let her know he wasn't buying it.

"It's just this thing Harry mentioned. It probably doesn't even apply to me, so there's no need to get all worked up over something that'll never happen."

His eyes widened with understanding. "He said there's something you can do—something *we* can do—didn't he?"

"See? You're already excited, and I can't deal with that!"

"Maybe if you just told me what he said, rather than expecting me to decode your ramblings, we could have an honest conversation here."

Sam folded her arms in defense against the gamut of emotions storming around inside her. "He mentioned a new treatment for endometriosis. Surgery that's been apparently yielding great results."

"And you're going to try it?"

"I don't know! I just heard about it today."

"Why wouldn't you?"

"Because! You have no idea how awful it was to go through three miscarriages. I thought this door was closed to me, and I've made peace with that. Now there's this tiny little crack, letting it all in again." She looked up at him. "I don't know if I'd survive if it happened again, Nick."

He dropped to his knees in front of her. "Then don't do it. Close the door, put the lock on and we'll go on with our lives as if we never heard about this. When we're ready, we'll adopt or hire a surrogate. Whatever we have to do."

Astounded, she stared at him. "You'd do that? Even if it might be possible for us to have our own?"

"I've told you before and I'll tell you again—*how* we have them doesn't matter one bit to me. That we have them— someday—that's what matters. As long as we're on the same page there, the rest is details to me."

Once again, she said a silent prayer of thanks to whatever higher power had arranged to have their paths cross again, years after they first met and connected on every possible level. He always knew just what to say to her, just what she needed to hear. "It's all I can think about," she confessed. "That I could have what Harry calls a simple surgery and then maybe…"

"Were you going to tell me?"

"I didn't want to get your hopes up only to see them crushed when it doesn't work out. And it *is* crushing. Take my word for it."

"I can't even imagine. But I can't help but remember what you said before."

"What?"

He shook his head. "Never mind. I don't want you to think I'm pressuring you, because I meant it when I said it doesn't matter to me if they're our biological children."

"Tell me anyway."

After another moment of hesitation, he said, "It's just what you said, about what kind of people we're going to be. Are we going to do what's easy or are we going to take some chances?"

Sam released a jagged deep breath. "We're not talking about a job, Nick. This is *much* different."

"Is it? Is it really?"

"So you're only *saying* you'd be okay adopting?"

"No, babe. I mean it. But I'm not thinking about me. I'm thinking about you, and I know this is something you want so badly, even if you'd never admit it. You say you've made peace with it, but you haven't. Not really. How could you?"

She didn't want to cry, but the tears seemed to have a mind of their own. They came in a great torrent that reminded her of the aftermath of her third miscarriage. This subject could be counted on to make her cry every time it came up.

Nick wrapped his arms around her and held her until she got it all out. "It's okay, Sam," he whispered, stroking her hair. "I'm here now, and no matter what happens, we'll deal with it together. Whatever you want to do is what we'll do."

"I don't *know* what I want to do," she said, sobs hiccupping through her. "I can't even talk about this without bawling my head off. Can you imagine what a mess I'd be if I had the surgery and managed to get pregnant? I'd spend the whole time panic-stricken, waiting to lose it."

"I can't picture that. The Samantha I know and love is ballsy and fearless and so courageous it often takes my breath away."

Touched by his faith in her, she attempted a smile. "You haven't seen her pregnant."

"I'd *love* to see her pregnant, but only if it's what *she* wants." He leaned in to kiss her and wipe away the remaining tears. "I love you, no matter what, and I'll support whatever you decide to do."

"Thanks," she said, "for getting me, and for understanding how this would hit me without needing me to draw you a map."

"Don't put pressure on yourself to decide anything right away. We've got plenty of time."

"My eggs aren't getting any younger."

"Puhleeze, you're a spring chicken." He kissed her again. "Are you going to tell me what else Harry had to say?"

"Do I have to?"

"Uh-huh."

"He said to say hi to you," she said with a big smile.

"Fabulous." He poked her ribs. "What else?"

She made a face at him. "He's making me give up soda."

Nick's mouth fell open. "You're kidding."

"I wish I was. Be prepared to see me at my very worst, starting tomorrow morning when I don't get my daily kick start."

"Thanks for the warning."

"You think it's funny now."

"So that was it? Just give up the soda and see what happens?"

"For now. He was very thorough, your pal Harry. I hope

you're not planning on having him over or anything. I doubt I could make eye contact."

Nick hooted with laughter. "That sounds like a dare."

"*Don't* you dare!"

"Do you feel better, babe? About the other thing?"

She exhaled a long deep breath infected with the hitches that follow a good cry. "Yeah." Rolling her shoulders, she sat back in the chair. "But I feel all revved up. You know what I'd really like to do?"

He raised a swarthy eyebrow. "Again?"

Laughing, she gave him a little shove. "Get your mind out of the gutter. I want to go back to Julian's hotel room and take another look. Sometimes when I'm stuck it helps to start all over."

"How about I go with you?"

"You don't want to do that."

He reached out to help her up. "There's nothing I'd rather do, and besides, maybe I'll be the one who figures this whole thing out."

She rolled her eyes at him. "Whatever. Stick with me, rookie. I'll show you the ropes."

Nuzzling her neck, he said, "Oh, ropes. That sounds promising."

Sam punched in the police code to unlock the hotel room door. Inside, she flipped on the lights and took a long look around at the large, elegant room where everything was neat and orderly.

"Looks like he was never here," Nick commented, "but I can smell his cologne."

Sam turned to him. "If it's too hard for you to be here—"

He rested an index finger on her lips. "I'm okay."

Even though crime scene detectives had already done it

once before, she went through the room again with methodic precision. She checked suit coat pockets, zippered linings in the suitcases and briefcase, and poked through the shaving kit in the bathroom but found nothing out of the ordinary.

"Are all your friends as anal-retentively neat as you and Julian?" she asked.

Nick sat at the desk and flipped through Julian's date book. "Not all of them." He turned to the page from the day of the murder. "Lunch with Trip. That would be Ackerman, chairman of the Senate Judiciary Committee."

"We couldn't figure out who that was." Sam marveled at how quickly he had given her a lead to follow.

"Prep school nickname. They probably went over how the nomination hearings would go, and he answered any questions Julian had. Will you talk to Ackerman?"

"First thing in the morning." She leaned in to kiss his cheek. "Thank you."

"I told you I'd figure this out for you."

She laughed. "Don't get all full of yourself quite yet."

"What do you suppose this refers to?" He pointed to an entry in the book that said, "P/a.d."

"No idea. I wondered if the *P* referred to his brother. Preston said he'd been in touch with Julian and hoped to see him while Julian was in town."

"What could *a.d.* stand for?" Nick asked.

"After Diandra goes to bed?" Sam ventured. "Austin and Devon?"

"After dinner?"

"Could be. I just wish we had tape of what happened after Graham and Laine dropped him off."

"Is it possible he managed to get back to his room but didn't leave again on foot?" Nick asked.

"What do you mean?"

"He could've been taken out in a laundry cart, for instance. I saw that in a movie once."

"So you're saying someone came in here, tied him up, tossed him in a laundry cart and wheeled him out without anyone seeing a thing?"

"Could've happened."

"We can't even prove that he came into the hotel after they dropped him off. In this fictional scenario of yours, did Julian go willingly? Did he just hop into the laundry cart and say, 'Tie me up and take me for a ride'?"

"Of course not."

"So then where's the struggle?" She gestured to the immaculate room. "Wouldn't a lamp be toppled or the bed covers rumpled or *something* disturbed?"

"Not if the attacker had a gun pointed at Julian. He'd do whatever he was told to stay alive."

Sam hated to concede the point. "That's possible. A gun would explain the lack of struggle."

Nick's grin lit up his face. "See, I'm a natural."

"You're still a rookie, though."

"So then teach me, master."

Hands on her hips, Sam surveyed the room, trying to imagine how it had gone down. "I'd love to have the background check the administration must've done on Julian."

Nick reached for his cell phone.

"What're you doing?"

"Getting it for you."

She watched in silent amazement as he called the White House deputy chief of staff at home and requested a copy of the vetting document on Julian Sinclair.

"He's emailing it to you," Nick said when he hung up. He looked up to find her staring at him. "What? We play racquetball together. He's a friend."

"Who *isn't* your friend?"

"Are you complaining?"

"Nope. You might be pretty useful to have around, rookie."

"Is that your ass-backward way of saying thank you?"

"I'm sure I'll think of *some* way to thank you—but not until we're off duty."

His eyes went hot with lust.

"Don't even think about it." As Sam took a step back from him her cell phone rang.

"Hey, Lieutenant," Jeannie McBride said. "I went through two years' worth of financials on all the principal players. The only interesting thing I found was a ten thousand-dollar wire transfer from Diandra Sinclair's personal account to an account in the Cayman Islands."

"Owned by whom?"

"I'm still trying to figure that out. The bank is closed right now, but I've left messages. I also tagged the Cayman police to make them aware of our investigation."

"Good work, Jeannie. Go on home. We can pick this up in the morning."

"It's something anyway."

"Absolutely. I appreciate you staying late. Any sign of Preston Sinclair?"

"Not that I've heard."

"Thanks again, Jeannie."

"Have a good night, L.T."

Sam ended the call and filled Nick in on what she'd learned.

"What do you suppose it means?"

"She could've paid someone to off her brother-in-law."

"If she did, why wait until he's here for nomination hearings? Everyone knew he was on Nelson's short list for the court. His nomination was hardly a surprise."

"Who knows? Maybe she had someone on retainer in case

it ever got this far. At any rate, I'd like to speak to her again. What do you say we hit GW on the way home? I want to check on Devon, too."

"It's not exactly on the way."

"No grumbling, rookie."

"I'm just saying…"

Patting his cheek, she said, "I can always drop you off at home if it's getting too late for you."

"And miss all this excitement? No way. Besides, you promised me a reward for getting you that background check. I intend to collect."

Closing and locking the hotel room door, she shot him a look full of innocence. "I was planning to make you an ice cream sundae. My nieces and nephews love my sundaes. Is that what you had in mind?"

"Not exactly," he muttered. "Although you can feel free to include hot fudge and whipped cream in my reward."

Somehow he always managed to get the last word.

CHAPTER 31

Headlights filled the rearview mirror with a bright glare.

Sam winced at the light and slowed down. "What the hell?" she said to the car behind them. "Get off my ass."

Instead of backing off, though, the other car tagged her back fender.

"What the fuck?" she cried.

Nick spun around for a better look and nearly lost the top of his head to the bullet that shattered the back window and lodged in the windshield.

She pushed his head down and hit the gas.

Nick pushed back. "Goddamn it, Sam! Let go of me!"

"Keep your head down and hold on!" She released him, called for backup and slammed on the brakes, spinning the car around to face the shooter. She drew her weapon, turned on her emergency lights and opened the car door.

"Where are you going?" Nick cried, grabbing her coat. "Get back in the car!"

She tugged herself free and got out.

The driver of the other car revved the engine and came at them, smashing into her car and narrowly missing Sam, who dove for cover in her car. Slamming the car into Reverse, tires smoked as the attacking car backed up and bounced off a parked car before it took off in the other direction.

Sam jammed her car into Reverse and turned around to give chase. "Damn it, I couldn't see who it was with the glare of the headlights."

"Jesus Christ," Nick muttered, clinging to the handle above the window as Sam took a corner on two wheels.

"Get down!" she cried.

"What about you?"

"I'm driving."

Another shot blew the driver's side-view mirror off her car.

"Son of a bitch," she muttered.

"Who the hell would be shooting at you?" Nick asked, his heart pounding, adrenaline and fear coursing through him. Thanks to the shattered windows, the temperature inside the car plummeted as the speedometer climbed to eighty-five. Lights flashing, they flew through deserted streets, dodging parked cars and the occasional pedestrian.

"Get the fuck out of the way!" Sam screamed at one of them. "Could be anyone. I've made lots of 'friends' during my twelve years on the force." Her eyes darted to the rear-view mirror. "Where the hell is my backup?" Reaching for her radio, she made a second more urgent call for help.

Zipping through red lights on Fourteenth Street, Nick braced for side impact. Watching her, he saw concentration, determination and a complete lack of fear, which made him feel like a total wimp since he was scared shitless. "You're one ballsy chick, Holland."

"Just doing my job, Senator. Oh, fuck!" She grabbed his coat. "Get down, Nick!"

The shooter in the other car had turned around to aim the gun at them. They dropped down in their seats, and Sam eased off the accelerator—slightly. The shot took out their left front tire, sending them into a spin that Sam tried valiantly to control. She let out a scream when the car suddenly launched into a series of bone-jarring flips, coming to rest upside down.

Since the front end didn't hit anything, the air bags didn't deploy, and at some point during the spin, Nick took hard hits to his forehead and shoulder. Shaking off the stars that danced in his eyes, he hung upside down, held in place by a seat belt. Once he could see straight again, he looked over at Sam. Blood dripped from an open wound on her forehead, and she was out cold.

"Sam!" He managed to release his seat belt and fell to the ceiling of the car. Catching a whiff of gas, his heart kicked into overdrive. "Sam! We've got to get out of here!"

The glow of a flashlight appeared outside the scrunched passenger window. Nick saw a badge on the chest of the officer who leaned into the car. "Are you folks all right in there?"

"I am, but Lieutenant Holland is hurt, and I smell gas."

"I do, too. Try to stay calm. The fire department's extrication unit is on its way."

Based on the amount of blood coming from the cut on her head, Nick decided that releasing her from the seat belt was more important than keeping her still. He worked his way under her so he could catch her when she fell. Even though his shoulder throbbed and he trembled from shock as well as the frigid temperature, he broke into a sweat from the effort it took to free her from the belt.

Her dead weight landing on him forced his side into the shift handle. Nick cried out in pain and wondered if he had broken a rib.

Through the smashed window on the passenger side, the officer peered into the one-foot space.

"Can we get her out?" Nick asked.

"It's not big enough."

"Not for me," he said, gagging on the gas fumes that filled the air. "But she might fit." Grimacing at the pain coming from his shoulder and ribs, he shifted her closer to the window while using the sleeve of his new overcoat to wipe the blood off her ghostly pale face. "Babe," he whispered, kissing her cold lips. "Wake up."

"Is she breathing?"

Nick put his face down close to hers and went weak with relief when he felt a whisper of air hit his cheek. "Yeah." In the distance, he could hear sirens. "I want to get her out of here."

"The opening is too small. Hang tight, Senator. Rescue is almost here."

His own head throbbing, he rested it on Sam's chest, comforted by her faint but audible heartbeat. "What's your name?"

"Montgomery. Officer Montgomery."

"Did they get the guys that shot at us?"

"I haven't heard yet, but I can check."

"Yeah." Nick's chest ached from the effort it took to breathe. "Do that." His eyes burned closed, but he fought the blackness, knowing if he had a concussion he should stay awake. "Samantha. Wake up, honey. Please wake up." He wiped more blood from her forehead. "Montgomery, do you have something I could use on her wound?"

The patrolman handed him a clean handkerchief.

"Thanks." He pressed the cloth to Sam's forehead while talking softly to her. The gas smell seemed to be getting stronger, and Nick was convinced the car was going to explode any second. "You should back up. Get away from the car. Just in case."

"I'm not going anywhere," Montgomery said.

"Lieutenant!"

"Who's that?" Nick asked.

"Detective Gonzales. Are you all right, Senator?"

"I am, but Sam's not."

"Fire's here," Gonzo said. "They'll get you out."

"Someone shot at us," Nick said. "That's how this happened."

"We got 'em. They crashed on the bridge."

"Good," he said, relieved. "That's good. Why were they shooting at us?"

"We think it might've been a gang initiation thing. Extra credit for shooting the famous lady cop. Triple extra credit for getting the senator, too. They're still sorting it out."

"Fabulous," Nick muttered.

The fire department sprayed flame retardant foam on the car. Nick closed his eyes and mouth and covered Sam's face with the handkerchief. In deference to the frigid cold, the EMTs passed a blanket in to Nick. He spread it out over Sam and snuggled up to her to share his body heat.

"Babe," he said, dropping kisses on her face. "Wake up. I need you." Sparks from the Jaws of Life rained down on them. Nick drew the blanket up to protect her face.

Twenty minutes later, the firefighters peeled back the side of the car. Hands landed on Nick's shoulders.

"Take her first," he said.

"We need to get you out so we can reach her, Senator."

Nick kissed her cold lips. "The paramedics are going to take me now, but I'll wait for you outside."

He had never felt more helpless than he did leaving her unconscious in the car. Once he was on a gurney, paramedics swarmed around him, assessing his injuries. He couldn't see what was happening with Sam. "I'm fine," he said, trying to sit up. His head swam, his side felt like it had been stabbed with a knife, and his shoulder seemed disconnected from the rest of him.

"Whoa, Senator." One of the paramedics held him down. "You have to stay still."

"I need to see her!"

"We're taking good care of her. Don't worry."

Don't worry. Sure. "Gonzo!"

"Right here, Senator."

"What's going on with Sam?"

"The paramedics are working on her."

"Did they get her out?"

"Not yet. Looks like they're stabilizing her before they move her."

"God," Nick whispered. "Don't let her die. Please don't let her die. If she does, I will, too."

Gonzo placed a hand on Nick's uninjured shoulder. "Hang in there, man. She's tough. She's going to be fine."

Nick wanted to believe him, but the hitch he heard in Gonzo's voice told him he wasn't the only one who was frightened for her.

They were transported in separate ambulances. Halfway to the hospital, Nick's lung collapsed. He'd never, in all his life, experienced pain quite like that. As he gasped for air, the paramedics moved quickly to insert a chest tube to re-inflate his lung. The minute he could breathe again, he asked what was happening with Sam.

"She's stable, Senator."

"Is she awake?"

"Not yet."

Nick realized his mouth had dried up, and his head buzzed. "What'd you give me?" His tongue suddenly felt too big for his mouth.

"Something for the pain."

"Don't give me any more. I need to stay alert."

"It's gonna be bad."

"No meds." Nick tried to move his left arm and gritted his teeth against the agony. "Will you call and check on her? Please?"

The older of the two paramedics nodded to his partner, who reached for his radio.

"Nothing new," the younger paramedic reported a few minutes later.

They pulled up to GW Trauma, where a swarm of reporters had gathered outside the E.R. Nick heard the paramedics radioing to the police, asking for help with the crowd. Even from inside the ambulance Nick could hear Gonzo screaming at the reporters to get the hell out of the way. For the first time in more than an hour, Nick smiled.

"We're going to put this over your face to preserve your privacy," one of the paramedics said, draping a clean white towel over Nick's head.

"Make sure they do the same for Sam," he said. "She'd hate to be photographed when she's out cold."

"Of course, Senator."

"You could probably call me Nick at this point." He hated the way everyone fawned over him these days. It was the one thing about his new life that didn't sit well with him. It wasn't like he'd run for office and won. No, his friend had been murdered, and he was just filling in for him. Maybe he'd feel differently if he won in November. Until then, it just seemed weird to be afforded respect he'd done nothing to earn.

The next couple of hours passed in a blur of pain, doctors, nurses, X-ray technicians and needles.

"How're you feeling, Senator?" the doctor in charge asked.

"Like I got hit by a bus." Nick wished he hadn't been so obstinate about the pain meds. He hurt everywhere, and his chest felt like an elephant was sitting on it. Every breath required supreme effort.

"The X-rays show a broken clavicle and a fractured rib, both on the left side in case you didn't already know that."

"How's Sam?"

"We're talking about you."

"I don't care about me. Tell me what's going on with her."

"The plastic surgeon put forty stitches in her hairline. Remarkably, she doesn't seem to have any other injuries besides a severe concussion."

"Is she awake?"

"No."

"Is that normal? Shouldn't she be awake by now?"

"Head injuries are tough. It can take an hour or a day, but she should be fine."

Should be wasn't good enough for him. "I need to see her."

"I'll arrange that after orthopedics deals with your shoulder and wraps your ribs. I don't want you to move around too much until then. The fractured rib is what caused your lung to collapse."

Nick winced at the reminder of that painful ordeal. "You're sure she's okay?"

"Right now she's stable. That's all I can tell you."

Nick studied the doctor's face, trying to see what he wasn't saying. "I need to call her dad."

"I believe Detective Gonzales took care of that. There's quite a crowd forming in the waiting room."

"I'm sure the entire MPD is here."

"Some of them are asking for you, too. People are here from your office, and we received a frantic phone call from your father. He said to tell you he's on his way."

"Oh. Okay." Nick was surprised and touched by his father's concern. "Is Captain Malone out there?"

"I can check, but you have to rest and take it easy."

"I need to see him. It's important."

"I'll send him in."

Malone came into the room a few minutes later. "How're you doing, Senator?"

"If one more person calls me that tonight, I'm going to lose it. My name is Nick."

Malone's solemn expression shifted into a small smile. "Are you okay, *Nick?*"

"I will be. Sam, on the other hand, I'm worried about."

"She's in good hands," Malone said, but Nick could see the concern etched into the older man's face.

"When she wakes up, she'll be freaking out about the Sinclair case. We were on our way here when this happened." He filled Malone in on Sam's theory about Diandra possibly paying someone off to take out Julian and mentioned the wire transfer Detective McBride uncovered.

"How does the son's shooting fit into that?"

"She wasn't sure yet. She was waiting for ballistics to see if the same gun was used in both shootings. She felt like she was getting close to some answers. We also figured out that Julian had lunch with Senator Ackerman, chairman of the Senate Judiciary Committee, earlier in the day he was killed. Sam was going to talk to him in the morning."

"Don't worry. I'll put Gonzales on that. He's been a mess since he saw you two in the wreck. This'll give him something to do with his considerable energy."

"There was an officer there. Montgomery. He was a big help to us. If there's anything you can do for him…"

"I'll make sure he's recognized."

"Good," Nick said, his energy flagging. He closed his eyes for a brief moment. When he opened them, Malone was gone and Skip Holland had taken his place. "Hey," Nick said. His voice sounded gravelly, so he cleared his throat.

"How're you doing?"

"Okay." He shifted in the bed, trying to find a more comfortable position. Pain radiated from his head, ribs and shoulders, briefly taking his breath away.

"You don't look okay."

Gritting his teeth, he sucked in a deep breath. "How's Sam?"

"The same. Celia, Angela and Tracy are with her. I wanted to check on you."

"Thanks, but I'm fine. I'm sure you want to get back to her."

"I hear your dad is on his way."

"So they say."

"Then I'll stay until he gets here."

CHAPTER 32

Nick awoke a few hours later and insisted on being taken to Sam's room. They'd given him a pair of scrubs to wear since his clothes had been cut off in the E.R. Because he was more comfortable standing than lying down, he hovered next to Sam's bed, staring at her pale face, willing her to wake up. Her sisters had encouraged their father to go home when he showed signs of tiring. Nick's own father spent a couple of hours with him until Nick sent him home, too.

"You really ought to get off your feet, Nick," Sam's sister Tracy said at two in the morning.

"I'm fine." In truth, he hurt from the top of his head to the end of his toes and everywhere in between. But until Sam woke up, he couldn't think about anything but her.

The door opened, and Freddie Cruz stuck his head in.

"Come in," Nick said.

"How is she?"

"The same."

Freddie approached the bed and rested his hand over Sam's. "Why doesn't she wake up?"

"I don't know. They keep saying she will."

"When?" Freddie glanced at him. "That was a stupid question. Sorry. How are you?"

"I've been better."

"Why aren't you in a hospital bed?"

"Because I need to be with her."

Sam's sister Tracy squeezed Nick's uninjured arm. "Ang and I are going to find some coffee. Can I get you something?"

He shook his head.

"Are you sure?"

"Yeah, thanks." Shifting his injured arm in the sling the orthopedic doctor insisted on, he gasped at the shaft of pain.

"Nick, why don't you sit for a while?" Angela said.

He bit back the urge to snap at them. "I'm fine," he said through gritted teeth.

"We'll be right back," Tracy said, shepherding her sister from the room.

"Take your time," Nick whispered after the door closed behind them.

"Getting on your nerves, are they?" Freddie said.

"They can't take care of her, so they're determined to take care of me."

"You look beat up, man."

"Tell me something I don't know."

"Um, the media has taken over the hospital lobby?" Freddie said with a sheepish grin.

"Ugh. Bloodthirsty vultures."

"It's a big story—the lady cop and the dashing senator in a car crash."

Not wanting to think about the morning's headlines, Nick linked his fingers with Sam's and brought her hand to his lips. "I wish she would just wake up!" When his outburst failed to stir her, Nick tightened his grip on her hand. "How's your shoulder?" he asked Freddie.

"Better. I'm finally free of the sling."

"Now it's my turn." Brushing the hair back from Sam's face and trying desperately to get his mind off his worries, Nick said, "So I hear you have a girlfriend."

Taken aback, Freddie sputtered. "Ah, um, well, I guess."

Nick laughed softly. "Well, do you or don't you?"

"I have no idea."

The younger man's exquisite discomfort provided Nick with some badly needed entertainment. "What would she say?"

"Probably that I'm a jerk."

"Why's that?"

"Because I haven't seen her or talked to her since the last time we, you know…"

"Ah," Nick said, enjoying this more with every passing moment. "And why's that?"

"This isn't really the time to have this conversation."

"Give me something to think about other than why she won't wake up."

Freddie looked down at Sam for so long that Nick wondered if he was going to say anything.

"It's just, you know, things got kind of intense sort of fast."

"You're in love with her."

"No! I'm not. I don't mean intense like that."

"Then how?"

After another long pause, Freddie muttered, "This is so embarrassing."

"Just say it."

"I've discovered I like sex. I mean I *really* like sex."

Despite the pain it caused him, Nick laughed so hard he wondered if he'd broken a second rib. "And that makes you different from every other guy how exactly?"

"You don't understand," Freddie said, taking a sudden and fervent interest in Sam's blanket.

"What don't I understand?"

"This thing, with Elin, it's, um, kind of out of character for me. It's like I've lost my mind and now my dick's doing all the thinking for me."

"You sound like a teenager who just got laid for the first time," Nick said.

"Well…"

Nick stared at him, incredulous. "You're not saying—"

"Look, I took a vow, okay? It was important to me, but then I met Elin and I've become someone I don't even recognize. All I can think about—morning, noon and night—is sex."

"You're making up for lost time," Nick said, hiding his surprise at Freddie's confession. "That's all it is."

"So there's not something wrong with me for wanting it *all* the time?"

"No," Nick said, laughing. "Welcome to the club. What does she think of your, um, urges?"

"She's always willing to accommodate them," Freddie said, flushing with discomfort.

"Lucky you. You managed to hook up with the woman we all dream about first time out of the gate."

"You'd better watch what you're saying, Senator," Sam mumbled.

Nick gasped. "Sam. Babe, open your eyes."

"Only if you two are done talking about Cruz's raging hormones."

"Oh, *shit,*" Freddie whispered, his eyes wide with horror. "How much did you hear?"

The left side of her face lifted into a small smile but her eyes remained closed. "Enough to torment you for the rest of your natural life."

Weak with relief, Nick bent down to kiss her. "Oh, Samantha, I'm so glad to hear your voice."

"That'd better be Nick kissing me."

"Don't worry. It's me. How do you feel?"

"Like my head is going to explode." She finally opened her eyes and looked up at him.

Nick had never been so happy to see her light blue eyes, even if they were heavy with pain.

"I, ah, I'd better go," Freddie said, backing out of the room. "I'll let you get some rest, Lieutenant."

"Call Skip's house," Nick said. "Let them know she's awake."

"Will do," Freddie said.

The moment the door closed, Sam laughed and then grimaced at the pain even that small movement caused her. "Clearly, he lost his mind along with his virginity."

"Try to stay still." Nick lowered himself gingerly to the edge of her bed.

"You're hurt," she whispered. "What happened?"

"You don't remember?"

"We were in the car." She closed her eyes and took a deep breath. "Someone shot at us. I can't remember anything after that. Wait! We were going to see Diandra."

"Don't worry. Gonzo and Jeannie are on it."

"Oh, good. So what happened? Did we crash?"

"We chased them, but they shot out one of our tires and the car went airborne and flipped a couple of times. We landed upside down." Reliving it, his throat closed when he thought about what could've happened, what had *almost* happened. Overcome, he rested his hand on her chest, taking comfort in the steady beat of her heart. "You were bleeding like crazy, and you wouldn't wake up."

She reached up to caress his hair.

"Scared the shit out of me."

"What did you hurt?"

"Broke my collarbone and a rib. No biggie."

"Nick," she said on a long sigh. "I'm so sorry. I never should've chased them when you were in the car with me."

"Why not? Would you rather they'd gotten away after shooting at us?"

"I'd rather you hadn't gotten hurt because of me."

"While your driving clearly leaves something to be desired, they weren't just after you." Smirking, he filled her in on what he'd heard about the gang initiation. "I was worth triple extra points. You were just *regular* points."

"And you're quite proud of that, aren't you?"

"You know it."

"I hope you're not so freaked out that you're going to run away again."

The genuine worry on her face made his heart ache, and he reached for her hand. "I can't. I made a promise. Remember?"

"Yeah. I remember." Her fingers tightened around his. "You can't run. Ever again."

"Your scar is going to be more gnarly than mine," he said, referring to the scar over his eyebrow from the bombing incident involving her ex-husband.

Her lips lifted into a smile. "Lay down with me."

"I don't know if I can."

"I'm so tired, but I can't sleep without you."

After hearing that, nothing could keep him from trying. "I'll give it a whirl." Moving very carefully, he eased himself down on his right side and attempted to find a comfortable position for his left arm. By the time he got settled, he'd broken into a cold sweat.

"You're hurt bad, Nick." She wiped the sweat from his brow.

"I'm much better now that you're awake."

"Your chest sounds all wheezy."

"My lung collapsed in the ambulance. That kinda hurt."

"I'm so sorry."

"It's not your fault, Samantha." He brought their joined hands up to rest over his heart and finally allowed himself to give in to the exhaustion. "I thought I knew exactly how much I love you, but I found out tonight that it's way, way more."

"So does that mean you want me morning, noon and night?" she asked, mocking Freddie.

Nick cracked up. *"Don't make me laugh,"* he moaned, his ribs burning from the movement. "I'm begging you."

"Is that a yes?"

"You bet it is."

Freddie leaned against the wall outside Sam's room, his heart racing. *I can't believe I just had that conversation with a United States senator. And Sam was listening! I'm never going to hear the end of this.* He wanted to curl up and die of embarrassment. *They must think I'm a freaking idiot!*

"Everything all right, Detective?"

Startled out of his thoughts, Freddie straightened at the sound of Captain Malone's voice. "Yes, sir. Lieutenant Holland is awake."

"That's great news."

"I'm going stir-crazy sitting around. There's got to be something I can do to help in the Sinclair case."

"The doctor cleared you?"

"Not technically, but I feel fine."

"You can come back when the doc says you can."

"I'm not due to see him until next week, but I'm ready to come back."

Malone studied him for a long moment. "All right. Desk duty only. Check in with Gonzo in the morning. See what he needs on Sinclair."

"Great," Freddie said, releasing a sigh of relief. "Thank you."

"You're sure you're all right? You look kind of funny."

The conversation with Nick came back to him in a rush of humiliation. "I'm fine."

"Go home and get some sleep."

"Yes, sir." Freddie decided to get the heck out of there before the captain changed his mind about letting him go back to work. In the lobby, reporters came swarming at him.

"Detective, what can you tell us about the condition of the lieutenant and the senator?"

"No comment." He pushed through them, amazed to realize they had doubled in number since he'd arrived two hours earlier.

"Are they alive?"

"Yes. That's all I'm saying."

"Have you recovered from being shot by Reese?"

"I'm fine." After only two minutes in the scrum, Freddie couldn't imagine how Sam and Nick stood the constant intrusion. Outside, the cold air was a welcome relief. Keeping his head down, he headed for his car. One of the reporters chased after him. Freddie saw it was Darren Tabor. Knowing Sam couldn't stand him, Freddie kept walking.

"Detective. I just need a minute."

"You're not getting anything out of me."

"Wait, Freddie. Seriously, I need to talk to you."

Tabor's use of his first name and his urgent tone got Freddie's attention. "You have one minute."

"There's a rumor floating around about Lieutenant Holland."

"I don't want to hear—"

"They're saying she had an abortion years ago."

Freddie stared at him. Shaking his head, he started to walk

again. "That's ridiculous. Everyone knows how badly she wants kids."

"This was when she was in college. The source is solid."

"So what're you going to do with it?"

"It's not me you need to worry about. It's one of the tabloids."

"Why are you having a sudden burst of conscience? After the way you savaged her during the Johnson case, I expect less from you."

"I deal in news, not gossip." Tabor grabbed his forearm. "Freddie. This is going to blow up big-time in the next day or two. Someone needs to warn them."

The idea of someone intentionally hurting Sam—and Nick—killed him. "Why now? I don't get it."

"A former receptionist from the clinic sold the story to the *Reporter*. Apparently, she made a killing thanks to their popularity."

Freddie felt sick. "How do you even know about it?"

"A buddy of mine is a photographer for the *Reporter*. He told me on the Q.T."

"So why do you care so much about giving them a heads-up?"

"I don't always agree with her, but she's a straight shooter. She doesn't deserve this. No one does."

"Thanks for letting me know. I'll take care of it."

"If, you know, the next time you guys need to use the media to advance your agenda, maybe you'll consider giving me a call?"

Nothing was ever free. "We'll keep that in mind."

Darren turned to walk away.

"Tabor."

"Yeah?"

"Thanks for the heads-up."

"No problem."

Freddie opened the door to his rattletrap Mustang and got in. He sat there for a long time processing what he'd been told. Tension gripped him as he thought about Sam, who'd been so much more than a partner and mentor. She was like a ball-busting older sister who he'd come to love over the past year of working closely with her. And Nick. Lately, he'd begun to feel like a friend, too. Even though he had a lofty job now, there was nothing lofty about him. Tabor was right when he said Sam didn't deserve this. Neither of them did.

Under normal circumstances, he'd go directly to Sam, tell her what he'd heard, and offer his help. But since she was in a hospital bed recovering from a serious head injury, that wasn't an option. What to do? He thought about going to Skip Holland, but due to the nature of the situation, he dismissed that idea.

Nick. He had to tell Nick, but remembering the crowd in the lobby, he didn't want to go back in there.

Freddie dug his cell phone out of his coat pocket and called Gonzo.

"Yeah. Gonzales."

"Gonzo. Wake up."

"I just got home," Gonzo mumbled. "Got to be back in two hours. This'd better be good."

"Is Christina with you?"

"What's it to you?"

"Can I talk to her?"

"What the fuck, Cruz?"

"It's important."

After a long pause, Gonzo said, "Hang on."

Freddie could hear Gonzo waking her up.

"This is Christina."

"I'm sorry to disturb you." He swallowed hard. "This is Detective Cruz. I'm Lieutenant Holland's partner."

"Yes, I know."

"I was wondering if you could give me the senator's cell phone number. It's urgent that I reach him."

"He's in the hospital. You know that. I saw you there earlier."

"I just left him with Sam, but the hospital is overrun with media, and it's very important that I speak to him tonight. In fact, after I talk to him, he's probably going to want to talk to you."

"What's going on, Detective?"

"May I please have the number?"

"Fine," she said, rattling it off.

"Thank you." Freddie ended the call before she could grill him some more. His stomach grinding with nerves, he dialed Nick's number and pressed send. It rang four times before going to voice mail. Since he knew Nick was injured and moving slowly, he called back.

He answered on the third ring. "Hmm, Nick Cappuano."

"Senator. It's Freddie Cruz. Are you awake?"

"No."

"Senator. Wake up. I really need to talk to you."

"There's nothing wrong with you, Freddie. I told you that."

"Senator! Listen to me. Come down to the parking lot outside the Emergency Room, but don't go through the lobby. It's full of media."

"You've got to be kidding me," Nick said. "I can barely move."

Freddie hated to ask him to come outside, but he couldn't take a chance on Sam overhearing what he had to tell Nick before they could figure out how to handle it. "It's about Sam. You have to come, Nick."

Freddie could tell that Nick was now fully awake. "I'll be right there."

"I'll wait for you in my car."

CHAPTER 33

Fifteen minutes later, Nick opened the passenger door and grunted from the effort it took to lower himself into the car. Glancing over at Freddie, he said, "This had better be good."

Freddie flipped on the inside lights so they could see each other in the murky predawn. "The *Reporter* is going to run a story that Sam had an abortion years ago."

Nick's pale face drained of what little color it had left. "What? What did you say?"

"It's not true. It can't be true. She could never—"

Nick sat perfectly still. "Tell me what you know. Everything you know."

Freddie relayed Darren Tabor's warning.

"Patient records are private. They couldn't possibly get the record."

"Are you saying it's true?" Freddie asked tentatively.

"I can't talk to you about this. I'm sorry. It's her personal business."

"Which is about to be splashed all over the news."

"Oh, my God. This can't be happening."

"You need to warn her."

"No." Nick shook his head. "She's hurt. I don't want her to know about this." He reached for the door handle. "I'll take care of it."

"What're you going to do?"

"I don't know yet."

"Call me if I can help."

With a quick nod, Nick worked his way out of the car and disappeared into the night.

Freddie sat there for a long time. He didn't envy Nick the task he had before him, but he did envy his love for Sam. What they seemed to have was something most people only dreamed about. Freddie started the car to head home, but home held zero appeal. Even though he knew he had no right, he called Elin.

"Hey," she said, sounding sleepy and sexy.

He yearned for her. "Sorry to wake you."

"S'okay."

"Can I come over?"

"Now?"

"Yeah."

With only the briefest of hesitations, she said, "Okay."

"I'll be there in a few minutes."

When she opened the door to him ten minutes later looking adorable and disheveled, he realized he'd missed her. Not the sex. *Her.*

"I'm sorry. I acted like an idiot."

She looked up at him with those bottomless blue eyes. "I missed you."

He reached for her, and she dissolved into his embrace. With one arm around her, he walked her into the bedroom, dropped his clothes into a pile on the floor, crawled into bed with her in his arms and fell instantly into a peaceful, dreamless sleep.

★ ★ ★

Nick stared out the window in Sam's room but could see nothing through the rage. That someone could do this to her… He checked on her, confirmed she was still asleep and stepped out of the room. Scrolling through the numbers on his phone, he found his attorney friend Andy, one of the guys he played basketball with. Andy and his wife had recently had a baby, so he hesitated to wake them up. But then he thought of Sam, sobbing at the Lincoln Memorial the night she told him her darkest secret, and made the call.

"I'm sorry to bother you, Andy. It's Nick Cappuano."

"Senator," Andy said, sounding groggy and surprised to hear from him—especially at that hour. "Are you all right? I heard about the accident."

"I'm banged up, but I'll survive. Sam's a little worse off."

"Sounds like it was quite a wreck."

"Yeah, it was. So listen, I've got a problem I could use your help with."

"Sure, Nick, er, Senator. Whatever you need."

"Nick is fine, and it's about Sam." Nick told him about the tabloid. "Tell me there's something we can do. An injunction. Something. If this comes out, it'll kill her."

"Is it true?"

Nick hesitated, hating this more with every passing second. "Yes and no. She had an appointment for the procedure, but miscarried beforehand. It sounds like the source only passed along the first half of the story."

"If it's true, it's harder to claim libel. And since she's a public figure, that further complicates things."

"How can that be? This is her private medical history that someone sold to a tabloid for personal gain. How can that be legal?"

"You can file for an injunction since medical records are private, but I doubt you'd get it in time to stop publication."

Nick released a ragged deep breath. "So because she's with me, because I'm in the Senate now and we've gotten all this attention, she forfeits her basic right to privacy?"

"It's more like it can be taken from her without notice. I can file for an emergency injunction in the morning. The best we can hope for is a sympathetic judge who will move swiftly. Be advised, though, the injunction will make news, too. It'll all but confirm that the story is true—and in this case, partially true is enough to be damaging. She can also sue the asses off the clinic and the tabloid—and she absolutely should—but again, that'll only perpetuate the story."

Nick ran a hand through his hair. "I can't believe this is happening."

"You'll want to get with your staff to figure out how to respond from a political standpoint."

"There's no way I'm dignifying this with a response."

"Your communications people will no doubt advise otherwise."

"This has nothing to do with my job."

"It has everything to do with it, Nick. We're talking about the most divisive issue of our time. The public will be looking for your position on this."

"I love her, I support her right to choose. I support every woman's right to choose."

"Then that's what you say."

"I can't protect her, Andy." The helplessness overwhelmed him. "I hate that I can't protect her from this."

"I haven't met her, but from what I've read about her in the papers, I can't imagine that she'd expect you to protect her."

"That doesn't mean I don't want to," Nick said. "Could

I offer the tabloid more money than they paid for the story not to run it?"

"No doubt that would get out, too, adding gas to the story's fire."

Nick sighed. "I'm really sorry I woke you up."

"I'm glad you called. I'm heading to the office now. I'll get that injunction filed first thing and let you know when it's done."

"I really appreciate your help. Send me the bill for your time."

"Don't worry about it. I'll be in touch."

Sam floated somewhere between dreams and nightmares. Victims and perps and hideous crimes cycled through her mind. Scenes from the Sinclair investigation flashed one by one, parts and pieces that refused to add up to a whole. Julian's body in Lincoln Park, his estranged brother and sister-in-law, the beloved nephews, one of them shot, his roommate killed. Preston Sinclair missing. Where had he gone? Why had he gone? What was she overlooking?

She could feel the answer circulating close to the surface. If only she could find the final pieces to the puzzle. If only she could find Preston.

The pulsing pain coming from the cut on her head interrupted the flow, demanding her full attention. Her eyes fluttered open. "Preston."

Nick turned from his post at the window. "What's that, babe?" In obvious pain, he moved slowly to the bedside and lowered himself down.

"It's Preston."

"What is? I don't follow."

"Preston shot Julian and Devon."

Nick curled a lock of her long hair around his finger. "What? Why?"

"To protect Diandra. I can't believe I didn't figure it out sooner."

"But why would he shoot his own brother and son?"

"Think about it. For thirty years, he lives with this domineering woman who has unpopular beliefs that caused him to be estranged from his brother. He had to make a choice—her or Julian. She was his choice. Now here she was, weeks away from her book being published, and Julian was going to steal the limelight from her. Everything about his life was going to come out, and Diandra would be embarrassed. She might even lose her TV gig. What if the publisher got squeamish about taking on a new Supreme Court justice and cancelled her book? She wouldn't have wanted to risk it."

"So he lured his own brother out of a hotel, hog-tied him and shot him in Lincoln Park?"

"Julian never went into the hotel." The whole thing clicked into focus with such amazing clarity it was all she could do to keep up. "That's why we couldn't find him leaving on the tape. Graham and Laine said they dropped him off at the hotel, but neither of them could confirm they saw him go in the door. No one in the hotel could recall actually seeing him after he returned from dinner."

"So he snuck off and met Preston somewhere?"

"They'd been in touch. Preston said he hoped to see his brother while he was in town."

"Do you think he intended to kill Julian?"

"Yeah, I do." Sam stared at a spot on the far wall, imagining the crime going down.

"Did Diandra know?"

"She planned the whole thing. She would've been freaking out about the timing, Julian coming to town for contentious hearings just as her book was released. She worried that she'd lose her TV show. How could she continue to spew hate and venom about gays when her Supreme Court justice brother-in-law was one of them? She worked on Preston until he saw no other option but to get rid of his brother. No one would suspect him. They hadn't spoken in years."

"What about the money in the Caymans?"

"She did that as a backup. In case Preston couldn't do it. She probably had someone else lined up."

"How do you explain their son being shot?"

"Austin might've told their father what Devon confessed to us when we interviewed him."

"I don't get why Austin would tell their father that."

"Who knows? Maybe he was rattled from being inter-viewed by cops. Maybe Preston somehow pressured him into recounting everything they told the cops. Hard to say. How-ever it happened, Preston found out Devon was gay, and all he could see was how it would affect Diandra."

"So she didn't know Preston intended to shoot Devon?"

"She had no idea." Sam recalled Diandra's reaction to the news about her son. "But she knew right away that Preston had done that, too. What she doesn't know is why."

"He's gone mad, and she drove him to it."

"Yes, he pulled the trigger. Both times. He was the one with the gun, but I'll bet we can prove she was an accessory to Julian's murder."

They stared at each other, adrenaline pumping through them.

"I think you've got it," Nick said.

"It took a knock to the head and forty stitches, but yeah, looks like we've got it nailed. Finally. Is Captain Malone still here?"

"He's asleep in the waiting room."

"Would you mind getting him for me?"

"Sure."

While he was gone, Sam closed her eyes in an effort to calm the pounding pain in her head. It had definitely gotten worse overnight. The smallest of movements made her nauseous.

Nick returned with Captain Malone in tow.

"How're you feeling, Sam?" Malone asked.

"As long as I don't move, I'm fine."

"Ouch. Nick tells me you've managed to crack the Sinclair case from your hospital bed." His face lifted into a proud smile. "Only you, Holland."

Sam told him her theory. "Here's what needs to happen. We need to get Austin Sinclair away from his mother. Get him to confirm that he told his father about Devon being involved with his roommate, Tucker. I need to know how and when that happened." A blast of pain reminded her of the need to stay still.

"Take it easy, babe," Nick said.

She took a shallow breath, fought back the nausea and continued. "We have to find Preston. He's armed and unhinged. We need to get him before he hurts someone else. If he has any capacity left, he's probably aware of what he's done and feeling desperate about his son. Maybe we can use Devon to somehow lure him in."

"What about the wife?" Malone asked.

"Have Cruz trace the purchase of the rope that was used to tie Julian. I'll bet my life she bought it. She set this whole thing up. She convinced her husband that killing his brother was the only way. The brothers were estranged because of her. She violently disapproved of Julian. He came to town for Supreme Court nomination hearings just as she was due to realize the dream of a lifetime by seeing her book published. No way was she going to let him deny her that. When Preston found out about Devon, he went off on a rogue mission to neutralize that threat, too."

"He shot his own son," Malone said, incredulous. "Preston saw him as a threat to the wife and took action."

"Yes," Sam said. "His lawyer will argue diminished capacity, and it'll probably fly. He'll end up in the psych ward. She's the one I want behind bars. She didn't pull the trigger on Julian, but she made sure her husband did."

"We'll get them both," Malone assured her. "You worry about getting better."

"I hate that I can't go after them myself."

"I'm sure you do, but we've got it covered."

"Keep me posted?"

"You know I will."

After the captain left, Nick could see that Sam's burst of energy had faded and the pain had her full attention.

Clutching her hand, he studied her precious face, aching from what he needed to tell her. If he had his way, she'd never know about the tabloid. But they had a deal about keeping things from each other, so he owed her nothing less than the truth, even if telling her would break his heart—and hers.

"What?" she asked. "What's wrong? Is it Julian? I know it's so hard for you to hear about how he was killed."

"No, babe. It's not Julian. Something happened while you were asleep before, and I wish I didn't have to tell you this."

"Not my dad," she said in a small voice.

With his good arm, Nick hugged her as best he could. "No, honey." Holding her against him, he pressed his lips to her temple and very softly, very gently told her about the tabloid.

As his words registered, she stiffened in his arms. "No," she whispered.

"I'm so sorry, Sam. I'd do anything in my power to protect

you from having to deal with this. My lawyer is filing for an emergency injunction this morning, but he doesn't think it'll happen in time to stop the publication."

"My dad," she said, frantically. "I have to tell him before he reads it in the paper." She struggled free of Nick's embrace, and then nearly fainted when her head injury fought back.

He eased her to the pile of pillows. "Sweetheart, you can't go anywhere right now."

"I have to tell him."

"I'll call Celia. She'll bring him here. I'll make sure she brings him in a side door so no one gets to him before you do." He brushed the hair back from her face. "It's going to be okay, Sam. You didn't do anything wrong."

"Everyone will know what I was going to do," she whispered.

"How about we steal their thunder?"

"What do you mean?"

"We could release a statement that tells the story your way, on your terms, rather than waiting for it to explode in the *Reporter*. We could pull the legs out from under them."

"Come right out and admit it? I don't know if I could do that."

"Tell your story, Sam. Tell the same story you told me. We'll issue a joint statement saying this is the only thing either of us will ever have to say on the issue. And then we'll sue the asses off the clinic, the woman who stole your record and the *Reporter*. I'll bet you all can come up with something to charge her with criminally."

She looked up at him. "How do I make a statement?"

Proud of her courage, he said, "Christina and Trevor are on their way over here now. We'll take care of everything."

"You can't be involved with this, Nick. You're running for office. This'll be a nightmare for you."

"Of course I'm involved with it. I told you before I ever accepted this job that you come first and you always will. Political fallout is the very last thing on my mind right now. This is happening to you because of me and my job. You have to let me fix it. I *need* to fix it, Sam."

Biting her lip, she studied him for a long time. "Okay."

Nick called Celia and asked her to bring Skip over as soon as possible. Returning the phone to his pocket, he reached for Sam's hand and brought it to his lips. "It's going to be okay. I promise."

CHAPTER 34

"No way, Senator," Christina said. "You can*not* go out there and read this. It's political suicide to attach yourself so vocally to this issue."

"I'm attaching myself to her, not the issue."

Astounded, Christina stared at him. "Are you really that naive?"

Trevor cleared his throat.

"Speak," Nick said.

The communications director glanced at Christina. "I, um, I agree with the senator." Before she could pounce, he said, "The entire region is caught up in their romance. People will respond to him sticking up for her."

"You've lost your minds—both of you," Christina retorted. "He's a *United States senator* who's going to tell the world that his girlfriend planned to have an abortion before a well-timed miscarriage saved the day. An *abortion!*"

"I'm going to say that fifteen years ago, when she was still a student, my girlfriend planned to have a legal medical procedure to end a pregnancy she was unequipped to handle at that time in her life. I'm going to tell them she miscarried before the procedure was performed and she's regretted the decisions she made at that time ever since. I'll say I love her, I support her and I support the right of all women to choose. Then I will tell them that neither the lieutenant nor I will have another word to say about this. Ever."

"Why can't someone from her family read the statement?" Christina asked. "Why does it have to be you?"

"Because I *am* her family, and this is happening to her because of me."

"How do you figure?"

Nick rolled his eyes. "Seriously, Christina? You don't see the connection?"

Trevor cleared his throat again. "If he hadn't agreed to finish Senator O'Connor's term, no one would care about Lieutenant Holland's past."

"Thank you, Trevor," Nick said, his eyes fixed on Christina.

"Fine." She handed him the statement. "Have at it. Just don't say I didn't warn you when the party tries to run you out of town on a rail."

"Unfortunately for them, I'm all they've got." Turning to Trevor, he said, "Let the media know I'll be making a brief statement in the hospital lobby at ten."

"Will do, Senator."

"Relax, Christina," Nick said. "It'll be fine."

Her expression rife with trepidation, she said, "Sure it will."

From her bed, Sam heard the whir of her father's chair coming down the hallway. Pushing herself up, she winced when pain bounced off every corner of her skull. She had a whole new respect for concussions.

Celia held the door open for Skip. "Morning, honey," Celia said. "How are you today?"

"Fine as long as I don't blink."

"You need to stay very still, which of course will be a challenge for you," Skip said, his sharp eyes assessing his daughter's condition.

"Did you have any trouble with the media?" Sam asked.

"Nope," Skip said. "We came in through the Emergency Room."

Sam's stomach tightened with the familiar pain, although she had to admit it wasn't as sharp since she gave up soda. Then again, *she* wasn't quite as sharp, either. "There's something I have to tell you."

"Why don't I wait for you outside, Skip?" Celia said.

"No," Sam said to her future stepmother. "Stay. Please."

"All right." Celia moved to the bedside and rested her hand over Sam's. "Are your injuries worse than they thought?"

Sam tuned in to the worry on both their faces and hated that she'd caused it. "No, nothing like that. It's about something that happened years ago, something shameful. The media has caught wind of it."

"Whatever it is, Sam, we love you," Skip said, but she could see the trepidation on his face. "You know that."

Sam cleared the emotion from her throat. "Yes, I do, and that's why I never wanted to disappoint you."

"And you never have. What's wrong, honey?"

"Do you remember the French guy I dated in college? Jean Paul?"

"Vaguely. As I recall, there was no shortage of young men interested in my little girl."

Sam wouldn't have believed it possible to smile just then. Taking a deep breath, she told them about the terrible decision she'd been forced to make, the miscarriage she'd suffered and the consequences she had lived with every day since. "I didn't know what to do, Dad," she said softly. "I felt like I had no choice."

Both Skip and Celia seemed stunned.

Nick stepped into the room, came over to the bed and slipped an arm around Sam. Kissing her temple, he whispered, "You okay?"

She closed her eyes for a moment, absorbing the tender comfort only he could provide. "Yeah."

"Why are you telling us this now?" Skip asked, his expression unreadable.

"Because it's about to hit the news," Nick said.

Celia gasped.

"Someone from the clinic sold the story to one of the rags and told them I went through with it. We have no idea what they'll actually report, but we suspect it won't be the truth."

"But that's illegal!" Celia huffed.

"You have to do something," Skip said, his eyes darting from Sam to Nick and then back to her.

"We're doing what we can," Nick assured him, outlining the plan.

"Still," Sam said softly, "everyone will know." After a long pause, she glanced at her father. "Say something, Dad. Please."

"I'm sorry you didn't come to me when this happened."

"Don't you remember how it was then? Mom had left, Tracy had just had Brooke, everyone was upset and stressed. I thought it was my only option. And then I lost the baby. Not a day has gone by that I haven't wondered what might've been."

"I have no doubt."

"This is embarrassing to you. I'm sorry."

"Don't be ridiculous," Skip said tersely. "I couldn't care less what anyone thinks. All that matters is that you're okay."

Nick squeezed Sam's shoulder.

Overwhelmed, Sam said, "It's mortifying to have everyone know about my personal business, but I don't want you to worry, Dad. We'll get through this." On top of her other regrets, she hated that her past was going to cause political grief for Nick.

"I think it'd be best if you leave before the press conference," Nick said to Skip and Celia. "I'd hate for them to get ahold of you."

"We'll take our chances," Skip said.

"I'd rather you go," Sam said softly. "If you stay, I'll be worried about getting you out of here."

"Sam's right," Celia said to Skip. "We can come back tonight."

"Absolutely." Sam sat up slowly. Leaning down, she kissed her father's cheek and hugged Celia. "I'll see you later."

"Sam." When he had her attention, Skip said, "There is nothing, and I mean *nothing,* you could ever do or have ever done that would disappoint me or make me love you less. *Nothing.* Do you hear me?"

"Yes," Sam said softly. "Thank you for saying that."

To Nick, Skip said, "Go out there and give 'em hell, Senator."

"I will. Don't worry."

After Skip and Celia left, a nurse came in. "That very cute partner of yours called to check on you," she said as she scanned Sam's monitors. "He said he didn't want to wake you up by calling, and he'll be here shortly."

"Good," Sam said, drained by the conversation with her father. Her head pounded, and her mouth was dry as the desert.

"Is he single?" the nurse asked with nonchalance. "Your partner?"

"He's seeing someone."

"Oh, well. My loss. He's *adorable.*" Under her breath, she

added, "So is your guy." She glanced at Nick, who stared out the window at the gray, frigid day. "Yum."

Sam smiled but her heart ached at the thought of what he was about to do for her.

An hour later, Sam watched on television as Nick stood before the press to read the statement she had approved. Off to the side, Christina and Trevor watched anxiously. "I have a brief statement, and then neither I nor Lieutenant Holland will have anything further to say on this subject."

The gathered reporters all but salivated with anticipation.

Sam muted the TV. She couldn't bear to listen. Fixating on Nick's handsome, serious face, she noted how pale and drawn he appeared. He'd suffered serious injuries of his own the day before, and yet taking care of her was his top priority. Despite the firestorm his announcement would set off in both their lives, she wasn't as freaked out as she would've been without him by her side.

Anxious to think about anything other than what Nick was saying to the press and the pounding in her skull, Sam wondered if they'd found Preston yet. Where in the hell would he go? A man like him, used to the creature comforts, wouldn't last long on the streets. Had he checked in to a hotel? Had anyone thought to look into that?

"I need to get back on that case." She pushed herself up as slowly as she could and then took a moment to contend with the accompanying swell of nausea.

Freddie tapped on the door and came in. "Morning, boss. How're you doing? *What* are you doing?"

"I gotta get out of here, Cruz."

"No way, Lieutenant." He stepped over to the bed and rested his hands on her shoulders, clearly intending to resettle her in the bed. "You're supposed to be still."

Gritting her teeth, she snarled at him. "Remove your fucking hands and get that bag of clothes over there." She pointed to the bag Celia had brought. "Hurry up. Before Nick gets back."

Startled by her tone, Freddie jumped back, jostling her in the process.

"The *clothes,* Cruz." It was all she could do to get the words out. "Now."

"If you ask me to dress you, I'll quit the force."

"Dream on. Go out to the nurse's station and sign for my personal effects. Tell them I'm twitchy without my gun since a bunch of gang punks put me here. What if they show up to finish the deal?"

"They aren't going to give me your stuff."

Sam closed her eyes, seeking mercy from the pain. "Ask for Holly," she rasped. "For some unknown reason, she thinks you're adorable. Charm her, but make it snappy." She glanced at the TV and saw Nick stepping away from the podium. "We're running out of time."

With a wary glance at her, Freddie put the bag of clothes on the bed and left the room.

Swallowing the sickening waves of nausea, she got dressed in a sweat suit and sneakers. Thankfully, Celia had also brought a warm parka.

Freddie returned a few minutes later with a satisfied smirk on his face. A plastic bag containing her gun, badge, cuffs and wallet landed on the bed next to her.

Sam jammed the gun into the back of her sweats, put the other items in her coat pockets and stood up. Just as quickly, she sat back down when her head exploded in protest.

"Sam—"

"Shut up," she growled. With one hand on the bed, she pushed herself back up and took a second to contend with the now-predictable burst of pain. Reaching up, she snatched the knitted skullcap off his head and dragged it over her injured dome, tucking her long hair inside. "Let's go."

"That's okay, I wasn't using that."

"I need it more than you do."

"Nick's gonna kill me for this," Freddie muttered.

"No, he's gonna kill *me*. So let's make it worth it."

Moving down the hallway, dodging nurses, Sam discovered her body hurt everywhere. The diagonal seat-belt bruise, stretching from shoulder to hip, protested every movement. Apparently, she'd also managed to hurt her knee, but no one had noticed that thanks to the head injury.

At the elevator bank, she pressed the up arrow.

"Where're we going?" Freddie asked, puzzled.

"To see Diandra. Did you get anything on the rope that was used to bind Julian?"

"Diandra purchased a spool of rope from the Home Depot in Gaithersburg two weeks before Julian was murdered. Gonzo is getting a warrant to search the house for the rest of it."

Sam wished she had the strength to dance a jig. "Excellent! I knew it. What else have you heard today?"

"Gonzo talked to Austin. Devon is still critical. Could go either way. Austin confirmed that he told his father about your conversation with Devon."

"Bingo. I knew it. Preston heard Devon was gay, and lost it. We *have* to find him. He's the key to this whole thing."

They rode the elevator to the ICU, where Sam flashed her badge and asked for Diandra. "It's critical we speak to her," she told the nurse on duty. They were granted entry to Devon's room where Diandra sat hunched over her son's bed.

"Mrs. Sinclair," Sam said from the doorway.

The face that looked up was barely recognizable as the stylish, put-together woman who made her career as a TV commentator. When Sam first met her, Diandra believed she had the situation fully under control. Her husband had done her bidding and taken out his inconveniently nominated brother. Everything was right in her world. Until the moment Preston went too far and shot their son. That, most definitely, had *not* been part of Diandra's plan.

"What do you want?" Diandra asked, her voice and posture defeated.

"How is he?"

"How does he look?"

"Not too good. May I speak to you outside for a moment?"

"I don't want to leave him."

"It'll only take a minute."

Diandra bent to press a kiss to Devon's forehead. In the hallway, she crossed her arms and leaned back against the wall, exhaustion all but rippling from her.

Aware of the nurses clustered around the monitoring station a few feet away, Sam kept her voice low. "Where's Austin?"

"He went home to change."

"What about Preston?"

"I have no idea." Clearly her concern from yesterday had morphed into anger overnight.

"Where would he go?"

Diandra shook her head. "I wish I knew. He doesn't even know about Devon."

So, Sam thought, *still in denial, are you, Diandra? Still not sure your husband could really shoot his own son? Still not aware of just how much power you exert over Preston or how far he'd go to ensure your happiness?* Being on top—or thinking you were on top— made the fall that much harder and longer. This woman had a huge fall coming her way, even if Devon survived.

"We'd like to speak to him." Sam nudged Freddie. "Give

her your card. Call Detective Cruz if you hear from him. Do you understand?"

"What does Preston have to do with anything?"

"I don't know yet. That's why I want to talk to him."

"What's wrong with you?" Diandra asked, zeroing in on Sam's face. "You're trembling and ghostly pale."

"She was in a car accident last night," Freddie said.

"And you're working on Devon's case?"

"I'm working on both cases—Devon's *and* Julian's."

Diandra appeared startled to hear that. "What does one have to do with the other?"

Sam took a moment, sized up the other woman, measuring her every movement. "I don't know yet." Despite what the motion cost her aching head, she leaned in closer. "But I'm going to find out, Diandra. You can bet your ass I'm going to find out. Detective Cruz? Let's go."

Emerging through the ICU double doors, Sam gripped Freddie's jacket to keep from falling down. Her legs had the consistency of cooked spaghetti. "Get on the horn with the lab," she whispered. "Tell them they have one hour to get me the report on the weapon used on Devon. I already know it was the same gun that did Julian. I just need confirmation. One hour."

"Lieutenant, maybe you should sit for a minute."

"Not 'til we're out of this place. Get me out of here without going anywhere near the lobby."

"Can I ask you something?"

"Yeah."

"Why didn't you nail her just now? You've all but got her on accessory to murder."

"Because we still need to sew up a couple of loose ends, and then I'm going to let Preston nail her. It's the least of what he owes her. All we have to do is find him." She staggered, and Freddie tightened his hold on her. "Make the call."

Freddie gripped her arm while dialing the cell phone with his free hand.

CHAPTER 35

"Where the hell would he go?" Sam asked the minute they were safely in Freddie's Mustang. Refusing to puke in the hospital parking lot where the press might see her, she fought back a vicious wave of nausea. "You're sure they checked all the hotels?"

"Every one within twenty miles of the city. The theory is he wouldn't go much farther knowing his son was wounded."

"And Austin couldn't think of anywhere else his father might be?"

"Only places we've already looked."

Sam punched the door and then instantly regretted it. Gasping from the pain that rippled through her in sickening waves, she closed her eyes and took shallow breaths through her nose.

"Damn it, Sam. You should be in the hospital."

"Drive. Now."

"Where to?"

"Out of this fucking parking lot! Before we get snagged!"

"Jeez, you're bitchy when you're in pain."

"I'm always bitchy."

"True."

"More so since I quit soda."

"*Very* true."

"So how's that whole 'I'm a crazy horn dog after all' thing going?"

"You're never going to forget that, are you?"

"Not in this lifetime." She rested her head back against the seat, pleased that at least something in her life had returned to normal—or what was passing for normal these days. Ever since the moment she first walked into John O'Connor's apartment and encountered Nick's grief-stricken face, her life had changed forever. Imagining the news of her long-ago near-abortion whipping through the city, she released a jagged sigh. "So, Nick said Darren Tabor spilled the whole thing to you."

"Yes. He was actually extremely cool. For him."

"Good of him to tip us off." She knew she had to ask, that this would be the first of many times she'd have to revisit the most painful moment of her life, a moment she thought she'd left behind a long time ago. "Are you disgusted with me?"

His eyes darted from the road to her and back to the road. "Of course not."

"Not even a little?"

His jaw tightened with tension. "You must've had no choice."

"I really didn't. But I know your faith runs deep. You should feel free to speak your mind, Freddie."

"I already have."

The tone of his voice indicated the conversation was over, that there would be nothing more said about it. Ever. He no doubt had strong feelings about the issue, but apparently he had strong feelings about her, too.

"You know what's disgusting?" she asked, looking to lighten things up.

"What's that?"

She kicked at the candy wrappers, chip bags and soda cans on the floor of his car. "Your disgusting eating habits."

"I'm a growing boy," he said with that charming smile of his. "I need my sugar."

"It's gross."

"You're just jealous because you wish you had my metabolism."

"I continue to hope I'm around to see your crappy diet catch up to you." The old car hit a huge pothole, and Sam gasped. "*Dude*. Watch the bumps."

"Um, do you think maybe you could tell me where we're going?"

"Just drive. Let me think. Where are you Preston? Where's the last place you think we'd look for you?" She let the thought run around in her mind for several minutes. "Call Gonzo. I want the log from Devon's house."

Dialing while driving, Freddie passed along the request.

Keeping her eyes closed, Sam said, "Ask him if Preston Sinclair came to the house after the bodies were found."

A minute later, Freddie confirmed that Preston had, in fact, come there looking for his son while crime scene processed the house. According to Gonzo's report, Preston acted suitably distraught and left after packing a bag for his son. He said he was going straight to the hospital. While they were on the phone, Gonzo also confirmed the same gun had been used in both Sinclair shootings.

The buzz of all the pieces falling into place rippled through Sam's battered body. "I *knew* it! Dupont Circle. Stat."

"There might be bumps."

"I'll risk it."

Ripped to shreds by what he'd just endured with the media, Nick returned to Sam's room to find it empty. "What the hell?"

Storming down the hall to the nurse's station, he inquired about her.

"She was in her room, Senator. I was just in there."

His ribs ached, his collarbone was on fire and his nerves were totally shot. Making a supreme effort not to rip the nurse's head off, he bit back a nasty retort and summoned a calm tone. "She's not there now. I want to know where she is."

"So do I." The nurse picked up the phone and called for security. "If she's in this hospital, they'll find her."

"Thank you."

He returned to Sam's room, dug his cell phone out of his pocket and called her. Hearing the tune of "Living on a Prayer" coming from under the pillow made him want to throw his own phone across the room. Then he noticed the bag Celia had brought.

Empty.

"Goddamn it, Sam. *Goddamn it!*" He reached under the pillow for her phone, scrolled through the numbers, found Freddie's and pressed Send.

"I bet he was in the house just long enough to unlock a window or door," Sam said.

Freddie pulled up to the townhouse and parked. "So you think he came back after the cops left?"

"That's exactly what I think." Sam reached for the door handle.

Freddie's hand on her arm stopped her. "What's the plan, boss? To go in there balls to the wall and ferret him out?"

"Well, yeah. Exactly."

"Um, no offense or anything, but a certain lieutenant near and dear to me recently ripped me a new one for going in without backup."

"You have backup. You have me."

"Again I say no offense, but I'd rather go in with my fat Aunt Doris than you in the condition you're in right now."

"Ouch. I'm hurt."

"Yes, you are, and I'm not going in there with just you to apprehend a man who's already shot his own brother and son." Stretching his injured shoulder, Freddie added, "I'd like to think I've learned my lesson. The two of us are hardly equipped at the moment."

"Christ, you're such an ass pain, Cruz. Call it in, but the collar's mine, you got me?"

"I got you, and I've asked you not to take the Lord's name in vain."

She growled at him.

Just as he reached for the radio to call for backup, his phone rang. Checking the caller ID, he glanced over at her. "Funny. It's you."

"Shit. It's probably Nick, and I'll bet he's pissed."

"*Gee,* do ya think?"

"Your sarcasm is of no use to me right now."

"Am I answering?"

Sam stared at the phone. "No. I'll call him after this goes down. Get the backup here before Preston slips through our fingers."

"You are so dead when Nick gets ahold of you. I hope I get to watch that."

"Shut up and call!"

The SWAT team scampered out of two black vans. They moved with the precision of a NASCAR pit crew, each member knowing exactly what they were supposed to do and when they were supposed to do it. Early in her career, Sam had considered SWAT but decided against it when she realized they did a lot of waiting for situations to arise while detectives were constantly in the thick of things.

With officers in place on the roof, in the street and on the ground they stormed the front door.

"Damn," Freddie said reverently. "I never get tired of watching them in action." A rumble of activity lit up the radio, and he reached for the door handle. "They're coming. Stay here."

"Screw you." Sam got out and was hit with another wave of nausea that nearly brought her to her knees. She forced the stars from her eyes and watched them bring a broken, bawling, handcuffed Preston Sinclair out of his son's house.

The SWAT lieutenant handed her a 9-millimeter handgun zipped into a plastic bag. "We got there just in time. He was going to off himself."

Malone and Gonzo arrived on the scene.

"I'm not even going to ask what the hell you're doing here, Holland," Malone said. "But why am I not surprised?"

Sam took the bag containing the gun. "Got the guy, got the weapon," she said with a smug smile. Even that small movement cost her. To Gonzo, she added, "Get him to HQ, put him in a room and stay with him until I call you. Don't even step out to take a leak, got me?" She handed him the gun. "Have Jeannie trace it. I want proof that Diandra bought it. Get it for me."

"Yes, ma'am." Gonzo took Preston by the arm and escorted him to the car.

Malone raised an eyebrow as he studied Sam. "What're you up to, Holland?"

"I need someone to pick up Diandra Sinclair at the GW ICU."

"That doesn't answer my question."

"I'll do it." Freddie flagged down a uniformed officer directing traffic around the scene. "We'll take his squad car and leave my car here. I'll meet you at HQ."

"Don't bring her in until I tell you to. Wait for my call."

"Got it." His face full of concern, Freddie turned to Malone. "Captain, you'll escort Lieutenant Holland back to HQ?"

"I'll escort her back to the hospital," Malone said.

"Then I'll grab a cab," Sam said, raising her chin—painfully—in defiance, "but either way, I'm going to HQ." The blinding light of the sun over his shoulder brought tears to her eyes, but she didn't look away.

"Fine, but the minute you finish this, you're on medical leave until I say otherwise."

"Fine."

"Fine," he retorted as he led her to his car. "You may be aware that there's a very unhappy United States senator looking for you."

"So I've heard." Closing her eyes, she rested her head against the seat. "Do me a favor? Help me dodge him? I need an hour to finish this, and then I'll take my punishment and my suspension and whatever else you all want to dole out."

"I'll look forward to seeing that."

"You and everyone else." She glanced over at him. "So, nothing to say? About the other thing?"

Malone shrugged. "None of my business. None of anyone's business."

"Is HQ all abuzz with it?"

"Maybe."

She sighed.

"Give it a day, maybe two—and you'll be on leave for most of it. It'll blow over."

"It's horrifying," she said softly. "That they all know."

"What's horrifying is that your privacy has been breached this way just because of who your boyfriend is."

"Yeah."

"But he's worth it, right?"

"He really is."

Malone smiled. "But that doesn't mean we won't nail the bitch who sold your medical record to the rag."

The unexpected laughter had Sam reaching for her head with both hands. "Oh, my God, don't make me laugh. *Please.*"

On the way to HQ, she used the captain's phone to call ahead to the U.S. Attorney's office. Hope Dobson, one of the three identical triplets who served the District as assistant U.S. Attorneys, answered. Sam laid out the case against Preston and detailed Diandra's role.

"Do you believe she knew he was going to kill his brother?" Hope asked.

"Not only did she know, she put him up to it, and I'm going to prove it. Can you be in the detectives' pit in thirty minutes? There's gonna be one hell of a show. You won't want to miss it."

"I'll be there."

"Thanks, and Hope? She's the main event as far as I'm concerned. Preston is diminished capacity all the way. He's totally under the control of his wife. It's disturbing."

"I'll see what I can do. How does the son's shooting fit in?"

"All your questions will be answered very soon. I'll let you hear it from the horse's mouth." She ended the call and handed the phone to the captain. "You might want to let the chief know this is going down."

"Again I ask, what are you up to, Holland?"

"Just closing a case, sir," she said, indulging in the chance to close her eyes and sink into the seat for just a minute. Among her many other woes, the line of stitches at her hairline was on fire. One minute of complete stillness to soothe her aching head and body. That was all she needed.

Captain Malone nudged her awake when they arrived at HQ. "This is insane, Holland. You need to be in the hospital."

Forcing herself to wake up, Sam tried to shake off the grogginess and gasped from the ricochet of pain. "Give me thirty minutes, and I'll wrap this one up with a bow on top just for you."

He cast a wary glance at the throng of media gathered outside the main door to HQ. "We need to go in through the morgue."

That would mean a longer walk to the pit—a much longer walk. "That's fine," she said, gritting her teeth. Anything to avoid the savages looking to take another piece out of her wounded hide. "Actually, I'm glad to see them here. They'll help my plan." She smiled at the idea of Diandra Sinclair, in handcuffs, being marched through the scrum into HQ.

"Which you *still* haven't shared with me."

At some point during the interminable walk, Sam became aware of his hand on her arm, all but holding her up as he directed her down the long hallways.

In the pit, she was greeted with none of the usual hubbub she'd come to expect. Rather, a subdued silence had descended over her troops as they no doubt tried to process what they'd learned about her that day. Refusing to be distracted, Sam shrugged off her coat and reached for the handheld radio on her desk.

Malone lowered himself into the other chair in her office.

"Detective Gonzales, what's your twenty?" she asked.

"Interrogation A with Mr. Sinclair."

"Detective Cruz?"

"In the parking lot with Mrs. Sinclair."

"Detective McBride?"

"On the way to your office, Lieutenant, with the information you requested."

Sam put down the radio and smiled. "Excellent."

Jeannie knocked on the door a minute later and handed Sam a file. Inside was a copy of a gun license, registered to Diandra Sinclair.

"Good work, Detective," Sam said, trying not to worry about the fact that Jeannie couldn't seem to make eye contact with her.

AUSA Dobson stepped into the room, followed closely by Chief Farnsworth, who took one look at Sam and blanched.

"What, in the name of God, are you doing out of the hospital, Lieutenant?" he asked.

"Thank you," Malone muttered. "She's up to something, won't tell me what, but I take it we're in for a show, Chief."

"What've you got, Lieutenant?" Hope asked.

Sam sensed an odd vibe coming from the assistant U.S. Attorney and wondered how long it would take to "blow over" as the captain predicted. She handed Hope the file with the license.

"The owner of the store recognized her and remembers her buying the gun," Jeannie said. "Diandra told him she was buying it as protection against the crazies who take issue with her views. She told him she'd been repeatedly threatened. He's willing to testify."

"So she put the gun in her husband's hand and told him his brother had to go?" Hope asked.

"That's exactly what she did, but she got more than she bargained for when he also used the gun on their son." Reaching for the radio, she called Cruz. "Bring her in, but wait to un-cuff her until you get inside." Sam waited exactly two minutes before she called Gonzo. "Please escort Mr. Sinclair, un-cuffed, into the pit." To the others in her office, Sam offered a gracious smile. "Ladies and gentlemen, will you join me in the hallway?"

Seconds before Freddie was due to bring Diandra in, Nick came around the corner, his handsome face tight and furious. Sam raised a hand to stop him, using her eyes to implore. He halted, noted the gathered group and stayed put.

Sam released a jagged sigh of relief. "Here we go," she said softly as Diandra and Preston approached each other from opposite sides of the detectives' pit.

As if gas had been thrown on a fire, Diandra took one look at her bedraggled husband and charged, just as Sam had hoped she would. Claws out, Diandra shrieked. *"What were you thinking?* You miserable excuse of a man! How could you shoot your *own son?"* She beat his chest with her fists. "Why? *Why?* We never said anything about Devon!"

His arms hanging loosely by his sides, Preston did nothing to defend himself against her tirade.

"Why?"

"He's gay," Preston said so softly it was almost inaudible.

As if he had struck her, Diandra stepped back from him. "What did you say?"

"Your son is gay. He and Tucker weren't just roommates. They were lovers."

"That's not true. You're making that up to get back at me for Julian."

Sam was pleased that Diandra seemed to have completely forgotten where she was and who was listening. This was even better than she'd hoped. Across the room, she met Nick's glance and was relieved to see that some of the rigidity had left his posture as he realized what was unfolding in front of him.

"I didn't want to," Preston sobbed. "I didn't want to do it, but you said Julian would ruin everything if he went before

Congress and told the world he was a gay man. You said we couldn't let that happen. So when Austin told me Dev was gay, too, I just did what I thought you'd want me to do."

"You shot Devon, Dad?" Austin asked in a dull, flat tone. He stepped through the doorway, having obviously followed his mother from the hospital to HQ.

Uh-oh, Sam thought. He hadn't been part of the plan.

"Mom's book is coming out." Preston fumbled over his words. "She's getting her own show. She's worked so hard. Everything she's ever wanted is finally within reach. I couldn't let them ruin it for her. She was afraid they'd ruin it for her."

"I never said anything about Devon!" Diandra repeatedly slapped Preston's face.

Austin grabbed her from behind, pulling her off his father. "Leave him alone. For God's sake, Mom. Hasn't he done enough for you? Haven't we all done enough?"

Preston descended into brokenhearted sobs.

"I've certainly heard enough." Sam stepped out of the crowd and nodded to Freddie, who cuffed Diandra.

"What're you doing?" she cried, fighting him. "I didn't shoot anyone. He did! I was with you when he shot Devon! You know that!"

"Mrs. Sinclair, you're under arrest for accessory to the murder of Julian Sinclair," Freddie said. "You have the right to remain silent. Anything you say can and will be used against you in a court of law."

Realization seemed to settle on Diandra all of a sudden. *"You fucking bitch,"* she seethed at Sam. *"You motherfucking bitch!"*

"You have the right to an attorney," Freddie continued. "If you cannot afford an attorney, one will be appointed to you. Do you understand these rights as they have been read to you?"

"Fuck you."

"I'll take that as a yes."

Sam turned to Preston. "Mr. Sinclair, you're under arrest for the first-degree murder of your brother, Julian Sinclair, for the attempted murder of your son, Devon Sinclair, and for the murder of Tucker Farrell." She repeated the Miranda warning as Freddie cuffed him. "Do you understand these rights as they have been read to you?"

"Yes, ma'am," Preston said wearily.

He was so defeated that Sam felt her heart go out to a murderer for the first time in her career.

"Detectives Cruz and Gonzales, please escort Mr. and Mrs. Sinclair to central booking."

After they were gone, with Diandra shrieking and fighting the whole way, Sam turned to Austin. "I'm sorry."

"I just can't believe he shot Dev," he said, the shock echoing through his voice. "She had him so under her control that he honestly thought that's what she'd want."

Sam rested her hand on his arm. "Your brother needs you to be strong for him. If he recovers, he'll need you to help him through this, as well as the loss of Tucker."

Austin seemed to make an enormous effort to shake off the stupor. "Yes, you're right. I'll see about getting an attorney for my dad."

"What about your mother?"

Austin fixed cold eyes on the doorway into which his parents had been taken. "She's on her own." He glanced at Sam. "Thank you for getting justice for my uncle and my brother and Tucker. In a million years, I never could've imagined that my parents were involved, but with hindsight I should've known my mother had something to do with it. I should've known that."

"You had no reason to suspect either of them was capable

of this. Go on back to your brother, Austin. That's where you
need to be right now."

He nodded and turned to leave.

Nick stepped up to her and put his arm around her.

Sam leaned gratefully into his embrace.

With his good arm, he took the coat Captain Malone
handed him and the two of them got her into it. "I have a serious bone to pick with you, Lieutenant," Nick said.

"So I've heard," Sam said, the burst of energy leaving her
as suddenly as it had come.

Nick steered her toward the door.

"Hey! What're you doing? I've got to do the report!"

"I'm taking you home, Samantha, so shut up before I bend
you over my knee and spank the life out of you right here in
front of all your coworkers."

Since she didn't have the energy to fight him, she rested her
head on his shoulder and let him take charge. "Mmm, that
sounds like fun. Can we try that sometime?"

"I said to shut up," he growled but she could tell that she'd
flustered him. She could hear it in his voice.

"Speaking of going home, I've been meaning to talk to you
about that," she said, her voice thick with exhaustion.

"We'll get to it. When you can keep your eyes open."

"'K. Don't let me forget."

"Don't worry, babe. I won't."

EPILOGUE

After two weeks of forced medical leave, all Sam wanted to do was get back to the action, but everyone seemed to be conspiring against her. Nothing infuriated her more than being mollycoddled by a bunch of overwrought men. All she'd managed to get done on her first day back was to confirm that Devon Sinclair was expected to make a full recovery. Malone and Cruz shoved her out the door at the stroke of five o'clock as if she wouldn't have had the good sense to go home on her own.

Home. Where was that exactly? Every time she'd tried to talk to Nick about moving in with him over the past two weeks, he'd dodged her, telling her they'd talk about it when she felt better. She was feeling *fine,* but if one more person treated her with kid gloves she was going to punch them. Her temper had been her biggest problem lately as she learned to live without caffeine. Her stomach, on the other hand, had been much better, which she hated to admit.

She'd been so bored during her leave that she'd even accompanied Nick to kick off his campaign in Richmond and to several events in southern Virginia. Following an initial burst of interest from the media about her long-ago almost-abortion, she and Nick had settled back into the usual grind of fending off just a small horde of reporters everywhere they went.

Buckling under enormous pressure, they had agreed to give Darren Tabor their first exclusive sit-down interview as a couple next week. Sam had major reservations about the idea and was doing it only to help Nick's campaign.

She parked on Ninth Street and contemplated where she wanted to be. Her dad's house was dark, as it often was these days as he and Celia finalized the plans for their Valentine's Day wedding. The thought of her father getting married on Valentine's Day made Sam want to gag, but they were so excited that she couldn't bring herself to object. She'd even grudgingly agreed to wear the red satin bridesmaid dress Celia had chosen for Sam and her sisters. Double gag.

While her dad's house was dark, Nick's was lit up like he was having a party. Sam locked her car and headed for Nick's. Inside, she found her sisters waiting for her.

"What're you guys doing here?" she asked, dropping her coat over the sofa. It drove Nick crazy that she couldn't hang it in the closet like a "normal" person, which was why she so enjoyed dumping it on his sofa.

"We're helping Nick with something," Angela said.

"With what?" Sam asked.

"Oh, a little project named Samantha," Tracy said as she linked her arm with Sam's and led her to the stairs. "Right this way, *Samantha*."

"He's the only one allowed to call me that," Sam snapped.

"When can you go back on caffeine?" Angela asked. "I liked you better with a bad stomach and a happy disposition."

"Bite me." In the doorway to the bedroom, Sam stopped and gasped. "What the hell?" Hanging on the closet door was the most exquisite ice-blue gown Sam had ever seen. She broke free of her sisters and pounced on the dress. "Oh, my God, is that *silk?* Where did this come from?" She let out a most uncoplike girlish squeal. *"Oh, my God!* It's Vera Wang? *Seriously?"*

"He said, 'the sky's the limit,'" Tracy reported, her face set in a grave expression. "We took him very, very seriously." She pointed to a box on the floor.

Sam screamed. *"Manolos!"* Tearing into the box, she withdrew delicate heels with beaded crystal accents—a perfect match with the dress.

"A delightful size nine," Angela said, gazing reverently at the shoes.

"I'm a nine-and-a-half," Sam reminded her.

"I know, but I'm a nine, and Spencer has this thing coming up at work, so don't stretch them all out with your big old hoofs, you hear me?"

"I'll see what I can do. And remind me to execute a warrant next week on your closet. I bet I'll find my missing Jimmy Choos there."

"You weren't using them," Angela retorted.

Sam sighed, unable to tear her eyes off the shoes. "This is better than sex."

"You need to have better sex," Tracy said.

"Not possible," Sam said. "What's this all about? I don't get it."

"He said to have you ready by seven, and he'll pick you up," Angela said.

"Pick me up? He lives here."

Tracy shrugged. "We're just doing what we were told. We were giving you five more minutes before we called to order you home."

"This isn't my home," Sam said, looking around wistfully at the bedroom where they'd spent so many blissful nights over the past month. Their near-death adventure in the car crash had driven their passion to all new heights. Sam hadn't known it was possible to feel so much. What was already amazing had ascended to stupendous lately, but she'd been frustrated—and baffled—by his refusal to let her tell him she was ready to officially move in. Whatever he had planned for tonight, Sam decided, there'd be no nookie until they had that conversation. She wasn't going to let him pull back from her now. No way. Not after everything they'd been through together.

"What do you suppose she's thinking about, staring at that big bed?" Angela asked Tracy.

"Her face got kind of red for a minute there," Tracy replied. "I bet I know what she's thinking about."

"All right, you two. That's enough. You've got ninety minutes to fix me up. Let's get busy."

Sam stood before the mirror. The dress fit as if it had been cut for her. The shoes, a little tight thanks to Angela's scheming, wouldn't cause blisters, but even if they did, they were worth it. The girls had corralled her impetuous curls into an elegant French twist and had even given her an emergency manicure and pedicure.

"Oh, wow," Nick said, releasing a low whistle from the doorway.

Sam turned to him.

"Wow," he whispered.

The sight of him in a tuxedo left her weak in the knees. "Not too shabby yourself, Senator."

He stepped into the room, reached for her hand and brought it to his lips. "You're beautiful."

"I'm not sure how I feel about you scheming behind my back with my sisters, although Vera and Manolo told me I should go easy on you."

His face lifted into the smile she loved so much. "Did they now?"

"Where's your sling?"

"Don't need it anymore." He made a big show of twirling his arm around, but she caught the grimace he tried to hide when his collarbone protested.

"It'll be back on tomorrow."

"If you insist."

"I do. Where're we going?"

"That's a surprise." He offered his good arm. "Shall we?"

Ready to go anywhere he chose to take her, Sam slipped her hand into the crook of his arm. "By all means."

He had a limo waiting at the curb.

Sam stared at it, suddenly filled with trepidation, nerves and a strange sense of foreboding. What was going on? What did he have planned? Didn't he know she hated surprises? Shouldn't he know that by now? The dress and the shoes were one thing...

"What's wrong, babe?"

"Where're we going, Nick?"

He put his arms around her and brought her in close to him.

Sam was grateful that the press seemed to have taken the night off from stalking them.

"Trust me?"

"You know I do."

"Then let's go have some fun."

She tried her best to relax. "All right."

As the limo worked its way slowly through the congested city, he asked about her first day back to work, told her about a low-income housing bill he'd been asked to cosponsor and re-fused to say another word about where they were going. They

glided along Pennsylvania Avenue, past the Old Executive Office Building and came to a stop in front of the White House.

"Nick?"

"Go with the flow, babe."

"You never said anything about the White House," she
stammered.

"Didn't I?"

"You know you didn't!"

"If I had, would you have come?"

"No!"

"Exactly."

The driver came around to open the door for them. Nick
scooted out ahead of her and held out a hand.

Sam sat stubbornly still, her heart racing and her stomach
hurting for the first time in weeks.

"Samantha?" He gazed in at her. "Please?"

He never asked for anything, so something about that softly
uttered "please" had her reaching for his hand.

"I'll deal with you later, mister," she growled.

"Yay. Something to look forward to."

"This was very sneaky," she said, oddly let down by the
whole thing. She'd hoped for a rare night alone together with
neither of their jobs interfering, and here they were at a work-
related event, even if it wasn't your average work-related event.
"Did my sisters know where we were going?"

"Nope. I was afraid you'd find a way to beat it out of them
and refuse to come."

"What's the occasion?"

"State dinner for the prime minister of Canada."

As they were sucked into the crowd, Sam's stomach hurt
worse than it had in weeks.

"What's wrong?" he asked, his lips brushing her temple.

"Stomach."

He swore under his breath and directed her to a bench outside the security area. "I shouldn't have forced this on you. I'm sorry. I just figured once you were here you'd love it, but if you had to think about it, you'd freak. I'm sorry."

Brushing her fingers over his hair, she leaned in to kiss him. "You handled me just right. I will think this is very cool, and yes, I would've freaked if I had known where we were going."

Clutching her hand, he said, "Then what's wrong? Why do you still look so worried?"

"It's just that all these people, even the president and first lady. They know. About me. About what happened years ago."

"Sam, honey, no one will be thinking about that tonight. I promise you. Let's just go in there and act like we belong there. Can we do that?"

"I guess so."

"We don't have to. If you don't feel up to it, we'll go somewhere else and have dinner, just the two of us."

"You can't diss the president of the United States," she said with a droll smile.

"Oh, no? Watch me."

"Thank you for being willing to bolt, but that's not necessary." She stood up and held out a hand to him. "Let's go, Senator. Duty calls."

He flashed her that one-in-a-million smile, and her nerves disappeared. As long as he was right there with her, she could get through anything. Even a state dinner at the freaking White House.

Hours later, they had been wined and dined and dazzled by the pomp, the ceremony, the sheer magic of the White House. Sam had to admit that she was glad she'd come, even if this was *so* not her scene. It was something she'd remember always.

And now, as a reward for her astounding patience with

the formal aspects of the evening's program, she had Nick's arms tight around her as they moved together on the crowded dance floor.

She looked up at him. "I need to talk to you about something."

"I know. Can we do it a little later?"

"As long as we do it tonight, that's fine."

"Oh, we'll do it, all right."

Laughing, she poked him in the belly. "Do you ever think about anything else?"

"Not really, and definitely not since the first second I saw you in that dress."

Over his shoulder, one of the White House valets seemed to be trying to get his attention. "Friend of yours?" Sam asked, nodding to the other man.

The valet gestured them over to where he stood by the door to the ballroom.

Baffled, Sam held Nick's hand and followed him.

"Everything's all set, Senator. Right this way."

"Thank you, Mike."

The older man's smile lit up his face. "You're quite welcome, sir."

"What's going on, Nick?"

He brought his lips down close to her ear. "Just come with me, and try not to make a scene, okay?"

She scowled at him but did as he asked. They followed Mike through several corridors before coming to a stop at a set of French doors.

Mike opened them and gestured for Sam and Nick to go out ahead of him. "I'll wait for you right here, Senator." He flashed another dazzling smile. "You take your time now, you hear?"

Nick shook his hand on the way by. "Thanks again, Mike."

"My pleasure, sir."

Outside, Nick slipped his tuxedo jacket over Sam's bare shoulders.

Steeped in his essence, Sam burrowed into his warm jacket as the faint scent of something else filled her senses. Roses. Even out of season, the fragrance drifted lightly through the air. She gasped. "Oh, Nick, is this the Rose Garden?"

"It is. What do you think?"

The light of a three-quarter moon silvered the leaves and grass in the garden where the roses lay dormant for the winter.

"It's amazing. How did you do this?"

"I told you. The deputy chief of staff is a buddy of mine."

"Who *isn't* a buddy of yours?"

His sheepish grin touched her heart.

"What're we doing out here?"

"Come over here, and I'll tell you." He led her to a stone bench along one of the walkways and sat next to her. "Are you warm enough?"

She nodded.

"I had a meeting today with the chair and vice chair of the Democratic National Committee."

"What did they want?"

"To gauge my interest in a run for the White House in four years."

Sam's mouth fell open. "They did not."

He laughed at her reaction. "They really did."

"But…I don't get… I mean… *Wow.*"

"Yeah," he said, chuckling again. "That's what I said, too."

"What did you tell them?"

"I suggested they talk to me in a year or two when I have a chance to see how things go in the Senate. My numbers are really good right now, but I'm just getting started. Who knows what they'll be a year from now?"

"I'm sure they'll be higher than ever."

"You have such faith in me, Sam."

"Of course I do. There's nothing you can't do when you set your mind to it."

"Only if I have you by my side." All at once, he dropped to his knees in front of her.

Sam gasped and raised a hand to her chest to keep her galloping heart from leaping through fevered skin.

"Samantha, I love you so much. Since you've been back in my life, I feel like anything is possible." He glanced at the grand old house behind them. "Even things I never dreamed of. Our life together will be crazy and chaotic and wonderful. Will you marry me and take the trip of a lifetime with me?"

"Yes," she said. *"Yes!"* As he gathered her in his arms, she had no thoughts about the past, about the marriage that had failed or anything other than what was right in front of her—the love of her life.

He reached for the inside pocket of the coat she wore and withdrew a dazzling square-cut diamond ring that took her breath away.

"I can't wear that to work," she said as he slid it on her trembling finger.

Smiling, he said, "I wouldn't expect you to. But you *will* wear the other one after you say 'I do,' you got me? I want the whole world to know you're taken."

Framing his face with her hands, she touched her lips to his. "I've been trying to tell you I'm ready to move in with you."

"I know," he said, returning to the seat next to her and leaning in for a lingering kiss.

"You had this whole thing planned."

"And you tried to ruin it."

She grinned. "Of course I did. I wouldn't want you to think I'm easy."

Hooting with laughter, he said, "No worries there, babe."

"So, we're really gonna spoil everything by making it official?"

"We really are." He helped her up and drew her into another long, passionate kiss. "I love you, Samantha."

"I love you, too. So, *so* much."

A big smile lit up his handsome face. "Just think of it this way—at least you can't say I never promised you a rose garden."

Sam laughed, her heart full of joy and anticipation and excitement. "You have a way with words, Senator. You really do."

★ ★ ★ ★ ★

ACKNOWLEDGMENTS

Thank you to my husband, Dan, and our terrific kids, Emily and Jake, for supporting my writing career every day. To my readers, thank you for being the best part of this crazy ride. To my editor, Jessica Schulte, and the amazing, dynamic team behind Carina Press, thank you for your support and encouragement. It's a pleasure to work with each and every one of you. And finally, to my darling puppy, Brandy, thank you for helping me to build my presence on Facebook. Your mischievous antics have provided entertainment for people neither of us will ever meet but who now call both of us "friend."

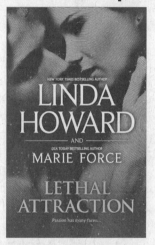

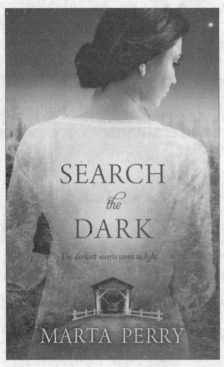

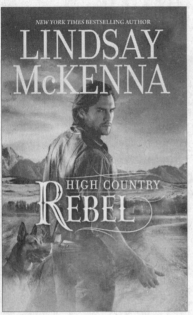